PORT CITY CROSSFIRE

PORT CITY CROSSFIRE

A BRANDON BLAKE MYSTERY, BOOK 1

GERRY BOYLE

Book and cover design by eBook Prep
www.ebookprep.com

August 2019
ISBN: 978-1-64457-055-5

ePublishing Works!
644 Shrewsbury Commons Ave
Ste 249
Shrewsbury PA 17361
United States of America

www.epublishingworks.com
Phone: 866-846-5123

To the memory of Mary Catherine Boyle:
loyal sister, devoted fan.

"French said, 'It's like this with us, baby. We're coppers and everybody hates our guts. And as if we didn't have enough trouble, we have you. As if we didn't get pushed around enough by the guys in the corner offices, the City Hall gang, the day chief, the night chief, the Chamber of Commerce, His Honor the Mayor in his paneled office four times as big as the three lousy rooms the whole homicide staff has to work out of. As if we didn't have to handle one hundred and fourteen homicides last year out of three rooms that don't have enough chairs for the whole duty squad to sit down in at once. We spend our lives turning over dirty underwear and sniffing rotten teeth. We go up dark stairways to get a gun punk with a skinful of hop and sometimes we don't get all the way up, and our wives wait dinner that night and all the other nights. We don't come home any more. And nights we do come home, we come home so goddam tired we can't eat or sleep or even read the lies the papers print about us. So we lie awake in the dark in a cheap house on a cheap street and listen to the drunks down the block having fun. And just about the time we drop off the phone rings and we get up and start all over again.'"

RAYMOND CHANDLER, *THE LITTLE SISTER*

ONE

Mid-September, not quite fall but the Maine summer slipping away. A chill rain had kept the Thursday night bar crowd subdued at closing time, guys pulling hoodies up, young women in heeled boots slipping on the slick cobblestones.

No brawls tonight but Brandon and Kat, driving west on Fore Street a little after 2 a.m., keeping an eye out for stragglers, the drunks who figured the cops were gone and it was safe to make a run for home.

A couple of blocks with just the radio talking, Brandon at the wheel, Kat riding shotgun, the actual shotgun racked to her left. She glanced over and said, "Quiet tonight, Blake."

"The weather," Brandon said.

"No, I mean you."

Brandon didn't answer.

"I rest my case," Kat said.

"Why I keep saying you should go to law school," Brandon said. "At least you'd get to say that for real."

"I'd rather catch bad guys. Cling to my delusion that they all get what they deserve."

"You and your damn rose-colored glasses," Brandon said.

They were quiet for the next block. Brandon slowed and turned the cruiser onto Center Street.

1

"Everything okay?" Kat said, giving him a longer look this time. She turned back to the street. Waited. Waited some more, knew something would come. Finally, a grudging reply.

"Not everything."

Brandon slowed to watch a couple standing near the curb, the woman trying to hold the guy upright. A red Passat slowed and the woman waved. The car stopped. An Uber driver, gray in his hair, might be a moonlighting school teacher. He leaned over, looked at the drunk guy dubiously, picturing vomit on his back seat. He drove on. The woman flipped him off and peered at her phone.

Kat glanced over at Brandon, felt him forming the first words in his head. He swung left onto Center Street, headed for Commercial and the piers. Brandon slowed as they passed Fianna, the Irish pub. The lights were dimmed, three cars left in the lot, workers closing up. Brandon took another left at the end of the block, Kat patient.

"I don't know," Brandon began. "It's just that——"

A long, deep breath. Then Kat's gentle prod.

"Just that what?"

"Mia, I think there's this—I don't know exactly how to say it. It just seems like there's this distance between us."

"You've been working a lot of OT. Haven't been around," Kat said.

"It's not that. You undo that when you get back together. You know, a day or two, back to normal. No, this is like there's this gap that we never quite make up, you know?"

"Huh," Kat said. "Maybe you need to go somewhere together. Some romance in your life. Maddie and I go to Camden. Stay in this cute Airbnb, sleep late, eat a delicious breakfast."

"I don't know. Maybe. But it's like lately we just don't agree about some things. And neither of us will budge."

"Hey, nobody agrees all the time. Not on everything. If I had to agree with everything Maddie does or says, and vice versa, we'd have split up years ago."

"I know. I guess I'm not explaining it very well."

"Give me an example," Kat said.

Brandon pulled out, headed east on Commercial, back up the peninsula. "Okay, it rained Monday night. We're sleeping and I hear this drip, drip, drip. I wake up, get up and go up on deck. The bow hatch is wide open. I come down, say, 'The bow hatch was wide open. Did you open it?' She says, 'Yeah, I opened it so I could air the cabin out. It stunk like your boots.'"

"No doubt," Kat said.

"I say, 'Well, didn't you know it was gonna rain?' She says, 'No. I haven't been looking at weather reports.' I'm tired and wet and grumpy. And I say, 'We live on a freakin' boat. Weather is kind of important.' She says, 'Then why didn't you check it?' I say, 'I just did. But I didn't open the hatch cover and just leave it.' She said, 'If you knew it was going to rain, why didn't you check sooner?'"

He stopped talking, glanced to his right. Kat looked unconvinced, confirmed it by saying, "So she's not a boat person. What's the big deal? I'd last about two hours in that thing."

Brandon drove, the two of them seeing two women making out in front of a condom shop. "Irony there," Kat said, but Brandon hadn't given up. He said, "Okay, the other day Mia came home with this book. She's always bringing books home."

"She's a writer. They read a lot. Maddie's like this book hoarder. It's an English professor thing."

"No, that's fine," Brandon said. "Except when you live on a boat. The space is limited."

"What about you and all your history stuff? Don't I keep telling you to get your head out of the past?"

She looked at him and grinned. "Get it? Get you head out—"

"I'm using my Kindle more. But whatever. It wasn't that. It was just that this book, it was this diary. Like an old-fashioned thing. Before my time but I've heard about it. Nessa had one when she was a kid."

"Sure, your grandmother would. Girls, mostly," Kat said. "Dear Diary and all that. You'd write in it every day, say what was on your mind."

"Right," Brandon said. "Harry Truman wrote in one and all that. This has a flowery cover made of cloth, like a cushion."

"Did it have one of those straps on it, with the little lock? My mother had one like that. I picked the lock."

"No, no lock. So maybe it was more of a journal than a diary. Anyway, this girl, she wrote these long sort of letters to herself in it."

"Who was she?"

"Her name was Danni Moulton. That's what it says, anyway. She's in high school, or she was, and she's writing about who she's in love with, who she wants to ask her out, who she slept with, who dumped her after she slept with them.

"Guys suck," Kat said. "Have I told you that?"

"Reading this thing it's hard to argue."

An oncoming pickup with a headlight out. It passed, three young guys, a good stop. Brandon wheeled the cruiser around.

"So Mia, she reads every word. I mean, fine. It's interesting, I guess. But then she brings it to her writer's group and they take turns reading it out loud."

"Huh."

"They said it was a very authentic voice, or something like that. But to me it didn't seem right. An invasion of privacy. It's this girl's innermost thoughts, you know? I mean, she's pouring her heart out."

Brandon eased up behind the pickup, an old Ford with a dented tail-gate, a bumper sticker that said, EAT MAINE LOBSTER. Brandon hit the blue lights.

The driver braked, only the left light going on as the truck pulled over. Brandon swung in behind, called it in. They waited for Choo-Choo, the dispatcher, to reply with the driver's name and record. It was a long one.

They'd just unsnapped their seat belts when Choo-Choo said, "Units in the area of Center and Spring. Report of masked subject exiting Fianna bar, showed a gun."

"Oh, yeah," Brandon said. "Rock and roll."

Kat reached for the radio, said, "Five-three. We're right there, ten seconds."

Brandon pulled around the pickup, accelerated hard. Kat reached over and killed the blues. On the radio, she said, "Direction?"

"Caller said he went behind the building, last seen running through the parking lot, east bound."

The radio noise had units converging, Tommy Park saying, "We're on Middle. Thirty seconds."

Kat murmured into the mic, "Five-three out coming up out front. Nobody showing."

Brandon slowed at the entrance to the gravel lot, hit the right-side floodlight. Nothing moving.

"Trying to get somebody inside. No answer," Choo said.

Brandon looked up at the rearview, saw a dark figure flash by, said, "There he goes."

He whipped the cruiser around, tires squealing, Kat calling in, "Subject in sight, running down Center, headed for Commercial."

Other cops converging, the sound of roaring motors behind the radio traffic.

"Subject dressed in black," Kat barked. "Handgun showing."

The guy was running hard, the gun swinging like a baton. The cruiser was almost alongside, Brandon on the P.A. shouting, "Stop! Police! Drop your weapon."

The guy went left, into a gravel lot. Brandon turned hard, jumped the curb, slid the cruiser to a stop in front of a concrete barrier. They flung the doors open, Kat saying, "We're in foot pursuit. Subject headed for that Mexican place."

To Brandon she called, "I'll go left, cut him off on Fore. Blake, the camera?"

But Brandon was gone, running hard. The sound of shoes crunching gravel, the chink of the guy hitting a chain link fence. He was up and over like a pole vaulter, Brandon thinking, "Shit, he's in shape."

He went over the fence, hit the ground and stumbled, got to his feet and sprinted down the alley. He called in, "Subject going north now, headed for Fore. Still in sight."

Cops calling in, murmurs and motor noise. The guy flying, disappearing behind corners, reappearing on the straightaways. They were behind a sports bar now. Strike Two. A dumpster overflowing, cars parked in the lot, the window lights dim. Brandon caught a look as the guy went right around the corner of the building, saw he still had the mask on. Brandon drew his gun.

He heard Christianson, his K-9, Laser, barking in the background. Other units chiming in with locations, the sergeant saying he was at Center and Free, almost on scene. Brandon slowed, drew his gun.

No footsteps.

A sudden and eerie silence.

Brandon slipped his finger inside the trigger guard.

It was the back side of the bar. A brick wall. A motorcycle parked against a chain link fence, the seat wrapped in a clear plastic bag. Cars and a pickup parked to the left. Brandon eased along the wall. A doorway to his right. He stepped to the corner, flicked his flashlight in. Recycling bins. Empty beer cases in a jumbled pile. Darkness to the right at the back of the alcove, a passageway.

Brandon stood still.

Listened.

Nothing.

He called, "Come out, hands above your head."

Nothing.

He listened another five seconds. The guy was trapped in there in the dark, a good spot for the dog, go in and flush him out. Brandon decided to wait for Christiansen. Backed out of the alcove, toward the cars. He leaned to his mic, said, "Need the K-9. He's holed up, back side of The Finish Line bar." Blurted responses, Christiansen on his way.

Brandon stood and listened. Nothing from the doorway. From the back of the bar, a door slammed. Then a clank. A digital melody, three notes. Then a whooshing sound.

A dishwasher.

He listened harder, moved slowly. There was a box truck parked along the wall, just past the opening. Gun raised, Brandon bent and checked underneath. Nothing. He swiveled, the gun trained on the darkness. From the other side of the building he heard radio traffic, tires scrunching and chirping, cruisers pulling in, Laser barking. Brandon reached for his shoulder mic to direct them in—and heard a scratching sound.

A shuffle.

He looked to his right. The guy was standing by the wall, fifteen feet away. He had his gun clenched in two hands.

It was aimed at the ground at Brandon's feet.

Brandon turned, a half step, his gun coming up. Everything had slowed, his breathing, his heart pounding like a gong. The guy still had the mask on. Something was strapped on his head, a faint red light glowing like a headlamp. The gun still aimed at Brandon's feet.

"Put it down," he said. "Just toss it."

There was a moment of silence, neither of them breathing. And then the guy made a sound, somewhere between a cough and a chuckle. The gun was still pointed at the pavement, the barrel wavering, an almost imperceptible jiggle. It was all he could see, the gun, the guy's masked face.

"Put the gun down, dude," Brandon said. "Just drop it right there. And we can all go home. Call it a night."

There was movement around the guy's mouth—a smile?—and then he shook his head slowly, the red dot on his forehead moving back and forth like a firefly. He was muttering. "You can do this, you can do this."

"Just let it go. Drop the gun and we can figure the rest of it out later," Brandon said.

"Oh, god," the guy said, still muttering. "Okay, you can do this."

"Don't need to do anything, dude," Brandon said. "Just put the freakin' gun down. Easy as that. Right now. Just pull your fingers apart and it'll fall. Easy."

The guy looked at him, the gun still pointed low. And then he took a deep breath and said, "I didn't want to hurt anyone at the bar."

"That was good," Brandon said. "Really. You're a good guy. I can tell."

"No such thing, dude. It's all fake. Everything. Everybody. It's all this fucking show."

"Maybe," Brandon said, "but let's put the gun down and really talk about it. It's the guns make it hard to really talk, you know what I'm saying?"

"Show's over, dude. Tell them I didn't want to play any more," the guy said.

"No," Brandon said. "We can tell them. You can tell—"

The guy took another deep breath, then clenched his teeth, his jaw moving the mask. He swung the gun up, saying, "You're dead, cop, and so am—"

Brandon lunged right, firing as he moved. Once. Twice. Three times, the shots coming in slow motion. The guy staggered, eyes wide under the mask. He stood for a moment, then went over backwards, the gun flying, hitting the wall, clattering on the ground.

The sound, Brandon thought. It wasn't right.

He called in, shots fired, subject down, Medcu ASAP. Falling to his knees he yanked the ski mask off so the guy could breath, but he wasn't really a guy. He was a kid, maybe sixteen, pale whiskerless face, skin icy gray against the gravel. Brandon could see the holes in the kid's black jacket, three of them, a triangle of small punctures in the nylon fabric. But the blood was soaking the ground underneath him, big holes there, Brandon knew. He started to reach under the kid, try to get a hand in there, keep him from bleeding out. And then the kid coughed and choked and a black-red spurt erupted from his mouth like vomit. Three gushes, his heart pumping the blood up his trachea like oil from a well. And then the blood stopped gushing, just ran down his cheek and onto his neck.

And he was gone.

"No," Brandon said, and he started to pump the kid's chest, all hard bone and thin flesh. But nothing happened, and he leaned back as he heard boot steps behind him. The kid stared up at him, eyes open, half smiling, like dying here in this place was expected, part of the plan.

It was Kat who came on the scene first, trotted past him, picked up the kid's gun. He knew. The way she handled it, no weight to it.

A toy.

TWO

Medcu had been there, paramedics crouched over the guy, going through the motions. Now the body was covered with a sheet, cops moving around it. Uniforms. Detectives. Brass. Out at the sidewalk, on the other side of the police tape, gawkers were gathered, drawn to the lights like moths. A TV truck, reporters and photographers, strobes flashing, the floodlight beaming from a video camera. Some on their phones, Tweeting, posting to Facebook.

Brandon was in the passenger seat of O'Farrell's SUV, the door open. He went over it. And then again and again.

The ten seconds replayed in Brandon's head, pausing in between loops for him to think, I can't believe this is real. I can't believe this just happened.

The same questions, spinning around in his head. What had the kid been thinking? What was with the GoPro camera on the his head? Didn't he know that if you pointed a gun at a cop, refused to put it down, acted like a crazy person, you'd get shot? "What choice did I have?" Brandon said aloud. "Stand there and wait for him to shoot me?"

And then, back inside his head: I mean, I had no other options. At the academy, they'd say I waited way too long. I could have been killed.

If it had been real.

He heard it again—the brittle, plastic clatter as the gun hit the brick wall and skittered lightly across the gravel.

The kid was lifted onto the stretcher now. When they moved toward the ambulance, Brandon could see his face again. Young. Longish blonde hair swept back behind his ears, like Mia's lacrosse-player friends from college. Black running shoes splayed outward. Feet too big for the rest of him, like paws on a puppy. A half-hour earlier he'd been alive, somebody's son, brother, friend. Now he was just a body, a slab of meat, a cadaver for the M.E. to dissect.

Fluids draining. Organs in bowls. The clink of the misshapen .45 Gold Dots dropped into a stainless steel bowl. The slugs from Brandon's gun. Unless they went straight through.

He looked down at his empty holster, the Glock taken for ballistics.

God almighty.

Brandon rested his face in his hands. Cops came by one at a time and patted him on the shoulder, leaned close to say, "Hang in there, Blake....We're with you, Brandon....You had no choice, man.... Anything you need, B. Blake....You did what you had to do, man."

Johnny Fiola, a stand-up guy, said, "It was a good shoot, Blake. Good shoot."

Brandon stared, still stunned. He said nothing.

And then Kat. Her hand on his shoulder, clasping tight.

"How you doing?"

Brandon exhaled. Shrugged.

"I'm here for you," she said.

He nodded. "Thanks."

"Let's go."

Brandon looked at her, thinking she wanted them to go back out, finish the shift. His mind still whirling.

"I can't," he said. "Not now, they're still—"

"No," Kat said. "I'm supposed to drive you back."

Cops cleared a path through the crowd and Kat tried to ease the cruiser through. A young woman with a big phone—flannel shirt, blue bandanna on her head like a pirate—stepped in front of the car, started shooting video. She darted around the cruiser so she was on the passenger side, the phone up to the glass at Brandon's face. Kat hit the klaxon horn and the woman jumped, screamed, "Fucking cops, fucking murderers." TV converged, video of the woman getting video. Fiola moving the woman out of the way, the woman slapping at him, screaming, "Get your fucking pig hands off me."

The cameras swung back to Brandon, the siren whooping as Kat pushed through. And then they were back on the dark and deserted streets, Brandon thinking, *We were just here. Right here. Everything was fine.*

Kat looked over and said, "It's going to be okay."

"I just killed a kid. He had a plastic gun."

"A replica. You can't tell the difference."

"He's dead. What was he? Sixteen? My god, Kat."

"I would have done the exact same thing," Kat said.

"Oh, dear Jesus, I knew it when it hit the ground."

"What were you supposed to do? 'Excuse me, but might I check to see if that gun that you're pointing at my face is real?'"

"What was he thinking?"

"He wasn't, Blake. Maybe he was nuts. Maybe he was high or tripping or a freakin' meth head. Whatever. He made his bed."

"I gave him two warnings," Brandon said. "I said, 'Just put it down. Just put the gun down.'"

"Two too many," Kat said. "Could be you lying dead back there."

"I told him to just toss it. We could all go home. I said that. It would be on the video. Was that thing recording?"

"I don't know."

"God, me on the camera, shooting him. It would be right on there."

"On your body cam, too."

Brandon reached to his shoulder, but the camera was gone. With his gun.

"I don't know if I turned it on."

From behind the wheel, Kat gave him a hard glance. "Friggin' A, Brandon."

"I know."

"It's alright. They'll figure it out."

They stopped at the light at Spring and Middle, three guys crossing in front of them, all three staring at him, knowing who he was, Brandon was sure.

"The word's out already."

"Gonna be fine," Kat said.

"I couldn't tell it was a kid. You couldn't see how old he was, under the mask."

"Doesn't matter if he was twelve or eighty. You'd still be dead."

"I'm sorry," Brandon said.

"You have nothing to be sorry for."

"That it happened, I mean."

"I know. Me, too."

They swung off Middle Street and up Pearl, then around into the police lot. Kat pulled the cruiser up close to the doors and parked and they got out. Brandon felt like his right side was floating, without the weight of his Glock. He took his bag out of the trunk, his water bottle and his left-overs from dinner—a taco salad from Whole Foods. A lifetime ago. Kat patted his shoulder, said, "O'Farrell and the lawyer will meet you. I'd get out of that uniform."

Brandon looked down at the front of his shirt, the kid's blood drying, sticky and stiff like varnish.

"Right," he said.

"You gonna be okay, partner?" Kat said.

"Yeah."

He paused and looked at her.

"What if Mia doesn't understand?" he said.

"She will. Hey, what's not to understand? Someone pointed a gun at you and refused to put it down."

Brandon turned away, then back.

"You know he had the drop on me. He must have been in the back of that little doorway and he slipped up behind me when I was checking under the truck."

"Then look at it this way, Blake," Kat said. "If you had nine lives, now you have eight."

"He said, "You're dead.""

"All I'd need to hear, Blake. I'd empty the goddamn magazine, I'm telling ya. I'm going home, that's all I know."

"And then he said, 'And I'm——'"

"I'm what?" Kat said.

"I don't know. That's when I fired, at that second. What if he was gonna say, 'I'm just goofing on you.' It's a paintball gun.' Or——"

"Who knows what he was thinking, Brandon? You don't know. Suicide by cop? Maybe he had a mental illness. Or he was just stupid. You may never know."

Brandon looked at her. "All he had to do was drop it. Throw it down. That's all. We'd be doing paperwork right now. He'd be out in two hours. Don't get in any trouble for a year, they file it."

"Crazy," Kat said. "He didn't even get any money."

"Scared off?"

"No, more like some weird movie. He ran through, said, 'Hands up.' Told everybody to get on the floor but people thought it was a joke or something so nobody did. Bartender dials 911 and he runs out."

"A paintball gun," Brandon said, his voice soft and low. "I knew it when I heard it hit the wall. Too light. A replica. Sig P226. But no red on the muzzle."

"He ground the orange down, painted the tip black," Kat said.

Brandon processed it, said. "Why the hell would he do that?"

"The GoPro," Kat said. "They'll just have to check the card."

It was all sinking in, Brandon sinking with it. "So it was just a kid screwing around? Friggin' put it on YouTube?"

"Playing a dangerous game, if he was."

"What if I'd decided to wait for Christiansen and the dog, not go deeper into that doorway," Brandon said.

"I know. You said that."

"Dog would have just grabbed him. End of story. Instead..."

"It was the right decision, Blake. The only decision. It's okay."

A long pause, the garage curiously empty, even at this time of night usually something moving. In the distance there was a Medcu siren. Then, from the darkness, the call of a gull. What the hell was a gull doing, flying around in the middle of the night? Brandon said, "What do you think? Tenth grade?"

Kat shrugged. "I don't know."

"Fuckin-A," Brandon said.

"You did your job, Blake. You went by the book, using the information you had at the time, at that moment."

"I wish I'd missed," Brandon said. "Hit the ground and kept going."

"Blake."

"Maybe if I'd just fired once, maybe he would have lived."

"You fire until the threat is neutralized, you know that. All he needed was time and strength to squeeze that trigger."

"I could've called in sick, not been there at all."

Kat walked over to him, took him by both shoulders and turned him square to her.

"It's gonna get harder," she said.

Brandon looked at her. "I know. Ferguson. Every other goddamn place."

"Don't read the news."

"Right."

"Or the comments on line."

"Yeah."

"Drink a lot of water."

"Okay."

"Stay away from alcohol."

"Yup."

"You can do this,Blake. You've done it—"

She caught herself.

"Before?" Brandon said. "Well, yeah, but not like this. Not even close."

THREE

There were three of them in the duty room: Charlie Carew, the shop steward, Esli Hernandez, the city lawyer, and Officer Brandon Blake, the principal in officer-involved shooting, Portland, Maine, September 15, 2018. Carew, an Irish-looking guy with red cheeks and hair, had brought three coffees from Dunkin' Donuts. He set them out, slid one across to Brandon. Hernandez—silver-haired, terse, tough, and smart—ignored her coffee and said she had two questions:

Brandon waited, feeling like she was scrutinizing his face, his reaction, even to that.

"One, are you okay?"

"Yes," Brandon said. "I mean, as much as you can be."

"Two, what happened? Just tell us."

He told them, from getting the call, to the foot chase, to pulling the trigger—once, twice, three times. And the kid dying in front of him. "The blood. It just kept spurting," he said. "And then it stopped. It was all over the place, all over me, all over him, it was..."

He paused. They could fill in the blank: horrible, unbelievable, a mess.

There was a long pause. Carew took a swallow of coffee. Brandon picked up his cup, just held it.

"Are you sure you're okay?" Hernandez said again.

"Yes."

She asked about distances: from Brandon to the kid when he fired, from Brandon to the kid during the chase.

"Totally straightforward," Carew said. "Subject points an apparent handgun at the officer's face, refuses repeated orders to put the weapon down. When Officer Blake chose to use deadly force, he clearly and understandably felt his life was in danger."

Hernandez was writing on a legal pad. She stopped, put down the pen. Her diamond engagement ring was very glittery, like it might have magic powers. It couldn't undo this.

"Complicating factors, Officer Blake," she said. "One, your body cam. It wasn't on."

"I know. I saw him running, jumped out to pursue him on foot. I just didn't think of it."

"Two, still looking for the SD card for the subject's GoPro."

"Was there one?" Brandon said.

They looked at him.

"I don't think the kid would wear the GoPro if he wasn't filming," Hernandez said.

"What are you saying? I didn't touch the camera. I was just trying to stop him from dying."

"Nobody's saying anything," Carew said. "We'd just really like to have that card."

"So would I," Brandon said. "It would be on there. Everything."

They looked at him, and it clicked. The reason it was gone. That it would all be on there.

Hernandez said, "Three. On the way over here, I got a call. The subject of the deadly force is Thatcher Rawlings. Mom and Dad live in Moresby and have serious money."

"You will be sued," Carew said. "You would anyway. Only difference is rich people get better lawyers."

"And your history," Hernandez said. "It's gonna come up. Big time. You've done this before."

"I wasn't a cop then."

"Exactly," she said.

They left him alone, Carew going to the men's room, Hernandez to call the city manager. "Hang tight," she said. Brandon sat at the table, his hands folded in front of him. Sitting there in the silent room he heard the shots, saw the holes, the torn jacket, the shocked expression frozen on the dead guy's face.

Not the kid, not Rawlings. This was Joel Fuller, almost three years ago now. He didn't think about it often, could go weeks without even a glimmer. But now it was playing full-screen, as vivid as it had been that night.

The Royal Arms Hotel, three blocks away from where he sat. Fourth floor, the far end of the corridor. Room 423. Fuller and Kelvin, their ransom plans unraveling. Mia bound and gagged and stuffed inside a big black suitcase, Brandon stopping them in the hallway. Fuller aiming the big revolver at Mia's head, muzzle pressed on the round lump in the black fabric.

Three shots that time, too, all in the chest. Center mass, they call it. Brandon knew that now. Back then he was just shooting to kill, to put Fuller down before he pulled the trigger.

Fuller blown back into the wall. No blood spurting from his mouth, just three quarter-sized holes in his shirt that turned to one plate-sized splotch. And then his cry, the crazy psycho wailing like a terrified child. And then breaths coming quicker and quicker, shallower and shallower. And then a last breath followed by nothing.

Gone.

Brandon holding Mia tightly in the corridor—no tears, just her dry, retching sobs. Cops, counselors. Talk, talk, talk, them trying to figure out this new normal. It took months for Mia. Brandon had a few days of bad dreams, one reoccurring one—a nightmare where he pulled the trigger and nothing happened. And then life went on, the killing of Joel Fuller an unspoken bond between them.

Regrets? Brandon had none. The counselor said, "It isn't healthy to keep it bottled up inside."

Brandon said, "There's nothing bottled up. I'm glad he's dead. I'm glad Mia's not."

So had he done it before, like Hernandez had said? No, not this. Not even close.

The first time he hadn't shot a kid playing some stupid game. A kid

17

holding a toy gun from WalMart. He hadn't left a sixteen-year-old dead, when he could have walked right up to him, taken the gun out of his hands. Put him on the ground, game over.

Brandon could picture it, so real it was tantalizing: the kid face down, cuffs snapping on. Brandon lifting him to his feet, pulling the mask off, saying, "Dude, what the hell do you think you're doing? You know how close you just came to getting killed?" Thinking, jeez, won't his parents be some pissed when they get this call. Brandon and Kat finishing the booking, leaving the idiot at intake, talking it over back in the cruiser.

What the hell's wrong with kids these days? Richey Rich gonna have a rude awakening if he ends up in Long Creek. Nah, the parents will bring in some high-priced lawyer, get him released to their custody. Probably that was the problem. No consequences for the spoiled little bastard. Parents aren't doing them any favor when they—

The door to the conference room swung open. Hernandez stepped in, another guy behind her. He was shortish, wiry, salt-and-pepper hair in a cop haircut. Brandon got up as the guy moved toward him.

He introduced himself, "Jim Beam, like the whiskey. AG's office." Brandon knew the name.

Beam shook Brandon's hand, made eye contact and held it. His expression was neutral.

The three of them sat. Hernandez had her yellow legal pad ready. Beam put his pad on the table, too. It was smaller, light green paper, in a leather folder. He slipped a recorder from his pocket, asked Brandon if he minded. Brandon shook his head. Beam hit the button and the recorder's orange light glowed.

"This is a voluntary statement," Beam said. "You have the right to decline to answer."

Just got Mirandized, Brandon thought, a ripple of unease moving through him. He pushed it back.

"No, I'll tell you everything I know," he said.

Beam smiled, hit the recorder again and the orange light began to flash.

"Good. Here we go, then. We're here as part of the criminal investigation of the legality of the use of lethal force, September 15, 2016, Portland, Maine. Please state your name for the record."

Brandon did, added that he was a patrolman for the Portland Police Department.

Beam nodded. "Tell me exactly what happened," he said.

They waited, pens poised. Brandon started at the beginning, went straight through to the end. Diving right, the kid going down, his blood gushing. The kid dying right there and then, staring up at him. Gone.

He paused, the sound of scribbling filling the room. And then Beam said he had questions. Brandon waited, concentrating, watching Beam's eyes like they'd give him a clue of what was coming.

How far away was the subject of the lethal force when Brandon saw him with the gun? What did Rawlings say? What did Brandon say to him? How long was it from the time of their encounter to the time to when the shooting took place, just an estimate? Was it clear it was a gun? How dark was it?

Brandon answered and then Beam paused. He looked at Brandon, held his gaze and said, "Why did you shoot?"

They waited, Beam and Hernandez, intent and alert. "I thought he was going to shoot me in the face," he said.

"You felt that your life was in danger?"

"Yes. I thought he was about to pull the trigger. I thought he was going to kill me."

Beam reached for the recorder and hit the orange-lighted button. It went black.

Forty-five minutes later Brandon relived it again, this time at the scene. The alley was smaller with the spotlights shining on it. The ground where the two of them had stood was flagged with evidence tags: the three shells ejected by Brandon's Glock, the place where the fake gun had come to rest, the black sodden ground where Rawlings had bled out.

Brandon retraced his steps, showed where he'd stepped into the alcove, then backed out. He stood by the truck and bent and looked under it again. He turned and looked back, froze at the spot where he'd seen the kid, the gun aimed at his feet. He raised his hand, forefinger pointed like his gun.

He repeated the words. "Just put it down. Just drop it and we can go home." And then he recited the kid's last words on this planet. "Bang, bang, you're dead. And so am—"

Brandon moved right, shot with his finger, saying, "Bam, bam, bam." Went to the spot where he'd knelt by the kid, pulled the mask off, saw the blood spurt. Brandon knelt and looked down, smelled the blood in the ground, the kid's blood. He stumbled to his feet, made it to the wall before he vomited.

Brandon stood with his hands on his knees, slowly raised himself up. He turned. They were waiting for him, Beam, Hernandez, a couple of crime scene investigators.

"I think we're good," Beam said.

"Nothing good about it," Brandon said, his certainty left on the ground with the blood and vomit. "It's a freakin' nightmare."

Which he relived yet one more time, with the critical incident debriefing team. They were in the same conference room: Sergeant Perry, Lieutenant Searles, Detective Sergeant O'Farrell, Chief Garcia, a police counselor named Townsend who'd come to Maine from NYPD. Townsend asked how Brandon was feeling. He said he felt stunned, like he couldn't take it all in.

Townsend said that was natural. Brandon opened up, said it was different from the last time, when he was overwhelmed by relief that Mia was alive, and glad that Fuller was dead. This time he felt like he'd lost someone from his own family, even if it was this kid he didn't know. They listened, Townsend nodding like it all made sense. Like hell. She said it would take time, that this was something akin to the grieving process. Wrapping up, there was the same advice:

Don't block people out. Keep talking.

Find a way to stay busy.

Don't read the news reports, and most definitely don't read the comments online.

Drink a lot of water.

Stay away from alcohol.

"Yup," Brandon nodded and they all got up, the cops patting him on the shoulder on the way by. "Hang in there, Blake," O'Farrell said. "You're not alone."

They left the room, headed down the hallway single file like soldiers in a trench. Brandon was at the head of the stairs when O'Farrell said, "Blake, wait."

He turned. O'Farrell came alongside him, leaned close. Brandon expected some more advice, a pep talk. Instead O'Farrell said, "You need a replacement weapon. Stop downstairs before you go."

And then he trotted downstairs. Brandon stood there for a minute, the hallway silent except for distance sound of voices, the hum of dispatch when the door opened. Another gun. To do what with? Shoot somebody else? But he had to carry one, it was his job. Armed law enforcement officer. Protect people from bad guys with guns. Protect himself.

He swallowed hard, said, "Oh my god."

Brandon went slowly down the stairs, went left and right and made his way to the equipment room. Vests. Weapons. SWAT gear.

Sylvia, the equipment manager, swung the door open from the inside. She turned away without him saying a word, came back with a Glock 22, an older one. She slid the gun across the counter, then two magazines, then a form for Brandon to sign. He did. She took the form back and finally looked Brandon in the eye. "Hang in there, Brandon," she said. "You're not alone."

"Sure," he said.

And then Brandon walked back down the corridor, out the door to the parking lot. He walked to his truck, put his stuff and the new gun on the seat. He put the key in the ignition and fell back. Not alone? Who you kidding?

FOUR

It was a few minutes before five, the marina lot glistening in the morning mist off the harbor. Brandon swung the pickup in, parked by Mia's Volvo. Had she heard? A text from Kat? Would he have to wake her, break the news? What do you say? "Hi, baby. How was your night? Me, I killed an unarmed kid. Any of that sushi left?"

Brandon unlocked the gate, pulled it shut behind him. He walked across the yard, bag in hand, his holster against his hip. He'd never fired this gun. Should he go to the range? Or would that make him look like some cold-hearted bastard. If he went, could he pull the trigger. The sound. The feel of the Glock nudging him. One, two, three.

Three shots, three hits, the kid taking one step backward and then going over, his arms flung up over his head. It played in his head, a continuous loop. Brandon closed his eyes. Opened them. Walked across the yard, started down the ramp to the floats, the place smelling like mud and salt, gasoline and diesel. Along the ramp, lights showed against the Portland skyline, glistening across the harbor. A few live-aboards showing, lights on in the cabin of *Bay Witch*.

Mia was up. She was waiting. She knew.

He approached the stern, stepped up the steps and over the transom. He looked up, saw Mia sitting in the helm seat. She was dressed, jeans and a fleece and her L.L. Bean slippers, holding a mug of tea in both hands. She put the mug down, slipped down off the chair, hurried to him. Putting her arms around him, she hugged him hard and long. When she moved it was to put her mouth to his ear and say, "It's going to be okay."

Still in her embrace, Brandon shrugged. Took a deep breath and exhaled slowly.

"I'm with you," Mia whispered.

"Thanks," Brandon said.

"What do you need right now?"

"I don't know."

He took a breath, felt everything begin to well up, and began to cry. Sobs racked him as Mia held him tightly, patting his back, saying, "It's okay." His tears ran down her cheek, and finally the sobs subsided. He swallowed hard, took a deep breath, and said, "He was only a kid. A stupid idiot kid."

"You didn't know that," Mia said.

"I could have—"

"You couldn't have done anything differently."

"I killed him, Mia," Brandon whispered. "I took his life."

"He killed himself," she said.

"All he had to do was drop it. I said to him, 'Just drop the weapon.'"

"I know you did. He had every chance."

Mia leaned back and looked at him. Her cheek was wet but she didn't wipe it.

"You can't blame yourself, Brandon," she said.

He didn't answer.

"Actions have consequences," she said. "That's the way life works."

Again, no answer.

"He set the whole thing in motion. You were just caught in the middle of it."

Brandon sighed.

"I didn't turn on my body cam. That's gonna be a huge problem."

"It'll be okay."

"But he was wearing a goddamn GoPro," he said. "On his head."

"I know. Kat called me."

"There should be a video. Of the whole thing."

"That's good," Mia said. "It'll show you didn't do anything wrong, that you had no choice."

"His parents," Brandon said. "They'll be able to hear their son, his last—"

"That's not your fault."

"I mean, can you imagine? Your kid and there's a video of me as I—"

"Stop it, Brandon," Mia said. "Just stop."

He closed his eyes. Sighed again. Mia pressed herself against him, held on tight. "You need to sleep," she said.

"First I need a drink," Brandon said.

"I don't think that you should—"

He moved past her through the hatch door to the galley, went to the locker where the liquor was kept. He took out a dusty bottle of Irish whiskey, Jameson Black. Poured an inch into a tumbler, drank it down in two swallows. The whiskey burned and he waited for the numbness that would let him step away from it all. It didn't come so he poured another and swallowed it in a gulp.

He turned and saw Mia watching him, her eyes narrowing with concern. "Kat said no alcohol," she said. "It'll make it worse."

"Easy for her to say," Brandon said. "She's never killed anyone."

She didn't answer because it was true, he thought. He sipped the third whiskey, then thought, screw it, and downed the rest. What do you do after you kill somebody? Check your email? Read a book? Listen to music? What the hell do you do?

They went forward, to the berth in the bow. Brandon took off his equipment belt, the remainder of his uniform, his boots. In his boxers, he crawled into the berth, the port side where he always slept. Mia, in her clothes, slipped in beside him. She reached over and took his hand and kissed it once and then held it.

They lay there, staring up at the wooden bulkhead. The boat rocked gently from a passing wake, the fenders squeaking against the float. A gull cried, sailing over as dawn brightened. Neither of them spoke. Mia held his hand tightly, like she didn't want him to slip away, to fall into the depths.

But he already had, the shoot replaying yet again in his mind, the unending loop. Bending to look under the car. Turning to see the kid right there, the gun trained. Brandon's order to drop it, the kid's reaction, his last words. *"Bang, bang, you're dead. And so am——"*

Even with the mask, Brandon had seen him smile.

Had the kid been joking? Oh, my god. God almighty.

———

There was a moment, just as he woke up and his brain was still loading, when it had never happened. The boat rocked as a big wake—a tugboat heading for the oil terminal, Brandon thought—jostled the floats. Public radio babbled from another boat in the marina, the woman host talking in a silky voice about a sonata in D minor. Gulls called back and forth. The sky, showing through the portholes, was battleship gray. Rain pattered on the deck above him.

Brandon felt for Mia beside him but the berth was empty. And at that moment it all came flooding back.

The kid, the shots, the blood—it enveloped him, pressed down on his chest, filled his head. Sitting in the car, the cops filing past like mourners at a wake. Kat's pep talk, the repeated advice. Don't drink. Don't read the news.

He closed his eyes. Sighed..

It was a little after ten. Brandon slid out of the berth, went to the shelf and picked up his phone, flicked his way to the *Portland News Review*, the local news blog. And there he was, sitting in the SUV, his hands partly over his face. He looked grief-stricken, like he'd done something terribly wrong. It was the only photo on the home page.

The caption:

Portland Police Officer Brandon Blake sits in a supervisor's vehicle after fatally shooting a 16-year-old boy who police said was brandishing what appeared to be a gun in Portland's Old Port. The gun was reportedly a toy used in a video that the youth, Thatcher Rawlings of Moresby, was filming. Blake was placed on paid administrative leave pending an attorney general's investigation.

———

"A toy?" Brandon said. "It wasn't a goddamn squirt gun."

The story was number one on the list of most read and most shared. Brandon skimmed.

The boy shot and killed. Police called after the kid went into Fianna, an Irish pub, wearing a mask and carrying what appeared to be a gun.

A foot chase ensued, a police spokesman said. According to police, Blake claimed the boy, when confronted, refused to drop his weapon and trained it on the officer. There were no witnesses and the boy was pronounced dead at the scene.

A Fianna employee, who asked that her name not be used, said the boy burst into the bar and said it was a hold-up. "It was weird," she said. "He had a GoPro on his head so we figured it was just some goofy thing for YouTube or something. We kind of went along with it until one of the girls said, 'You know the cops are coming.' That's when he ran out."

And then the kicker. The sidebar story:

Second Fatal Shooting for Portland P.D.'s Blake

By Matthew Estusa

And there it was, Brandon's inescapable past. The three-year-old story retold, the botched bizarre extortion attempt by Joel Fuller, a scheming local criminal just out of prison.

Fuller was aware of acquaintances of Blake's who were later found to be involved in trafficking of young women from Eastern Europe to Maine. Blake, who lives on a cabin cruiser at a South Portland marina, knew the traffickers through the Portland boating community, authorities said. Fuller planned to rob the traffickers, police said, but the plan went awry. In desperation he and an accomplice abducted Blake's girlfriend, Mia Erickson, and held her at an Old Port hotel.

The plot ended when Blake, then a criminology student at the University of Southern Maine, shot and killed Fuller in the corridor of a downtown hotel. Blake claimed that during a confrontation Fuller had aimed his own handgun at Erickson, who was trapped in a suitcase. Like Rawlings, Fuller died of multiple gunshot wounds to the chest. A witness to the shooting, Kelvin Crosby, Fuller's partner in the robbery plan, was uninjured and received a reduced sentence for his reported "cooperation."

There were no other witnesses to the fatal shooting.

Sources said that while Blake's violent history and criminal acquaintances were seen by some as a red flag at the time of his hiring by the Portland Police Department, some said he was given the job as a reward for killing Fuller, who was wanted for questioning in the 2008 shooting death of Moresby County Deputy Sergeant Kyle

Griffin. "You take out a cop killer, you're golden," one officer said, requesting anonymity.

While the two shootings are not believed to be related, sources within the Portland Police Department say some officers have raised concerns about Blake's propensity for use of deadly force. "Some guys are just shooters," the source said. "It's their first choice, instead of being the last."

"That's total bullshit," Brandon said. "That son of a bitch."

"Brandon," Mia called, from the hatch. "Don't read it. He's just making stuff up, you know that."

"Deever, that piece of crap. What goes around, comes around, goddamn chicken shit—"

"Brandon," she said. "Stop."

He did, looked to Mia and saw the gray shadows under her eyes, the haunted expression that had stayed with her so long. It was back, like an illness that had been lurking, a virus dormant in her body and now revived. The terror of being abducted, being stuffed alive into a suitcase. Hearing the shots but waiting interminable moments before knowing it had been Fuller, not Brandon, who had died in the hotel hallway. The nightmares that kept her into counseling, forced her to sleep for weeks with lights and music on because she couldn't be alone or in the dark.

"I'm sorry, baby," Brandon said.

"No, it's okay," Mia said, turning away. "I just can't—we can't—do this all over again."

"No."

"But you can talk to me. You know that."

"Yes, I do," Brandon said, but he didn't. In fact, he now knew that when he tried to unburden himself, he put the weight directly on Mia. He moved to her and, standing on the steps to the hatch, hugged her and said, "It's going to be okay."

He didn't know that. He did know that the consequences of this shooting were his and his alone.

Mia hugged him back, and he went to the locker, pulled out jeans and a Portland P.D. sweatshirt. He pulled them on, slipped into a pair of battered Topsiders, and climbed up the steps and into the galley. Sun was streaming through the parted blinds and Mia was cracking eggs into a fry pan. Brandon brought the kettle to the sink, was filling it when he heard, "Hey, Brandon."

Estusa was on the float.

Brandon stepped out onto the stern deck, felt Mia close behind him.

"How you doing, man?" Estusa said. "I'm sorry to bother you and Mia, but I really hope we can talk."

He had his concerned look pasted on, like he'd come to check on their well-being.

"The marina's private property," Brandon said. "You're trespassing."

"Oh, sorry. The gate was wide open so I thought——"

"Close it on your way out."

"Sure, but can't we talk? I can't imagine what you're going through. I mean, it must be just awful, with what's happened. But I'm thinking of a story about the hazards of your profession, that every time you go to work, this kind of thing is a possibility. And with what's going on nationally, the police shootings and Black Lives Matter and all, I mean, your job has gotten harder and harder. It must be——"

"Fuck off," Brandon said.

"Brandon, don't," Mia said.

"No, I understand," Estusa said. "You have a right to be angry."

"Hey, I'm not angry," Brandon said. "I'm just telling you to leave."

"Well, it doesn't have to be now. I get that I just sort of showed up. Didn't know how else to reach you. But maybe we can find a time——"

"I'm gonna call South Portland P.D. If you're still here when they show up, you'll be charged with criminal trespass."

"Hey, easy man," Estusa said. "I'll leave you two alone. I'm sure you have a lot to talk about."

"What we talk about is none of your business," Mia said.

"Oh, but it kind of it," he said. "I mean, Brandon is a public figure by profession, and you're one by extension and involvement in a public event, a serious crime in a public place. The Fuller shooting. And now, I mean, a kid dying and all."

Brandon moved to the stern, pointed his forefinger at Estusa's face, said, "Get the hell out of here before I——"

And he heard a whirring sound, looked toward the yard, the open gate. A woman was standing there, camera raised, long lens aimed like a missile launcher.

"Her, too," Brandon said.

Estusa smiled, said, "No, I understand. I really do. It's gotta be very upsetting thing, shooting somebody, I mean, a child. It's not like it was some hardened serial killer."

"I'm calling," Mia said, turning and slipping through the hatch.

"I'm going," Estusa said. He reached inside his jacket, then yanked his hand back out and held it up, palm out. "Easy now. Just taking out my business card."

He slipped his hand into the jacket, took out a card. Holding it in front of him like a white flag, he took a step forward and laid the card on the transom.

"We'll be talking," he said.

"I don't think so," Brandon said.

"Okay. Your decision. I respect that. But we're going from here to interview Mr. and Mrs. Rawlings at their home. They want to tell us about their son. I think they're gonna have a lot to say, even in their grief."

"Go," Brandon said.

"It would be great to have your side of the story, just for balance."

"Now," Brandon said.

Mia stepped out onto the deck. "They're coming," she said.

Estusa smiled and backed away, then turned and started up the float.

The South Portland cruiser rolled in a minute after Estusa drove off. Brandon walked up the float and across the boat yard, stepping through the gate as a second cruiser slid to a halt behind the first. The cops—a big guy named Robichaud who'd played football somewhere, a smaller woman named Otongo whose husband was in the Marines—got out and approached. Brandon felt naked in plain clothes, like he was in his underwear.

"Hey," Robichaud said.

"He left," Brandon said.

"Estusa?" Otongo said.

"Yeah."

"Piece of shit," Robichaud said.

"Total slime bucket," Otongo said.

"Walked right up to the boat," Brandon said.

"We could round him up but he'd write about it," Robichaud said.

"Nah," Brandon said. "I just don't want him on the property. Or his photographer."

"Once they're warned, we can cite 'em," Otongo said. "Probably across the bridge by now, but your guys could track him down."

"He'd say I threatened him or something," Brandon said. "May say it anyway."

They paused, looking at him. The moment extended, an awkward sort of standoff, the two curious but not sure what to say. What was it like to kill someone on the job?

A car rolled by slowly, a gray-haired couple eyeing the cops, headed home to lock their doors.

"So," Otongo said. "You okay then?"

"Yeah."

"That dirtbag comes back, call us," Robichaud said, his thumb in his belt. "We'll write his sorry ass up."

"Yeah, thanks," Brandon said. "And it's not just me. My girlfriend, she doesn't need to be hassled. This has nothing to do with her."

Even as he said it, he knew it wasn't true. It had everything to do with Mia, with the two of them. Brandon felt the cops' curious gaze again, Otongo staring. He shot her a look, and she turned away, her black hair pulled back tightly, posture military straight. Everything under control—until it wasn't.

"Yeah, well, you need anything, we're here," she said. "Got your back, man. Press steps across that property line, even if they don't. You call."

Brandon nodded. Otongo took a couple of steps toward her idling cruiser. She stopped, turned back, started to say something and hesitated.

"How does it feel?" Brandon said. "Pretty friggin' strange. Even if you know you did the right thing. One minute everything's normal, the next minute everything's changed. And there's no going back."

Otongo looked at him and nodded. Robichaud looked at the ground, embarrassed at having his mind read. The unspoken truth was that it could be them, any day, any time.

Back among the floats, a diesel boat motor started, rumbling and gurgling. Otongo put her hand on the butt of her gun, then pulled it away.

"Yeah, well, sucks to be them 'cause I'm going home end of my shift," Robichaud said.

Brandon smiled. "Right," he said.

When he got back to the boat, Mia was standing in the stern. She was holding her school bag in one hand, keys in the other.

"You going?"

"Will you be okay? 'Cause I can stay," she said. "It's just that I've got students coming and I can't cancel them now. And it's Abukar at eleven and I texted him but I don't know if he saw it so I have to go. He could be waiting for me."

"Sure. I'm fine," Brandon said.

"What did South Portland say?"

"Not much. Call if they come back."

"That's good."

"Estusa will twist it around. Say cops are sticking together, protecting their own."

"You sure you don't want me to stay?"

"No, you go. You can't stand them up."

"They're bringing in their first revisions. They'll be looking for my reaction. Most of them, it's their first time doing this so I want to establish some trust."

"Right. So go. Really, I'm good."

"You sure?"

"Yeah."

"You know I'm with you on this."

"Right."

"On everything."

"Likewise," Brandon said, and he leaned in, kissed her cheek. She put the bag on the deck and hugged him. "You hang in there," she said, pulling back and looking at him, scouring his face for clues to his mental state.

"Oh, yeah."

"It's gonna be okay."

"Right."

"Call Kat if you need to talk."

"Sure."

"And I'll be back between four and five."

"Okay."

"Work around here, take your mind off of it," Mia said. "Stay busy."

Brandon paused, said, "Is that what you're doing?"

Mia looked out at the boats, the shimmering harbor waters, the Portland skyline. "I can't just sit here," she said. "If I don't keep moving, it'll catch up with me."

"I'm not sure we can outrun this," he said.

"Yeah, maybe. But I'd rather be a moving target," Mia said.

It was what they taught you at the academy. If you're in the open, return fire and keep moving. A shooter, even if they're hit, will often get a shot off, so don't make it easier.

How 'bout this, Brandon thought. A dive to the right. Three quick shots, a two-inch cluster. Eliminate the threat from the goddamn plastic gun.

———

Mia hurried down the float and up the steps to the yard. She clanged through the gate, turned to give Brandon a last wave. When her Volvo SUV had pulled out of the lot and disappeared, he stepped back onto the boat.

Keep busy, Mia had said. Hard not to on a wooden cruiser. Want to stay busy for the rest of your days? Buy a vintage Chris Craft.

Brandon had a list for fall: touch up the topsides paint, fill in the gouge in the planking on port bow where Sammy Sandoval had stalled *Sea Stallion* backing into the adjacent slip and drifted stern first into *Bay Witch*. Sammy had said he'd pay for somebody to do the repair but it was easier for Brandon to just do it. The switch for the blower was balky and he could go over to Hamilton Marine and pick up a new one.

He pictured it: driving down Commercial Street, looking up the block to the shooting scene. He grimaced, went below, opened the paint locker and started rummaging. Epoxy. Hardener. Sand paper...

And he heard it, even with his head in the cabinet.

The marina entrance gate clanging and rattling. A woman's voice screaming. He straightened up and listened. A woman, crying, hysterical, a piercing wail. Screaming, "You bastard. You killed my son."

FIVE

As Brandon hunched over the open locker, frozen in a half-crouch, the crying subsided. He straightened and turned, moved to the hatchway, climbed the two steps up and froze again.

"You filthy pig. You piece of shit. You goddamn murderer!"

Then a jagged cry, a moan. Brandon closed his eyes, waited. It was quiet, just the creaking of the boat. He opened his eyes, took a deep, long breath and pushed the hatch doors wide. Stepped through and moved part way to the stern. Looked up at the yard.

A woman was pressed against the fence to the left of the gate. She was spread eagle, fingers locked around the chain links. Her head was bowed and she looked like she'd been crucified. Brandon watched through the starboard rain curtains, thought maybe that's what it felt like, to have your son shot and killed. Hung on a fence, bared to the world.

No one had come off their boats, the live-aboards cowering below decks like Kitty Genovese's neighbors, he thought, then it occurred to him that nobody there would remember Genovese, murdered in New York while the neighbors put pillows over their heads. Guy got life, the piece of crap. Look it up.

There was nobody in the marina office, Brandon's assistant, a high school kid named Luke, taking a few days off between summer traffic and fall pullouts. Thatcher's mother hung on the fence like she was about to be flogged. Brandon hesitated, then moved to the stern, stepped over the transom, started up the ramp.

He was crossing the gravel yard when she raised her head. She looked at him, eyes narrowing.

"You," she said.

"Yes," Brandon said.

He was 20 feet away, walking slowly. Their eyes were fixed and he could see that her face was red, the eyes swollen. The diagonal pattern of the chain links was embedded in her left cheek. She looked at him blearily, like he'd awakened her from a dream. She said, "He was my baby."

Brandon stopped and stood in front of her. Her fingers, with red-painted nails, clenched the metal like she was an animal in a zoo. She pulled herself upright, the reek of alcohol wafting through the fence, mixing with the boatyard smells.

"Did you hear what I said?" she said. "I am Tiff Rawlings and Thatcher Rawlings was my son."

"I did hear you. And I'm sorry."

Her hair was blonde, with bangs askew. There was a pinkish slash across her lower lip. Smeared lipstick. She smiled and the pink streak twitched.

"I started to put makeup on when I decided to come see you," she said. "Can you believe that? Like it matters? Like anything matters?"

"I'm sorry," Brandon said. "I'm sorry it happened. I'm sorry for you and your family."

"You're sorry," she said. "*You're* sorry. What are you sorry about? Your mother still has a son." She gave him the bloody grin again and Brandon had a flashback, Thatcher on his back, blood pumping out, running down his chin like water from a fountain.

"Your mother can call you. Your mother can talk to you. Your mother can hug you and make you dinner and ask you how your day was. 'Hi Brandon.' It is Brandon, right? 'Hi Brandon, kill anyone today? How many kids did you blow away?' Kids, goddamn it. Stupid kids doing stupid things. Making stupid movies to put on stupid fucking YouTube so other stupid kids can look at them and give them a follow or a like or whatever the fuck it is they do."

Brandon took a deep silent breath. Waited.

"Unless some yahoo cop comes along and kills him, leaves him dying in some God-forsaken fucking place, all by himself, this little boy who never hurt anybody, never had a bad word to say. You know what the worst thing was that you could say about Thatcher? That he was a geek. That's all. Video games and his geeky friends and never the cool kid, never the big jock. My husband and I used to say, 'You think he'll ever have a girlfriend?' I'd say, 'Maybe in college, some other geeky person just like him. And they'll have little geeky kids and they'll all live happily ever after. But now..."

She sobbed and retched. A boat owner came out of the parking lot, Kyle Drake from the big Grady White sportfisherman, lugging a cooler. Bait, Brandon thought. Eels for stripers. Drake looked at Mrs. Rawlings, then at Brandon, and clicked the gate open with his card. He turned sideways and squeezed through, let the gate bang shut. Continued across the yard like it was normal for a distraught woman to be hanging from the marina fence.

Tiff Rawlings pulled herself together enough to talk. "He'll never be there when I look into his room to check on him. I still did that. I did. 'G'night, Thatch.' I still did that and he'd say, 'G'night, Mom.' Two nights ago. I didn't know it was the last time I'd speak to my son."

Gulls soared over, eyeing them the way gulls did when there was anything unusual going on because unusual might mean food. Brandon said, "I didn't want to hurt your son. I did everything possible to—"

"Where's your mother, Officer Blake? Let's call her right now. I want to talk to her, you know, mother to mother, see if she can put herself in my shoes. I mean, she probably loves you. Thinks you're a big brave cop, protecting society from skinny kids with toy guns."

Brandon knew he should leave, just turn and walk away. But he felt rooted, nailed in place.

"Call her, Blake. She'll be glad to hear from you. Probably make her day. Let me talk to her. We'll have a nice chat. Maybe we can make a date for coffee. Hey, we could get to be friends, having so much in common, you killing my son and all. Yeah, that's it. We could bond. She can come over to the house, I'll invite some of my friends, introduce her around. Tell her not to worry, we're pretty casual. My friend Sarah, she's a little old for Lily Pulitzer but she's the only one who—"

"My mother's dead," Brandon said. "She died when I was three."

Tiff Rawlings paused, looked at him and smiled.

"Good," she said. "I'm glad."

The smile fell away.

"Except she'll never know what it's like to bury your son."

Louder, she said, "She'll never know what it's like to never hear your son's voice again."

Still louder, shouting, she said, "She'll never know what it's like to get that knock on the door and hear the fucking cop say, 'Mr. Rawlings. This is the Portland Police Department. I'm afraid we have some bad news.'"

She shook the fence, the chain links jangling. Brandon heard an outboard rev behind him, a small one, someone at the float by the ramp. The motor shut off and there was just the fence rattling, Tiff Rawlings shouting, "Bad news? Bad news? Bad news is your car got towed. Bad news is your son got arrested for drunk driving. Or pot. Or maybe he was in a car crash and he's in the emergency room getting patched up and can we come get him. That's bad news. That a cop shot him and killed him for no fucking reason and now he's dead and there a hole in him, and he's gone."

She sobbed, retched, and her head dropped to her chest, her fingers still entwined in the metal links. "My beautiful, beautiful boy."

Brandon stood still, let her words pelt him like stones. He felt the stare behind him, whoever was on the float. And then someone came around the side of the boat shed, the roadside. The photographer who had been with Estusa. Tiff Rawlings turned to look, the photographer shooting video. Then Estusa materialized beside her, notebook and recorder in hand. He held the recorder up as Tiff Rawlings bellowed into the camera, "He killed him. He killed my sweet, wonderful, beautiful boy."

And as she started to cry, part sob and part moan, Estusa moved closer, the recorder held out in front of him like it was guiding him in, a misery detector. Thirty feet, twenty, then ten.

"Just go," Brandon said.

"Public property on this side, Officer Blake," Estusa said.

"Interview this man," Tiff Rawlings said. "Ask him what it feels like to shoot someone in cold blood."

"How does it feel to meet the mother of your shooting victim?" Estusa said, pointing the recorder at Brandon. "Does it make you regret your actions?"

Brandon bit back the words welling up inside him. Go to hell you piece of shit. He finally moved, peeling his shoes off the ground, turning his back on them, and he heard Estusa say, "Mia. How are *you* doing?"

She'd come from the parking area, had her book bag in one hand, a Starbucks cup in the other. "Abukar texted me," she said to Brandon, took two steps toward the gate. The photographer was shooting, the camera like a single eye, shutter snapping.

"Mia, could I talk to you for just a few minutes?" Estusa said, veering toward the gate, cutting her off. "Because this is almost as much about you. Your past. Your experience as a victim. Your intimate relationship with a man who has killed more than once."

"Leave her alone," Brandon said, moving to the gate.

"Just a few minutes," Estusa was saying, moving toward Mia, following her as she retreated, the photographer shooting from beside her, getting both Mia and Brandon in the shots, maybe Tiff Rawlings, too, now leaning against the fence and watching.

"No comment," Mia was saying. "I have nothing to say."

And then Brandon was through the gate, heard Tiff Rawlings say, "Is this your little honey? How does it feel to sleep with a murderer?"

"That's not fair, Mrs. Rawlings," Estusa said, close to Mia now. "Mia didn't shoot your son. She's as much a victim as——"

Brandon grabbed him by the shoulder, spun him around.

"Brandon, don't," Mia said.

"Get your hands off me," Estusa said, shoving back.

"You're a psychopath," Rawlings yelled.

"Brandon, don't," Mia shouted.

"You piece of shit, I should kick your fucking ass——"

And then a car hurtled up, slid to a stop behind Rawlings, still against the fence. A shiny black Grand Cherokee, the driver's door flung open. Big blonde guy rolled out, jeans and a pink polo shirt, trotted to the woman, pulled her down like he was taking her off a cross.

"Tiff, stop it," the guy said, holding the woman by her armpits. Tiff Rawlings pointing at Brandon and screamed, "It was him. There he is."

The guy looked at Brandon, kept backing up, dragging the woman with him. He called out, "You're finished, you son of a bitch. You goddamn coward. We're gonna put you away. You're fucking done, you hear me. Gonna own your sorry ass, you pathetic piece of shit."

"Not gonna get away with this," Tiff Rawlings screamed over her shoulder. "They're gonna lock you up. See how you like it then, Blake, you fucking murderer."

The guy stuffed her into the passenger seat and shoved the door shut. As he was coming around the front of the Jeep a cruiser pulled up. South Portland—Otongo and Robichaud again. The Jeep backed up and swerved out into the road. Rawlings braked, pulled up to the fence, slammed the truck into reverse. For a few seconds, their gazes were locked, Brandon and the parents of the kid he had killed.

And in that moment, Brandon expected to see seething fury. Blind hatred. Two people who would kill him with their bare hands. But he didn't.

He saw the woman look at him, then at her husband. She was impatient, like it was time to go, what was he waiting for? The guy shot a glance back, like he was annoyed with her. He said something and she spat something back, and he turned as the Jeep began to back up. She turned and looked at the patrol car, then back at Blake, and, as the Jeep started to drive off, then braked hard to stop, she flipped him off.

In that glimpse, she wasn't crazed by grief or hysterical or seething with anger. Brandon's last glimpse was of Tiff Rawlings suddenly shouting at him, the words muffled through the glass, the Jeep pulling away, Brandon thinking it was like she's been playing a part and had just gotten back into character.

Estusa was twenty feet to one side, had his recorder out and the photographer had backed off to the other side of the road, snapped a longer lens on, kept shooting. Otongo told Estusa to vacate and Estusa protested and Otongo said, "Don't make me lock you up because you'll be mailing your stories in from the county jail."

"The roadway is public property," Estusa said.

"Where you're creating a public nuisance," Otongo said.

She started toward him and Estusa started to back away.

"Brandon," he called. "You change your mind, know where to reach me."

Brandon shook his head, saw Mia walking back toward her car. He caught up, came alongside her and said, "I'm really sorry."

"I know. Me, too. But I can't stay here. Not with this."

"They'll be leaving."

"And then they'll be back. And tomorrow everyone will know. We'll be trapped, Brandon, stuck on a goddamn boat."

"I can't leave. I won't," Brandon said.

"You can stay at the apartment," Mia said.

"They'll follow me there. Estusa, then whoever comes next. At least here there's a fence."

"Whatever, Brandon. I'm going. I'm sorry. But it's just too much."

She was wide-eyed, her voice quivering.

"I'll call you later," Brandon said.

"Right."

"After they're gone."

"Okay."

And then Mia started walking faster, almost broke into a trot. The doors cheeped on the Volvo and the lights flashed and she yanked the driver's door open, slung her bag across the front seats, and slid in. The motor started with roar and she swerved across the lot and out. As she skidded onto the pavement, the photographer ran five steps closer, crouched and fired.

Brandon started to run toward her. Caught himself. Pivoted right and slowed, walked to the fence and the gate, barely looking at the Rawlingses, now in their Jeep, the cops leaning into the windows on both sides. Estusa was beyond the Jeep, back turned, on the phone. "Yeah, he grabbed me," he was saying. "Oh, yeah. Clamped right on."

And then Brandon was through the gate, slamming it shut behind him. He walked down the ramp, saw people eyeing him from the other boats. Kyle on the Grady White, sitting in the stern, pretending to rig a fishing rod. The MacMasters, sitting on deck chairs on *Ghost Dancer*. Tommy Kim, from *Junkman*, a sloop moored beyond the floats, was approaching pulling a dock cart.

"Hey," he said, flashing a brief smile as he passed, no chitchat today, not even a comment about the cops beyond the fence. He knew not to ask.

Tommy kept walking and Brandon stepped over the transom and onto *Bay Witch*, the cruiser rocking almost imperceptibly under his weight. He looked back toward the yard, saw that the cruiser and the Jeep were gone, presumably Estusa and his photographer, too. Or they could be waiting, the photographer staked out with a telephoto aimed at the boat, waiting for Brandon to come out on the deck with a beer.

Killer Cop Drinks While Victim's Parents Grieve

Brandon scowled, went through the hatch door and down into the galley. He threw himself heavily on the settee on the port side, away from the road. Put his head in his hands and took a long deep breath. Exhaled.

"Shit," he said.

He got up and crossed to the galley, took the clean dishes out of the rack and set them in the cupboard. Took a mug out of the cupboard, the French press off the shelf, and filled the kettle. Turned on the burner and the kettle hissed against the flame.

Brandon filled the press with coffee, waited for the water to boil. It didn't, not fast enough, and he turned away, started neatening the stuff on the chart table: a boating magazine, one of Mia's literary journals, a book on teaching poetry.

"You've got to be kidding me," Brandon said.

He put Mia's stuff in one stack, feeling an ominous premonition. Shook it off and the kettle began to whistle. He crossed the three steps to the other side of the cabin, turned the gas off and poured the water into the press, then turned back to the settee, sat back down in the same spot. Stared out the starboard side and eyed the yard. No cruisers, no distraught people in sight.

Brandon held the mug to his lips and blew. Sipped. The coffee singed his lips and he blew again. Sipped again. Looked across the top of the mug to the writing desk.

His laptop. He looked away, replayed the advice in his head: stay away from alcohol, don't read the paper or read the online comments, don't watch news on TV. He was drinking coffee. He didn't have a television. He wouldn't read the *Review*, Estusa's crap.

But the laptop sat there like a beacon, the silver MacBook seeming to glow in the dim cabin. Brandon took a sip of coffee and stared. Put the mug down on the table and got up, pulled to his feet like he'd been hypnotized. He picked up the laptop, walked back to the settee and sat. Flipped it open.

A deep breath.

A pause.

He opened the browser, went to Facebook.

Typed in *Thatcher Rawlings.* Waited.

There were two. One was in Chico, California. The other in Moresby, Maine.

Brandon tapped the keyboard, his hands like a puppet's, attached by strings to some invisible puppeteer. He waited as the wheel turned, and then Thatcher Rawlings profile page appeared.

Where there should have been a profile photo of Rawlings, there was a picture of Harrison Ford. He was young and was holding a stubby handgun with red lights showing under the barrel.

Brandon stared, tried to place it.

Blade Runner.

Rawlings had been tagged in a dozen posts, high school kids. *RIP, Thatch....I know you're in a better place.....It's only a movie, man....Don't worry, Thatch. That cop's gonna fry....got your back thatch....Love u, bro....since when is there a death penalty in Maine? For shooting a freakin' video?...Blake's gonna like it in prison. Not....shoulda had a real gun, dude, but who knew you'd be gunned down in cold blood....you know what happens to cops in jail. Don't drop the soap!...You're at peace, Thatch. That cop will have this on his head the rest of his pathetic life.... My heart goes out to the Rawlings family.*

And this, from H. James Kelly, Esq.:

On behalf of the Rawlings family, we thank you for your support. Please respect the family's privacy at this time. We will be releasing more information about Thatcher's tragic death, the circumstances surrounding it, and next steps when that information becomes available. In the meantime, please remember Thatcher in your prayers. He is gone but will never be forgotten.

Brandon felt his jaw clench. He swallowed hard. The puppeteer flicked the strings again and Brandon's finger tapped.

About Thatcher Rawlings.

His favorite movie was *Blade Runner*. His favorite activity was paint-ball. There was a photo of Rawlings in protective goggles, a paintball gun aimed at the camera. He was smiling, the same enigmatic grin that he'd flashed just before he died. His goal in life was "to hunt replicants, like the ones that are all around us, including the jocks at Moresby High. You know who you are, d***heads."

Back to the profile page. Rawlings had 45 friends, a very small circle for Facebook. They were mostly his age, looked artsy, like they might do high school band or drama. Not jocks. Three or four of the friends were older, one with another *Blade Runner* character for her photo—the blonde woman with black makeup across her eyes. A replicant, Brandon thought. An actress whose name he should know. This was a serious fan, and was that what Thatcher Rawlings had been? Was that what he had been doing at the bar? Some *Blade Runner* scene? Living out his fantasy?

"Jesus," Brandon said.

He sagged back on the cushions, threw his head back. Had that been Thatcher's fatal mistake? Being a geek with very bad judgment?

Brandon looked around the cabin, felt the bulkheads start to close in. The boat seemed small, the reality suffocating him. He couldn't think his way out of it, couldn't distract himself enough to shake it loose. The three shots, the three dark blotches in the kid's chest, like paintball except not paintball at all. The kid's amazed expression as he fell backward, the unblinking eyes that stayed wide open as he died.

"Oh, god," Brandon said.

He stood, crossed the cabin to the starboard side and looked out. There was another TV crew on the other side of the fence, a van with the station's call letters on the side. A guy this time, his back to the boats, cameraman with the camera on his shoulder, aimed, it seemed, at Brandon's face.

He stepped back, was reaching for his phone when it buzzed. Mia? Kat?

Brandon picked it up, didn't recognize the number, read the message.

How can you sleep at night, you filthy piece of shit?

He clicked the screen dark. The phone buzzed again. A different number.

Hope you go to prison with the rest of the murderers you piece of human garbage. You're lower than scum Blake. Prison is filled with better people than you, asshole.

Brandon flicked the message away, started to put the phone down but it buzzed again.

What were you afraid of Blake? That the plastic gun would shoot plastic bullets? You're a coward Blake, like all cops. Need that gun and badge to make you feel tough. But you're not tough Blake. You're a pussy.

Brandon looked away, then back. The phone hummed again.

Officer Brandon Blake: He was a good kid. He never hurt anybody. Why didn't you just try to talk to him? Why didn't you tell him to stop fooling around? Why didn't you tell him to just put the gun down? He used to come over our house since he was 4. He was the sweetest boy in the world and now he's gone.

He put the phone down but the texts kept coming, the phone buzzing like an upended beetle. And then it burbled, the ringer. Brandon leaned closer.

Mia.

He waited and the phone rang five times then stopped. There was a chime: voice mail. Brandon picked the phone up and flicked the screen. Waited. Listened.

"Hi, Brand. Just calling to make sure you're okay. Why don't you come over here? We can order Thai, watch a movie or something. Estusa was parked out front for a while but now he's gone."

Brandon closed the voice mail, then his eyes. He put the phone back down. He was staring at it when it buzzed again—a text, the words MURDERER and COWARD legible even upside down. Brandon reached for the phone and texted Mia:

I'm fine. Hope you are too. Don't talk to Estusa. I'll call you later.

He tapped *send*, waited a few seconds and put the phone down.

The television crew left and was replaced by another one, local Fox News. Brandon crossed to the galley, put the milk back in the tiny refrigerator. He shook the coffee grounds out of the French press into the trash can and rinsed the press in the sink. Then he wiped the counter down, folded the dishcloth neatly and hung it on its hook.

He stood there and looked out the window at the sunny September day, a good day to be on the bay. Brandon considered it, taking the boat out of the harbor, way beyond the islands, where nobody could find him. He hadn't had *Bay Witch* out for a couple of weeks, the last time limping back from Chebeague Island with the motor misfiring. Not bad, just a little skip, enough to be unsettling. Water in the fuel maybe, because he'd drawn the tank down. He'd been meaning to change the fuel filter, add a can of dryer to a new tank of gas. Hesitating, he decided against a cruise, because of the boat and not wanting to be stranded out on the water, another way to get his name in the paper. He could write the story himself:

Brandon Blake, the Portland police officer who shot and killed a Moresby teen Thursday, was assisted by the Coast Guard Friday after his cabin cruiser had engine trouble in Casco Bay.

Blake's 28-foot Chris Craft, Bay Witch, *was just east of Peaks Island when the cabin cruiser developed engine trouble. Blake's destination was not known. He is on administrative leave with pay pending investigation of the shooting. Portland Police said that his movements are not restricted, though he is expected to be available to investigators.*

Meanwhile, the family of 16-year-old Thatcher Rawlings, the teenager shot Blake shot and killed Tuesday night after the youth reportedly refused to drop a plastic gun outside a Portland bar, was preparing for his memorial service...

Brandon went back to the settee. Sat. Rested his head in his hands and closed his eyes. He saw the blood. Thatcher's eyes, the moment when they faded and went blank. That instant played and replayed. Where there was life one second, then there was none. Just like that. All of the life that Thatcher Rawlings had contained, all that he'd been for 16 years—liking movies, paintball, being a jerk or a geek or a nice kid—was gone. The person he had been was erased. Thatcher Rawlings no longer existed.

Because he had pulled the trigger.

Because he had fired rather ducking. Doing nothing. Letting the kid play his stupid game with his plastic gun, then chase him down, put him on his belly, snap the cuffs on and say, "You little bastard. You know how close you just came to getting shot?"

Brandon could see it, that scenario. It was like wishing could make it come true. The kid on the ground. Brandon calling in, suspect in custody. A collective exhalation. A little disappointment. The cops who itched for a chase missing out on one. The cops who had been in one before breathing a sigh of relief.

It was excruciating, seeing the way it could have played out. And then the fantasy faded and reality filtered back in until it was thick as fog, choking as poison gas.

The phone began to rattle again. Texts coming in one after another, the phone buzzing like an alarm. Brandon eyed it like it was a living thing, then lunged and grabbed it. Where were they getting his number? He flicked through the latest barrage—*God will punish you even if the cops won't…hope you die slow…it isn't over*—until he found it. A group text, the recipient list trailing off. *This is his number. Got it from a good source. The press isn't all bad. Text and let him know his life will be hell too.*

The mom, most likely. Estusa had Brandon's number from early on, when he'd been with the *Portland Press*, before he'd shown his true colors, gotten canned.

Brandon scowled, thought of replying to the texts, at least telling Estusa to go to hell. But he thought better of it, reached for the phone and turned it off. Let them text themselves into a lather, he wouldn't see them. Wouldn't go online at all. No news reports. No nothing.

But what?

He looked around. Crossed the cabin and looked toward the yard and the road beyond. The news crew was packing up. A car eased into view and stopped. Brandon reached binoculars off the shelf and looked. A blacked-out BMW, four guys inside. High school kids, all craned to look toward *Bay Witch*. They were talking, pointing. The driver, a scraggly-haired kid with dark-framed glasses, reached out the open window and held up his middle finger in Brandon's general direction.

There was shouting. "Fuck you, cop."

"You suck."

"Asshole."

The car lurched forward a couple of times, then there was a screech of tires, and it sped out of sight. Brandon lowered the glasses. Thought of making a note of the make, model, time. Then another car rolled up from the other direction, then two. A white SUV, a Tahoe. A mini-van. He raised the glasses again. Girls in the SUV, peering toward the boats. Angry faces. Guys in the mini van, more shouting but more subdued than the guys in the BMW. These cars stopped.

And then the BMW was back, skidded to a stop. The driver leaned on the horn. The other two did the same, a blaring cacophony like a Manhattan traffic jam. The kids were shouting but the horns drowned them out. And then a cruiser rolled up. Otongo. She put on the blues and the honking stopped. The BMW started to drive away but Otongo pulled in front of it, cut it off.

She got out, touching her shoulder mic, headed for the BMW. Another cruiser pulled in, blocked the van and the Tahoe. Robichaud. He got out, big and burly, and strode to the driver's side of the SUV. Robichaud said something and Brandon could see the girl digging for her license. The driver of the BMW was out of the car, doing the same. He was tall, thin, skinny jeans and black T-shirt with something on the front. He started to gesture toward Otongo and she said something that shut him up. She took his license and headed for the cruiser. Robichaud was at the mini-van, leaning in.

A white VW came into view, stopped. Estusa and the photographer got out. The photographer raised her camera, started shooting. Estusa went to Otongo's cruiser, said something and Otongo said something back, not looking up. Estusa went to the BMW, started talking to the driver, Estusa scribbling on a notepad.

Brandon watched for 15 minutes as the cops sorted things out. They talked to the kids, Brandon knowing the drill. They could be cited for disorderly conduct, a misdemeanor punishable by a fine of up to $500. A repeat offense could result in a jail sentence, prosecution for criminal trespass. He could hear Otongo: How would that look on your college applications?

The cops handed the licenses back, no citations. The kids got into their vehicles and headed off. The cops pulled their cruisers around so they were facing Bay Witch and flicked their lights. The cruisers pulled away and were gone, and only Estusa and the photographer were left, the woman peering at the back of her camera at her shots, Estusa looking toward the boat. Peering through the binoculars, Brandon saw him wave and smile.

He stepped back into the shadows of the cabin, laid the binoculars down. A couple of boat owners passed by the stern, pulling dock carts and glancing into *Bay Witch*, knowing the reason for the ruckus. Brandon sat back down on the port side settee, looked at his phone, quiet now, the laptop screen dark.

He could feel his mood spiraling downward, like something dropped overboard at sea, the waters growing darker and darker. He shook himself loose, considered whether he should just fill the tank, add some dry gas, and go. Find a cove out around Chebeague or Peaks and anchor.

The logistics of it ran through his mind. Fuel, food, water. Telling the boat owners he'd be gone for a couple of days, the usual grumbling when he wasn't available at the fuel dock, to take reservations for guest moorings, to help people hook up to shore power, tell them where to dump their waste tanks.

He scowled, looked down at the deck at this feet, saw the edge of something sticking out from under the settee. It was a print: dark pink flowers and green leaves. He leaned down and pulled it out.

The diary.

SIX

The cover was soft, flower-print fabric over some sort of padding. Brandon flipped the book open. Written inside in purple ink was the name Danni Moulton, and Woodford, Maine, a former mill town 20 miles south of Portland. The pages were filled with a careful, looping cursive that fit precisely between the ruled lines. Each entry was addressed to Danni (Me) with a handwritten smiley face. The entries were dated. The first was 4-1-93; the last, December 11, 1994. Brandon held the diary upside down and shook it. A couple of loose folded pages fell out, and a clipping slipped from the papers. He picked it up off the deck and turned it over.

A newspaper photo of a high-school age guy with a big smile and a mullet. Someone, presumably Danni, had written below the face, *I love Jackson*, then crossed that out and scribbled on the face with a different pen.

He started at the beginning.

April 1. April Fool's Day.

I guess I got fooled. Matty said he loved me and that was why he wanted to sleep with me. I think I loved him too or I could of if he hadn't gone back to Starr even tho he said it was just to tell her they were finished. But Starr said he slept with her

49

again and told these guys at the Qik Lube that he works with, including this dude who goes out with her cousin. Even that guy said it was a shitty thing to do, keep two girls all strung along on lies and then act like it's a big joke. I don't know if I'm glad Starr told me, maybe better if Matty just went away and I never knew.

Brandon's phone buzzed. He glanced at it. A text from Estusa. Brandon put the phone down. Turned the page.

April 4: Danni got in a fight at school, a girl calling her a slut. The girl lied and Danni got three days suspension.

I don't care. I hate Woodford HS. I hate all those assholes. I'm never going back to that dump.

April 8: Danni went back to school.

I said I felt sick so I could go to the nurse and sleep. I saw Sashay in the hall but she looked the other way.

April 19: Danni's father, who lived in Albany, New York, bought her a car, a used Toyota Corolla with 210,000 miles. He drove to Maine and dropped the car and left. Danni's mother said Danni had to pay her own insurance and Danni got a quote for $1,800, which was $1,657 more than she had. Her mother's boyfriend said it would teach her responsibility to pay for it herself. *Cheap bastard leeches off my mom like all the freakin' time, don't tell me about being responsible.* The car was parked behind the garage. *I hate my life*, Danni wrote.

May 7: Danni had a crush on Zack and even bought him some weed but he tried to have sex with her and couldn't. *He said it was the pot but I think he just doesn't think I'm sexy. I feel so stupid. So what else is new.*

June 23: graduation. Danni's mother couldn't attend because she had to work mandatory overtime at the nursing home. Danni got drunk at a party afterward and ended up walking around town all by herself trying not to throw up. *Which was no surprise, high school ending on a sucky note cuz the whole time pretty much sucked and when it didn't it was about to.*

The phone buzzed again. A text from a reporter at WPRT TV, probably got his number from Estusa. Brandon ignored it.

July 4: Danni met a guy named Roger St. Clair at a party before the fireworks. Everybody smoked pot and then went to the park and Roger sat with her on the blanket all night and ended up making out with her in his car afterward. *He's different. From Mass. He said he'd never met anyone like me before. I gave him my number. Is he the 1? I just know he was way sweeter than Matt or Zack, that shit.*

Brandon read on.

Roger didn't call. Danni decided he was a jerk after all, she should have known. She and her friend Vanity drank wine coolers and went to Target at the mall and Vanity stuffed a scarf and a bra inside her shirt and got stopped at the door. *They hauled her off to Moresby County jail and I waited and waited and than he said 25.00 bail great all I had was 10 so I had to go bum 15 off my grandfather to get her out thank god he was home. It took her 1 hour after just to let her be released. My date with Roger is Friday. I pray it goes O.K.*

It didn't. Roger texted her to say he was sick. And so it went, one disappointment after another. Danni was pregnant but then she wasn't after all. Gonna marry Roger, but then she wasn't. She went to night school to get her CNA but didn't finish because her mother's minivan broke down on the way to the final exam, and *screw it anyway, wiping up people's crap and spit.*

Brandon's phone buzzed, another text. Mia.

```
I'm staying here, you coming over?
tired, been a long day.
you sure you're alright by yourself?
I'm fine. Just need to decompress. It's been
a lot.
you sure?
yeah.
really?
yeah, really.
call me then.
I will.
love you.
love you too.
```

Brandon got up from the settee, went to the starboard side windows and looked out. A TV van was parked outside the gate, a blonde woman doing a stand-up with the marina and boats in the background. He pulled the curtain shut, went to the writing table and opened his laptop, then Facebook. Searched for Danni Moulton, Woodford, Maine.

First hit: A photo of a heavyset blonde woman in her 40s. The picture was a selfie taken in a bathroom mirror, a flare of light showing beside her head like a muzzle flash. Danni was wearing a tank top and a sad smile, like she'd been burned way too many times.

Her profile said she'd gone to Woodford H.S., was in a relationship. She liked watching NASCAR with her cat, Dale (Earnhart). It didn't say whether her relationship was with the cat or with a person.

Flipping the diary open, he read more: *No ring. No baby. I'm afraid he's going back to Rachel. I hate my life. I do. I do, I do, I do.*

The boat rocked. Brandon closed the laptop, got up and quickly moved to the stern. It was Kat, in jeans and T-shirt, bulge of her carry gun under the shirt on her right hip. Brandon came up through the hatchway and out. Kat smiled.

"Am I supposed to wait to be piped aboard or something? I can never keep this nautical stuff straight."

"If I'd known you were coming, I would have had the crew lined up in their dress whites," Brandon said.

Kat stepped over the transom, onto the boat.

"Well, at least you swabbed the poopdeck," Kat said, eyeing the gleaming varnished wood.

"Nothing else to do," Brandon said.

Kat moved close, clasped his shoulder.

"How are you?"

"Fine."

"Considering?"

"Yeah," Brandon said. "Considering."

"Everybody's thinking about you."

"Thanks. Want coffee?"

"Sure," Kat said. "Didn't come all the way to SoPo for idle chit chat."

They moved inside, Brandon holding the hatchway door open behind him.

"Cozy," Kat said. "Mia home?"

"Went to the apartment. Things got a little crazy around here earlier. She'd had enough."

He lit the kettle again, retrieved the coffee and French press.

"Heard the family and friends paid you a visit."

"Oh, yeah."

"How was that?"

"They were upset. It was upsetting," Brandon said.

"Hang in there."

"No choice."

They stood in the cabin, watched the kettle as it rattled on the burner.

"Hope you're not watching the news."

"No."

"Or reading the papers."

Brandon shrugged.

"That's nothing compared to Facebook."

"You're supposed to stay away from all that," Kat said.

"After the screaming mother, the rest of it's no big deal."

"Sure it is. It's a very big deal. You know it and I know it, so don't go locking everything up inside."

Brandon got out two mugs, didn't answer. He stared at the kettle as it started to hiss. Kat smiled.

"Like I said."

They stood and waited, Kat hunched below the bulkhead above her head. In the cruiser they would ride in silence for hours but there was something awkward about these couple of minutes. Finally, the kettle steamed and Brandon poured, waited for the press to drip. It finally did and he handed Kat a mug. She sniffed the mug, creased her eyes. Sipped. Smiled. "Way to a cop's heart," she said.

They chinked mugs like they sometimes touched paper cups in the cruiser, Kat saying, "Here's to the good guys," Brandon replying, "Good guys. What good guys?"

Standing there, they blew and sipped, just like in the cruiser. Brandon thought that it seemed like months ago that he'd put on his uniform, loaded up the cruiser, hit the streets.

"I've got a little news," Kat said.

"I've been cleared for duty?"

"No. The parents hired Jim Kelly."

"I know. He's been on Facebook already," Brandon said.

"He'll be looking for big bucks, suing everybody in sight."

"Gotta pay for that yacht somehow."

"They also hired a social media consultant."

Brandon looked at her.

"Like for their Instagram page?"

"Like they already have a hashtag. Kids lives matter."

"Jesus. How'd you hear about that?"

"The university uses the same outfit for an ad campaign or some marketing thing. One of their admins is friends with the admin in Maddie's department."

"Christ," Brandon said. "It's not like I shot an unarmed kid. Or shot him in the back. Or panicked and shot him because he was reaching for his wallet. I had no choice."

He looked at her. "Right?" he said.

"I know," Kat said. "Don't have to tell me. But they're launching a Twitter campaign."

Brandon drank some coffee.

"Probably go viral," he said.

"You've got to stay strong," Kat said.

"I'm fine."

"Stop saying that."

Brandon didn't answer.

"And don't shut down on me, either."

"You said that already, too. I think you're getting dementia."

"You need to find something to do," Kat said.

"I know. I was going to take the boat out but I figured they'd say I was partying on my cabin cruiser while they buried their son."

Kat thought. "That's exactly what they'd say."

"Estusa was outside Mia's place already. I don't want to drag her into this anymore than I already have."

"How?"

"By going anywhere near her."

"Because of the last time."

"Right."

Kat sipped, stepped to the starboard side, flipped the curtains open and closed.

"Anybody out there?" Brandon said.

"Not at the moment."

"There will be. So here I sit."

"Anywhere you can go?"

Brandon shrugged, drank coffee, lowered the mug.

"I could go on a road trip but I don't want to look like I'm running," he said.

"Might be good to get away from all this."

"Hard to hide from a Tweet," Brandon said.

The boat rocked with a passing wake and Kat shifted on her feet. She put the mug down on the counter by the sink. "I gotta go get ready," she said.

"Good luck. Stay safe."

"You too. Mentally, I mean."

"I'm—"

He caught himself, smiled.

"You know something about this hashtag thing?" Brandon said.

Kat waited.

"I'm young too."

"Only in years," Kat said, and headed for the hatchway, lowering her head. "I'll be checking in."

Kat got off the boat, walked up the ramp to the yard. Brandon watched from the stern, then went back below, sat at the desk. Flicked his phone on, opened Twitter. He searched for it and there it was:

Thatcher Rawlings, December 1, 1999-September 8, 2016. Dead at the hands of the Portland, Maine Police Department. #kidslivesmatter

The tweet was from @tiffrawlings. In less than five minutes, it had gotten 132 likes and had been retweeted 39 times. Brandon clicked the phone dark. Sat and stared, looking toward the starboard windows but seeing only as far as the inside of his head.

Minutes passed. A half-hour. His phone rattled like it was trying to rid itself of something. Texts. When the phone wasn't buzzing, the only sound was the scolding cry of gulls and the lap of water against the wooden hull.

Brandon felt himself hardening, frozen into a dark place. The night whirled around in his head, followed by the day. Thatcher. The shots. The blood. Tiff Rawlings, her snarling, lips-curled snarl, the visceral hatred. And then memories of his own mother, wild child Nikki Blake lost at sea when he was three. The images were so fragmentary and elusive that he didn't know if he had imagined them, dragged them from old snapshots, turned them into facsimiles of actual memories.

He only thought of her when he was sinking, and then he would wonder if that was because she had sunk herself, executed on a sailboat for a pile of drug smuggler's cash. Now they sank together, mother and son, the only thing that seemed to link them. Bad luck? Bad judgment? Some of both?

"Damn," he said, and shook himself loose. He got up from the settee and paced the cabin, shouted, "Why didn't you just drop the goddamn gun?"

And then there was quiet again, gulls and water. Brandon criss-crossed the cabin until he felt the black rage start to fade. And then he looked at the writing desk, went and sat.

He flipped the laptop lid, the screen lighting to show Danni's Face-book page, her sad, smiling face. He hesitated, then started to type a message:

You don't know me but I feel like I know you. I found a diary and I think it's yours. From high school in the 90s. Your best friend was named Starr. She was arrested for shoplifting at the mall. If you'd like the diary back, just shoot me a message and I'll get it to you. I live in Portland.

Brandon hit return and the note was sent—from the Facebook account of Chris Craft of Portland, Maine. He picked the diary up from the desk, went back to the settee and started to read. Danni working at MacDonald's. Danni meeting her best friend Nelly at Domino's. Telling Nelly about a new guy she'd met, Marcus, who seemed wicked nice. Turned out he wasn't.

My mind is so confused its unreal. I hate life and especially myself. I hate men. They are all jerks, assholes, users. I am very hurt. My heart feels like it has been stamped on by everyone. Is their something wrong with me?

The entry ended not with a smiley face, but with a grimace. Brandon read a few more pages, snapshots of Danni's sad and lonely life. But every few days, she'd pick herself back up, meet a new guy, party with her friends, draw a few smiley faces until the next betrayal. Brandon wondered what she'd think if she read the message, knowing a stranger was reading her most private thoughts, seeing her when she was most vulnerable.

He'd give the book back to her, say, "Here you go. Your secrets are safe again." It was a small thing but these days small things were all he had.

And then Brandon fell asleep on the settee, lulled by the slap of the waves, the cool September breeze blowing off the harbor and through the cabin. He was out cold, gone, exhausted by all of it, maybe driven to the deepest sleep by the need to escape. He didn't dream, didn't move, slept with his head lolled back on the settee pillow, the diary open on his chest.

And when he woke it was dark. He had a moment of peace before it all landed on him again, compressing his chest, clamping down on his skull. He took a deep breath, hoisted himself up off the settee, lurched to the galley sink. Reached over the sink to turn on a light, filled a glass with water, rinsed his mouth and spat.

Brandon picked up his phone, and climbed the steps to the bridge. Sitting at the helm, he looked out at the lights of Portland, glimmering across the harbor. Behind him, the red markers glowed on the bridge and headlights streamed across. The world was moving around him, like he was the only thing that had been anchored in place. He tapped his phone on, saw a missed call from Mia, another from Kat, still another from Sergeant Perry. He checked his voice mail: Mia wanted him to call her. Kat told him to stay away from alcohol. Sarge said he was just checking in, call if he needed anything, he'd call back.

And then another message, this one forwarded to his email. It was from Danni. She said:

hey, chris. yeah its me. I'd really love to have that back. Embarrased! Blush!!! Where do you want to meet up? Im in Woodford. Around tonight. Thanxxx!

A smiling emoji. Brandon hesitated, the typed out a reply:

Great. I'm headed down that way anyway. Just let me know where and when you want to meet.

He hit send. Waited. Ten seconds later:

Hey, Chris. Can you make it for 8? Dunkin on Route 1? Buy u a coffee for yr trouble.

Brandon looked at his watch, the glowing dial showing 6:23.

See you then. I'll be driving a blue Chevy pickup.

White ford focus. Number 3 in back window.

Nascar fan. Friends over to watch Talladega.

And another message appeared:

just park in the lot and wait. I'll find u.

Brandon stood. Hesitated there in the cabin, weighing his choices. Stay on the boat and replay it a thousand times. Leave and go meet this person and maybe get away for an hour or two. He could be Chris Craft. Leave Brandon and his problems behind.

He went to the locked cabinet on the starboard side, fished the key from its hook behind the curtain. Unlocked the wooden locker and stood there. Inside were five boxes of .45 ammo, the department Glock, his personal carry gun, a smaller Glock 26 9-millimeter in a waistband holster. Brandon picked it and held it in front of him. It looked foreign, not the familiar thing he'd picked up every day. Wallet. Keys. Radio. Gun.

Brandon put the gun down and stared at it, like he was window shopping. He hesitated, then reached back into the little cupboard and took the gun out. Stripped off his belt and slipped the holster on. Clinched the belt and stood. Could he do this? If he could carry it, could he ever fire it again?

SEVEN

Brandon made his calls on the ride south, Mia first. She didn't pick up. He left a voice mail: "I'm fine. Just had to get out of Dodge, go for a drive. I'll call you later. No worries."

Then Kat, the sound of the police radio in the background.

"I'm fine, Mom," Brandon said.

"And you're a lousy liar, Blake. You can be a lot of things right now, but fine isn't one of them."

"Okay, I'm fine considering. Going for a drive. Change of scenery."

"Good idea. Call me later, if you want."

"Will do. How's the night going?"

"The usual assholes and inebriates," Kat said. "You're not missing anything."

"Sure I am," Brandon said. "I'm missing the whole goddamn thing."

"Got your back."

"I know."

And then Perry, with Christiansen's K-9 barking in the background.

"What you got, Sarge?" Brandon said, like he could be there in five.

"Runner from a traffic stop. Passenger panicked. Condom full of heroin up his butt."

"That'll raise the anxiety level? Dog get him?"

"Oh, yeah. They can run but they can't hide."

"Right."

The dog barked louder, voices in the background, someone saying, "Keep him back." Then the barking subsided, replaced by the sound of a cruiser moving, the motor revving up.

"How you doing, Blake?" Perry said.

"Fine."

"Staying away from the news?"

"Oh, yeah."

"Just gotta ride it out," Perry said.

"Right."

"Stay close to home."

Brandon was getting on I-295 south.

"Right."

"Watch the Red Sox on TV or something."

"Gotcha."

"Low profile, Blake. Under the radar."

"Will do, Sarge."

And then Perry was gone. Brandon was passing the Scarborough exit. It was 7:15.

He had rules for meets like this, which were usually with informants or potential ones. Get there way earlier than the C.I. Park with your rear bumper to a fence and scan the area.

Wyatt Earp always sat facing the door of the saloon.

He rolled into the parking lot of the Dunkin' at 7:35, cruising through slowly once and then exiting, watching to see if anyone followed. No one did. He doubled back.

The second time in he parked at the back of the lot near the Dumpsters, turned off the motor and lights and sat. The place was quiet, a half-dozen cars parked in the back row beside him, beater Honda sedans and a lifted Toyota pickup that probably belonged to employees. Closer to the entrance there were four more cars and two Harleys. As Brandon watched, the bikers—big-bellied guys with black do-rags—came out and climbed on and revved, roared off.

He waited, the diary on the console beside him like a gift for a high school girlfriend. Cars came and went: an older couple holding hands; a Somali family, the women and girls in headscarves; the guys in shirts and ties. A skinny kid came out of the back of the restaurant with a bag of trash, walked toward Brandon, the kid making eye contact as he lifted the lid of the Dumpster and dropped the bag in. Brandon nodded and the kid did, too, started to cross the lot and stopped as a white Ford Focus swung into the lot and wheeled around the corner. Brandon saw Danni at the wheel, blonde hair pulled back. The car passed and parked nose in, four slots down the row. The lights went out, and Danni walked quickly from the car to the restaurant.

She was stocky and muscular, like somebody who did physical work. Waitress or CNA in a nursing home. Jeans tucked into black high-heeled boots, a black sweater. Brandon waited. At 7:58 Danni came out of the restaurant on the far side carrying two coffees, walked along the building and started for her car. When she reached the car she looked around, stood for a moment, and then walked over to Brandon's truck.

He opened the driver's door as she approached. Danni pulled it wider with the pinky of one hand and held the coffee out.

"Chris," she said.

"Danni," Brandon said.

"I was hoping you weren't just some weirdo in another blue Chevy pickup." He took the coffee and slid out, Danni holding out her hand to shake. They did and hers was strong. They stood awkwardly for a moment, both sipped. Smiled. He handed her the diary and she looked at it, said, "Oh, my god. I never thought I'd see this again." She glanced up at him, flipping pages with one hand, the swirling cursive showing in the parking-lot light.

"Did you read it?"

"Some, not all."

"Jesus Christ, this is so embarrassing. I can't believe I wrote this stuff down," she said.

"Sometimes it helps to get things out, I guess," Brandon said.

"Where did you find it?"

Brandon opened the coffee and sipped. Danni did the same, the breeze bringing a waft of mocha.

"Somebody I know bought a desk at a second-hand place in Portland. This was in the back of one of the drawers."

"And you tracked me down?"

"Wasn't hard. Facebook knows all."

She snapped the book shut, said, "Jeez, that brings some stuff back." She gave a shudder, looked at him.

"I had my ups and down in high school," Danni said.

"Didn't we all," Brandon said.

"You go to Portland High, Chris?" she said. "I knew people went there."

Brandon shook his head. "No. Home schooled, actually. Long story."

She looked at him curiously.

"I'll bet."

Dannie stared and said, "You ever live around here? You look kinda familiar."

"No. Portland, South Portland."

"Boy, seems like I've seen you somewhere."

"Maine's a small place," Brandon said.

He sipped the coffee. Milk, no sugar. A good guess.

"Well, awful nice of you to bring this down. Hope it didn't take you too far out of your way."

"Nah, no big deal."

"I'm glad to get it back. May burn it, though."

Brandon smiled. "You can spread the ashes."

"Hate to think of somebody reading about my love life, such as it was. God, I was a disaster."

It was getting awkward again.

"I'm sure it all worked itself out in the end," Brandon said. He lifted the cup to take a drink. Saw movement to his left, someone coming fast down the line of cars, Danni blurting, "Oh, my god!"

A guy running toward them, fist cocked back. Brandon turned to meet him, got his forearm up, stepped inside the first looping punch, the coffee cup flying. Their forearms slammed together, Brandon's arm going numb. The guy was close in, threw a wild left that hit Brandon in the shoulder, glanced off. He stepped in and hooked a leg, got the guy's right arm in a lock, jammed it backwards. The guy grunted. Brandon drove him back into the front of his truck.

The guy pushed off and they wrestled standing, just like Brandon with a drunk in the Old Port. He was big, stocky, a barrel chest and thick arms. Head shaved and a goatee with gray, his breath smelling of alcohol. The guy shouted, "Cheating bitch," and Danni stepped in, tried to pull him away. "Stop it, stop it. Are you out of your fucking mind?"

Danni was thrown off as they spun around, the diary falling and skidding on the pavement. She tried to reach for it but they stumbled into her and she staggered backwards. Brandon got a foot in again and drove his shoulder into the guy's chest, and this time the guy stumbled and fell. Brandon rode him down, blocked another punch with his forearm and hit the guy twice in the face. Two short jabs. The guy's face spurted blood and he saw Danni circle around them, drop to her hands and knees, looking under his truck.

The diary.

"You bitch," the guy shouted, and Brandon felt people watching. The guy went slack like he'd given up and when Brandon eased off, the guy thrashed and got another punch off, this one hitting Brandon on the cheekbone.

Brandon put his forearm across the guy's throat, scissored his legs and held the guy down. The guy got an arm loose and started to reach for something at his waist and Brandon grabbed the guy's left arm and twisted hard. The guy gasped, "You fucker," and Brandon took his arm off the guy's throat long enough to hit him in the face again. Once. Hard.

A small crowd was gathering. A few people from the restaurant, the kid who had taken out the trash. "Cops are coming," he said, like they should scatter. Danni reached under the truck, came up empty, her shoulder flecked with gravel. Got to her feet, trotted toward her car.

The guy's face was slick with blood, Brandon's fist red as he raised it again. Danni's car started and the tires squealed as she pulled out of the space and accelerated toward the exit. The guy fell back and went slack and this time stayed down. Brandon reached behind him for his cuffs, felt nothing but belt and Glock. He jumped to his feet and said, "You crazy bastard. She's not cheating on you. I returned something to her, that's all."

"Yeah, right. The goddamn slut—"

"You're an idiot. It was some book from high school. I picked it up, found her on Facebook and gave it back to her. Never laid eyes on her before. Never will again. Now get the hell out of here before I lock your sorry ass up."

The words slipped out, and the guy stopped resisting. Like you'd thrown a switch. His expression changed, the tension draining out of him. Sometimes people came to their senses. Not often.

The guy wiped his face, looked at his bloody hand, then at Brandon and said, "Misunderstanding, dude." He stepped back as he got to his feet, wiping blood from his nose and mouth. "I just figured the bitch was—" the guy muttered.

"Listen to me," Brandon said. "She didn't do anything wrong. Don't take it out on her."

He started for the truck, saw something on the ground. The diary was near the driver's door, splayed open in a puddle of coffee. He leaned down and snatched it up, hurried to the truck and got in. The guy was walking away, his hand over his bleeding mouth. Brandon started the truck and pulled out, heard someone say, "Hey, stop," but then he was around the corner, swinging into the Route 1 traffic.

The diary was beside him on the passenger seat, the flowered cover splotched with the guy's blood. Brandon pulled off into the lot of a Burger King, leaned over and took napkins from the glove box. He wiped the blood from his hands, hoped the bastard didn't have HIV. Then he wiped the blood from the diary, smearing the flowers with brown streaks. He got out and dropped the bloody napkins in a trashcan, pulled back out and headed north.

"Shit," he said, settling back into the seat, looking at his scraped knuckles.

It wasn't supposed to go down that way. Danni probably had the son of a bitch on her case now, beating her up as soon as he got home. She looked like a longtime abuse victim, had that reflective eagerness to please, to mollify. Bringing Brandon coffee, thanking him, talking about what a mess she'd been. The guy looked like a classic abuser, the kind Brandon had seen a hundred times at domestic violence calls. Enraged, controlling, sadistic bullies, fear showing in the woman's eyes, the look of someone locked into a sick relationship with no easy way out.

Brandon wondered if they had kids. How long they'd been together. Had Danni had affairs? Had she looked for someone better, kinder, gentler? She seemed like a nice enough person, judging by the diary just somebody who hadn't caught a break. A bunch of loser guys and then she gets stuck with this one. "Dump the piece of crap," Brandon said, taking a left to get back on the interstate. He gunned the engine, glanced at the rearview, saw headlights coming up the access road fast.

"Damn," he said as the blue strobes blipped on.

He pulled over, saw the cruiser, an Explorer SUV, slide up and out beside him. He opened the window, reached his wallet from the console. Flipped it open to his badge. Waited. It was a minute before the cruiser door popped open, the cop running his plate, getting it back.

Brandon Blake. Isn't that...?

A flashlight beam swished through the cab and then the cop was at his left shoulder.

"I'm Portland P.D.," Brandon said, held up his badge. The cop leaned closer.

"Blake," he said.

"Yeah."

"Aren't you—?"

"Yeah."

"Admin leave?"

"Right."

"Marlon Davey. As in Brando"

Brandon looked at him. Chubby guy, maybe 40. Military haircut, baby face, glasses with thick dark rims. Looked soft but appearances could deceive.

"Seen your name around," Brandon said.

"Sorry for your troubles. Freakin' pellet guns. After your...your thing, I looked it up. Something like forty a year, people carrying replica guns shot by cops. Took one off a kid you couldn't tell from a Glock 26. That's in broad daylight, never mind the dark. Oughta be outlawed."

"A little late," Brandon said.

"For you," Davey said. "Sorry, man."

"Yeah."

He moved up beside him, lowered the light.

"So we got a call."

"Yeah. A bit of a cluster back there."

"Right, so tell me what happened, Brandon."

He did, the quick version. A good deed gone astray.

"Why bother?" the cop said.

"Sitting around. Seemed like the right thing. And I had time."

Davey eyed him, considering it.

"Stir crazy already?" he said.

"Yeah. The worst thing about it, nothing to do but sit around and think."

The cop nodded, traffic flashing past behind him.

"Who called it in?" Brandon said.

"Couple people. One was a Dunkin' employee."

"No complaint from the guy?"

"No."

"Classic domestic violence perp."

"You get his name?" Davey said.

"Hell, no. He just started in swinging."

"Caller said you beat him up."

"I just put him down. You know how it looks. Probably already up on YouTube."

"I hear you," he said.

"He was drunk, pretty big. Tried to explain but he wasn't having any of it. Kept saying she was cheating on him."

"But not with you?"

"Never saw her before in my life."

Davey hesitated. "Didn't arrange to meet her for sex? Escort thing?"

He shook his head. "No, I have a girlfriend."

Davey looked at him, boring in. Brandon knew the routine, the way a cop's mind works.

"What's her name?"

"My girlfriend?"

"No, the woman at Dunkin."

Maybe he wasn't so soft.

"Danni. With an I. Last name Moulton. At least it was in high school. She's on Facebook. From your town. Grew up here."

Brandon saw a flicker.

"You know her," he said.

Two cops reading each other's minds. Davey looked back at the cruiser, his face illuminated by the strobes.

"So what's the deal?" Brandon said.

"No deal, really. I know Danni by sight. Works in a sandwich place. Know the boyfriend some."

"Lucky you. Frequent flyer?"

"Not really. Name's Clutch. Last name is Tedeschi. I don't remember his real first name. Joe? Joel? I'm not sure. Has a wrecker. Used to do a lot of repos, around when the bakery closed. People lose jobs, can't make payments. Vultures swoop in."

"So you'd get calls?"

A little shrug.

"Nothing big," Davey said. "Just a lot of disagreements, people seeing him hook up to their vehicles, getting irate."

"So no domestic violence record?"

"Not that I know of," Davey said. "Of course, I've only been here like four years so I can't tell you the long history. But other than the repo stuff, he keeps a pretty low profile. What I can tell, picks up a few cars at the auctions, cleans them up, sells them off the lot at his garage."

"Lock the doors and terrorize the wife?"

"I don't think they're married. But no, nothing I've seen. From the little I have seen, Clutch is kind of an odd combo. With the repos, he could get angry, acts tough with the owners. But then we show up, he backs right off, all polite and respectful, yessir, yes ma'am. Like he doesn't want trouble."

"Didn't back off with me," Brandon said, "not at first."

"And then you told him you were a cop?"

Brandon thought back.

"Yeah, in a way. Said I'd lock his ass up. He was fighting and when that came out, he just went slack."

"Right. Some people, they seem like idiots but they're smart enough they just don't want to mess with law enforcement," Davey said.

Brandon thought of Thatcher Rawlings, the gun pointed.

"And some people don't know any better," he said.

Davey caught it. There was a lull in the conversation as cars passed, red lights glowing as drivers braked for the tollbooth. The light reflected off of Davey's glasses. What did they call them? Rec Specs?

He cleared his throat and then, still looking out at the traffic, said, "I hope this doesn't come off as weird. My wife says I'm nosy. But I have to ask you. What's it like?"

Brandon looked at him, not surprised.

"To shoot somebody?"

"And have them not live," Davey said.

Brandon hesitated, not sure how much to open up. But a fellow cop, could be in the same situation...

"Surreal," he said. "Just when you think you're starting to get used to it, you still can't believe it happened."

"I've never fired my weapon," Davey said. "I mean, just on the range."

"You and most cops."

"Never even touched a gun until the academy. I mean, I sold insurance. Didn't hunt. I worry about it, to be honest."

"That you'll have to kill someone?" Brandon said.

"Or I won't be able to do it if the time comes."

"I waited too long to fire."

"I have two kids," Davey said.

"I let him hold onto the gun, even though I thought it was real."

"For how long?"

"Ten seconds. Maybe more. I was telling him to put it down. Most of the time he had it pointed at my feet."

"Jesus. You know how quick he could raise and fire? The academy, they said a third of a second. My god, you could be—"

"I know."

They pondered it for a moment, both knowing a millisecond difference, a shot that didn't take the perpetrator out, and...

"How old are your kids?" Brandon said.

"Two and four. Boys. Tyler and Jacob."

"Nice," Brandon said.

"I know the procedure. A warning and then if the armed perp doesn't comply, you fire. You keep firing until the threat is neutralized."

There was a pause, the two of them standing there in the darkness, the headlights and taillights streaming by.

"I heard it all at the academy," Davey said, more quietly now. "But with everything that's been going on."

Ferguson. Videos of knucklehead cops, racist cops, cops who just lose it. All of it going viral, whipping up a war on the police.

Brandon hesitated, then decided to open up, just a little more. Something about Davey's directness, his unassuming way. "Nope, not the same at all. When we had training it was, like, boom, boom. Over in a flash. When it's really happening it's totally slow motion. Like you're watching yourself in a movie."

Davey listened, every word.

"You can't undo it," Brandon said. "Not any of it. The kid's dead and I caused that to happen. And you know you I had no choice, everybody saying I did the right thing, I could have been killed. But still, it doesn't feel like the right at all."

He paused.

"And these days a lot of people instantly hate your guts."

Davey looked away and said, "I'm going home to my boys."

Brandon nodded.

"I hope you don't have to ever make that decision," he said.

"Could be tonight. Could be in an hour," Davey said.

"Why they pay us the big bucks," Brandon said.

Davey reached for his mic, telling dispatch he was back on the road.

"Hey, before you go," Brandon said. "This guy Clutch. Where's his garage?"

Davey looked over at him and said, "No offense, Brandon Blake, but I don't want to see you again."

Brandon put the truck in gear, said, "You won't."

"I know your type, my friend. Once you get on to something, you don't let go. You ride it into the ground even if you go down with it."

He started to pull away, stopped and reversed. "With all due respect,

I'm gonna give you some advice," Davey said, "even if you don't want to hear it. Go home. Tomorrow's another day."

Brandon nodded. "Right."

Davey pulled out and Brandon watched him jump into the left lane, put the blue lights on as he made a U-turn in front of the tollbooth, head back into Woodford. He flicked his phone on, typed Clutch Tedeschi, wrecker, Woodford.

Waited. The search turned up a record from a court case, somebody taking Clutch's Wrecker and Repossession Service to court for taking the wrong car and damaging it in the process. The suit said the owner's reputation had been damaged because friends and associates saw his car being repossessed from his place of employment. The post didn't say how the case turned out. It did list an address for the business: 878 Western Highway. Brandon typed that in. Started the truck. Considered making the U-turn by the tollbooths but got off at the next exit instead.

And circled back.

Western Highway had been a what passed for a highway fifty years ago. Now it was just a two-lane road with businesses and homes scattered like they'd been scattered randomly like seeds. Brandon passed small ranch houses with oversize garages, an appliance repair shop tacked onto a mobile home, a shuttered hot dog stand, plywood hammered over the windows. And then a lighted sign, one of those portable rigs with replaceable letters.

CLUTCH AUTO
CLEAN RIDES, REASONABLE PRICES
WE FINANCE

Brandon braked, passed slowly. The sign had an arrow that pointed at a row of six used cars and a pickup, lined up with colored pennants clipped onto their windshields. The cars were older, an assortment of nondescript sedans. The pickup was a bright red Ford, the name of a fire department painted over on the door. There was a breeze out of the northwest and the pennants fluttered in the glare of a spotlight mounted to a tree, the tree trimmed so it was just a trunk, like a limb-less torso. Beyond the row of cars was a two-story garage, a metal pre-fab sort of building with three bays. Parked next to it was a wrecker, black or dark blue with no visible lettering. When you do repo, you go stealth.

To the left of the garage was a ranch house, with lights on. There was a lawn out front with a wishing well at the center, the kind with the bucket hanging under a shingled roof. Brandon wondered what Danni and Clutch wished for. Layoffs? Economic collapse?

He coasted by, continued a quarter-mile down the road and turned around in a lot full of rubble, six-foot mounds showing like the place was home to giant moles, the mounds sprouting a fringe of weeds. He drove back, slowed as he approached the house. He could see a carport out back. Underneath it, a pickup and the white Ford were parked side by side. The pickup was a silver Dodge, a metal rack mounted behind the cab.

The windows glowed yellow, making the house look deceptively cozy. What was going on in there, Brandon wondered. The guy punishing Danni for wrecking his evening? Danni warning that if he ever did anything like that again, she was gone? The two of them sitting in stony silence? Or had he beaten her up, was sucking down beers and nursing his anger and jealousy while she cried herself to sleep.

An average guy might have been taken down by Clutch's wind-milling arms and fists. He probably pictured standing over the sprawled boyfriend, telling him to back the hell off or next time it would be worse. Then he could take his woman home, lock her away where she belonged.

Instead, it had to be Brandon, who fought for a living.

"Sucks to be you," he said to himself.

He gave the house a last glance, then hit the gas and started for home. As he settled in, he looked to the passenger seat. The blood on the diary had turned dark, like the cover had been smeared with black ink.

What was it that Danni had said about that time? "God, I was a disaster."

Hard to argue, and if she was a disaster then, what was she now? What had the forlorn and hapless girl in the diary become twenty years later? Finally found a man, it appeared. But behind those shaded windows, was he controlling? Abusive? Did she live in fear?

Brandon drove the bleak stretch of back road, past the shuttered businesses, the rest of them doomed, awaiting their fate. He slowed for the turn for the interstate.

Brandon figured he'd hear from her again. He didn't know if that was a good thing.

EIGHT

Brandon was getting off the connector, headed into the west end, when his phone lit up. Mia texting. He picked up the phone and glanced at it.

Where are you? I'm worried.

He put the phone back down on the seat. It lit up all the way through the west end, onto Commercial. He picked it up at the light at the corner of Fore.

text me as soon as you can.

Onto Fore Street and into the Old Port, the crowd headed for the bars. Guys and girls on the sidewalks, nobody staggering yet. Early days.

The phone buzzed and Brandon picked it up. Kat this time: Text me back. Don't be an idiot.

Brandon tossed the phone aside, muttered, "Nag, nag, nag." Picked the phone back up. Stopped at the crosswalk on Exchange, he texted:

I'm fine. Went for a ride, clear my head. Headed back to the boat. Don't worry.

Another text, this one from Kat again:

I know what you're doing. You can't do this alone.

Brandon put the phone down, stopped at the crosswalk at Exchange. The crowd filed past, a couple of guys looking up at him, squinting into the headlights. Brandon pulled his hat lower, slid down in the truck seat.

The phone buzzed and this time Brandon didn't look. "Yeah, right," he said. "Like you've ever killed somebody. Gonna tell me how to handle it."

The route to Mia's place was straight through, up Fore Street and a left on Munjoy. Brandon started to cross the intersection, braked and went left. He made the light at Congress, continued west and took a left on Marginal Way. From there it was a few blocks to Forest Avenue, where he took a right and drove. Two miles out was a convenience store, the Forest Avenue Pop-In. Cambodians ran it, the older ones barely speaking English.

They wouldn't read the paper. Probably didn't watch the news, working 18 hours a day.

Brandon pulled in, parked by the back fence in the dark. He got out of the truck and walked back to the front of the store. The parents were behind the counter, the mom running the register, the guy rummaging around beside her. A hipster-looking guy with glasses and a beard was buying cigarettes, the lady asking for ID. Brandon hurried past, went to the beer cooler and reached out a 12-pack of Baxter IPA.

He paused in the aisle in front of the chips and pretzels until the hipster guy had left. Then he walked up, put the beer on the counter and looked down as he fished a loose $20 bill out of his pocket. The lady looked at him, said, "You got ID?"

Brandon looked off to the side as he dug out his wallet. His police ID flashed as he opened it, the guy seeing it and smiling and saying, "Hi officer. Beer on sale. Ten dollars." The guy grinned at Brandon and then his grin fell away. Brandon looked at the woman and said, "No, I'll pay the full price."

And then the both of them were staring at Brandon, who stared back until they looked away.

The woman gave Brandon his change, didn't make eye contact. He slid the beer off the counter and headed for the door. On the way out he heard the guy say, "That's the cop shot that kid."

Brandon grimaced, headed for the truck. He yanked the door open, heaved the beer across the seat. Got in, slipped his phone out and texted:

Hey, baby. Me again. I'm done in. Exhausted. I'm going to sleep. Don't want to leave Bay Witch unattended, the kids from the high school out there and all. I'll call you first thing in the morning.

Hit send.

He was still in the parking lot when Mia texted back:

You sure? I can come over. Be with you.

The motor idling, Brandon replied:

It's OK. I'm just going to sleep. No worries.

Back out onto Forest and into town, the beers clinking in the carton beside him. Through Monument Square, the panhandlers on the corner, one guy with a sign that said, DESTITUTE. NEED HELP.

"Yeah, right," Brandon said. "Like you've got problems."

Down the hill and across the bridge, the lights of the harbor twinkling in the wind, the surface of the water shimmering in the spotlights of the container docks. He swung into South Portland, followed the harbor east and zigzagged his way through darkened streets to the marina.

He slowed as he approached. The parking lot was dark. There was nobody in the yard. Lights glowed from the cabins of the few liveaboards. He pulled the pickup into the lot, drove to the far side and backed the truck up to the fence. He turned off the motor and shut off the lights. There was a moment of blindness and then the shadows emerged from the blackness.

Brandon looked out on the lot for a minute, then another. He eyed the road beyond the fence, looked for anything moving, anyone parked. It was dark and still.

He reached up and turned off the truck's dome light, opened the door and slid down. He reached back for the beer and started to close the door and stopped. He opened it again and reached across and came away with the flowered book, the stain black now, like the flowers had been killed by frost or some pestilent blight. With the beer in one hand, the diary in the other, he started walking across the lot. The light by the gate was askew, the far side of the fence in shadow. He shifted the diary to his left hand, started to reach for the touch pad.

Stopped.

Something moved in the shadows, something dark along the ground. Brandon reached for his waist, slipped his gun out.

"Don't move," he said.

But the dark clump did, raising up slowly until it became a figure. It was seated, then Brandon saw arms reach out for the ground as the person started to stand.

"Stay on the ground," he barked. "Arms out in front of you."

The figure slowly stood, Brandon's gun raising, pointed at the center of the dark mass, thinking, please god, no, not again.

"Hands up," he said, and then saw a glimmer of brightness, teeth, a mouth.

"What are you gonna do?" a girl's voice said. "Shoot me?"

He lowered the beer and the book to the ground, and with the gun still leveled, slipped his phone out and flicked it on. A girl showed in the blue light, maybe 16, her dark hair disheveled under a dark sweatshirt hood. She was glaring at him, her eyes puffy, her cheek speckled with dark bits of something. Gravel from the lot.

"Go ahead," she said. "Kill me."

"Why would I do that?" Brandon said, lowering the gun but only slightly.

"Because of this," the girl said, and she slipped a knife from the front of her sweatshirt. She held it in front her, blade out, waist high.

"That's a terrible idea," Brandon said.

"I'm not afraid of dying," she said.

"Why would you want to die?"

"Thatch wasn't afraid, was he?"

Brandon didn't answer. The girl took step toward him, the knife still extended, the blade glinting in the light of Brandon's phone. It was a kitchen knife. Wooden handle, serrated broad blade. Something you'd use to slice a ham.

"You're a friend of his."

"Not a friend," the girl said, louder and shrill. "We were in love."

"I'm sorry. But doing this isn't making things any better."

"I'm not trying to make things better," the girl said.

She took another step. Brandon backed up.

"What's your name?"

"Who cares?"

"I do. I like to know who I'm talking to."

"Before you kill them?"

"I'm not gonna kill you. So what *is* your name?"

"Amanda," the girl said. "But it doesn't matter."

"Sure it does. Now you're more of a real person. You're Amanda. From Moresby?"

"I'm asking the questions," the girl said.

"So ask away, Amanda," Brandon said.

She took a wavering step toward him and he backed away, lowered the gun.

"What are you doing, cop?" she said. "I could kill you."

"No, you can't," Brandon said.

"I can and I'm going to," Amanda said. "Unless you kill me first."

"You should drop the knife, Amanda. I know you're upset, you're grieving. And I don't blame you. Not one bit. But you're just making an awful situation even worse."

"It can't get worse."

"If you're in Long Creek?"

"I'm not going to Long Creek. I'm going to heaven. With Thatch. I'm going wherever he is right now, this second. We're gonna be together. He promised. That we'd be together forever."

If Thatcher was Romeo, this was Juliet.

She took a step closer, then another. Skinny black jeans, pants legs rolled up. Black Converse All-Stars. A theater kid. Brandon matched her, still retreating.

"Just toss it away," Brandon said. "And we can talk."

"I don't want to talk. Did you talk to Thatch before you killed him?"

She was moving steadily, small careful steps, her shoes scrunching softly on the gravel.

"What did you say to him? Before you killed him. Shot him over and over."

"Told him to put it down, just like I'm telling you."

"And I'm saying you're a murderer," she said, starting to sob. "You piece of cop garbage. You filthy piece of—"

She broke for him, the knife held out awkwardly in front of her like a horn on a charging bull, Brandon sidestepped, dodging back as she awkwardly waved the blade in the general direction of his belly. And then he was on her from behind, wrapping her up with one arm, reaching around her with his gun hand and hacking at her forearm. She screamed, dropped the knife and stumbled over it. Brandon spun her around, hustled her fifteen feet back to the fence and pressed her against the chain links.

"You bastard," she screamed. "I'll kill you. I'll kill you. I'll fucking kill you."

He holstered his gun as she started to sob, pushed her harder as she flailed at him with both arms. She was skinny under the clothes, a child. Brandon held her in place with one hand while he searched her with the other.

"Oh, Thatch, I tried. Oh, my god, Thatch. Oh, my god," she cried.

He ran his hand across her chest and belly, swept the inside of her legs. Now she was crying, a braying wail of despair. Brandon stepped away from her and she turned and slumped to the ground, her back against the fence. She snorted and sobbed, wiped her nose with the back of her hand. The hand was pale in the darkness, a flicker of light.

"How did you get here?" Brandon said.

A snort.

"Uber," Amanda said.

"Why did he do it?" Brandon said. "You guys were together, right? What was it? Some sort of suicide pact?"

Another shrug.

"Did he want to die?" Brandon said.

She didn't respond, then lifted her thin shoulders in another shrug.

"You don't know?" Brandon said.

"He had stuff going on."

"What sort of stuff?"

"Just stuff."

"Enough to die for?"

No response.

"Please tell me."

She looked at the ground, her head in her hands.

"You know why I want to know?"

A slight shake of her head.

"Because I want to know if I was just a tool, a way for him to kill himself."

No reply, just a sniff from the darkness. Brandon looked at her, felt a wave of anger and frustration.

"Because he's gone. Sure, it's sad. Horrible. A tragedy. But you know what else? I have to live with that. I'm not the same any more than you are. You lost your boyfriend or whatever the hell he was. I lost..."

Lights came on out on the float. Brandon figured somebody was calling 911. He leaned down and said to her, "I'm asking you."

She looked at him, their faces ten inches apart. Her cheeks were streaked with tears and dirt and her face was flushed.

"He didn't want to die," she said. "He loved me."

"I'm sure. Then why did he do it?"

"He didn't. It was a video and you came in all tough and acting like a cop and killed him. Like the rest of them. You're all the same. You get off on it. Gives you a hard-on, killing innocent people."

Brandon let off, took a step back and to the right, bent low and picked up the knife. He turned and threw it into the darkness, turned back.

"You don't believe that, Amanda. What was it? What was wrong with him? He pointed the gun at me and said, 'Bang, bang. You're dead. And so am I.'"

A stretch by one word.

"He was joking. Don't you get it? He was funny, like totally ironic. He thought life was so absurd. Especially around here. All these pathetic plastic people."

A siren in the distance. Brandon said, "He wasn't joking. He knew I was going to shoot him."

"He didn't."

She'd pulled her hood back up and over her head, had her hands in the pockets at the front.

"Did he have some problems? Was he addicted to drugs? Was he being bullied? What was it?"

"He had me," Amanda said, shaking her head. "He didn't want to die."

"He may have had you," Brandon said, "but he wanted to die. No question about it."

"No. He loved me."

"Maybe he loved you *and* he wanted to die."

"No," Amanda screamed, "he didn't," and she slipped a hand from her pocket, yanked at her sleeve, and started hacking at her thin, pale wrist.

"Jesus," Brandon said, leaping at her, grabbing her arm, squeezing her wrist, screaming, "Drop it. Drop it." A razor blade flashed to the ground and he grabbed the other wrist, squeezed it tight, blood seeping between his fingers, then dripping onto his palm. It was warm and slippery and she yanked her hand away suddenly, blood spurting, then shoved him and tried to run. He overtook her in two steps, kicked her legs out and put her on the ground on her belly. She had both arms underneath her and he yanked the left arm out. It was slick with blood, crusted with dirt and pebbles. He turned the arm, held it palm up against the ground and pressed the wrist. He could feel the cuts, the soft flesh splayed open. He held the wrist tight, waited as the siren got closer.

Amanda writhed weakly, her head turned toward him, her cheek pressed to the gravel. "I'm coming, Thatch," she whispered. "I'm coming to you."

"Sorry, but you're not," Brandon said. "You're not going anywhere."

It was Robichaud, the big guy. He put the spotlight on them as the cruiser slid to a stop, slid out and loped toward them. "Off her, hands in the air," he shouted. And when Brandon stayed crouched over Amanda, Robichaud barked, "Get the fuck off her."

"Attempted suicide," Brandon said. "She needs—"

And then Robichaud scooped him up, flipped him to the ground, screaming, "Show me your hands. Show me your hands."

Brandon did, and they were red with Amanda's blood.

"Blake," Robichaud said.

"She's a friend of Thatcher Rawlings. She slashed her wrist."

"Oh, Christ," Robichaud said, falling to his knees, picking up the bloody forearm, looking for the wound, pressing her wrist. With the other hand he pressed his shoulder mic and said, "We need Medcu here asap. Royal Point Marina. Woman with serious laceration."

A blurted response. Blake and Robichaud hunched over the pale, bleeding waif.

"Talk to us, Amanda," Blake said.

"Amanda, look at me," Robichaud said. "Why'd you go and do this, nice girl like you? You live around here?"

She looked at him vaguely, sweat beading on her forehead, her breathing shallow and rapid.

"She's going into shock," Blake said.

Robichaud lifted Amanda's legs up to increase blood flow, leaned close to her and said, "Listen to me, honey. Gonna fix you right up. What's your last name, Amanda?"

She looked at him, eyes going in and out of focus.

"Shakespeare," she said, squeezing the word out.

"Really?"

Amanda gave a bleary nod.

"No kidding. You must be related to William."

She was turning gray, dark splotches under her eyes.

"Any other injuries?"

Blake shook his head.

"Just showed up here and cut herself?"

Blake nodded.

"Christ," Robichaud said. "Just a kid. My daughter's age."

Amanda's breathing was coming more rapidly and her eyes were rolling back. They could hear the traffic on the bridge, the rattle of the metal grating as cars and trucks crossed to Portland. And then a siren, a whoop and then a howl, and then the siren turning off. The ambulance skidded into the gravel lot, rolled up close to the cruiser. The EMTs got out of the cab, trotted to the trio on the ground. Robichaud and Blake fell back, Robichaud saying, "Left wrist. Deep."

They bent over her, wrapping the wrist, putting in an IV, rolling a gurney over and lifting Amanda up and on. She lifted easily, like a child, which she nearly was. When the ambulance pulled out, lights flashing, two other cruisers pulled in, a blue SUV from South Portland, a black and white cruiser from across the bridge.

Kat.

She stayed back as the South Portland sergeant, an older guy named Leopold, walked with Brandon to the SUV. They stood there in the strobe light, the sergeant's silver hair turning momentarily blue.

"From the beginning, Officer Blake," the sergeant said. Officer Blake. Like the sarge wanted him to know he thought he still was a cop.

Brandon told the story. Amanda waiting for him in the darkness. Amanda pulling a razor blade from her pocket and cutting her wrist.

"Came here to make you watch?" Leopold said.

"I guess so."

"How'd she get here?"

"Uber, she said."

"What else she say?"

"That Thatcher was just fooling around, that he thought everything was absurd."

"Absurd. Point a gun at a cop in a dark alley. What else?"

"Said she was going to Thatcher. Join him."

"Goddamn, kids do stupid shit," the sergeant said.

"Sometimes they do," Brandon said.

"How you doing?"

"Been better."

The sergeant leaned closer. "You hang in there, buddy. Anybody comes around here, you hit the phone and we'll be here. I'm gonna keep a unit close all night. Got your back, Blake. The next one might want to do more than cut herself."

Brandon nodded. The sergeant turned, climbed into the driver's seat, swiveled his laptop over and started typing. Kat moved closer.

"Company?" she said.

"Don't you have to protect and serve?"

"We get a dinner break."

"Galley's pretty bare."

"I've eaten."

"Coffee then."

"Sure," Brandon said.

"You can tell me the story," Kat said.

"I think you just heard it."

"That was the sanitized version, Blake. I can tell those a mile away."

NINE

There were dark drops of blood on the gravel, scuff marks where he and Amanda had so briefly grappled. Brandon picked up the beer and the diary, walked to the gate and punched in the code. He pushed the gate open and they stepped through and he closed it behind him, making sure it latched. There was a puff of cool breeze from the water and it carried the smell of the harbor, oil and brine and the fetid, rotting seaweed that lined the shore. They walked side by side down the float to Bay Witch. Brandon stepped over the transom first, went to the cabin door and unlocked it, turned on the stern floodlight. Kat came on board, said, "I still don't get what's wrong with dry land."

She followed him below, sat back on the settee on the starboard side. Brandon put the beer and diary on the table, slipped the Glock from his waistband and laid it beside them. He filled the kettle, put it on the burner and lit the gas. The flame puffed and flickered, blue wavelets in the dim light.

"Who you riding with?"

"Tommy Park," Kat said.

"How's that?"

"Mostly talks about high school soccer."

"His kid," Brandon said.

"No worse than you talking about boats," Kat said. "How it took you two hours to replace the boondoggle on the foreskin."

He smiled.

"Only one cup?" she said.

"It'll keep me up."

"You sleeping?"

"No, but if I can, I want to be ready."

She waited as he watched the kettle, his back to her. It hissed, then steamed, then whistled. He poured the water into the French press. Stared at the press as the water dripped through. After a minute he poured the coffee into a mug and turned and hand it over.

"Not the best looking barista I've ever seen," Kat said.

"I get by on my personality."

She leaned into the steam and touched her lips to the coffee. Pulled back.

"That the diary?" she said.

Brandon looked at it, wished he'd left it in the truck.

"Yeah."

"Carry it around with you?"

"I was going to give it back to Mia."

"Where is she?"

"The apartment."

"Don't tell me. You told her you wanted to be alone."

Brandon went to the carton and took out a Baxter. He opened it with the coffee spoon. Drank.

"What are you doing, Brandon?"

He didn't reply, knew the question was rhetorical.

"Gonna play the stoic."

"Kinda hard to understand if you haven't been there."

"Kinda hard to help if you're shut out."

"I'm not shutting you out, Kat. You're right here. We're talking."

"You put the wall up, Blake. Just like you did..."

A pause. She put her mouth to the edge of the mug.

"The last time?" Brandon said.

"Didn't really know you then but that's what I heard. Did the macho tough guy thing. 'I don't need anybody.'"

"It's not a group project. I pulled the trigger all by myself."

"Could just as easily been me. I went left and you went right."

"Luck of the draw," Brandon said. "And now I play out my hand."

He drank. The beer was half gone. He felt it starting to hit him—a warm and enveloping wave of calm. Kat sipped the coffee, lowered the mug and fixed him with her hard stare, the one she used when she was about to say something he wouldn't want to hear.

"You're feeling sorry for yourself, Brandon," she said. "Sliding into the abyss of self-pity."

He swallowed. Smiled.

"What the hell am I supposed to be? Be glad this all happened? Hey, look at all the OT. Maybe I'll get paid for the deposition."

"Don't give me your wise-ass shit, either. You can't do this alone. Nobody can. Not even Brandon Blake, the loner cop raised by wolves."

"A dead mom and a drunk grandmother, to be more precise," Brandon said. "Wolves would have been more fun."

"The orphaned waif who wandered the docks of Portland harbor. It's a movie. Not a good one, but a movie. And you're falling right back into the role."

Brandon gripped the can.

"In your best moments you're honest with yourself, Brandon. So be honest now. You're hurting. This totally sucks. It's tragic and sad and you're wondering why the hell it happened to you. Could you have done something differently? Again, fair enough. But don't think you can just take this on as your personal burden. Don't be a goddamn martyr."

Kat looked at him. Took a deep breath and a swallow of coffee.

"So there it is," she said. "I like you too much to let you do this to yourself."

Brandon held the beer with one hand, looked down and away.

"Orphaned waif," he said. "Very literary. Stole that from Maddie."

"Horatio Alger's got nothing on you, Blake," Kat said.

They both smiled. The boat rocked slowly, the water slapping softly on the planks. Brandon sipped the beer and ran through the night in his head. Dunkin' Donuts. Danni and her boyfriend. Amanda looming from the darkness like a zombie.

"She had a knife," he said.

"That girl?"

"Yeah. Looked like she took it from the kitchen drawer."

"She pulled it on you?"

"In a half-hearted sort of way. She wanted me to shoot her."

"What did you do?"

"Took it off her. I searched her but didn't feel the razor blade."

"Hard to pick up something like that in a heavy sweatshirt," Kat said.

Brandon considered it. "Should have. Getting rusty already." He drank more, the ale seeping into his head.

Kat waited, then asked the question.

"You tell South Portland PD about the knife?"

"No."

"Why not?"

"She didn't need to go to jail, have a felony on her record. Never get into college. She was just upset because her friend died. Got all melodramatic. Any Old Port drunk is more of a threat."

"Not your call, Blake. D.A. can figure that out."

"Yeah, well, I already made it," Brandon said. It sounded belligerent, insubordinate, with his senior partner.

"Save the attitude," Kat said.

There was an awkward silence, then the faint sound of a boat motor in the distance. An off-shore lobster boat headed out from the Portland side, Brandon thought.

"Sorry," he said.

"It's okay. But one last bit of advice."

Brandon waited.

"I know you're hurting. But don't take it out on the people who are trying to help. Like Mia."

Kat stood.

Brandon looked at the half-full beer in his hand, put it down on the galley table.

"Something I didn't tell you," he said.

Kat took the last swallow of coffee, put the mug on the table beside the beer. Looked at him and waited, hand on her belt.

"The kid. Amanda. Rawlings' friend."

"Uh-huh."

"She said he had 'stuff.' Some sort of baggage he was carrying."

"Enough to want to die for?" Kat said.

"That's what I asked her. She said he wouldn't want to die because he loved her."

"Nothing else about this so-called stuff?"

Brandon shook his head. "No."

"AG investigators will try to recreate his last twenty-four hours. They'll talk to this girl, his friends, his parents, siblings, whatever. If there was stuff there, it'll come out."

"Listen to you, Ms. Glass Half Full," Brandon said.

"You can come to me with any of it, any time. Day, night, whatever. Don't keep it inside, Brandon. It'll eat you up."

And with a last pat on his shoulder, Kat was through the hatchway, out onto the stern deck, and gone.

Brandon sat for a moment, considered the beer, picked it up and finished it in two swallows. He put the can down, looked over at the writing table, his laptop closed on top of it. Like a magnet it pulled him across the cabin. He flipped it open, waited for the internet to load. He opened the news pages. Portland. Bangor. Headlines barking at him: *Investigation of Fatal Police Shooting Continues…Victim's Family Charges Cover-up…Portland Police Mum on Shooting…Police Critics Demand Answers…Rawlings Known for Creativity, Humor…Blake's Past Marred by Violence…*

And this from Estusa's Mainefeed website, posted at 9:54 p.m. *Body Camera Off, Victim's Video Card Missing in Police Shooting*

"Shit," Brandon said. Standing over the laptop he read on.

Sources close to the investigation said Brandon had neglected to manually turn on his body camera, equipment recently provided to all Portland police officers. Department policy says patrol officers must activate the camera during interactions with the public. If Blake had done so, the shooting and the events that led up to it would have been recorded. In addition, the source said, a digital memory card that would have been inserted in Rawlings' GoPro camera to enable it to record was not in the camera and could not be found at the scene.

"No witnesses," the source said. "It's pretty much his word because the only other witness is dead."

"Jesus," Brandon said. "Hanging me out to dry or what?"

He slammed the laptop closed, opened it back up. Read the story again and then, his fingers moving like they were remote controlled, clicked to the comments. *If Blake gets away with this, we'll know we live in a police state…of course he didn't turn on the camera. He was about to execute a teenager...this cop's a psycho, lock him up...AG should nail his ass, so Bubba can nail it in prison...no witnesses means the cop skates, so what else is new?...who knew Maine had the death penalty for a kid acting goofy?...*

Brandon closed the laptop. Went to the counter and took out another beer. Opened it and drank half of it down, then stepped out onto the stern deck, illuminated by the lights of the float. He slipped up on the deck and moved forward, sat on the folding chair on the bow where Mia would read papers in the sun. It was dark there and quiet, water lapping at the hulls, the traffic humming on the bridge. Brandon sat and stared out at the harbor lights, a plane descending into the jetport, another crossing the sky high above him like a slow-moving shooting star.

He barely saw any of it, everything whirling around in his head.

The shooting. The other cops. "It was a good shoot, Blake." Kat's hand on his shoulder. Mia's voice on the phone, the pitying tone like he was damaged or sick. Danni and Clutch, the feeling of being pulled into somebody else's mess. Mia again, not knowing what to say, him having no way to explain. The Rawlings parents, the mom, Tiff, prostrate on the fence like she'd been crucified. Amanda, in that moment willing him to shoot her, too. Thatcher Rawlings, the look of surprise on his face as he died.

It was inescapable, all of it, filled his head, coming at him relentlessly. Guns. Blood. Crying. Cops. "Goddamn it," he said.

He sat for a few more minutes, stared at the flickering headlights across the harbor, the glow of skyline, the flicker of the buoy lights bobbing in the channel. He slipped his phone from his pocket, started to send Mia a text. But then he thought it would scare her, leave her wide awake with worry. He flicked the text away, saw the red dot over the Facebook icon. Stuff happening there, but did he want to see it?

Hesitating, he opened it. A message:

`Chris. really sorry about tonight. Now I think I owe u a beer, not just a coffee that u never even got to drink! Get in touch. I'll come to u this time. Sorry again!!!! Danni. PS I'm really not a bad person. And my bf said to tell you he hopes no hard feelings. Just a freakin cluster!! U know these jealous types! PS again. U have the book, right?`

Lemme know cuz I'll totally freak if some kid at
Dunkin is readin my diary!!

That would stink, those high schoolers passing the thing around, having a good laugh. Brandon looked over at the book, the cover with soiled flowers like somebody had trampled the garden. Now he had to get rid of the thing, at the very least get Danni off his back, finish what he started. Probably should have tossed the stupid thing to begin with, but too late now.

He hesitated:

Hey Danni. Yeah I still have it. Kinda scuffed up.
Sure we can meet up. Lemme see what next cpl days
looks like.

He hit send. Put the phone down. Stared at it and waited. Ten seconds and it buzzed.

Great chris. I'll wait to hear frm u. don't forget
me now!! I'll think of a way to repay you!!!

Whoah. Was she hitting on him? Just being appreciative? All he needed, give that freakin' idiot a real reason to be jealous. Or maybe this guy Clutch had reason, just guessed wrong that night. Brandon reached over and picked up the diary, flipped it open.

Well, Karl came down Saturday. We talked and went out to eat. We made love twice and in the morning he was still there. The love between us is stronger than ever. Our bodies and minds and hearts have become one. I want it to stay like that forever.

He flipped the pages. More about Karl. Danni's car towed in Portland. Worries that she might be pregnant. Karl saying he wasn't ready to be a father. Danni finding she wasn't pregnant. Karl breaking up with her over the phone. Forever turned out to be three weeks and eleven pages.

He looked at his watch. It was three minutes after midnight. He stretched his legs out, put his head back on the cushion. Started to replay the fight with Clutch in his head, grappling with the guy, his drunken breath, putting him down on the pavement. Clutch going slack. The way it was supposed to end, on the street. Not the way it ended in the alley, the Rawlings on his back, the geyser of black blood.

Brandon heaved himself upright, went out onto the stern deck. The marina was quiet, slip lights glowing, water slapping gently under the floats. He dreaded sleep, knowing it would take him back to the shooting, leave him to relive it again and again. The Portland lights were sparkling, reflecting on the shimmering water. He moved to the ladder, mounted the four steps to the helm. Parting the canvas, he crouched and slipped in, went to the helm and sat.

He put the diary down on the console, leaned back in the seat. Suddenly exhausted, he slipped down, went to the settee and flopped down. Stretched out there, the boat rocking, he fell asleep.

Drained. Spent. Done. And his brain kicked in.

He was back in the alley, gun drawn, trying to shout, "Drop the gun, drop the gun," but no words would come out, just an awful wail, and out of the blackness came the kid, Thatcher, and he was smiling even as the slugs hit him.

He didn't go down, just kept walking toward Brandon and laughing but when Brandon looked again, it wasn't Thatcher, it was Mia and he was screaming run, run, still no sound would come out and his gun was still firing, the marks popping out on Mia's shirt, and then the blood gushing from her mouth, hitting Brandon like it was from a hose. And he was screaming, but he couldn't control any of it, not the gun, not his voice, not Mia, who turned into Amanda, then Kat, then Thatcher's mother, vomiting blood through the fence.

Brandon woke up.

He was drenched in sweat, his hair stuck to his neck, his shirt soaked. It was morning, light streaming into the boat through the side-lights, the cabin light still on. He lurched to his feet, his mouth dry, tongue thick, kicked the beer bottle across the deck. He pushed through the canvas, stepped out and lurched down the ladder. On the stern, he went to the transom, leaned on both hands, felt like he might vomit, too.

The images from the dream whirled through his head and he tried to shake them off, opened his eyes and turned to look out on the harbor. It was cloudy and cool, a thin mist on the water, the tide high and ebbing. Brandon looked up at the marina yard, saw a car parked on the far side of the fence. Two people were standing beside it, looking his way. Estusa. A woman wearing a dark baseball hat, holding something. A laptop? No, smaller, and then Brandon heard it. A humming sound above him. He looked up, saw a drone. It was two hundred feet up, circling. And then it hovered, began to descend.

"Go to hell," Brandon shouted, first at the drone, then Estusa and the woman. When he looked back up the drone was 50 feet above him, buzzing like a giant bug. He raised his middle finger to it, turned and went back down and into the boat. When he turned to latch the hatch door, the drone was hovering over the stern.

Part of him wanted to get the shotgun out of the bow locker, blow the thing out of the sky. Instead he strode through the cabin, grabbed his phone.

Four missed calls, three from Mia. And a text from Mia:

worried about you. Coming over. Just leaving.

It had been sent 8:01. Brandon looked at his watch. It was 8:16.

He went to the stern hatch, eased his way out. Turning to the yard, he saw Mia's Volvo parked on the road thirty yards from the gate. And then he saw Mia, punching in the code, coming though the gate, crossing the yard. Too late to call. She was on the float, coming toward him. The drone came from behind her and Mia turned at the sound and looked at the thing hovering 20 feet over her head. She turned back, hurried to *Bay Witch*. Brandon took her arm, helped her over the transom, pulled her inside and up the steps to the helm.

"What the hell?" Mia said.

"Estusa. A drone."

"Can they do that?"

"I don't know. But it's too late."

"So what do we do? Stay trapped in here?" Mia said.

"If I were you, I'd take off. You don't want to get sucked into this."

"I am sucked into this. We're a team, right?"

"Not your fight, not with that guy."

"That sleaze," Mia said. "Somebody ought to—"

She stopped.

"What happened to the diary?"

It was on the console.

"It fell on the ground, got kinda dirty."

"What ground? Did you take it outside?"

Brandon hesitated. How to explain?

"In a parking lot."

"What parking lot? Here?"

He thought, everything else was crap, why not add a little more?

"No, in Woodford. I tried to return it to the girl who wrote it. She's not a girl now. She's probably thirty, but she looks older, what hard—"

"You what?" Mia said. "Why?"

Brandon sighed.

"It's hers."

"How did you find her?"

"Facebook."

"Christ," Mia said.

"Christ what?"

"I don't know. Christ, it wasn't yours to take. And Christ, why would you be out there, now of all times."

"I can't work. I've got to do something."

Mia frowned, then said, "What did she say?"

"She was embarrassed, wanted to have it."

Mia walked over and picked the diary up. She held it close, eyed the cover.

"What's this?"

A long pause this time. Pile it on, Brandon thought.

"Blood."

Mia looked at him, her mouth open.

"Her boyfriend followed her. Thought she was cheating on him."

"So what happened. He punched you or something?"

"Not really. Tried to get a little physical. His nose ended up bleeding a little."

"Are you crazy, Brandon?"

"I was trying to do something good. Give her stupid book back."

"And you could get arrested for beating somebody up."

"I wasn't. I left. It's no big deal."

"Jesus, Brandon. That gets on line? Along with everything else?"

"I didn't know it was going to happen. I didn't know her. I didn't know she had some nut-job boyfriend."

"You read any of this? It shouldn't come as any big surprise that she'd be in a dysfunctional relationship. In high school she had, like, six guys in a year. She's nuts."

"I think she was just lonely. Insecure. Wanted a Prince Charming to take her away, live happily ever after."

Mia moved to him, still holding the diary.

"Come stay with me."

"Why?" Brandon said. "So you can keep an eye on me?"

Mia's hesitated. "No, so I can help you."

"I'm fine. I just need for people to stop trying to take care of me. Kat was here, same thing. She's here for me, blah, blah, blah."

Mia took a step back.

"Is that what this is? Blah, blah, blah?"

"No, it's just that, I don't know. You can't help, Mia. I appreciate you trying but you can't change anything. The kid's dead. I did it. He was sixteen. Life over. End of story. Kaput. Sorry, kid. Tough break. Shoulda pointed your toy gun at a cop who can't shoot straight. There's a couple I know woulda missed you by ten feet."

"Brandon," Mia said. "It wasn't your fault." She put the diary back on the table, took both his hands, tried to get him to meet her gaze. He looked away.

"It doesn't matter. My fault, not my fault. That's what nobody gets. This is mine now. I own it. So let me get on with it. I'll figure it out. You can't help me with that. So just...."

"Just what?" Mia said.

"Just go. You don't want to be around me now. It's no fun, I'm a pain."

"Our life together isn't just about fun."

"Yeah, well, our life together isn't about this mess, either," Brandon said.

He took a long breath and then said, "I'll call you tonight."

"You want me to leave?"

"I don't know. I need to think."

"Brandon, I can—"

"You've got things to do. So go do them. I'll talk to you later."

"Come on, babe, this isn't the way to—"

"Just go, Mia," Brandon said. "Please, just go."

She looked at him but he turned away, looked out the harbor. Mia watched him, then turned and started for the stern. She turned and said, "I'll call you."

Brandon nodded, flipped a cushion onto the settee. He felt the boat rise and fall as she stepped off, heard her footsteps recede up the float. He walked out onto the stern deck, watched her as she went through the gate and across the lot to her car. There was no sign of Estusa or anyone else, no sound of the drone. The day was cool and damp, a sharp cutting breeze out of the northeast. Brandon crossed back into the cabin, went to his laptop.

Estusa's site.

A huge headline: *Did Killer Cop Also Kill the Cameras?*

He read on: the card missing from the GoPro. His own body cam turned off. The same quote from the newspaper about no witnesses. Rehash followed. Brandon heard a bing, a text tone. He leaned over and picked up the phone. Chooch at the PD.

`Girl called looking for you. Said it was impor-tant. Wouldn't say what it was about. Said you would know. Her #....`

A girl. Would Chooch call Danni a girl? Did Danni know he was a cop? Not Mia. Chooch knew Mia.

He texted the number:

`You trying to reach me?`

Put the phone down and wondered some more. A girl. Some kid he'd ticketed? A drunk and disorderly in the Old Port? There had been a teenage girl from Westbrook whose bag was stolen from her gym, seemed to think he was on the case, that he would...

His phone buzzed. The number the girl had left.

"Yes."

"Is this Police Officer Blake?"

"Yes."

"This is Amanda. The one who tried to kill you."

As opposed to any other Amandas he knew.

"Hey. How are you doing, Amanda?"

"OK, I guess. Except I'm alive."

"That's a good thing, right?"

"Maybe. I don't know."

"Take my word for it," Brandon said.

"You didn't tell them about the knife. How come?"

"It wasn't much of a knife."

"Are you trying to be nice to me?"

"Nice? Not really. Just figured you needed a break."

"So I'm supposed to, like, thank you?"

"No need. Over and done."

There was silence, then voices in the background, then silence again.

"I'm supposed to get out of here in a while. The hospital part. My mother went to get me some clothes. These are still from yesterday. They're gonna put me in the psycho ward."

"They just want to make sure you're doing okay. They can help you."

"I doubt it," Amada said. "I still don't, like, want to go on living. Without Thatch."

"Yeah, well. Give it a chance. I'll bet Thatch would want you to."

"I guess. I don't know."

She coughed and then he heard her breathing. He waited. The boat ground against the fenders like it was impatient.

"Anyway, I think, maybe you're not so, like, evil. It could be the meds, though. They're mellowing me out. But I'm also thinking that's fake, you know? Underneath it I still want to die."

"I hope not."

"Anyway, I think I need to talk to you."

"What about?"

"Can we talk face to face?" Brandon considered it.

"I don't know. I'm sort of a witness. And I'm not supposed to be working."

"Oh," Amanda said. "Even if it has to do with Thatch?"

"Especially if it has to do with Thatcher. I mean, I can't just march in there and go see you."

"Oh. Then maybe I should just tell you."

"Tell me what?" Brandon said.

"It's like, something with his parents."

"Oh."

"But the thing is, he told me I couldn't tell anyone. He made me, like, swear. But now he's gone and I don't know if that counts anymore. The swearing part. If you swear to be married to someone, and then they, like, die. Then you don't have to be sworn to be with them anymore, right?"

"I suppose it would be hard to be. If they were dead. Don't they say, Until death does you part?"

95

There was a rustling on the line and Amanda said, "I think I gotta go."

"Listen, Amanda, why don't you just talk to somebody there? They can tell you if—"

But she was gone. Brandon looked at the phone. 8:48.

"What the hell?"

Something with Thatcher's parents. Something he'd told Amanda but sworn her to secrecy. What would Thatcher be ashamed of? They abused him? They were embezzlers. They had orgies? He swears his girlfriend to secrecy then goes out and gets himself killed?

He walked out to the stern, phone in hand. There were two strings of floats that led to a third string that paralleled the shore and extended out on both ends, like a double T. People were pushing carts out on the far float, the first two stopping at their slips on the far side. And then Brandon noticed a third group, the Andersons with their little boy, Hans, take the long way around to their big Grady White, five slips beyond Brandon and *Bay Witch*.

He seemed like a nice guy, but shooting somebody to death? What do you say?

Brandon looked back to the yard, saw a car pull in, a TV station logo on the door. A woman got out, walked to the gate and waved. The boat owners were avoiding him; the media couldn't stay away.

He should have gone up to the office, checked the mail, made sure the clunky ice machine was operating. Instead, he climbed the ladder to the flybridge, sat down at the helm seat. Now he could see how much activity there was, people on their boats, the owners of the adjacent boats to *Bay Witch* staying away. He looked out over the harbor, told himself he wouldn't check the news on his phone. There were dark clouds rearing up to the northeast, the breeze stiffening.

Just the weather, he thought, flicked his phone on, saw the three-day forecast. Rain in the afternoon, continuing through the early morning hours. Seas 2-4, building to 3-5 by sunset, then diminishing. Another touch and there was his email. Google alerts for "Brandon Blake" and "Portland Police."

Rally Planned in Portland Police Shooting
Critics charge police cover-up; family and supporters of teen victim say death followed harmless prank

The rally was outside the P.D., three o'clock. The story talked about rogue cops, excessive force, no accountability. The missing GoPro card. Patrolman Brandon Blake turning his body cam off.

"It was never on," Brandon muttered.

The shooting has sparked a groundswell of protest on social media under the hashtag #kidslivesmatter. Activists charge that this latest death shows a continuing pattern of excessive force like the shootings elsewhere in the country. 'Police officers cannot be allowed to indiscriminately levy the death penalty on innocent people,' said Roger Williams of the National Union for Civil Liberties. 'Law enforcement can't function as some sort of Third-World death squad.'"

"Jesus," Brandon said. He clicked the screen dead, put the phone down on the console. Sat back in the chair and gazed out over the harbor. The wind was picking up, kicking up silvery chop on the Portland side. A crane was loading containers onto a ship, swinging like a movie dinosaur. A dragger was coming back into port, a cloud of gulls following it like a swarm of deer flies. Beyond the floats, a big ketch coming in under power had picked up a mooring. The Jaegers in *Gypsy IV*, back from a cruise up to Deer Isle. Brandon could see David Jaeger clinching the mooring line tight, his wife Liz pulling the inflatable up to the stern.

None of it mattered. It was like it was all from a previous life, everything before the shooting just some odd and distant memory, like it belonged to someone else. The kid who worked in the marina and bought *Bay Witch*, scraped and sanded, painted and varnished. The guy who had busted his butt to become a cop. The cop who loved putting on his uniform, who liked his partner, the cruiser, the streets, the people he met, even the people he arrested.

It was like he was looking back through a haze.

Brandon looked at the phone.

A demonstration. #kidslivematter. No shit. It was why he was a cop. Had been a cop? Would it ever return to any sort of normal? He blew out a long, weary breath, took another look out over the water. The Jaegers were snapping a sail cover over the boom. A tug was headed upriver, passing under the bridge. Gulls were hovering on the wind like kites.

He turned. The woman from the TV station was standing with her back to the boats, the cameraman standing behind a tripod. She turned and gestured toward the water, then stopped. The guy reached for the camera and they started to pack up. What did they call it? B-roll?

Brandon slid down off the seat, grabbed his phone and climbed down the ladder and went below. It was cool in the cabin and he turned on the heater. Opened the fridge and saw two beers. Considered it for a second, then reached for orange juice. He drank out of the carton, put it back, turned and reached for his police radio and turned it on.

The sound of the department filled the boat: Chooch and the other dispatchers at their consoles, directing traffic. Somebody giving a parking cop a hard time on Middle Street. A missing barbeque grill on Munjoy Hill. Domestic disturbance in the West End, Brandon recognizing the address. Guy was a dirtbag. Car accident with injury, Brighton Avenue. Drunk harassing the cashier at a Somali market on Forest Avenue.

Subject fallen off parking garage, Maine Med.

TEN

Brandon froze. Listened. Picked up the radio and held it in front of his face. Waited, the sinking feeling growing. Medcu rolling. Cops on the way, Kat calling in. Sergeant Perry asking for better location. Chooch saying victim on embankment just west of the Congress Street entrance.

"Medical there from the hospital," she said.

"Where'd she fall from?" Kat said.

Brandon waiting, praying for the second floor. Chooch saying, "Witness says level four."

"Oh, no," Brandon said.

He pulled his phone out, hit Amanda's number. Phone at his ear he grabbed a baseball cap, sunglasses, truck keys. He vaulted the stern, sprinted down the float, through the yard, slammed through the gate. The TV crew was pulling out of the lot but they stopped. Brandon ran past them to his truck, slammed the door, started the engine, stomped the pedal, spun out of the lot in a spray of gravel.

Units were off at the scene, voices calm on the radio, cops and Medcu,

Chooch, too. Brandon was approaching the bridge when his phone buzzed. He glanced, saw Kat's ID.

"Shit," he said. "Shit, shit, shit."

He picked it up.

"Is it her? Amanda?"

A pause before Kat answered.

"Yeah."

"Dead?"

"Yeah."

"Goddamn it. Goddamn it all to hell."

"Went off the fourth floor of the garage," Kat said.

"She just called me, like twenty minutes ago. Shit."

"Brandon, where are you?"

He was coming off the bridge, headed for State Street.

"On my way."

"Brandon, you shouldn't—"

"She said they were gonna keep her. The psych unit. Her mother had gone to get her clean clothes."

"She didn't want to stay?"

"No, she seemed okay about it. She said she wanted to tell me something. Thatcher told her something and swore her to secrecy."

"Did she tell you?" Kat said.

"No. She said she had to go."

"Damn."

"She was just a kid, Kat."

"This isn't your fault. None of it is," Kat said.

"Yeah, right. All strung together, he dies, she dies, who's next? The mom? Goddamn it."

"You coming here?"

"Five minutes."

"Sarge is gonna flip out."

"Yup."

"Oh, Christ, the mom's here. I gotta go."

Kat rang off, Brandon drove. Flashers on, he swerved around turning cars, a city bus. And then there were the blue lights, cops blocking the street. He pulled over and parked and Park, Kat's new partner, approached to tell Brandon to move it. Saw Brandon and said, "Sorry, man," and gave Brandon a pat on the shoulder as he strode by.

Amanda was on a landscaped embankment, the kind with juniper bushes and pine mulch. Medcu had covered her with a green sheet, and there was a woman on her knees beside the body, sobbing into her hands. The mom. Kat was crouched beside her, her arms around the woman's shoulders. One Converse hightop was sticking out from under the sheet. There was no visible blood. The mulch soaked it up.

Brandon, hat and sunglasses on, stood thirty feet away, watched as an EMT wheeled a stretcher along the entrance ramp, and she and another EMT picked it up and carried it up the embankment. They wrapped the sheet around Amanda Shakespeare and, on three, lifted her up and onto the stretchers. Her mother wailed and then sobbed and then wailed again. "My baby. Oh, my baby."

Brandon felt his eyes well behind the sunglasses. He swallowed hard, forced himself to watch as they carried the stretcher down the embankment, dropped the wheels onto the pavement. Amanda's mother got unsteadily to her feet and, Kat still with her, and started to follow. Stepping over the curb she stumbled, caught herself and looked up.

"You?" she said.

She was looking at Brandon.

"You son of a bitch. You did this, you bastard."

She started for Brandon, her fists clenched in front of her.

"You killed her," she screamed. "You killed both of them."

Brandon didn't answer. Kat took the woman by the shoulders, held her back. She was still screaming and people were watching, hospital people in printed shirts and green scrubs, cops and EMTs, a couple of scroungy guys from that end of Congress.

"Arrest him," Amanda's mother screamed. "He killed my daughter. He did it. He did it."

And then she collapsed to her knees again, her body wracked in sobs, her fists pounding the pavement. Brandon started to turn away, felt a hand on his shoulder. Perry.

"Blake," he said. "Get the hell out of here."

Brandon turned with him, felt himself pushed along.

"What the hell are you thinking?" Perry said.

"I just talked to her," Brandon said, both of them still hurrying toward the line of cruisers.

Perry jerked to a stop. Brandon turned.

"You talked to her? The dead girl?"

"Amanda Shakespeare. Yeah."

He explained. Amanda calling the P.D., asking for him. Chooch calling, his text back. Amanda calling, wanting to talk about something Rawlings told her. Perry stopped him.

"Friggin' A, Blake," he said. "Is there anything you don't wind up in the middle of?"

———

The front seat of an unmarked Impala, still on scene at the hospital. Amy Smythe, a detective on the day shift, at the wheel, a legal pad on her lap. She was making a time line. Brandon had his phone out.

"It was 8:48," he said. "When she rang off."

"Said she had to go?"

"Abruptly. Like she had another call. Or someone had come in. I sort of expected her to call back, say, 'Sorry about that.' Keep talking."

Smythe wrote the time on the pad. Drew a line to make a column. Word was she did her reports in Excel. Before she was a cop she studied accounting. Fortyish. Widow, husband killed in Iraq. No outward display of emotions. Some of the cops called her Mrs. Spock but they liked her because she was cool under pressure, smart, dependable, consistent.

"What did she want, Brandon?"

"I think she wanted to tell me something, some sort of secret. Something to do with Thatcher and is parents."

"Did she start right in with that or work her way up to it?"

Smythe. Methodical and thorough. Nothing slipped through.

"Worked her way up to it, I guess."

"Tell me the whole conversation, step by step," Smythe said.

Brandon considered it, knew he had no choice. So he laid it out. The girl had attacked him with a knife, or tried to. He hadn't included that in his account to South Portland P.D.

Smythe scribbled, didn't flinch.

"So you're saying you omitted that part?"

"Yes."

"Why?"

"I felt bad for her. She was upset, had lost her boyfriend and all. I didn't think she deserved whatever she'd get for it. Assault with a dangerous weapon, criminal threatening, whatever. A felony."

Smythe was writing.

"So she wasn't distraught when she called? Didn't threaten you again?"

"No. She was pretty calm."

"Despondent?"

"Yeah, but more exhausted. She said she was medicated."

"Did she say anything to indicate she was going to kill herself?"

"No. Nothing like that," Brandon said. "She said they were going to put her in the psycho ward, as she called it. She didn't indicate she wasn't going to go. She said her mom had gone to get her clean clothes."

He watched her writing, then stop. Still staring at the page, Smythe said, "Are you omitting anything now, Brandon? Is there anything you haven't told me?"

"No. That's the whole thing."

Smythe looked up. The ambulance transporting the body of Amanda Shakespeare was pulling away. Lights, no siren. CSI was taking photos of the garage from across the street. More cops were up at the fourth floor. Two of them poked their heads over the concrete wall and peered down. One of them took more pictures.

"Not to tell you how to do your job," Smythe said.

"Right."

"And this shooting, I'm with you. I think what's going on is way over the top."

"Uh-huh."

"But you start cutting corners, Brandon. Even if you're trying to be a good guy, it's gonna come back to bite you."

He nodded, took the lecture. It was odd but he felt better here, didn't want to leave the sanctuary of the unmarked car.

"So what do you think it was? What this girl wanted to tell you?"

"I don't know. What would a sixteen-year-old guy tell his girlfriend about his parents? Then have her promise not to tell anybody?"

"One of them having an affair?" Smythe said. "Dad beats the mom. You met them?"

He looked at her.

"Sort of. The mother came out to where I live and screamed at me. Father said they were going to have me locked up."

"Other than that?" Smythe said.

"Perfectly normal."

She wrote on the pad.

"Yeah, well, I have to talk to the hospital people before they scatter. How the girl got out to the garage. Did she say anything. Her demeanor leading up to this."

She gave him a last glance.

"Remember what I said, Brandon. Word to the wise."

And then she out of the car, the door slamming behind her. Brandon sat for a minute, hiding behind the sunglasses and hat. And then the door snapped open and Kat was standing there.

"Are you out of your mind?" she said.

"No."

"You can't be here, Blake."

"I had to."

"You didn't have to do anything. Jesus, jumping into the middle of this shitstorm?"

"I'd just talked to her."

"So run the other freakin' way."

"It's not about me," Brandon said.

"Sure it is. All about you wallowing in your bad luck. Well, listen to me, partner. You're gonna wallow your way out of a job and into a whopper of a lawsuit. Listen, you gotta get the hell out of here. Estusa is coming down the street. I heard him ask if you were here."

"Screw him," Brandon said, but he was out of the car. They hurried to Kat's cruiser, his old cruiser. Park was in the front passenger seat and Brandon got in the back. Park was silent. Another awkward cop.

Kat threw the car in gear and wheeled out into the street. She headed west on Congress, past the morning-beer bars, down the hill toward the Greyhound station. Brandon stared out the window like a suspect in custody. Which, in a way, he was.

"My truck," he said.

"We'll swing around and drop you."

They circled and came back east of the hospital. A TV news truck was parked fifty yards from the spot where Amanda had fallen. A dark-haired woman was leaning close to the rearview on the passenger side, putting on lipstick. The crowd had grown, people stopping, blocking the sidewalk. Estusa was on the side of the embankment, shooting video over the police tape. There was an indentation in the mulch, like a sunken grave.

Kat pulled the cruiser up close to Brandon's pickup, looked over at him.

"You gonna be okay?"

"Yeah."

He got out and opened the truck door. Kat came around the front of the cruiser.

"Go see Mia."

"Okay."

"Don't be alone. I'd go with you but..."

"I know."

"Gonna get worse before it gets better."

"Right."

"Internal will be starting up."

"I know," Brandon said. "Tell the story a few more times."

"You didn't kill this girl."

Brandon shrugged.

"Had to tell Smythe about the knife," he said.

"Jesus."

"Yeah."

"You were distraught. Because of the shooting."

"That argument will keep me out for months."

"Might be the best thing," Kat said. "This media crap, goddamn Twitter."

"Yeah. No end in sight."

"And you're a sitting duck on that boat. Where can you go?"

"Boats move," Brandon said.

She gestured with her eyes for him to move away from the cruiser and stepped to the front of his pickup, away from Park.

"Something's all wrong with this," Kat said.

"You got that right."

"Nobody's acting like they should. This girl. The kid with the toy gun."

"The parents," Brandon said. "They seem fake, like they're acting."

They looked away from each other, surveyed the quieting streets, the lingering cops, the dwindling crowd. Amanda Shakespeare had had her fifteen minutes. Maybe it was the spotlight. Somebody points a phone at you, you perform.

"We're working on something," Kat said. "Think of it as Team Blake."

She turned away, said, "Maddie's waiting to talk to you. The garage off Forest. She's there now. Second level."

"Same car?"

"Blue Outback."

"So what's up?"

"I'll let her tell you. You're on leave. I gotta go."

She glanced toward the cruiser. "Park's a good guy but he sucks at keeping a secret."

Kat walked back to the cruiser, slung herself into the driver's seat and pulled away.

The Subaru was backed into a corner space that looked out toward the downtown. Brandon pulled the truck in three spaces away, got out, walked over, and got in. Maddie looked over and smiled. She had a metal travel mug of coffee between her legs.

"Hey," Brandon said.

"Hi, Brandon. How are you doing?"

She was forty, pretty, with dark hair in a runner's ponytail and an easy, open smile. Kat said Maddie's students spilled their guts to her in office hours, talking about everything but 20th century American literature.

"I'm doing okay," Brandon said.

Maddie put her hand on his shoulder and said, "No, really."

It wasn't just the smile, it was her eyes. They were green with flecks of gold and when she smiled they fixed on you like she could look inside your head, nestled there so you weren't alone. Brandon could see why rough-tough Kat loved her.

Brandon looked at Maddie, then away. The sign on top of the Time & Temperature Building showed 11:01 a.m., 53 degrees. A jet passed over it, headed east. He looked back and she was still watching him, waiting. He said, "Not so good."

"I heard about the girl."

Brandon blew out a sigh and his eyes began to water. He blinked and fought that back. "Yeah. Totally stinks. She was a nice kid. Seemed to be."

"Surprised?"

"Yeah. She'd just called me. Thanked me for not arresting her and all. She said things were going okay, considering. I felt like I'd made the right call, you know? Like she'd crashed and was on the way back."

"Did she want to talk to you again?"

"She didn't say that. Just said she had to go. But it wasn't like, 'I have to go kill myself.' It was like, 'Somebody's at the door.'"

Maddie squeezed his shoulder. "You can't blame yourself."

"Kind of hard not to. Maybe she would have gotten some help."

"Or maybe she would have hung herself with a bed sheet, Brandon."

Brandon took another long breath, let it out. Maddie took her hand off his shoulder and sipped her coffee. The smell of it filled the car. Vanilla.

"A guy in my American short-story class. Randy. He was a friend of Rawlings. A year ahead of him in high school."

So this was it, what they were working on. Brandon waited.

"Missed class the day after Thatcher died. And Randy's never skipped. Came to office hours the day after that and wanted to talk. He knows I'm with Kat. Read the stories about you, and she was in there."

"What'd he say?"

Maddie drank more coffee. Brandon waited. The temperature had gone up a degree.

"He said Rawlings had some serious problem with his parents. Something that really shook him up."

"Say what it was?"

"No. Just that Rawlings seemed totally thrown by it. And troubled."

"When was this?"

"A couple of weeks ago."

"And he didn't say anything else about them?"

"Randy said Rawlings said his parents were total assholes. Randy said, 'Like more than usual?' I guess they're this pair of narcissists. He said they ignored Thatcher all growing up, just care about money and appearances. Dad is this big macho type, hunts endangered species in Africa and wherever, and hangs their heads on the wall. The son wouldn't have anything to do with it. Randy said the dad pretty much told the kid he was a huge disappointment."

"But something else recently?" Brandon said.

"Yeah. Randy said Rawlings said, 'Like totally messed up.'"

"Huh. And now he's dead. I wonder who else he told?"

"The girl?" Maddie said.

"Amanda? Yeah, they seemed pretty tight."

"What did she say?"

Brandon pictured Amanda, tears streaking her pale face.

"That he had stuff," Brandon said. "Like something weighing on him. That he'd promised they'd be together forever."

She paused. They sat. A truck swung through the garage, a black F150 with a young guy driving. Maine Law sticker on the back window. Maybe he'd be cheap.

"I'm teaching *For Whom the Bell Tolls*," Maddie said. "You know it?"

"Vaguely. I mostly read history."

"You know the poem from the title? What it means?"

"Yeah. No man is an island and all that."

"John Donne. So you do know literature."

"It must have been in a military history or something," Brandon said.

"But you know what I'm getting at."

"Yeah. Don't be a martyr. Kat already gave me the lecture."

"We're going to help you."

"What? This Team Blake thing? Please don't."

"Not up to you, Brandon. You can't help yourself, so we'll do it."

Brandon shook his head.

"I'm not a cop," Maddie said.

"You're married to one. You could still get in trouble. Kat can, for sure. Just leave it alone. I'll be fine."

Maddie looked at him. "You know you're one of the most independent people I know. In this case it's not a good thing."

Brandon shrugged. "It's how I was brought up."

"By your grandmother?" Maddie said.

"By myself."

ELEVEN

He was glad Nessa hadn't lived to see this. The silver lining in her liver quitting after fifty years of hard drinking. "You're such a good boy," she'd say before she passed out on the couch in the shabby sunroom in the big house overlooking Casco Bay, wine bottles scattered on the floor like spent artillery shells. Brandon would have the rest of the day to himself. Read his books. Explore the shoreline. Make up games with hard and fast rules, invent his own structure for his unstructured life.

It played in his head as he drove back down Congress and up onto Munjoy Hill. He'd told Kat he'd go to Mia's place so he did. He took a right on Munjoy Street. Two blocks down he rolled past her place, saw that her car wasn't in the driveway.

He kept going.

The past still scrolled as he drove down to the Eastern Prom, doubled back toward the Old Port. His mom—strikingly pretty, impulsive, funny—played it just as loose as Nessa. Nikki partied, went where the wind took her, literally. She hung with a young boat crowd, people born to money but with no inclination to make more—at least not legally. Party girl Nikki went along when they cruised to the Caribbean, sailed back loaded with pot. When the money got too big, there were casualties and Nikki was one. She left Brandon behind but she'd always done that. His biggest regret was that she died without ever naming his father.

It was like being orphaned twice. Now, for the first time in a long time, he felt just as alone.

At the cruise ship terminal he pulled in and parked facing the harbor. The wind was still out of the southeast and the chop had built on the peninsula side, boats pointed into the wind, sterns swinging toward him. Brandon rolled down the window, listened to the rattle and jingle of the stays, the hurried slap of the waves on the rock shore. He closed his eyes and it was just as he feared. Amanda's foot sticking out from under the tarp. Her last words to him, maybe to anyone on this earth: "I gotta go."

Brandon opened his eyes. The boats still were swinging. A yellow ferry was creeping across the harbor to Chebeague Island. It all seemed pointless, the coming and going, the boats on their moorings. He looked left, saw two cars parked. A drug deal going down, Brandon figured, a couple of days worth of heroin. And then they'd be back.

He picked up his phone. Missed calls: Kat, Mia, Mia's dad, Alex. The hotshot D.C. lawyer offering legal advice with the usual strings attached. Mia again. He texted.

I'm OK. Don't worry. Just don't feel like talking. Will call later. xoxo

Another tap at the screen. Email. The shop steward, Charlie Canavan, wanting to set up a time to meet. The AG's investigator, Jim Beam, with a question. The department shrink, Harriet Foote, wanting to have "a sit down."

A message from Facebook. He opened it.

Danni.

Hey, Chris. hoping we can meet up, no hard feelings. can I buy you another coffee? In Portland tday for the dentist. good times! done by 10:30. If ur around txt me. 861-9080

It was 10:45. Brandon looked out at the water. It had started to rain, a front blown in on the south wind. The windshield was sprinkled with drizzle, then drops, then the drops started to run together. He hit the wipers, one swipe. The kids doing the drug buy were gone. Ditto for the smiling guy in the mini-van. Brandon tapped at the phone.

Hey, there. Okay. Where?

He waited ten seconds. The phone buzzed.

Great Chris. Dunkin' forest ave?

He texted back.

See you in 15.

Chris Craft would be there.

The Dunkin' was tucked up against a white apartment block. There was a patio out front with two tables with folded umbrellas and ornamental maples surrounding the patio. They had turned a pale yellow green, some of the leaves shriveled and fallen to the ground. Brandon drove up slowly, scanned the lot for Clutch's truck. It wasn't there but he did see the white Ford Focus, toward the rear under another yellowing maple. The Focus was empty. He parked beside it, texted.

I'm out here. Medium coffee, milk. I'll pay you back.

You don't want to come in and sit?

Lot is fine.

Brandon waited, wondering if he should have warned Danni that he was coming empty-handed, no bloodstained diary to hand over. He hadn't wanted to drive all the way to South Portland, he told himself. Or maybe it was more than that. Once he gave the book back, it was over for Chris Craft and he'd be stuck with Brandon Blake, killer cop.

He glanced over, relieved to see Danni coming out of the door with two coffees and a bag.

Her reddish-blonde hair was pulled back at the nape of her neck, her part showing sandy brown. She was wearing jeans, a black turtle-neck sweater, black work boots. The sweater fit her snugly, showed her belly, the roll of flesh that squeezed out above the waist of the jeans. She was big all around, four inches taller than Mia, 50 pounds heavier. If she'd been a guy, she would have played football.

Danni smiled as she approached the truck, Brandon leaned over and popped the passenger door open and she elbowed it the rest of the way open and handed him a coffee. He took it and she climbed in, put her coffee in the console holder and opened the bag. She took out a jelly doughnut and handed it to him. He took it and she took out another and took a big bite, wiped jelly and powdered sugar from the corner of her mouth with her finger. Her nails were painted purple. There was a tattoo on the underside of her right wrist. Two padlocks, their hasps hooked together.

"So," Danni said. "This is a little better."

"A little bit," Brandon said. "How was the dentist?"

"Fine. Guy with peanut-butter breath picking in my mouth. Told me to lay off the sugar."

She held up the doughnut.

"I don't follow instructions real good."

Brandon said, "Ha. Right." Danni took another bite, chewed and swallowed.

"I'm wicked sorry about last time. Just a cluster all around, you know? You didn't deserve that."

"No."

"Not after you came all that way to give me the book."

Brandon sipped the coffee, took a bite of doughnut.

"I don't have it," he said. "So you know."

Danni glanced around the cab of the truck like he might be mistaken.

"It's at my house. I was downtown and didn't have time to go get it."

Danni looked stressed but only for a split second. She smiled over at him and said, "I owed you a coffee anyway."

Brandon sipped.

"You live far?" she said.

"Far enough," Brandon said.

"I'm free pretty much all afternoon," Danni said.

"I have things I have to do."

They sat and chewed for a few seconds. Simultaneously they raised their cups and washed down doughnut.

"I don't blame you for being pissed," Danni said.

"I'm not," Brandon said. "It wasn't that big a deal."

She looked at him more closely.

"You acted like it was kinda normal, having some guy come outta nowhere, take a swing at you. Most people are afraid of Clutch. He's a pretty big guy. When he's hauling a car off, he gets out of the wrecker, they're like, whoah."

Brandon shrugged.

"You kinda kicked his ass," Danni said.

Another shrug.

Brandon was picturing Amanda in the marina lot, big eyes peering out at him from under her hoodie like an animal in a cave. Amanda. Gone.

"You okay?" Danni said.

He glanced at her.

"Yeah, sure. Why?"

"No reason."

She ate more doughnut, just a small chunk left. There was something refreshing about the way she ate.

"I really appreciate you bothering," she said, still chewing. Her lip gloss seemed pinker, or maybe it was the jelly. Under the makeup her skin was faintly pockmarked on her cheeks, like she'd had acne. She smelled like fruity shampoo.

"I mean, you coulda just tossed the thing into the recycling. Instead you came all the way to Woodford, you know? And you coulda blown me off today, too. So thanks."

"For what it's worth," Brandon said. He hit the wipers.

She popped the last bite of doughnut into her mouth and chewed. Then she swallowed and wiped her mouth with a napkin.

"That's okay. We can meet up. I can come back up and pick it up. I know you're busy."

Brandon was sipping the coffee. He lowered the cup and looked over at her and said, "How do you know that?"

Danni started to reply, then stopped. She took a quick hit of coffee, looked out as the Passat pulled away.

"I know who you are," she said, still looking away.

Brandon waited.

"You're Brandon Blake, the cop who shot the kid."

She turned toward him.

"Clutch figured you were something like that. The way you took him down and stuff. And you looked sort of familiar. So he went online. Your picture is all over the place."

"So I hear."

"I don't think it's fair what they're saying. I mean, what if it was a real gun?"

"Thanks."

"I know it must be pretty heavy and all. To carry that with you. It's gotta eat at you something wicked. Even if it wasn't your fault."

Brandon nodded.

"If you really did something wrong. I mean, if you knew it was a bb gun or whatever, that would be one thing. But even this must really chew you up."

Danni reached back and gathered her hair, doubled the elastic with a flick of her wrist.

"So I'm on your side, Chris. Or Brandon Blake."

"Thanks," Brandon said.

They sat, but not awkwardly. They were more like two people who had known each other a long time. Brandon was thinking this, wondering how it could be, when Danni said, "Why *did* you come? Not having the book and all."

He took a bite of doughnut, washed it down. Looked out at the terra cotta wall of Starbucks, the yellowing trees. The answer was coming to him as Danni waited.

"I guess I needed a break, from being Brandon Blake. Chris Craft is way easier."

She looked at him.

"I know what you mean," she said. "About wanting to be somebody else."

Brandon thought of the passages in the diary. *My birthday sucked as usual....I am ready to give up and surrender....I am confused. I am tired....I would like to settle down and have children. I'll probably be a crappy mother.*

"Why's that?" Brandon said.

Danni didn't answer, just stared straight ahead. She took a breath, stopped. It was like she was trying to say something and couldn't figure out how.

"I don't know."

A pause.

"My life, it's pretty shitty sometimes."

Brandon waited, finally said, "Problems with your boyfriend there?"

"Oh, jeez. Problems? I don't know. More like the whole thing. It's not like something happened. I mean, like, lately."

She took a quick sip of coffee and it spilled a little on her chin. She wiped it with the back of her hand.

"It's just...I don't know. It is what it is. I mean, why should I complain? Doesn't change nothin', right?"

She smiled, the moment passed.

"Anyway, listen to me. You're the one with the shit coming down."

"All around me," Brandon said.

"You know, I don't know how much you get paid to be a cop, but whatever it is, it don't seem worth it."

Brandon shrugged. "Most of the time it is."

"But not now."

"No," he said. "Not now."

"And you know what's hard about stuff like that?" Danni said.

She looked over at him, like she expected him to answer, at least hazard a guess.

"No," he said.

"There's no way to get away from it. It's always there. It's like you wake up and there's this, like second or two, where you forget. And then it comes back to you. Like wham. Piling back on. You're like, fuck me. Can't I have just a minute of freakin' peace?"

Brandon was staring at her and she looked at him, caught herself.

"Sorry. I get wound up sometimes."

"Sounds like you know the feeling," Brandon said. "Shoot somebody?"

Danni looked down at her cup, raised it to her lips but didn't really drink. Put it back on her lap. "Yeah, right. What was it my father used to say? Life ain't a bowl of maraschino cherries."

He waited. Danni was back on the verge of saying something, teetering on the edge.

When her phone buzzed. She looked at it.

"Oh, Christ."

She put it to her ear. "Hey....No, I'm still in Portland....Half-hour... I thought you were gonna be at the auction all day....yeah, well, wouldn't be the first time you bought crap...."

Then a longer pause. Her expression hardening.

"Yeah....No....I told you....Right. I don't know. Twenty minutes. Listen, I said I'd get to it and I will....I know....Yeah."

She pressed the phone, ended the call. Looked at Brandon and smiled. Sheepish.

"Clutch. It's like, if I'm not home right on time, he goes ballistic. Probably thinks I'm bonkin' you. Going out and getting myself a piece of younger ass."

"Right," Brandon said.

"Yeah, for a while he had this tracking thing turned on in my phone. He's like knowing everywhere I've been. Finally I say, 'What? You following me?' He goes, 'No, the phone does it for me.' I got a phone downgrade after that. Said the other one broke. The fucker."

He looked at her more closely, saw a faint purple splotch under the pinkish white stuff on her cheeks.

"Does he beat you up?" Brandon said.

She flinched, looked at him. "Yeah, well. I mean, not really. Not for a while. But you know, a fist fight isn't so bad compared to just being treated like shit."

Brandon said, "I do know. I see it all the time, domestic calls, neighbors call the cops. Guys, even if they don't get physical, they treat the woman like dirt. Pick at her. Emotionally, I mean. Nothing's ever good enough. 'How can you be so stupid? Goddamn bitch. Where would you be without me?'"

He paused.

"'You cheat on me, you're dead.' That's a common one."

Danni swallowed, looked away.

"Shit happens, right?" she said.

"Doesn't have to keep happening."

Danni twisted in her seat, reached for the door handle. "Yeah, well. Good talking."

"Likewise."

"Listen, I can come to you. For the book, I mean."

She turned back to him.

"How's tomorrow?"

"I don't know," Brandon said. "Hard to predict what's coming these days."

"I'm sure," Danni said. "How 'bout I text you? Faster than Facebook. I'm not on there all the time."

Brandon hesitated, then wondered, what had she wanted to tell him?

She held out her hand. Brandon took it and gave it a shake. Her hand was bigger than Mia's, her skin rougher. She fell back into the seat and said, "You know there's like this march. A protest thing."

"I know."

"That must suck for you."

"Whatever," Brandon said. "It's like, bring it on."

"You going?"

"Not supposed to go anywhere near any of it."

She looked at him.

"That's not an answer."

"I don't know. First I have to go see my girlfriend. Not sure what's happening after that."

"She must be worried about you," Danni said.

"Yeah."

"Well, you know what? I am, too. Hope that doesn't sound weird."

He smiled, nodded.

"So you hang in there, Brandon. Don't let the bastards get you down."

Danni opened the door and slid out. Hurried to her car, started it and sped off.

Brandon sat in the car, half a doughnut in his hand. He lowered the window and dropped the doughnut. A seagull swooped down from the roof of the shop and snatched it up. And then Brandon was alone and it all came rushing back. Again.

Amanda. The garage. Thatcher on his back, the blood. Tiff Rawlings screaming through the fence. Amanda's mother, more of the same. Even Joel Fuller, the slugs pocking into his chest.

Like Danni had said, it all comes piling back on.

But what?

TWELVE

Brandon thought of heading south, out of Maine. Boston. New York. Someplace where nobody knew him. He could sit in a hotel room, a Motel 8, alone with his thoughts.

His demons.

His nightmares.

So he did, got all the way to Saco on the Interstate. And then he thought better of it, thought of Mia and Kat. He got off the highway and drove north.

He took Route 1, stayed in the right lane and drove at the speed limit. Cars rushed past him as the roadside rolled by. Used-car lots, Clutch's competition. Tired strip malls occupied by doomed businesses: computer repairs, tanning salons, swimming pool supplies. Motels with little cabins, something out of the 1930s. Chinese restaurants and go-kart tracks. A gun shop. He reached for his, took it out from under the truck seat and laid it beside him.

The Glock looked strangely small, crudely mechanical—but capable of unleashing such misery.

And then he was crossing the Scarborough marsh, which stretched for miles to the sea. There were puffy clouds to the east, floating like balloons. They seemed fake, fool you into thinking everything was just beautiful here: the sky, the green scrub, the birds skittering into the air. As if any of it made any difference.

He shook his head. Drove.

Brandon was in South Portland when his phone buzzed. He was in traffic and by the time he answered the call had been followed by a text, then another. He pulled up to a light, picked up the phone. Mia. He glanced at the text.

Where are you? Call me. I'm worried.

He did.

Mia answered with a clatter.

"Coming into town."

"Are you okay?"

"Yeah. I'm fine."

"You can't be fine," Mia said. "I heard about the girl. The one at the hospital. It's on the news. Estusa. The connection to the shooting."

"Jesus, already? Who's talking to that asshole?"

Mia waited.

"So I guess I'm not fine," Brandon said.

"Are you coming here?"

"Your place?"

"Yeah," Mia said. "We need to talk. At least I do."

Brandon almost said, "About what? How I'm leaving a trail of dead kids across Portland?"

He caught himself, said, "Okay."

Mia's apartment was the third floor of a tenement on Munjoy Street. It had views of Portland Harbor and the weird guy across the street who liked to walk around his apartment wearing nothing but Speedos and a snake.

Her Volvo SUV was in the driveway. She was at the door. The same TV crew that had been at the boat that morning was pulling away as Brandon pulled up. It was after 12:30. Time to set up at the demonstration.

Brandon stepped inside and Mia closed the door and then hugged him tightly for a long time. He felt inert in her grasp like he was an animal playing dead. Then he hugged her back, hoping it would be enough. It wasn't.

"Are you sure you're okay?" Mia said, holding him at arm's length.

Danni's exact words.

"Yeah."

"You don't seem it."

"Sorry."

"Don't be sorry. Just tell me what you're really thinking."

They were still on the stairs.

"Let's go inside," Brandon said.

"I've been worried," Mia said.

"I texted you. Told you not to."

"I had students. I didn't see it until a little while ago."

They walked into the apartment and Mia shut the door, took his arm and turned him to face her.

"Talk to me, Brandon. Really talk to me. Please."

"I'm fine."

"Kat called me," Mia said.

"Yeah. I saw her."

"At the hospital? Did you go there?"

A pause before he could say it. "Yes."

"Oh, baby, I'm so sorry."

"Maybe if I'd arrested her she'd be alive. Locked in Long Creek or whatever."

"Brandon, don't go there."

Mia took him by the shoulders. Behind her, out the window, he could see rooftops and an oil tanker making its way out of the harbor. She moved her hands from his shoulders to his cheeks, made him look her in the eye.

"That has nothing to do with you," Mia said. "It's the country. Everything that's happened. You just happen to be caught in the middle of it."

"I just happen to be the guy who pulled the trigger."

"Who had no choice."

"Who didn't have his camera on."

"It wouldn't have made any difference, Brandon," Mia said. "He'd still be dead. This girl would still be dead. She didn't—"

"Kill herself," Brandon said.

"Not because you didn't have your camera on. She killed herself because her boyfriend's dead and she's a kid and into melodrama and filled with self-pity and she was devastated and grieving and didn't know how to handle any of it."

"No, I mean I talked to her," Brandon said. "She fit all of that when she was at the marina. That night. She didn't sound like that this morning."

Mia looked at him.

"When did you talk to her?"

He told her when and what Amanda had said.

"And then, a few minutes later, she just goes off the side of the garage? Takes her secret with her?" Mia said.

"I don't know. I can't even try to find out. Just say what I know and walk away. Stay away."

Mia walked him to the kitchen. "You want coffee?"

"No, just had one."

He started to say where and with whom. Caught himself. Again.

"Kat told me about Maddie's student," Mia said.

"Right. Some other kid all screwed up."

"And—"

"And saying something's wrong with the Rawlings mom and dad," Brandon said.

A shake from Mia, her hands gripping his. Hers were small, soft, delicate compared to—

"Time to look out for yourself here, Brandon. Don't get run over by all of this—I don't know—this hysteria. Don't let these people turn you into something you're not. You're a good person. A good police officer. So many people are on your side. Remember that."

Brandon looked over her shoulder. The oil lighter had disappeared from view. A tugboat pushed it out toward the bay. The harbor was otherwise quiet, the rain keeping boats on moorings, at their slips. He looked back at Mia, who was searching his eyes.

"I saw somebody else who says she's on my side," Brandon said.

She waited.

"Danni. From the diary."

Maya froze.

"You saw her again?"

"She texted me. Wanted to buy me coffee to make up for the rest of it."

Mia fell back a half step.

"Did you go?"

He told her he had, when and where.

"She have a thing for you or what?" Mia said.

Brandon shook his head. "Maybe a little lonely. I think the boyfriend is beating her."

"Tell her to get some help. Call a hotline. Find another shoulder to cry on."

"You don't need to worry. She's built like a linebacker. Drank coffee and ate jelly doughnuts."

"Would I have to worry if she was a hundred and five pounds and had a salad?"

Brandon shook his head. "No, of course not. I was just telling you. So you could picture it."

Mia looked at him, her lips pursed.

"Did you give her the damn book?" she said.

"No. It's on the boat. I was in town."

"At the hospital."

"Yeah."

They were quiet for a moment.

"I don't know what she wants," Brandon said. "It's like she wants the diary back but she also wants to talk. Weird mix."

He hesitated, then said, "They figured out who I am."

"So it's some celebrity crush thing," Mia said. "Give her the goddamn diary and tell her to get lost. Mail it to her for god's sake. You don't have to save her from her messed-up life. Tell her to call some other cop. Maybe she's a uniform chaser."

Mia turned away, walked to the kitchen. Brandon followed, stood as she filled the kettle and put it on the stove. "I need tea before I head back?"

The kettle hissed, the water on the bottom burning off.

"This march on the P.D." Brandon said.

"Don't you dare go watch."

"Amanda dying is gonna ratchet things up even more."

"Don't watch the news," Mia said. "They told you not to."

"But she's gonna be gasoline on the fire. Pressure on the D.A. to do something. Somebody to throw to the mob."

"Stay here. Watch Netflix."

"That's okay. I'll go back to the boat."

"Just let Kat and Maddie and the rest of them do their thing. Stay out of the crossfire."

Mia caught herself. "Sorry," she said.

It was 1:15, raining steadily. Brandon sat in the truck, motor running, heat on low. He flipped through his email, responded to Canavan, Beam, Harriet Foote. "I'm around. Give me a time." He ignored the emails from the Boston Globe, the Portland *Review*, three TV stations, and a lawyer named Polceski, offering his services. There was a text from a woman named Addison Slate, Channel 5 out of Bangor:

I can't imagine what you're going through, Officer Blake. My heart goes out to you. Can we talk?

Brandon put the phone down on the seat beside him, turned off the heat. The rain had speckled the windows, turned the truck cab into a private capsule. It was like this was his life now—isolated, alone with his own reality. The doors were locked and no one could get in. Nor could he get out.

He put his head back against the seat and closed his eyes. Waited for the nightmare slideshow to begin. When it did—Amanda slicing at her wrist—he opened his eyes and sat up. Started the motor and pulled out, headed east toward the harbor.

At the Eastern Prom he turned right, rolled slowly down the hill toward the Old Port. He glanced left and caught glimpses of the South Portland shore, a smatter of boats that was his marina. He'd be there in fifteen minutes, hunkered down on *Bay Witch*, the rain pattering on the deck above him. He could call Mia, Kat, watch something online, read. He had a couple new World War II books—the tank war at El Alamein, the battle for Okinawa—from the South Portland library. At five he'd have a beer. Wait for it to get dark and the interminable night to begin.

Christ.

At Pearl Street he took a right, turned into the pay lot halfway up the block. The far end of the lot fronted Middle Street, a half block down from the P.D. He circled, found a space two slots in. Backed the truck in and waited. A few cars passed. The people with umbrellas. Then TV crews. Photographers. A few cops stood off to the side, like they were waiting for closing time in the Old Port. Brandon could hear the marching orders. Stay in the background. Don't respond. Don't get pulled in.

And then the marchers, a guy playing a snare drum. People stretching banners leading the way:

TWO DEAD, WHO PAYS?
OFFICER BLAKE IS NOT ABOVE THE LAW
THATCHER & AMANDA, RIP
U BET YR ASS #KIDSLIVESMATTER

Then more people, some just walking, some with arms linked, some with signs.

MAINE IS NOT
A POLICE STATE

NO WITNESS
NO JUSTICE

By 2 p.m. it was three hundred people, maybe more. Some had brought little kids. Some had brought their dogs. Somebody had made a sort of stage with a piece of plywood laid across milk crates. There was a microphone and an amplifier, like a busker would plug into.

A bearded guy with glasses, asking for a moment of silence for "Thatcher and Amanda, martyrs who will not be forgotten." The crowd was hushed and then people stepped up onto the plywood. High school kids, some crying as they described Thatch and Amanda as "incredibly awesome people." A guy with blonde dreadlocks calling for an end to oppression. A white-haired woman demanding disarming of Portland police, "just like in England." A kid waving a petition urging the police chief to fire Officer Brandon Blake. A woman chanting, "Brandon Blake, lock him up." The crowd joined in.

And then Tiff Rawlings stepped up to the microphone. The crowd quieted, people shifting to get a better look at her.

She was wearing a black T-shirt with a face on it. She pointed at it, jabbing with her finger.

"This is my son Thatcher. He was my best friend. He was sweet. He was kind. He had great friends, including Amanda, who is with him now."

Tiff Rawlings voice broke and she started to sink to her knees. Her husband, wearing the same T-shirt, jumped up and grabbed her, pulled her back to her feet. A man and woman followed him, took Tiff Rawlings by the shoulders and helped her down from the platform.

Crawford Rawlings stayed at the microphone.

"I'm here to tell you that there was no reason for my son to die," he said. "He was a funny, creative kid. He wanted to be a filmmaker. He made these crazy wonderful videos, which is what he was doing the night he died."

Someone shouted, "He didn't die. He was murdered." A few people clapped.

Rawlings held up his hand.

"So I don't believe the story the police are telling, that my son threatened Brandon Blake. I believe my son ran because he was scared. He was sixteen, for god's sake. He ran and then he was cornered there in the dark. And Blake panicked. Did he tell Thatcher to drop the paintball gun? We don't know. Did he just start shooting? Why didn't he use pepper spray, if he felt so threatened by this skinny kid with a toy gun? Why didn't he reach for his Taser? We don't know that, either, because, conveniently Blake didn't turn on his camera. Conveniently, there is no evidence. It's Blake's word against all common sense. I mean, why would a kid point a toy gun at a cop who was holding a real one?"

There was more shouting. The other guy hopped up and leaned into the microphone and said, "I'm told that Brandon Blake is here with us? We can just ask him."

Brandon looked, saw Estusa working his way through the crowd, people falling in behind him. He pointed to Brandon's truck and the crowd turned, started moving. Estusa was through the barriers and into the parking lot. He had his phone up, shooting video. A woman behind him shouted, "Get him. Get the killer cop."

Police were breaking for the parking lot, running across the street. Brandon started the motor, put the truck in gear, and lurched out of the space. Estusa sprinted alongside, filming. People were smacking the truck with their signs. In the mirror Brandon saw commotion at the back of the truck—cops stepping in, angry shouting, scuffles breaking out, signs flying. A siren as a police SUV appeared, Sergeant Perry on the P.A.: "Everybody out of the parking lot. Stop where you are."

Brandon hit the gas, left Estusa behind, sped for the exit, the gate down. He swerved right, jumped the concrete barrier, bounced the truck into the street. He went left down Pearl, screeched onto Commercial. A woman in a crosswalk jumped backwards and he rolled past her, hit the gas and was gone.

Down Commercial.

Up and onto the bridge.

His phone buzzed. Texts were pinging in. A ding that said he had voicemail.

"Shit," Brandon said.

He crossed the bridge, hit a green light on the South Portland side, then a late yellow, another green. And then he was cutting down to the marina, slamming the truck to a stop in the lot. There were a few cars there, the marina quiet in the rain. Brandon grabbed his phone and his gun, slid out of the truck and stuffed the gun into his waistband holster and covered it with his shirt. He strode to the gate, slammed through. The MacMasters from *Ghost Dancer* were coming up the ramp and they moved aside to let him pass.

"Hey guys," he said. "Not a great day."

"More than the shower they were talking about," Len MacMaster said.

And then Brandon was by them, hurrying down the float, jumping up onto *Bay Witch*, fishing in his pocket for his keys. He reached for the padlock.

It was gone.

THIRTEEN

The hasp had been ripped from the doorframe.

Brandon reached his gun out, eased the door open. He listened, bent down and stepped inside. Everything from the stern lockers—cleaners, brushes, lines, tools—pulled out and tossed. There were cushions on the deck, books and magazines strewn underfoot, charts torn and crumpled, teak polish poured out over the whole mess.

The galley cupboards were emptied, the refrigerator, too. Food flung across the boat, cereal boxes opened and emptied. Across the salon, jackets, hats, shoes and boots had been pulled from the cabinets. Ketchup and milk poured this time, a pink smelly mess.

Brandon kept moving toward the bow, stepped down into the cabin. Someone had used silver spray paint to write U SUCK KILLER COP on one side of the hull, BLAKE/MURDERER on the other. Bedding, clothes, books, all of it flung to the center of the deck. The bow locker was open, extra life jackets pulled out, coils of line. The life jackets smelled of urine.

"Damn," Brandon said.

He holstered his gun, eased his way back toward the stern. In the salon, he pulled up trapdoors to the engine compartments. Nothing had been touched. He opened the doors to the electrical panels. All good.

If someone had wanted to really damage the boat, that would have been the way.

He moved back to the stern deck, climbed the four ladder steps to the helm. The canvas was unsnapped. He pushed through and scanned the space. A couple of charts had been pulled from the slot under the controls, tossed on the deck. But the controls looked untouched, same for the electronics, the VHF radio off, mic still on its hook; depth finder and radar off.

Nothing had been trashed, the helm apparently too visible to the rest of the marina. Brandon pivoted for a quick inspection, started for the ladder. Stopped.

He moved to the helm seat, lifted the cushion. The diary was there. He turned and, standing at the top of the ladder, called the police.

It was Otongo and Robichaud again, standing at hatch door and peering in at the mess. Otongo slipped her phone out and took a few photos, Brandon stepping to one side. CSI guy arrived 10 minutes later, quick response for a fellow cop. The CSI guy—heavy set, grimacing as he crouched to dust the cabinet doors, the tabletops, plastic chart sleeves.

"Goddamn knees aren't what they used to be," he said.

"How much longer?" Brandon said.

"Until retirement? Seven months, two weeks, three days."

"No, until I can clean the place up."

"Ten minutes. I'm not getting anything. For someone who wanted to make a big mess, they sure wiped stuff clean."

"Wasn't high school kids then," Otongo said.

"High school kids with prints in the database?" Brandon said.

"Look at the footprints. Just big smudges, like they wore booties."

"Got surveillance cameras?" Robichaud said.

"Ancient ones by the gate. Haven't worked in years," Brandon said.

"Might want to invest," the CSI guy said.

"A little late," Brandon said.

He was wiping oil off the deck with a bath towel when Kat and O'Farrell appeared at the hatch.

"I think you're out of your jurisdiction, Detective Sergeant," Brandon said.

"You're our jurisdiction," Kat said.

"I heard no prints," O'Farrell said.

"Yup. A big mess, wiped clean."

"They do the whole boat?"

"Yeah. Pretty thorough."

"A lot of foresight for a kid," Kat said.

"But not for a parent," Brandon said.

"More to lose," O'Farrell said.

"Still," Brandon said. "Weird combo. Trash the place but be cool enough to cover your tracks."

"Maybe they weren't just trashing the place," Kat said. "Maybe they were looking for something. The card from his GoPro?"

"There wasn't one," Brandon said.

"Which you've said," O'Farrell said. "Looks to me like somebody doesn't believe you."

Brandon dumped the oil-soiled towel into a trash bag. Reached for a clean rag.

"Rawlingses were at the demonstration," Kat said.

"So was Estusa," Brandon said.

"Could have hired somebody," O'Farrell said.

"Video would be huge for his website," Kat said. "A police shooting? These days, it would go totally viral."

"Talk to him?" Brandon said.

"You can't," O'Farrell said.

"Stay away from him," Kat said.

"I've been trying," Brandon said.

He bent to the deck, kept wiping. Picked up a magazine, a box of mac and cheese, stuffed them in the trash bag. And heard a woman shouting. Then another.

Kat and O'Farrell ducked low and crossed the stern deck, leapt out of the boat. They were trotting up the float when Brandon emerged and followed. He could see a circle of people outside the gate, women shouting from somewhere within the scrum. Closer, he could see a kid with a phone out, then another and another. People on the ground.

Kat turned to him, barked, "We'll handle it."

The cops banged through the gate, waded in. Brandon saw the high school kids fall back, phones still out. Video.

And then a bare foot kicking on the pavement. A sandal that looked familiar.

He was closer. The sandal said Colby College. Mia.

"Shit," Brandon said.

Kat and O'Farrell were flinging kids aside, Kat slapping a phone out of a girl's hand. There was grunting and a muffled shout, and then Brandon was through the gate and into the crowd, kids saying, "It's Blake," and the phones stuck in his face. He pushed through, saw Estusa with his phone out, too. Mia on the ground, Tiff Rawlings straddling her and Kat yanking her up and off.

"You little bitch," Rawlings was hissing, teeth clenched. "Gonna go screw your killer boyfriend? Are you?"

Her nose was bloody, her mouth and chin, too. O'Farrell was lifting Mia off the ground. She writhed in his grip, shouted over his shoulder, "He had no choice. Your son gave him no choice."

"You slut."

"Why was your son so messed up?" Mia yelled. "Whose fault is that?"

A high school kid started to run toward Mia and O'Farrell and Brandon grabbed his shoulder, spun him around and shoved him back. "He's assaulting him," a girl shouted. "Police brutality."

Ten feet back, Estusa was shooting video, a half-smile on his face. He moved to Brandon, phone still up. "Officer Blake. What do you think of your girlfriend becoming part of the collateral damage for this shooting?"

Brandon slapped the phone away, said, "Fuck off."

And then a cruiser slid up close, siren whooping, and the crowd backpedaled. It was Otongo and Robichaud again, and they moved in, arms wide and corralled everyone toward the fence. Brandon went to Mia, O'Farrell holding her by the shoulders. Her cheekbone was scraped on one side, and her knuckles were bleeding.

"She came at me," Mia was saying. "She's crazy. She was saying horrible things about Brandon and she was right in my face and I pushed her back and she grabbed on to me and started slapping and punching."

She started to sob, fought it back, and then saw Brandon and said, "Don't they understand? This wasn't your fault. This is awful for you. It's awful…awful for us."

O'Farrell led her to the space between the Portland cruisers, Kat's black and white and his brown Impala. He said to Brandon, "Give us a minute," and Brandon turned, saw Kat and Robichaud with Tiff Rawlings. Her back was to the same fence she'd clung to a day before.

"He murdered my son," she was saying.

"Ma'am," Robichaud said. "That doesn't give you the right…"

"What rights did Thatcher have? Shot down like a dog for making a movie. What rights are those, huh? What goddamn rights are those?" She saw Brandon and screamed, "Look at him. Blake, you're gonna rot in prison. Walk around now, Blake. Walk around while you can, you murderer. Blake, how dare you…"

They turned her away from Brandon. He stood for a moment, unsure where to go. The high school kids were watching him, and a girl said, "You should be so ashamed, asshole." And then they all started to chant. "Shame, shame, shame. Asshole, asshole, asshole."

Otongo moved to Brandon and said, "Might be better if you go back inside."

"Mia," Brandon said. "My girlfriend."

"We'll bring her down when we're done."

———

Brandon sat on the transom, flipped through his phone. Kids had posted video of the scuffle, like Mia and Tiff Rawlings were fighting on the playground. The post was circulating on Facebook. "Mother of police-shooting victim fights back." One kid had live streamed it. 1,903 likes on Twitter and 56 shares. Make that 1,907 and 65. #kidslivesmatter #stopkillercops. Estusa had posted it on RealPortland's Instagram. 675 likes and climbing.

Brandon looked up, stood. Mia fell into his arms and said, "I'm sorry."

"Nothing to be sorry for," he said.

"She's just out of control. I mean, I understand why but—"

"You have nothing to do with this," Brandon said. "She can take it out on me."

"But yes," Mia said, "I do have something to do with this."

They stepped apart and Kat moved closer. The South Portland cops had cleared the lot, sent everybody on their way. A few people watched from their boats, standing with sponges and ropes, pretending to do chores. Gulls circled and swooped low, in case the aftermath to a police fracas involved food.

"Mia doesn't want to press charges," Kat said.

"No," Mia said. "I mean, I'm fine."

"Best thing, considering," Kat said. "Just be gasoline on the fire."

"And I don't think it was me she was after."

They looked to her.

"When I got out of the car I could see these people at the gate. They were yelling and a couple of them shook the fence. She was standing kind of back from them with her arms folded like she was in charge or something and then Estusa came up and they were talking. He saw me and tapped her on the shoulder and said something, and she turned and looked at me and then they talked for a second and she kind of shrugged and then she just came at me."

"Shrugged?" Brandon said.

"Like, 'if you say so.' But by the time she got to me she was crazy, ready to tear my head off."

"Like in the car last time she was here. She turns it on and off," Brandon said.

"This family," Kat said. "Something doesn't add up."

"Yeah, well," Brandon said. "Right now, they're untouchable. Take them on, they win."

Kat looked at him. "Only if they know you're there," she said, and she turned and walked down the float, across the yard, and through the gate.

Mia looked in at the remnants of mess, and then they climbed to the helm and sat, shielded by the canvas and plastic.

"Leave the boat and come stay with me," she said.

"I'd be trapped there," Brandon said.

"Like you're not trapped here?"

"Boats can move."

"You can't just take off," Mia said. "Don't you have to go through more, I don't know, police stuff?"

"Internal investigation. Get cleared by the shrink."

"How can you just go back to work?"

Brandon thought about it, said, "I don't know. It'll fade over time, I guess."

They sat for a moment, looked out at the harbor. Keeping *Bay Witch* on the South Portland side had been his sanctuary. Now the harbor seemed small, Portland just a narrow stretch of water away.

"I can find another slip, a mooring," Brandon said.

"The name. They'll see *Bay Witch*."

"I can cover it."

"Where would you go?"

"I don't know," Brandon said.

But he did.

———

Cushing Island was three miles southeast of the harbor mouth. Dusk was approaching as he cut south of the channel markers, running slow in 13 feet of water. The drizzle had turned to rain but the wind was still 5-7 knots out of the south, a two-foot chop. There were fishing boats headed into Portland from the east, a tanker anchored south of Little Diamond Island, and a big sailboat running up the channel under power. It was a Hinckley ketch and as it passed Brandon on his port side, he waved to the guy at the helm. The skipper was gray-haired in a red slicker—tanned, rich, indifferent—and gave the old wooden Chris Craft a dismissive flick of his wrist. Brandon turned to, saw *Poseidon II* and Marblehead, Mass. on the stern.

Bay Witch meant nothing to him. Patrolman Brandon Blake meant nothing to him. Out here, Brandon could hide.

Brandon waited until the ketch was five hundred yards astern and then he swung *Bay Witch* northeast, following the channel markers between Cushing and House islands. The lights on Peaks Island were showing in the rain when he caught the bell leading into Whitehead Passage. Just beyond the bell he throttled back. When he'd passed Catnip Island on the port side he swung southeast and into Spring Cove. The town pier was to starboard and he eased his way beyond it to a small rocky island just west of Whitehead. He cut the throttle in 18 feet of water, two hours from dead low tide, he slid down from the helm, went to the bow and released the anchor. The chain rattled out and the anchor disappeared into the green murk. The boat swung around, bow to the shore, and jerked gently on the anchor rode. Brandon went back to the helm and cut the engine.

It was quiet, the waves slapping the bow, the stern swinging. He was alone.

This was one of their spots, Brandon and Mia. Just a half hour from the marina but on most days deserted. Sheltered by the lee shore from the prevailing southwest wind in the afternoon, protected by Peaks and the crescent of the cove from winds out of the east and northeast. Away from the gaggle of boats around Great Diamond. It seemed odd to be here by himself, not opening a bottle of wine with Mia on the stern deck.

That all seemed a lifetime ago.

He slipped down the steps from the helm, went below. It smelled like bleach and dish detergent and polish, the deck still sticky. He went to the refrigerator and then remembered the two remaining beers had been poured on the pile. There was a bottle of Jameson in the back of the galley cupboard and they'd missed it. He reached it out, poured an inch into an aluminum cup. Sipped. Poured more and, taking the bottle with him, went out onto the stern and back up to the helm.

He sat in the seat at the wheel. Flicked on the VHF and tuned it for weather. The robotic voice said south winds would become southeast during the night, building to 15 knots after midnight, gusts to 20. Southeast winds were fine. They'd blow him back into the harbor in the morning. He drank. Grinned to himself in the dark.

What had they said? No booze. No news.

"Screw that," he said.

Brandon drank. *Bay Witch* swung on the anchor, bow pointed toward the rocky bluff, a dark band in the dusk. To starboard a light glowed on the end of the island pier. Solar lights flickered on a private dock. He flicked his phone on, a pale gray glow filled the cockpit. Everything else fell away.

He peered at the screen, scrolled through the news feed:
Demonstrations Roil Portland After Police Shooting
Parents of Police-shooting Victim Demand Justice
Critics Say Police Body Cameras Only as Good as Officers Who Wear Them
And this one.
Mother: Teenager Killed in Garage Fall Died of Broken Heart
Brandon stared at the screen, read the headline again. Reached for the cup and took a long pull of whiskey. He swallowed it. Put the cup back on the console and tapped the phone.

Estusa. realportland.com

A video, the still shot showing the mom, her face drawn, eyes red-rimmed and bloodshot. She was holding a tissue in both hands. Brandon reached for the arrow. Touched it like it were on fire. The video played.

"My daughter was a wonderful girl, so kind and loving." A sniff. A wipe with the tissue. "She and Thatcher were, I don't know if you call it love, but they were just so happy when they were together. What do they call it? Puppy love? It doesn't make it any less important, you know?"

A sniff and then a cut, the video edited.

"Do I blame Officer Blake? I hate to say this but I do. Thatcher was a good kid. He wouldn't hurt a soul. He wasn't some threat to society. Amanda was so lovely, so sweet. I mean, I'm a single mom. She was all I had. But now both of them are gone because this policeman made the wrong decision."

Another sniff and wipe, another cut of the video.

"Should there be consequences? Yes. There are no witnesses. Nobody knows what happened there. Why should we take this cop's word for it? He's got everything to gain and nothing to lose."

"By lying?" Estusa's voice.

"By lying. Yes."

The video continued. A tagline appeared: CHLOE SHAKE-

SPEARE, MOTHER OF AMANDA SHAKESPEARE, 16, WHO FELL FROM PARKING GARAGE TO HER DEATH

Brandon put the phone down, reached for the cup and drank. He picked the phone up again. He flicked through Estusa's stories, the next one on the feed: *Parents Demand Justice in Son's Death at Police Hands*.

A photo of the Rawlingses at the demonstration, the crowd in the background. Signs: NO DEATH PENALTY IN MAINE…THIS IS NOT A POLICE STATE…PUT A STOP TO TRIGGER HAPPY COPS

Another video: Brandon hesitated. Tapped again.

Tiff and Crawford Rawlings, standing close, his hand around her shoulders like he was holding her up. Tiff Rawlings lips were clenched and she was staring into the distance like she was oblivious to Estusa, to the crowd behind her. She looked battered, exhausted, bleary.

"When one of us stumbles, the other one steps in," Crawford Rawlings said. "Sometimes it's me who can't take any more. Today it's my wife. But we both refuse to let our son die for nothing. His contribution will be to make sure this doesn't happen to anyone else. That this police department does not continue to hire rogue cops. Cops who have a history of fatal shootings. Cops who have backgrounds that are one giant red flag."

Estusa: "You mean Brandon Blake?"

"Yes, I do mean Brandon Blake. He should never had been hired. He had a troubled childhood, was raised by his alcoholic grandmother, shot a man to death shortly before becoming a police officer. I mean, what were they thinking? He was carrying so much emotional baggage that he was a walking time bomb. And still is."

"So you don't think Blake should go back on duty?"

"I think Blake should go to prison for the execution murder of my son. I think this police department and this city should be held liable for the death of my son. I think this should stop now so no other family should go through what we are going through, what Mrs. Shakespeare is going through."

"It's a living hell," Tiff Rawlings whispered. She started to crumple and her husband reached across and held her with both arms as she sobbed into his shoulder.

"Bullshit," Brandon said.

Staring into the phone, he played the video again, but this time watched Tiff Rawlings as her husband talked. She stared into space for a few seconds, then her gaze sharpened and she looked at something off camera. She tracked something with her eyes and then seemed to make an almost imperceptible nod. Then her stare blurred again, like someone pretending to be asleep. And someone passed behind her, in front of the demonstrators.

Brandon played the video again. Saw the guy walk by.

The lawyer James Kelly. Portland's finest criminal defense. The Rawlings' lawyer. Coaching from the sidelines? "Just remember your line, Mrs. Rawlings. It's a living hell."

———

Brandon drank more whiskey. He went back and forth, one minute thinking the Rawlingses were cashing in on their son's death, the next minute slapping himself for thinking it at all. The wind picked up. The boat swung in a wider arc, caught in an eddy. He sat at the helm, looked back at his phone. Stories. Photos. Video. #kidslivesmatter trending on Twitter. People calling for him to be fired, convicted, killed in prison. Which he supposed could happen, him being an ex-cop.

The word froze him. Ex-cop. Never to be a cop again. His career, his life. The whole thing blowing up like Thatcher Rawlings had been a suicide bomber. Which he had been, in a way.

Brandon looked out into the darkness. He heard the bow slap as the boat swung, the soft swish of the lee surf on the rocks. And then a ring, the phone lighting up. A text.

Mia: You okay?

He replied: I'm fine.

139

FOURTEEN

Brandon woke up on the settee in the salon, his clothes on, shoes off. It was a few minutes after six and the sky was cement gray over the island, the sunrise looming behind clouds. The southeast wind had, indeed, picked up after midnight and he could feel Bay Witch was tugging on the anchor and making wide, quick swings. Brandon couldn't remember coming down from the helm.

His mouth was dry and his head felt tight, like a clamp had been screwed onto his temples. He rolled to his feet and lurched to the head. Filled a glass of water and drained it, drank most of another. He put the gas on for coffee and, as the kettle hissed, patted himself down looking for his phone. No luck. He glanced around the galley and salon, looked to the stern and slipped up and out. The wind was gusty, a chop building in the passage and west of Peaks Island. Brandon climbed to the helm, saw his phone on the console, the whiskey bottle, too. He grabbed both, came back inside and dropped the bottle in the trash. He plugged his phone into the charger, saw the screen fill.

Texts:

Mia, 5:16 a.m.:

`They called and spoke this time. Some kid said I'm harboring a criminal, a bunch of nasty stuff. Should I tell Kat? Call me.`

Kat, 5:02 a.m.:

Hope you're ready for today. Bring your A-game partner. Protests are putting some pressure on.

Mia, 4:14 a.m.:

Somebody's been calling every half hour all night, hanging up.

Mia, 2:35 a.m.:

I guess you turned off your phone. Call when you wake up.

Mia, 12:47 a.m.:

Sorry to bother you but where are you? You never said. Please let me know you're OK.

Brandon did. Mia answered, sounded exhausted.

"I'm sorry," he said.

"Where are you?"

"That cove on the west side of Cushing."

"Was your phone off?"

"I left it topsides."

"I was so worried," Mia said.

"Sorry."

"But are you really?"

"Of course."

"I know. I'm just exhausted. I need to see you."

"I know. Same here. What about these calls?

"Some guy, young sounding when he finally spoke."

"Number?"

"I'll text it. When are you coming in?"

"Shortly. Meeting at the P.D. Internal investigation is starting."

"What about the attorney general's office?"

"They do both," Brandon said.

"Why?"

"AG decides whether I broke the law. Internal decides whether I screwed up in other ways."

"What time?" Mia said.

"I have to be there at nine."

"I can pick you up."

"Don't you have to work?"

"Yeah, but——"

"This is gonna be a long run, Mia," Brandon said. "Save it for something big."

"Like court?"

"Yeah. Like court."

There was a pause, both of them picturing Brandon on the stand, a hotshot lawyer like Jim Kelly questioning him.

"I can meet you," Mia said.

"I'll text you when I'm done."

Brandon washed his face, considered shaving but didn't. He was three days into a beard, starting to feel less recognizable. He trimmed it, looked halfway respectful. Of the process. Of his superiors. Which he was. They had to ask questions. He had to answer them. One step closer to getting back on the job—if he wasn't going to be sacrificed to appease the demonstrators. The parents.

Chief Garcia? A police chief with an MBA? He was cold but Brandon didn't think he'd throw him under the bus. The D.A.? He didn't know.

He put on clean khakis, a little rumpled. A button-down shirt and a sweater. Looked like he was one of Mia's preppie friends. He wasn't, not by a long shot.

He went to the helm, ran the blower. Looked out as he waited, saw whitecaps in the passage, the chop building from the southeast. A fast run into the harbor. He started the motor and the V-8 gurgled, idled up and then slipped into a steady throb. There was a half-tank of fuel. He'd top it off at the marina after the meetings. No time to go there first, and no inclination. People at the gate. People on board. The drone flying over.

One of the owners, a plastic surgeon from Cape Elizabeth, kept forty feet of dock space at Custom House Wharf for his Sea Ray, like leasing a parking spot. He used it when he and his wife went to dinner in the Old Port. But the doc was on some sort of medical trip to Central America, fixing cleft palates. The Sea Ray was growing weeds in its

South Portland slip. The wharf space was empty. A 10-minute walk to the P.D. Beard, sunglasses. Baseball hat.

The wind was brisk, steady at 15 knots, higher puffs. When Brandon stepped out on deck, it caught him for a second and he steadied himself with the grab rail. He moved to the bow, stepped on the switch for the winch, after a second, felt the anchor come free. *Bay Witch* drifted back, as the anchor chain rattled onto the reel.

As the bow swung away from the shore, Brandon locked the anchor in place, slipped around and up to the helm. He eased the throttle up, steered for the bell buoy, and swept past the east end of Cushing, headed for the southern tip of House Island. It was 6:55. The seas were four feet and *Bay Witch* porpoised her way through the channel, past Spring Point, Bug Light. The Peaks Island ferry was headed out and passed thirty yards off on his starboard. A deckhand waved and Brandon waved back. It felt good to be just another boater, no judgment out on the water.

He angled into the ferry wake and *Bay Witch* heaved and pitched, and then he was around Bug Light and the Portland waterfront loomed, a cruise ship berthed like it had landed from space.

The city. A sinking feeling.

His phone buzzed on the console. A text. Then another. And another as the phone blew up. He reached for it and read:

fu killer cop…prison is 4 murderers like u…your life is down the shitter, blake…justice for Thatch and Amanda…we've got u surrounded u coward…your done blake…P.D. can't protect u, not this time…how many people do you need to kill?…how can you sleep?…Gonna be somebody's bitch, Blake.

And then:

Brandon Blake. Got your number from the realport-land website. I think we need to talk. I knew Thatcher. Like really well. He was a good kid. I'm not here to ream you out. Something you should know.

Brandon put the phone down, listened to it buzz. He couldn't talk, no way. His phone number on the website? That bastard, Estusa. Where did he get the number? God, he'd like to kick that guy's ass.

Something he should know, like what? But then he was coming into the harbor, a backhoe and dump truck on a barge chugging out to the islands, a dragger coming in, a tug crossing his bow, headed for the bridge and upriver, a big sailboat motoring out into the bay. A cruise ship towering over the whole thing.

And then he slowed, rose and fell over the tug's big wake. He idled into Custom House wharf, saw the space below the Port Hole restaurant. A tight fit for 32 feet of Chris Craft, with somebody squeezing a 40-foot yawl along the float in front of his slot. Brandon idled past the space, reversed and pulled the stern in, whipped the wheel around and goosed the throttle, *Bay Witch* settling close enough. He jumped down from the helm, slipped around to the bow, ran the line back, and leapt onto the dock. *Bay Witch* was drifting forward into the stern of a gleaming sport fisherman, and Brandon yanked hard on the line, took a loop on a post and pulled. The boat fell back against the dock and Brandon cleated the line, ran to the stern, which was drifting off. He jumped on board and off, cleated that line, too. Got back on board and climbed up and shut off the engine. Instruments.

A sigh of relief. His phone buzzed.

Kat: `Where are you? Let's talk before you go in`

Brandon: `pearl and commercial in 5`

Kat: `roger that. I'm off duty`

Brandon put the fenders out to protect the hull. Felt like he should wear some of his own.

He stood at the corner of Commercial and Pearl, looked up and down the street. A few early bird cruise ship passengers were doing the same, holding maps in front of them. Brandon waited, saw Kat's black Jeep approach. She pulled up like an Uber driver and he got in. Kat was in yoga pants, running shoes, a T-shirt that said Team Glock.

"I'd say coffee but maybe not," Kat said.

"Low profile," Brandon said.

"I like your preppy slacker disguise."

"Thanks. Should I have worn a suit and tie?"

"No," Kat said. "It's not like you're going to court."

He looked at her.

"Much," she said.

She drove down Commercial, swung up onto the Eastern Prom. They passed Munjoy Street, and Brandon pictured Mia, making coffee, cleaning the apartment. That made him think of her father and he said, "Think I should have my own lawyer there?"

"Carew will be there for you. So not yet. Not for this."

"Soon?"

"Oh, yeah."

"I could lose the boat," Brandon said.

"We can only hope," Kat said. She looked at him and smiled.

They parked by the ramp, looked out. The boats were all pointing southeast, into the wind. A couple was struggling to keep their kayaks from being blown around. The trip out of the harbor was going to be rougher.

"So here we are," Brandon said.

"You'll be fine. Just tell the truth. The whole truth."

"I always do," Brandon said. "The one thing my grandmother taught me that stuck. That and how to make her a Manhattan."

"I thought she drank wine," Kat said.

"Only before five. A couple of stiff Manhattans for the big finish."

"You miss her?"

"I'm glad she's missing all of this," Brandon said.

"She'd be on your team. Speaking of which..."

Brandon watched the kayakers. The guy was fifty feet ahead of the woman, who was still struggling.

"The mayor."

"Uh-huh."

"I heard she wants Garcia to come down on you hard on the body cam."

"Body cam doesn't change the shoot," Brandon said.

"Halsey pushed for the things. You didn't use it. It's like you were dissing her."

"I forgot."

"I know."

They sat. The guy in the kayak had turned back, almost flipped coming around. Brandon didn't feel like saving him, leave it to Kat the triathloner. He didn't feel like saving anyone. He was done.

"There's a lot of pressure on her. That comes down on Garcia."

"I know. You should see my phone. Estusa put my cell number online."

"That little weasel."

"Yup."

"You know it's got very little to do with you and Rawlings," Kat said. "It's like you're the scapegoat for all of the shootings all over the country."

"Timing is everything," Brandon said.

"Plus the failure to report the Shakespeare thing."

"I know."

"Lay it all out there. You had good intentions. You're a good cop."

"What's the line? When bad things happen to good people?"

"A reprimand, maybe. Thirty days suspension," Kat said.

"What happens to the bad cops?" Brandon said.

"Like Dever, always the last one in? Three guys pounding you and it's 'Where's Dever?' He was just here? That coward. People like him, they skate. Until they don't."

The kayakers were both running past the boat ramp, the wind blowing them upriver toward Back Bay. Smart. Don't beat your head against the wall.

"I got a text this morning," Brandon said. "Somebody said they knew Thatcher Rawlings. Something I need to know."

"You can't talk to anybody."

Brandon didn't answer.

"I'm telling you, Brandon. Don't make a bad situation worse."

"What if it's important? What if he told the guy he was going to go get killed by a cop? What if it was all planned?"

"Playing with fire, Blake. It could all go fine without it. This could cause the whole thing to blow up on you, you go nosing around. You're on leave. *You* can't be working."

She looked at him, held his gaze.

"You're as tied to this as me," Brandon said.

"Maddie's not."

She dropped him in the police lot, which was quiet between shift changes. A slap on the shoulder and Brandon went to the door, buzzed himself in. He heard voices, saw no one. Walked down the corridor toward the voices, but they were coming from upstairs. He went up the stairs, homing in on them. Steeled himself. Stepped into the room

They were drinking coffee. Charlie Carew, the shop steward. That was Brandon's team. The department side: Sergeant Perry, Chief Garcia, Lieutenant Searles, a detective named Broward. She didn't like O'Farrell and he'd brought Brandon in. Broward said the hotel shooting was a deal breaker. O'Farrell said if that's the case, what do we do with all of these cops who fought in Afghanistan? Broward lost. She and Brandon hadn't hit it off.

The group went quiet when Brandon walked in. Carew broke the silence, said, "Hey, Brandon," and came over and shook his hand. The others followed, Broward bringing up the rear, her handshake as tepid as her expression. They went to the table, where legal pads and yellow pencils had been set at each place. Carew motioned to the seat on the end, like Brandon was the dad at Thanksgiving. He'd never had one, but he'd seen it on TV.

They sat, said they might as well start at the beginning. He asked Brandon to walk them through the events of Sept. 6, 2017.

"Starting when?"

"When you started your shift," Searles said.

Brandon looked at him, thought of how Searles and his wife did ballroom dancing, won competitions. You never knew about people.

He took a long breath, focused on the day. First coffee. Then a call on Forest Avenue, a woman from Burundi complaining she'd been harassed by a passing driver. Her description of the car was that it was big and black. Or maybe blue. Kat and Brandon said they'd keep an eye out. A domestic at a condo in Deering, two guys, one with a bloody lip and a swollen eye, the other with ice on his hand. A summons for domestic assault, ice man told to leave. He started to pick up stuff piece by piece. A sock. A lamp. A dog dish. Passive aggressive. Kat told him to move his ass and vacate the premises or they'd lock him up. He did.

Kids on a stoop on Sherman Street, not their house. They moved on. A drunk in the road at Monument Square. She was unconscious on arrival, vodka pooled in the gutter from the bottle still in her hand.

Medcu hauled her off. Traffic stop on Mellen just up from the park. An empty syringe in the ash tray of the pickup, the passenger, a big guy in paint-spattered coveralls, starting to nod. Medcu again. Kat saying, "Are we the only ones in this goddamn town who aren't messed up?"

Dinner. The salad bar at Whole Foods. Kat was training for a triathlon in Vermont. She had a big dish of lentils, some chickpeas and cottage cheese thrown in.

And then the shooting.

"We don't need every detail, Officer Blake," Broward said.

"Right," Brandon said.

"Let's cut to the chase," Searles said. "Literally."

Brandon did. Told it again. The call. The guy coming out of the pub. The foot chase. The shoot. They had questions.

Searles: "The gun was clearly visible?"

Brandon: "Yes. In his right hand."

O'Farrell: "Foot chase was the best option?"

Brandon: "There were a bunch of fences."

Broward: "Okay, let's get right to it. Why no body cam? Didn't you complete the training?"

Brandon: "Yes. My mistake. I forgot."

Broward: "I heard your partner tried to call to you."

Brandon: "I was running. I didn't hear her."

Broward: "You didn't think of turning it on later?"

Brandon: "I was thinking of the guy in the alley with a gun."

Broward's eyebrows twitched and she wrote something on her legal pad. Her handwriting was neat and very small. "The shooting, again," Searles said.

Brandon nodded. Swallowed and took a deep breath. Everyone else sipped their coffee, their eyes looking over their mugs, except for Broward and Carew, who were still writing.

"You chased Thatcher Rawlings, or the suspect who would later be identified as Rawlings."

"Yes."

"Go on."

Brandon did, leading them over the fence, down the alleys, ending up behind the sports pub. Going into the alcove sort of thing, not seeing

148

anyone, backing out. Checking under the cars and looking up to see Thatcher standing behind him.

"So he was in there," O'Farrell said.

"I don't know. I would think so," Brandon said.

"You told him to drop the weapon," Searles said.

"Several times. I said, 'Just toss it, dude, and we can go home.'"

"Where was the gun at that point?"

"In his right hand, pointed at the ground."

"How many times is several?" Searles said.

"I don't know. Three? Four?"

O'Farrell shook his head.

"What did Rawlings do?"

"He started to raise the gun, said, 'Bang, bang. You're dead and so am—"

"He didn't finish the sentence?" Searles said.

"No, because that was when I shot him."

"How many times?"

"Three."

"He was neutralized at that point?"

"Yes. Three shots. He went down."

"He still had the mask on?"

"Until I took it off him. I was going to try to apply first aid."

"But you didn't?"

"His heart blew out, all the blood came up and out of his mouth."

Brandon paused.

"He was gone."

Another silence, the other cops eyeing Brandon closely. None of them had ever killed anyone in the line of duty, except Searles, the ball-room dancer, when he was serving in Iraq.

"The GoPro," Broward said. "Did you touch it?"

"It came off when I took off his mask. It was strapped onto his head."

"Did you touch it otherwise?"

"No," Brandon said. "I didn't touch it at all."

"You know there was no card in it?"

"I do now. I didn't know it then."

"You didn't remove the card," Broward said.

That one drew a dirty look from O'Farrell.

"No. I told you I didn't touch it. It fell on the ground."

"Was it turned on?"

"There was a red light on it, but I don't know if that meant it was running."

A pause and Searles said, "You're aware of the department policy regarding use of body cams. Any interaction with the public. Any time the lights or siren are activated."

"Yes."

"Wouldn't you say that this fell within those guidelines?" Searles pressed.

"Yes."

"But you—"

"Jesus," Carew said. "He's a young patrol guy. Somebody runs, it's like a dog chasing a squirrel. They just go. You've all been there."

"We don't put policies in place so they can be ignored," Garcia said.

"Did you think of waiting for the K-9?" Broward said. "Could have saved a lot of trouble."

"I did think that. Brandon said. "Later."

"How old are you, Brandon?" Broward said.

"Twenty-four."

"And you've never seen a GoPro?"

Brandon looked at her, shook his head. "Not up close."

There was more, the chief saying there were two purposes for the internal investigation. Find out what Blake did, and if he screwed up, how they could avoid that happening again. Failure to activate the body cam was a serious mistake.

"It wouldn't have changed the shoot, sir," Brandon said. "Camera or no camera."

"It unnecessarily exposed the department to serious liabilities."

"How are we liable if it was a clean shoot, sir?" Brandon said.

"Fuckin' A, Blake," the chief said. "You were out there. It's called the court of public opinion."

"They've already found you guilty," Broward said. "And don't think that doesn't spill over into the courts. Good luck with that jury. Failing to report the assault attempt in South Portland? Pattern of lying? They'll be talking high six figures."

Brandon looked at her, bit his tongue.

"Why did you fail to report the assault by Amanda Shakespeare?"

"It was barely an assault. She was upset. She couldn't hurt me."

"That's not an answer," Broward said.

"I felt bad for her. Putting something like that on her record, seemed unwarranted."

"You know that's not your call," she said.

"Yes."

"Do you withhold evidence all the time?"

Brandon swallowed.

"I'm serious," Broward said. "It's not our job to decide whether somebody deserves to be punished. It's our job to decide whether they've broken the law. If everybody—"

"Jesus, what are you? The D.A.?" Brandon said. "I thought you were a goddamn detective."

"Easy," Carew said.

"Sorry. I was thinking I'd already wrecked one kid's life," Brandon said. "I didn't want another one."

"Enough, Blake," O'Farrell said.

"I know what my job is. I did it when I pulled the trigger, for Christ's sake."

"It's not the shoot, Brandon," O'Farrell said. "It's the camera thing."

"K-9 would have hauled him out of there," Broward said.

"What ever happened to trusting your fellow officers?" Brandon said. "I told you what happened out there. He was warned. More than once. He wouldn't drop the gun. It looked real."

"And he made threatening statements and actions," Carew said. "If anything, Brandon waited way too long."

"And I didn't take any card from his goddamn camera. He was vomiting blood all over me. That's what I was thinking about."

"Enough, Brandon," Carew said.

"Blake," the chief said. "You're out of line."

"This," Broward said, looking at O'Farrell, "is what I'm talking about. Judgment."

The chief stood up. He raised his arms like he was about to bless the table. He said, "All of you. Shut the fuck up."

"Blake, my office. Charlie, you can stay or go."

He turned and walked out the door, left it open behind him. Brandon got up from his chair. Carew did the same. They followed Garcia down the corridor. Just outside the door, Brandon heard Searles say, "Good kid, but he's digging a deep hole."

The chief's office, his diplomas on the wall, certificates from the FBI school, some crude drawings from a school visit. *Thank you, Mister Police Chief.* Garcia behind the desk, hands on his hips.

"I'm sorry, chief," Brandon said.

"He's under serious stress," Carew said.

"We all are," Garcia said. "Freakin' demonstrations. People marching on the department. Making Rawlings to be the victim, some kind of Boy Scout."

"Exactly," Carew said.

"But you screwed up, Blake. We put the body cams out there to prevent just this sort of thing. No room for doubt. Gun in your face. You say, 'Drop your weapon.' He says, 'You're dead, cop.' End of demonstration. One story in the newspaper. Nip it in the bud. Let some lawyer take the parents' money but we don't have half the city on our asses."

Brandon started to respond but Carew reached over and grabbed his arm.

"Look. City Hall is looking for blood," the chief said. "Halsey is salivating. Thinks this will make her governor. First cop in the state to be prosecuted for a shooting."

"Christ," Carew said. "All we need."

"I'm gonna have to throw her a bone," the chief said. "Give her something to think she won."

"Throwing Blake to the wolves?" Carew said. "You shitting me? He's out there risking his life every goddamn night."

"Not throwing him to the wolves. Just playing it by the book," Garcia said.

"For the camera?" Carew said.

"Yeah. And South Portland."

"Kill the kid and then arrest his distraught girlfriend? How is that good PR?" Carew said.

"None of it's good PR," Garcia said. "That's why these dipshits are marching down the street with signs."

"So what are you thinking? Letter in his file? Suspension?"

Garcia looked away, then back. "Don't know."

"Any of that will screw Blake in civil court. You know that."

Garcia didn't answer.

"Are you firing me?" Brandon said.

"Won't let that happen," Carew said.

"He pointed the gun right at my face."

"Shoulda shot him after the first warning," Carew said. "Gun still pointing at the goddamn ground."

"I'm not disagreeing," the chief said. "Suicide by cop? Sure sounds like it. But it's your word, Blake. One guy against a world that's turned against cops. Buncha bad apples left you holding the bag."

"He can't help that," Carew said.

"A lot of things we can't help," the chief said. He leaned down, shuffled papers on his desk. "Let's call it a day, gentlemen. I've got other shitstorms to deal with. We'll be in touch."

Carew and Blake went out into the hall, cops' voices coming from somewhere. Carew led Brandon ten feet, turned and stopped him.

"You've got to keep control of yourself."

"I'm trying. It's hard with all of this crap. And then the girl kills herself. I'm thinking—"

"Don't think. Stop it. Watch the Patriots. Go for a run. Paint your boat, or whatever you do to the goddamn thing."

"Will I lose my job?" Brandon said.

"No. I don't know. Department is behind you, everybody is. Just caught in a tough spot. The politics. The camera. The kid. The girl thing, I don't know how that will play. Make you seem more human?"

"To her mother? The Rawlings parents? I don't think so," Brandon said.

"Probably say you were propositioning her," Carew said.

"Jesus," Brandon said.

"I know, but it's the public. When it comes to cops, there's a big part of the population wants to think the worst."

"Let them do this job for one night," Brandon said.

"I know."

"Think I liked shooting him? Think I like living with that the rest of my life? I'll never forget him looking up at me. Dying. Right there. His last second on earth and he's—"

"I know, Brandon."

"Then why can't they—"

"Hey, will you listen to me? Just take it easy."

Carew guided Brandon down the hall to the stairwell. He led him downstairs, turned him to face him and said, "It's gonna be fine. It's just gonna be a bit of a process. Don't worry. Get out of town. Turn your phone off. Just find a way to put it out of your head."

Brandon looked at him.

"Yeah, right," he said.

"I'm going back in there. I'll talk him down. I'll be in touch."

Carew hurried back the way they'd come. Brandon took a deep, long breath and put his hat on. Shouldered his way through the door. Estusa was standing there. He raised his phone and started recording.

FIFTEEN

"Disciplinary hearing, Brandon? How did it go?"

Brandon started walking. Estusa sidestepped, the phone still up.

"Are you going to be suspended? Do you think that's fair?"

Now Estusa was backpedaling in front of Brandon, headed for the steps and Middle Street.

"Failure to activate the body cam. That's serious, right? And what about reports that you didn't report an interaction with Amanda Shakespeare, the girl who jumped from the garage? What did she say to you, Brandon? Was she looking for answers? Asking why you killed her boyfriend?"

Estusa looked over his shoulder, started down the steps, the phone still up.

"No comment, Officer Blake? No comment for the livestream?"

Brandon said, jumped over a step, started to go around him. Estusa stayed with him, the phone still up. "This is your chance to tell your side, Officer Blake. Thousands of people are watching all over the country."

Mia appeared on the sidewalk at the bottom of the steps.

"Brandon," she said. "Is everything—"

Estusa started to pivot, train the phone on Mia. Brandon slapped it out of his hand, the phone clattering down the steps. "Leave her alone, you son of a bitch."

"Jesus, Blake," Estusa said.

Brandon pushed him on the way by and Estusa stumbled, went to one knee.

"That's assault."

"You'll know it if I assault you," Brandon said.

"That's criminal threatening."

"Fuck you."

"You're a public figure, Blake. I can photograph you anytime."

"She's not, asshole," Brandon said.

"Mia," Estusa called. "He's killed two people now, responsible for a third. How does that make you feel?"

Brandon took Mia by the shoulders, hurried her down the sidewalk. Estusa was picking up his phone. They crossed Middle Street, went around the corner.

"Where's your car?" Brandon said.

"Up here. At a meter. I was waiting and you didn't text so I thought I'd just see if—"

The Volvo was ahead, same side of the street. Mia had her keys in her hand and Brandon said, "Unlock it."

She did, the car chirping and blinking. Brandon crossed into the street, yanked the driver's door open. He pushed Mia inside, said, "Go."

"But what about you?"

"The boat," Brandon said. "It's here."

"But when will I see you?"

"Just go. Now."

"Brandon, please don't do anything. Don't hit him. It'll come back on you."

"Go," Brandon said. He slammed the door and crossed the street, broke into a trot. Estusa came around the corner, his phone in his hand. Mia floored it, whipped by him, flipped him off. Brandon was around the corner, zigzagging his way back to the harbor. Across from the wharf he looked back. Estusa was in the middle of Commercial Street, waiting for traffic. Brandon trotted down the wharf, stepped into the Port Hole restaurant, crossed the room, and went through the door and out onto the deck overlooking the harbor. He jumped a gate, and slipped down the ramp onto the float.

Jumping onto *Bay Witch*, he climbed to the helm, hit the blower. Counted to thirty and started the engines. They rumbled. He jumped back onto the float, whipped the stern line off, then the bow. Back on the boat, he reversed, cut the wheel hard, and powered forward and away. At the end of the wharf he hit the throttle. The V-8 roared and the boat lifted, the bow coming up. He skirted the first buoy, passed the stern of the cruise ship at eighteen knots. He followed the channel to the southeast, pounding into the chop, spray coming over the bow and slapping the windshield. Around Spring Point the waters were open to the wind, the chop four to five feet. The motors roared like lions, undulating with the hull as *Bay Witch* porpoised through the waves, wallowing and lunging ahead.

He was running. Thatcher and Amanda. Estusa and the mob. Broward and Garcia. Churning through the gray-green waves, he was leaving them behind.

South of House Island. Past Cushing. Portland Head. Cape Elizabeth to starboard, Brandon hanging tightly onto the wheel. Don't think, just go.

His phone was buzzing in his pocket but he left it. He swung out to catch the buoys, continued south. Scarborough, the beaches. The seas bigger out here, a lot for a 50-year-old wooden cruiser. He throttled back, for *Bay Witch*, not for himself. And then he began to calm, realized his heart had been pounding in rhythm with the waves against the hull. He reached under the console for a chart, flipped it open to the coastline: Old Orchard, Pine Point. Something sheltered.

Woodford Bowl.

It was an enclave at the mouth of the Saco River, five miles downriver from the mill town where Danni lived. Old money in the Bowl. A different world.

Brandon knew of it from Mia's friends, who had family summer houses there. He'd been to a barbeque. A guy named Chandler had footed the bill: inch-thick steaks, lobster and clams, cases of boutique beers, wine from the family cellar, fancy tequila. The place was sprawling, with two big shingled houses, some kind of compound. They partied next to the croquet pitch.

Across the road there was a tennis club, people playing in all-white outfits like it was 1950. Next to that was the golf club. The guys, all blonde and fit, had an eight o'clock tee time, were joking about how they played better hungover. They'd asked Brandon to join them but he'd never swung a golf club in his life. They knew it, that he wasn't from a place like this. From the bathroom in the house he'd overheard through the window:

A cop? You mean like riding around in a police car? No shit. Hey, but that's cool. Lives on an old boat. Some sort of screwed-up family with no parents and shit, but Mia's really into him. Nice guy but don't piss him off. He's a cop, you know? They pound people for a living.

Brandon pushed them out of his mind, pictured the harbor. Chandler's father had a boat moored there, a big center console with twin 150s. He'd said they could take it out but everybody had too many beers. Another time.

There were a handful of moorings in the Gut, Brandon remembered, picturing the deep part near the narrow entrance to the Bowl. It was mid-tide, two hours from high, no problem getting in. September, most of the summer people would be gone. He figured at least a couple of their boats would have been pulled for the season, but still too early for the mooring chains to be dropped to the bottom for the winter. He could hook up.

He was a half-mile east of Ram Island, Scarborough Beach showing as a white-sand strip. To the southeast were the two islands that sat out in Saco Bay. Brandon dug under the console for the charts, flipped the book open. Bluff and Stratton. Three miles beyond them was Wood Island, which marked the entrance to the bowl. The seas were bigger out in the bay and he slowed, marked a course for the island, hung on as *Bay Witch* rose and fell, shuddering as she knifed through the chop.

Three miles, twenty minutes. The island materialized, a green smudge that turned into spruce trees and rocky shore line, surf showing white on the eastern tip. Brandon checked the chart, traced the route to the harbor mouth. A rocky point to port south of the island, keep to the middle of the channel. He watched the island get closer, then he was past it, swung east, the chop calming in the lee of the wind. He saw a few boats on moorings on the outer side of the gut, steered for them in wide loop. And then he was idling in, past the sailboats, two moorings with dinghies swinging on them. Into the gut with the incoming tide.

A yacht club, red-spattered geraniums in boxes, sailing dinghies lined up on wooden stands. A lobster pound, crates on the float, restaurant on the deck above. A big catamaran on a mooring, a couple of lobster boats. He motored on, picked up the VHF mic and tried to hail the harbormaster.

No reply. He tried again. Waited. Hung up the mic and motored deeper into the bowl, away from the yacht club, saw an empty mooring to port, the nearest boat a buttoned-up 30-foot sloop, no sign of life. He swung around and came up alongside against the tide, threw the motors into neutral and slipped to the starboard rail, hooked the floating line with a boat hook. He hung on as *Bay Witch* lost momentum, and then he walked to the bow, cleated the line. The boat drifted back, then caught, and pointed into the current.

Brandon looked to the shore, both sides. No one was showing. He moved to the helm, shut off the engines. *Bay Witch* went still. The harbor was quiet, gulls slipping by, eyeing the boat for fish or bait. Brandon left the radio on, went below to the head. Came back out and went back up to the helm. He was hidden here, ten miles and a world away from Portland.

And then his phone buzzed again. He hesitated, then slipped it out and looked. His life came roaring back.

A list of texts and Twitter messages that went off the screen.

Mia: You okay? Let me know.

Kat: We need to talk asap. Heard you chewed out Broward, smacked Estusa. Gotta hold it together, Blake. Not good.

@righteous1: police state is crumbling, killer blake gonna be the first to go. #kidslivesmatter

O'Farrell: see me, tomorrow latest, Brandon. Gotta get this back on the rails.

Charlie Carew: Brandon, we need to regroup. Trying to rebuild some bridges. Will be in touch.

@realmaine22: I was assaulted by Officer Brandon

Blake @bblake95 and my phone was smashed by him. Have filed complaint with Portland P.D. See where it goes. #policecoverup #kidslivesmatter #portland-justice

@pshakespeare1979: how can you sleep? Maybe you can't. when you're lying there think of my beautiful baby girl and what you've done.

@munjoydude: can't cover this up anymore. put another notch on your gun blake? The people gonna rise up and take you down with the rest of the Gestapo cops.

@jesusfreak545: you may get away with this, officer blake. But you will be brought before your maker. "when justice is done, it brings joy to the righteous but terror to the evildoers." Proverbs 21:15.

@trawlingsmaine: you can't hide, blake. The world isn't big enough. There will be justice for Thatcher. You will spend many years behind bars. If you live that long. I hear they hate cops in prison.

Danni: Hey Brandon. How you doing? Worrying about you (the news). Hope you don't think that's weird! Gimme a shout, grab a coffee, pick up the book. I'm off today. Maybe you need a break.

The messages kept going, screen after screen. Brandon put the phone down, reached under his seat. The diary was still there. He took it out, flipped through the pages again. Closed it and put it down on the console. He picked up the phone, texted Mia:

How you doing? Sorry about today. You shouldn't have any thing to do with this. Or me, for now. I'm fine. Found a mooring, tied on. Just needed a break. I'll call you.

And then he called, said, "Hey there. This is Brandon."

Danni said, "Hey, you hanging in?"

"Yeah, thanks. I'm fine. How you doing?"

"Good."

"Listen, got your text. Thanks. I'm on my boat, but not in South Portland. Listen, how 'bout I just toss the thing. I could just burn it.

Mia's apartment has a fireplace. I'll even send you a video of it burning."

A moment of silence, then Danni said, "Nah, to be honest I'd kinda like to have it. Like a record of that part of my life, you know? I have a bad day I can look at that, say, shit could be worse. I could have a humungous zit on my forehead and my boyfriend just dumped me for my best friend."

She laughed but there was something desperate about it, Brandon thought. Like she absolutely had to have the diary in her possession.

"You sure?"

"Yeah, I mean, if you don't mind. I'll come to you, unless you're out in the middle of the freakin' ocean."

Another laugh, still with the edge on it.

"Okay," Brandon said. "Not in the middle of the ocean. I'm tied up in your town. Woodford Bowl."

"I'll come down."

"I'll watch for you."

―――――

He did, after he straightened up the cabin, shoved the trash bags forward. And then he went back up the helm and waited, the diary in his hand, blood dried hard and black on the cover. A random page, Danni sleeping with an older guy who was living with a woman. She found out and the guy went back to the girlfriend. *No boyfriend, no marriage. No babies*, Danni wrote. *I hate life. It sucks. Please let me die like my car.*

Brandon could relate, everything falling apart. But the tone in her voice was more than trying to avoid embarrassment. More serious, like if Clutch found out she'd slept with four guys in high school he'd kill her. Why? Did he know her then? Was she sleeping with all of his friends?

He flipped more pages.

Danni fired from Dunkin' Donuts for missing a shift. Bickering with her best friend because at a party the friend called her fat. Getting another old clunker car from her grandfather, caught driving it without a license.

Brandon held the book open, flipped from the back cover. Started to do it again and stopped. The pink page on the inside of the back: Danni had written names of boyfriends, crossed them out, like someone counting off days in a prison cell. The top right corner of the page was ragged, like someone had picked it with a fingernail. Brandon did just that, and the paper peeled back.

Inside was another piece of paper, the same handwriting but smaller. He slipped it out, read:

July 21, 2012

This lie is getting harder and harder to live with every anniversary. I want to leave Clutch, go somewhere where he can never find me. I could start over, work in a restaurant, change my name. But we're tied together, him and me, all cause of what happened. I wish I'd of known then what it was gonna be like, carrying this secret around. I would of gone right to the cops. Say to them, do what you want to me. I don't care. It can't be worse than this freakin life sentence. But you can't undo what's been done. Maybe that's your punishment, having to live with it, being stuck forever with a guy who could do that and not blink an eye.

Brandon turned the paper over. Blank. Turned back and read the note again. He flipped to the front of the book, started to pick at that page, too.

When his phone buzzed. He picked it up.

Danni: I'm here

He looked out toward the yacht club. Danni was standing on the float by the overturned dinghies. She waved. He waved back, went down the ladder, left the diary on the table in the salon, came back out and flipped the inflatable overboard, tied it off, pulled two lifejackets and the oars from the stern locker. He tossed the oars and lifejackets in, untied the dinghy and stepped in. It drifted off the stern and he rowed, thinking, what secret? Did the guy beat her, even back then?

Could have called the cops but went back to him? Accepted it? But she'd told him he didn't hurt her, not physically.

A lie to cover up the reality? Maybe the truth was too hard to admit to. She felt complicit. Embarrassed.

He turned over his shoulder and she was standing on the edge of the float. "Hey," she said. "That thing big enough for the both of us?"

Brandon got her aboard, steadying the dinghy against the stern. Danni said, "Jeez. This is like Gilligan," and sang, "This is a tale of our castaways." He smiled, tied the dinghy off and stepped onto the stern. Danni took a few tentative steps, peeked into the salon. "Hey, this isn't bad. It's like a camper but better."

He led the way down two steps and in, the salon still smelling like oil and polish. Brandon said, "One of my fans decided to trash the place yesterday."

"Are you serious?" Danni said. "What's wrong with these people?"

Brandon shrugged. Picked up the diary from the table and held it out. She grabbed it, said, "I'm not even going to open it, I'm so embarrassed. I hope you didn't read the whole thing."

"Bits and pieces," he said.

"Always having my heart broke. Some serious self-esteem issues. I know that now. Back then I was just a chubby high school girl, just wanted a boyfriend, you know? Somebody who thought I was special. Never quite found it."

"Have you now?" Brandon said.

She looked at him, surprised.

"With Clutch? Hey, he's rough around the edges but you get used to each other, you know? I mean, you didn't exactly see him at his best. We talked and kinda straightened things out. He's just got a wicked active imagination, thinks guys are all after me. Which is definitely not happening."

Danni looked at him. She was holding the diary in two hands against her chest, the flower-print cover clashing with her bright blue sweatshirt. The sweatshirt said "MAINE" in big letters across her chest. Her jeans were cropped above the ankle and her white running shoes were a store brand, like you'd get at Kmart. There was a tattoo of a butterfly on her left ankle.

"I saw the note you stuck in the back," Brandon said.

She flushed, stammered.

"Oh, jeez."

"Sorry. I was just holding it and saw the page had been picked at and did the same thing. Didn't mean to pry into your business."

Danni flipped the diary open, slapped it closed.

"Nah, that's okay, really. I mean, we had some rough patches there. Got 'em fixed back up. Whatever. So much for the fairy tale, right?"

"You said it was a life sentence, or something like that. You sure you're all right? Because there are people you can talk to, places you can go."

"Oh, I know. But we're okay now, really," Danni said. "No worries."

She stopped, looked around the boat as though to change the subject. Still looking away, she said, "The hard part is keeping it all to yourself, you know? It's like you're living this lie or something. After a while it gets to be a lot."

"I know it's not easy but you can get out," Brandon said.

"Hey, I can hang in. Nothing like it used to be."

"What's the anniversary? Of when you got together?"

She looked at him, eyes narrowing, alarmed.

"You said that in your note. Anniversaries."

The alarm passed.

"Yeah. Right. 'Cause we're not married. I mean, Clutch, he thinks we're either together or we're not. We decide. I wouldn't mind, too late for a church wedding, but maybe some small thing. In a park or Foxwoods or whatever."

She grinned. "Every girl wants to be a bride, right?"

Brandon gave Danni the tour, which, in a 30-foot boat, doesn't take long. She seemed interested but restless, like she wanted to go but then kept deciding to stay. She sat in the helm seat and Brandon stood beside her, explained the controls. They looked out over the basin, the boats all pointed to the harbor mouth into the tide. Danni said, "You must feel like you have nobody to talk to."

He glanced at her, hesitated, said, "Why?"

"I don't know. It's like, who's gonna understand? I mean, really. If they haven't been through it."

"Shot somebody?"

"Yeah. I mean, you can think you know what's it's like, you can imagine it, but it's not the same. As actually doing it, I mean."

"No, it's not the same," Brandon said.

"How's it going with your girlfriend there? She was on the news. Wicked cute."

"Mia? She's hanging in, I guess."

"You're not sure?" Danni said. She turned toward him on the seat, her white running shoes on the rail.

He felt himself draw back, away from the probing. Then something about her. It was like she understood.

"Well, it's hard," Brandon said. "I don't want to drag her into everything. But then she ends up dragged in anyway. It's like it's my problem—"

"And you have to carry it alone, right?" Danni said. "Because nobody can walk in your shoes. Nobody would get it 'cause they weren't there. And you have to carry the whole thing and it gets heavier and heavier until sometimes it feels like you're gonna bust in half."

She caught herself.

"You sound like you've been here," Brandon said. "In my shoes."

She slipped down from the seat, looked flustered, tugged at her ponytail. "Nah. I mean. Nothing like you're doing."

"Like what then?" Brandon said.

She looked like she was going to reply, then stopped. Took a deep, deliberate breath. Another. And then she moved to the ladder, looked at her phone and said, "Holy shit. I can't believe I've been here this long. I'm late. Can you row me back?"

Danni turned, stepped carefully down to the deck. She hurried to the stern, waited for him to untie the dinghy. He held it as she climbed in heavily, the diary clutched in one hand. Brandon eased down and in and sat and took the oars. He rowed away from *Bay Witch*, toward the yacht club float. Danni was quiet, looked away from him and out at the shoreline: the water lapping at the greasy rocks

They reached the float and Brandon swung the dinghy broadside, held on to a cleat. Danni put the diary on the float first, then heaved herself up onto her knees, stood and turned and said, "Don't mind me. I just have an imagination, you know?"

Brandon nodded and she turned to go. Then turned back.

"Maybe we could talk again," Danni said. "I mean, I'm not hitting on you. Not one of those cougar things. There's just something—"

A flash of motion, a guy coming from the shingled yacht club building.

"Hey," he called, approaching. "This is private property. And is that your boat on that mooring?"

He was onto the float, stopped next to Danni, looked down at Brandon. A tanned, stocky guy, maybe 70. Khakis and boat shoes and a dark blue polo shirt with an insignia Brandon didn't recognize. "You can't just come in here with that old thing, tie up anywhere. This is members only and that's the Griswold's mooring."

"Where's their boat?" Brandon said.

"It's out for the season but that's not the point."

Brandon slipped his wallet out, flipped it open and held up his badge.

"Police business," he said.

The guy stopped.

"We're conducting an investigation. Up river."

He waited for the guy to get it. He did.

"Drugs, huh? Woodford's full of 'em."

Brandon didn't answer. Danni looked at him and said, "Roger that," and turned and walked away. The guy looked out at *Bay Witch* and said, "Do what you need to do, but don't let the members know I said so." Brandon nodded and the guy hurried away before he could be seen.

He sat in the dinghy, took out his phone. He flipped through his contacts and tapped the number. Waited, the dinghy gently rocking.

"Officer Davey? Brandon Blake. Portland P.D."

He never had to worry about whether somebody remembered him.

"When you have a few minutes, I'd like to talk," Brandon said.

Davey said he had a few minutes. Brandon told him where he was.

"I came by boat."

"I know," he said. "It was on the news."

Brandon sat, waited. Reached into the back pocket of his jeans and took out the page from the diary. Folded it carefully and slipped it back. Wondered how long it would take Danni to call.

SIXTEEN

B randon watched it on his phone: a video of his boat rumbling away from the wharf in Portland, *Bay Witch* showing on the stern. The blurb said, *Portland Police Officer Brandon Blake sails away from an altercation with RealPortland editor Matt Estusa. Blake assaulted Estusa as he attempted to interview the embattled cop, who had just left a grilling by Portland police higher-ups. Portland police refused to comment on the incident, which comes just three days after Blake shot and killed Thatcher Rawlings, 16, in the city's Old Port.*

On Facebook, the video had 436 views. 39 shares. The comments went off the screen. "Why is this guy not in jail?"

"Jesus," Brandon said.

"Hey, Officer Blake," Davey said.

He was looking down at the float and the dinghy. He motioned with a nod back to his cruiser, idling in the parking lot. "Your place or mine?"

Brandon hopped up on the float, double-checked the bowline. Walking to the cruiser, he gave the yacht club guy, watching from the clubhouse deck, a discreet salute. Police business had commenced.

"You look like crap," Davey said, swiveling his computer away from Brandon and buckling his seatbelt.

"Don't like the beard?" Brandon said.

Davey reversed, turned the SUV around, wheeled out of the lot.

"Trying to grow a disguise."

"Things pretty rough up there, huh."

"Yeah."

"Come down here to escape?"

"Something like that."

"What's the rest of the something?" Davey said.

They were driving along the road off of the peninsula, stately shingled houses with long driveways and stone gates. They all looked the same, like a housing project for old money. Brandon gazed out, mulled the question. Problem with being around cops, they were all pretty good interrogators, saw right through the bullshit.

"Danni. The woman with the tow truck guy."

"And Clutch," Davey said.

"Right. Repo man."

"I just saw a story. Somewhere out west. Said repo guys used to carry guns, pull the thing out, calm a situation down. Now everybody's carrying. You pull the gun out, you'd better be shooting."

"Practice your quick draw."

"Guns friggin' everywhere," Davey said. He caught himself, looked over at Brandon. "Guess you know that. Your woman with the book there. And the jealous husband."

"Boyfriend. And it's a diary."

"Right. After we talked the first time, I did ask around. Word is they keep kinda to themselves, especially him. Man of few words."

"Just what a used-car salesman needs," Brandon said. "Makes his money off the wrecker?"

"I don't know. One of the old guys, sarge on desk, said he remembered a story Clutch got some kind of big insurance settlement years ago. What got him the wrecker and the garage."

"Car accident?" Brandon said.

Davey shrugged, "Don't know. Before my time. But give him credit. Most of these bums blow the money."

"Booze," Brandon said.

"Drugs."

"Vegas."

"All of the above," Davey said.

They were on the main drag, the old downtown. A café with an awning. A mill turned to condos. Scruffy people trudging down the sidewalk like they'd been displaced. Davey swung off Main Street, back into a neighborhood of tenements. Kids eyed the cruiser coldly. Cops, the occupying army.

"Ever heard of anything kind of big with them? Domestic assault?"

Davey shook his head.

"Not in my time. Kinda quiet, really."

"Anything in July? She said something about July. I was thinking maybe he beat her up particularly bad or something."

"If he did, they kept it to themselves."

They drove, Brandon settling into the cruiser, this viewpoint on life. Like riding herd.

Davey glanced over and said, "I think I know why you're here."

"Had to return the book," Brandon said.

"No, I mean, here. With me."

Brandon looked at him. "Cheaper than a taxi?"

"You miss being in a cruiser. You miss being around cops. You needed to come to a place where you're not so well known."

"You ought to be a detective," Brandon said.

"Welcome to ride along for a while."

"All you need, protesters down here, too."

Davey looked doubtful. "Long way from liberal land up there," he said. "Where do you want to go?"

"How 'bout the library?" Brandon said.

"You and the homeless people?"

He smiled.

"Me and the rest of the homeless people," Brandon said.

The library was a brick place on Main Street, vintage Carnegie on the outside, kindergarten colors on the inside, bright orange and green. The garish colors were muted by the drab people sitting at the tables, at a bank of computers. Women in sweatpants. Guys in camo. Some taking notes, some just staring.

Brandon followed the arrows in the carpet to the service desk, found a gray-haired woman peering at another computer screen. She said, without looking up, "Can I help you?"

"I hope so. You have the local newspapers on microfilm?" Brandon asked.

"There's only one. The Argus."

"May I take a look?"

"What are you looking for? Maybe I can help you?"

Still staring at the computer screen.

"Real estate stuff," Brandon said. "Foreclosure notices."

"Plenty of those around here, a while back."

"I imagine."

"Bakery shut down. Can't pay a mortgage with nothing."

"Right."

"People living check to check. Lose the house. Lose the car. Maybe even lose the kids. Drugs. Drink."

"That right," Brandon said.

"Money makes the world go round," the woman said. "Turn off the spigot, whole thing come to a stop."

"Right."

"Desperate times there for a while. Thank god for welfare."

"Better now?"

"A little."

"Jobs came back?"

"No," the woman said. "People left. To the right, all the way down, then to the left. Microfilm room. Drawers have them by date. If you can read, you ought to be all set."

"I'm good," Brandon said.

"Used to be a nice town," the woman said. "Now it's everyone for themselves."

There were two machines side by side, one occupied. An older guy wearing a ball cap, reading glasses perched on his nose. He looked up and nodded. Brandon could see sports pages on his screen, football photos. *Woodford Wins State Gridiron Title.* Glory days.

The cabinets were gray steel, big sliding drawers that shut with a bang. Brandon went back to 2012, found July. Then he went drawer by drawer, pulled July going back another five years. He went to the machine and sat, the other guy glancing over, shifting in his chair.

Brandon didn't know what he was looking for. Something that would warrant an anniversary. If Danni had meant their first date, their first sex, their first puppy, he was wasting his time. But he didn't think so.

He spooled the film on, pushed the lever. The days began streaming by, baseball scores, school kids winning awards, a house fire, a mother and toddler killed in a car crash.

And then July 22. Town council trying to bring business in. Not much luck. A local woman who found her long-lost sister in Arizona. There was a resemblance. A guy arrested for trying to burn his own house down. He was drunk and his name wasn't Clutch.

Brandon checked July 22 through 25, figuring a daily newspaper ought to report a July 21 incident by then. 2012. 2011. 2010. More chronicling of the life of a mill town: car accidents, businesses closing, roads closed for repairs, new books at the library. 2009, 2008. People resigning from town boards, replacements sought. A cat that jumped out of a car and walked 12 miles home. A dog that saved its owner from a house fire. A local musician who made it big and was playing small clubs in Boston. A high school principal arrested for having sex with a student.

Brandon pulled the reel off, put it on the used pile. Threaded 2007 onto the machine. The film whirred.

July 18, 19, 20, 21. And then on the 22nd:

A front-page story, three men found dead in a gravel pit. A local guy and two bikers from Lawrence, Mass., shot each other in what was believed to be a dispute over drugs. The bikers had long records; the local guy was Damian Sash, 20, arrests for possession of cocaine, drunk driving, and disorderly conduct, smashing a windshield during an argument with his mother. "While the case is still under investigation by the Woodford police, it is believed that Sash shot the two men before being shot himself. All three succumbed from their wounds.

"Sash worked as a mechanic at Woodford Tire & Wheel. Calls to the tire shop requesting comment were not returned. A woman at the

Sash residence on River Street declined comment, saying, "Get the f---off our property."

A mechanic in Woodford? It had to be a small world. And the guy was around Clutch's age. If he had been a longtime local, they might have known each other.

Or not.

What had Danni written? *A guy who could do that and not blink an eye.* Do what? Hurt her in some awful way? Strangle their puppy?

Brandon leaned back in his chair. He looked over at the sports guy, who was taking notes in a binder.

"How's it going?" Brandon said.

The guy looked over, startled.

"Good. You?"

"Fine. Hey, you play football here?"

The guy puffed up. "Four years. State championship in eighty-one." He nodded toward the screen.

"Wow. Must've been something."

"Never forget it. The feeling. Holding that gold ball."

Brandon smiled. "I'll bet."

"Play ball?" the guy said.

Not a time to explain being homeschooled.

"Basketball."

"Starter?"

"No. Sixth man. Then the younger guys got better."

The guy nodded. "Happens."

"Listen, you've lived here a while, right?"

"My whole life, 'cept for two years in the Air Force in Texas. Lackland."

"Here in 07?"

"Oh, yeah. Daughter graduated from the high school in 2006. Played field hockey. All-state two years."

"Really," Brandon said.

"R.N. now, moved away. Lives in Portland. Don't see her much or the grandchildren. Says I can look at their pictures on Facebook but, hell, I don't have time for that."

"Right."

Brandon's turn to nod to his own screen.

"Remember this?"

The guy leaned over, eyes narrowing as he peered through his glasses at the screen.

"Oh, sure. Scumbags killed each other. Saved taxpayers a chunka money, not having to feed 'em in prison."

He looked at Brandon, waited.

"Write for magazines. Thinking of doing a story on biker gangs trafficking in drugs."

"Christ, oughta line 'em all up and shoot 'em."

"Right," Brandon said.

He paused.

"Know this Sash guy? Damian Sash? He was 20."

"I did."

"Wow, really."

"Not that surprising, really. Christ, know most boys in this town, if they play ball. And that's most boys, at least when they're younger. This Sash kid played freshmen for a few weeks. Then he quit, like losers do. Turned into a druggie. I tell the kids on my teams, you can play ball or you can throw your life away. Your choice."

"Ever have a guy named Tedeschi? Sells cars out on Route 1?"

"Nope. Had his brother, though."

Score, Brandon thought.

"Yeah, big boy, had lots of potential. Linebacker type. I said, 'Toby, you have a choice. Right path or the wrong one.'"

"Which did he choose?"

"Drinking, partying. Sixteen, he got drunk, racked up his car, now he walks with a cane. Hate to say I told you so but I did."

He didn't seem to hate it at all.

"Had to learn the hard way," Brandon said. "You know, I met the other one. The guy with the wrecker. They call him Clutch."

"Toby's little brother. Pulled my wife out of a ditch once. Was driving by, she's stuck in the snow. Driving not her strong point. I said to the wife. 'Well, at least one of 'em amounted to something.'"

"Running a business and all."

"Right. And a wrecker, that runs you a pretty penny. Had that rig, Jesus, he couldn't have been more than twenty-two, twenty-three. Rest of the Tedeschi crew, a sorry bunch. Shacking up, robbing off some-body's welfare check."

Brandon nodded. "Always the way, isn't it?"

The guy held out his hand. "C.J."

"Brandon."

C.J. peered over his glasses. "You're a writer, huh? Musta seen your stuff somewhere. You look awful familiar."

Brandon stood, gathered up the microfilm reels.

"So when these biker guys were killed, was that a big deal around here?"

C.J. shrugged. "Don't recall it that much said about it. Good riddance to bad rubbish, you know?"

"And the local kid. Sash? He know Tedeschi?"

"I don't know. Like I said, once they quit the team, they were dead to me. But they were around the same time. 2006. Maybe 2005. Some-where in there. I mean, must have bonded a little before they wimped out."

Brandon smiled.

"So not much sympathy around town when this Sash guy got killed?"

The guy shrugged, pushed his hat back and turned to the screen. "Hey, like I always say to my players, you run with junkyard dogs, even-tually you get bit."

Brandon left the library the way he'd come in, past the woman at the desk. She had a newspaper spread out in front of her, the *Portland Press Herald*. Brandon could see his photo, a file pic from a shooting in the Old Port. He said, "Thanks for your help," and the woman looked up, said, "Hey, you're—"

And then he was out the door and onto the street, his phone buzzing as he got service. Three missed calls, three voice mails.

Danni.

Ten feet down the sidewalk, the phone buzzed again. Brandon kept walking, answered.

"Hey, this is Danni."

"Hey."

"Sorry to bother you, but you know that note you found? In the diary?"

"Yeah."

"It's not there."

"Really? I thought I put it back."

"Nope. So you think it's on your boat? 'Cause I could come back down."

"You sure it isn't there?"

"Yeah. Listen, where are you?"

"In town," Brandon said.

"Need a lift? I'll give you a ride back."

"Not quite ready to go. I'll be a couple of hours."

"I'll wait for you," Danni said. "You getting provisions or what not for the boat? I could help you."

"That's okay."

"No, really. Where are you? I'll swing by."

"You don't have to."

There was a muffled sound, like the phone bumping against somebody's face. "Brandon," Danni said. "Listen to me. I do have to. I have to have that goddamn paper."

"Or else what?" Brandon said.

There was a muffled rattle, then a door slamming. And the phone went dead.

SEVENTEEN

Brandon stood for a moment on the sidewalk, people veering around him. He tapped the screen, said, "Hey. It's me."

"Liking your home away from home?" Davey said.

"No. But I need a ride back to the Bowl."

"What do I look like? A taxi service?"

"And I need to talk to you."

"Where are you?"

Brandon told him.

"Gimme five."

—

The cruiser rolled up in four minutes, Davey swiveling the laptop aside, tossing his briefcase in the back. Brandon climbed in and Davey pulled out into what passed for traffic in Woodford. The radio burbled. Brandon could smell leather and gun oil. He was home.

Davey swung off the main street at the next light, headed south toward the coast and the Bowl.

"July 21, 2007," he said.

Davey glanced over, reached out and turned the radio down.

"So?"

"Danni wrote something in the diary about July 21 being an anniversary. Of something bad."

"And you found something bad on that date? At the library?"

"Your local newspaper. Three people killed in a gravel pit. Drug deal. Bikers from Mass. and one local guy. Shot each other up and it was kind of out in the middle of nowhere. They bled out."

"Case closed?" Davey said.

"Cut and dry. Kind of like a murder-suicide," Brandon said. "Good news is you know who did it. Bad news is you'll never know why."

Davey swung left at a fork, the houses spreading out, driveways with the occasional boat on a trailer. "You think this is Danni's anniversary?"

Brandon shrugged this time. "Could be something personal. But in her note she said something about him, Clutch, being capable of something. Like it had scared her."

"Did he know the local who died?"

"The kid who got shot, Damian Sash, played football freshman year. So did Clutch's older brother. Guy sitting next to me in the library was their old coach."

"C.J. Violette," Davey said. "There all the time. Supposed to be writing a book about the glory days of Woodford football. Half this town played. It's the low-budget Friday Night Lights."

"Gotta love small towns."

"That we are. So you're thinking they were buddies? Clutch knows something about this?"

"Where'd he get money for a wrecker?" Brandon said.

"Insurance settlement," Davey said. "Or dealing drugs. Who knows?"

"The outlaw path to prosperity," Brandon said. "Nobody robs banks anymore."

"Actually, they do."

"To get money for drugs. Not to get rich."

Davey drove and thought about it. The ocean flickered in and out of sight through the trees beyond him.

"Worst kind of cold case is one that's been solved," he said.

"Maybe there were alternative theories."

"Better than three drug-dealing bikers dead on the ground after a shootout?"

"It was just two," Brandon said.

They crossed the causeway past the Bowl. Brandon glimpsed *Bay Witch* on the mooring, her bow pointed east, the wind having shifted from the south. And then they were wending their way past the big houses with geraniums in boxes, Audis in the driveways. When they passed the golf course, a couple of silver-haired guys waved from their cart, like the cops were their private security force. No demonstrations here.

Davey swung into the entrance to the yacht club, the cruiser's tires crunching on the crushed clamshells used to line the drive. There were two cars in the lot by the float, a Mercedes SUV and Range Rover. When the cruiser pulled up, Brandon could see people on a sailboat on a mooring, a guy rowing toward the dock.

The car ground to a stop. Brandon popped the door and Davey turned to him, reached out and held his arm. He locked on, a cop's practiced hard grip.

"I can ask around. But I know what you're doing," Davey said.

"What's that?"

"Distracting yourself," he said. "When you're thinking about this woman and her crazy diary you're not—"

"There's more to it than that."

"Okay, but when you're chasing this stuff, you're not thinking about everything else. The shoot. The protests."

"There's more to that, too," Brandon said.

Brandon was halfway to *Bay Witch* in the dinghy when he saw Danni's car coming fast down the yacht club drive. He'd said two hours. She hadn't believed him. No dope.

As he slid under the stern, she was getting out of the car, waving to him. He swung up and onto the boat, tied the dinghy off. Danni was trotting down the ramp to the float as he climbed the ladder to the helm, slipped the key in and ran the blower. She was calling, "Brandon! Hey! It's me!"

He started the engines and felt his phone buzzing in his pocket. As he slipped down and forward, crouched to press the winch switch, he felt the buzzing stop, replaced by the single buzz of an incoming text. The anchor came loose and the chain rattled on board. He fastened it down and, as the boat started to drift back on the tide, moved around the cabin and back up to the helm. Danni was waving as he put the engines in gear and swung past the mooring buoy and headed for the passage to the bay.

Out in the channel, Brandon pressed the throttles forward and the motors rumbled as the boat pushed through the incoming tide. And then he was through the gut and into the bay. He steered for the entrance buoy, hit the throttles and the boat lifted, heaved once, and then settled into an easy rhythm. Leaning on the console, Brandon slipped his phone out, opened Danni's text.

`where u going? where's my paper?`

He texted back:

`police emergency. will be in touch.`

Seconds later the phone buzzed:

`But your on adm leave.`

Then:

`can we meet tomorrow?`

And finally:

`need that page, Brandon. and the other ones. if I don't have 'em, I'm fucked.`

Brandon said to himself, "Join the club." He texted back:

`be in touch.`

It was 4:15 when he passed the buoy, headed north by northeast. Twenty-four miles to Portland harbor at 12 knots. The gauge showed 30 gallons of fuel, maybe a tad less. At 10 gallons per hour, he was cutting it close. He slowed to 10 knots, the motors rumbling, *Bay Witch* easing along with a following sea.

It had clouded up from the south, leaving the sunset a band of pale gray sky. The waters were empty, a tanker five miles offshore, nothing else in sight. Brandon suddenly felt alone, and the dark thoughts closed in, like they'd been waiting. The kid's blood. The look on his face the moment before he died. Amanda in the parking lot, sobbing after he took the knife away. Amanda under the tarp because her head was crushed.

Just a kid.

The boat heaved over the chop, bigger now out of the lee of the Bowl. As he stood with his hands on the wheel, the doubts started coming like a whirling pack of hounds. Should he have backed off, waited for the K-9? Should he have sent Amanda off in the back of a South Portland cruiser, let the E.R. order up a psych eval? Should he have given Danni the note? Who knows what it referred to? Was this just going to get her a worse beating from that stupid son of a bitch?

Was Davey right? Was he just distracting himself by playing cop?

"Uh-uh," he said aloud, his voice lost to the rumble of the engines. "No way."

Brandon picked the phone up and, elbows on the wheel, texted Mia:

On my way up to Portland. Harbor before dark. I'll call you.

And then he hit another number, held the phone up to his ear.

"It's me," he said, shouting over the wind and engine noise. "We need to talk."

"No shit," Kat said. "Where the hell are you?"

"Coming north from Woodford. In the boat."

"Woodford? What the hell is in Woodford?"

Brandon hesitated. The diary. Danni and Clutch. The bikers in the gravel pit.

"Nothing," he said. "Just needed to get away. Sunset is 6:40. Be back at the marina before then."

"No you won't," Kat said. "Seen the news?"

"Trying to avoid it.

"Somebody took a shot at Dever."

"Jesus. Was he hit?"

"Upper arm. Reaching for a bottle of water."

"He alright?"

"Eventually."

Bay Witch throttled up the swells, heaved back down. Brandon felt a million miles away from Portland, the streets, engulfed by an urge to be back in it, be one of the cops swarming the city.

"What, stick a gun in the window?" he said.

"Sniper," Kat said.

"Shit."

"War on cops and all that."

"Sure it wasn't on Dever? Somebody targeting him?"

"He's an asshole but this was random. Shooting at a black-and-white."

A big swell, the props revving as the bow buried itself.

"How do you know?"

"Some guy called it in to the radio station WPTL a minute later. Said it was time to fight back."

"You mean—"

A long pause from Kat. Brandon's answer.

"Said, 'This one's for Blake. He can hide but his cop scumbag friends can't.' Sorry."

"Where?"

"Parking lot off Marginal Way. A medical building. He was out back. Eating dinner in the cruiser."

"Where they'd shoot from?"

"Still looking. Thinking from behind a fence other side of Bayside Trail."

"Distance?"

"Forty yards."

"Any brass?"

"Not yet."

"Residue?"

"Don't know."

"The caller? Any number?"

"Burner."

"Track it?"

"Peninsula. Probably drove up the hill to Congress, called, kept on going."

The marine radio squawked, a tanker looking for its pilot boat. Brandon turned the radio down, said, "Jesus. How is everybody doing?"

"You know. Circling the wagons. Them against us now."

"Hunt is on?"

"Oh, yeah. All the dogs turned loose on this one. Roadblocks. K-9 in the lot. Turning the neighborhood upside down. Everybody in."

Brandon swallowed once, started to say something and stopped.

"Spit it out, Blake," Kat said.

He did.

"Feel, I don't know, like I started this one."

"They started it. We'll finish it. But you can't just be sitting on that boat like a sitting duck. Not there, not with this nutjob loose. He could just pick you off from the bridge."

Brandon was coming around Cape Elizabeth, the lighthouse at Two Lights beaming like a laser sight.

"So where you gonna go?" Kat said.

"I can use a space on the wharf."

"Where Estusa got that video?"

"Yeah. I'll hang in the harbor until it's dark," Brandon said. "Nobody will know."

"What if they do, you trapped in that goddamn wooden coffin?"

"Okay, I'll pick up a mooring," Brandon said. "Where are you now?"

"Eastern Prom. By the ferry ramp."

"Down there all by yourself?" Brandon said.

"Park's with me."

"I should be there."

"We'll find him," Kat said.

"Or her."

"You thinking the mom?"

"Which one?" Brandon said.

Mia answered on the first ring. Brandon said he was coming into the harbor from the south, would swing around to the ramp at East End Beach.

"Be careful," she said.

"I know the way in."

"Not what I mean," Mia said.

She was parked at the ramp when he idled up to the float. There were two guys loading a skiff onto a trailer, buckets and striper rods on the dock. Mia stepped by them and hopped aboard and Brandon reversed, backed out into deeper water and swung the bow around. As he eased the throttles open, Mia came up the ladder to the helm. She leaned against him, put an arm around her shoulder.

"I'm glad to see you," Mia said.

"Me, too."

"This is awful."

"Yeah."

Brandon swung further offshore, headed for the marker off Pomroy rock.

"How are you doing? And please don't tell me you're fine."

Brandon half-smiled, said nothing.

A third of the way to Fort Gorges, he throttled back. The motor rumbled as *Bay Witch* settled deeper into the water, the bow swinging into the southeast wind. Brandon shut the motors off and he and Mia stood at the helm, looked out at the harbor mouth, the red lights blinking atop the downtown buildings. Mia put her hand on his shoulder and said, "You heard what happened?"

"Kat called."

"It could have been you."

"I'd rather it had been."

"Don't say that," Mia said.

"It's true. Dever will hold this over me for years."

They leaned against the console, the boat drifting, the sea slapping the hull. Dusk was lowering and Brandon flicked the running lights on.

"Where were you?"

"Woodford."

Mia looked away.

"Did you give her the diary?"

"Yeah."

"So that's over and done with?"

Brandon didn't answer. The boat drifted and rocked.

"What?" Mia said.

"Nothing."

"What do you mean, nothing?"

"Nothing. I gave her the book."

Mia looked at him closely, reading his face, his eyes.

"Why are you doing this?"

Another shrug, the only sound the wave slap and the murmur of the radio.

"I don't know. She seemed like kind of a sad person. I thought it was the right thing—"

"Not that," Mia said. "I mean, why are you shutting me out? I have no idea what's going on in your head. You haven't really talked to me since—"

"Since I killed Rawlings? Since that girl killed herself? Since the rest of this goddamn mess?"

Mia grabbed his upper arm, swung him toward her, held him by both arms.

"Didn't you sign up for this?" she said.

Brandon hesitated, clamped his mouth shut.

"Didn't you, Brandon? You knew this was all possible. You knew you might have to shoot somebody. You knew that person might die. You knew that would be hard. You'd have to live it once and then relive it, carry it with you for the rest of your life. Didn't you know that?"

Brandon looked at her. Angry eyes, lips clenched in a pale line.

"Yeah, I did."

"So what are you feeling sorry for yourself for? That it was you and not Kat? Not O'Farrell or Dever or any of the others? That it was you who had to have this happen?"

"I'm not feeling sorry for myself. I'm just sorry it happened at all."

"No you're not," Mia said. "You're just sitting there and letting this take you down. And everyone around you, too. You don't want to get past it. You don't want us to help you. You just want to wallow in your bad luck."

He steeled himself.

"What are the odds? The odds are exactly what you knew they were when you chose to become a cop. One in a thousand? One in ten thousand? I have no freakin' idea. But there was always the chance you'd be the one. And now that you are, you act like it's some conspiracy against you. That kid didn't know you. The girl didn't, either. It's just bad luck. And the world is full of bad luck. You know. You see it. Kids killed in car crashes. Babies abused. Women killed for marrying the wrong guy. So pick yourself up, Brandon. Get on with your life. Let us help you. Let me help you. And help yourself. You've been on your own your whole life. You've overcome everything else, you can get past this."

She shook him.

"Fight back, Brandon Blake."

Mia looked away toward the bay, breathless and flushed. Easing her grip, she let her hands fall away and looked out on the water.

"So there it is, Brandon. I love you. If you need me, just tell me. But right now I want to go."

"Home? I don't think—"

"Carrie said I could stay in Cumberland."

A writer friend. A big house in the country.

"Okay."

He glanced out at the harbor. The boat had drifted toward Cousin's Island. He reached for the key, ran the blower. Started the motors. They rumbled as he put the boat in gear and swung the bow around. Mia was leaning against the console, arms folded across her chest, mouth clenched shit. Brandon took it slow, motored around the buoy and into the float. He reversed and idled, and Mia stepped to the ladder and said, "I'm sorry."

"Don't be," Brandon said. "You're right."

"You know I'm with you."

"Yes."

"Where are you going tonight?"

"Back to the marina."

"You can't do that. What about this sniper guy?"

"I'll pick up a mooring. It'll be almost dark."

"And then?"

"I don't know," Brandon said.

"You've got to take care of yourself," Mia said. "Fight for your job. Your reputation. For everything."

He feathered the throttles, said, "Hey."

She turned.

"Two things. Thanks."

Mia nodded.

"And there's a gun in the hall closet at your place. Under the quilts. There's a clip with it. I think you should snap that clip in and keep it near the bed. You know how to use it."

"One time shooting tin cans?" Mia said.

"Good enough."

She shook her head, said, "I don't think so. Guns—they cause nothing but trouble."

"If this guy decides to take it out on you because he can't get to me—"

"I'll cross that bridge," Mia said, and she stepped down the ladder, onto the deck. The boat lifted almost imperceptibly when she stepped off. Brandon eased away from the float and looked back. He would have waved but she never turned, just walked across the parking lot to the car. She got in, the headlights came on, and she pulled away.

Brandon turned away from shore, and idled out toward the marker buoy. When he glanced back he saw the Volvo driving up onto the Eastern Prom and out of sight. He hit the throttles and *Bay Witch* lifted herself up, sliced into the chop.

The mooring was at the most easterly point of the marina waterfront, a quarter mile from the bridge. If the sniper could make that shot in the dark, Brandon thought, more power to him.

He motored in slowly, running lights on in the thickening dusk. The southeast wind was supposed to last all night, and would keep the bow pointed toward the shore, the telltale *Bay Witch* name facing the harbor. Would they attack by water? Brandon couldn't picture it. Still, he slipped his loaded Glock into the waistband of his jeans, tossed his backpack into the dinghy, climbed down, and rowed.

He slipped his way between the boats, silent in the gloom. The marina was quiet, most of the boats dark. A television glowed in the Galbraith's big Carver, and when Brandon rowed past, he heard a newscaster say, "Police continue to search for..."

Tying the dinghy to a cleat in his slip, he heaved himself onto the float, reached back for his pack. Straightening, he looked around the floats, started up the ramp to the yard. It was dark. Quiet. Something scurried along the fence and he touched the gun. A rat emerged, tumbled down into the rocks and headed for the water. Brandon hurried across the yard and through the gate. His truck was where he'd left it. He circled it once, checking to see the tires hadn't been slashed. Then he unlocked it and climbed in. He drove out of the lot and down the street toward the Coast Guard station. And then he turned on the lights.

He wouldn't wallow. He wouldn't be a sitting duck. For anyone.

His Red Sox hat pulled low, he drove over the bridge to Portland, looped around and headed for the West End. At the first red light, he pulled his cap down lower, leaned back in his seat, wished his truck had blacked-out windows. He picked up the highway and headed south, his police radio on. There was a new tension in every spoken word, every traffic stop doubled up. Day-shift detectives were on, the big brass, too. The new normal in Portland, Maine.

But Brandon was in South Portland, then Scarborough. He was slowing for the Woodford exit when his phone buzzed on the console.

A text. Danni.

`Brandon, buddy. We really gotta talk.`

EIGHTEEN

He paid cash for the room at the Motel Five, a place on Route 1 that only saw cops when they busted drug dealers. The guy behind the desk—bald on top with a gray pony tail, probably cool in some distant past—asked for I.D. Brandon said he left his license in his other car and held out $60 in cash. The guy took the money and shoved a clipboard across the counter. Brandon signed his name, George C. Patton, the last biography he'd read. The guy behind the desk didn't blink, said, "Here's the key, Mr. Patton." How quickly, Brandon thought, we forget.

The room was on the first floor at the end, the door fronting a walkway bordered by a scruffy hedge with plastic grocery bags impaled on its branches. Brandon let himself in, threw his backpack on the bed. He turned on the TV, flipped through the channels until he saw his face, turned it off. Standing by the bed he called Marlon Davey.

"Hi, there," Brandon said. "It's Brandon. You working?"

"Yeah. Where are you?"

He told him.

"Jeez, Blake. Only reason we go there is to kick doors in."

"I missed the smell of dirtbags," Brandon said.

"Hey, you should come out with me. Me and an SP detective just arrested a forty-year-old guy tried to set up sex with a twelve-year-old. Said he thought she was fourteen."

"Wipe the slime off your cuffs."

"Seriously," Davey said. "Ten minutes."

"I'll meet you in the lot of the McDonald's down by the road."

———

He did, Davey pulling his cruiser in beside his truck. Brandon got out and slid into the passenger seat and Davey pulled away. Brandon felt a pang as the cruiser accelerated, another as the radio hissed. Dementia patient wandered away from a nursing home.

"Yours?" Brandon said.

"Maybe, or they call in the K-9."

Davey was in the left lane, headed south on Route 1. Mattress stores, ice cream shops, lots of pizza.

"What's the word on the shooting?"

"Everybody pulled in, going at it hard."

"Good thing. That asshole needs to be locked up for a long time."

"I guess," Brandon said. "Dever was about six inches from buying it."

"Christ."

They were quiet for a minute, moving with traffic. The guy with dementia had turned up in somebody's house eating their cereal. Davey turned off Route 1, headed toward the downtown.

"Going to tell me why you can't stay away from this thriving metropolis?" he said.

Brandon considered which answer to give, decided on, "People are telling me to get off my butt, stop feeling sorry for myself."

"So there wasn't enough to keep you busy in the big city?"

"I'm pretty well known there. At least it feels that way. Go to Home Depot feel like I should wear a disguise."

"What else?" Davey said.

Nothing like a cop to cut to the chase.

"The dead bikers."

"Yeah?"

"I don't know. I just feel like it's worth pursuing."

"Long time ago."

"People around here move away?"

"Not much," Davey said. "When they do, they eventually come back. Like lost dogs."

They drove, Brandon settling into the cruiser, basking in the glow of the laptop. He could learn to like this town, this P.D. Not that they'd jump to hire him, not if he were disciplined. He'd be damaged goods. An ex-cop. He fought off the thought and asked Davey, "Think you could check something for me?

See if Clutch was in a bad accident? Something with a settlement?"

"Can query DMV."

"Thanks. Also, since you're being so helpful, people who know this Sash guy, where would they hang out?"

They were coming into the downtown, a big renovated mill on the left, lights on in the towering wall of brick. Davey pointed right, a side street with dark storefronts, a sign for a bar: Twilight Lounge.

"Be my first stop," he said. "All locals, no kids from the college, no yuppies from the apartments in the mill. Go there to see your old buddies from high school, if they're not in jail."

"How do they like strangers?" Brandon said.

"Way more than they like cops."

"Drop me up here?"

Davey looked at him.

"You sure? Other ways to keep busy. Rake leaves. Walk the dog."

"Don't have a dog. And I live on a boat."

"Scrape barnacles, then."

But he pulled to the side of the street, killed the headlights, reached up and switched off the dome.

Brandon opened the door, said, "I'll let you know how it goes."

"Call if you need company."

"I'll be fine."

"A stranger asking about old murders in a small town?" Davey said.

"It's not that small," Brandon said. He smiled. Davey smiled back.

———

The Twilight Lounge was darker than that. There was a baseball game on over the bar, Red Sox and Tampa, four guys hunched over beers, two together, two more apart. They didn't look up when Brandon sat down between them, beside one of the singles. The bartender, a barrel-shaped woman with a red 80s shag, looked over from behind the bar and said, "Yeah?"

Brandon said, "Budweiser."

She turned away and snagged a glass in one motion. Started pouring. Brandon glanced around the room. There was an older couple at a table in the corner—the guy looking at the game, the woman at her phone. She had the same hair as the bartender, like the place was frozen in time. Three young guys were playing darts on the far wall, a man and woman at the pool table. Brandon looked back at the TV as Mookie Betts hit a line drive to the opposite field, headed for second. "Oh, yeah," the guy beside him said. "Mookie can motor."

Brandon nodded.

"Sox farm system," he said.

"Grow their own," the guy said.

He was in his thirties, shaved head and a goatee. Smallish with big shoulders and biceps, ingrained dirt on his fingers, like maybe he worked in a tire shop. The bartender clopped Brandon's beer down, said, "Tab?" Brandon nodded, looked to the guy's nearly empty glass and said, "Him, too."

The guy looked over and Brandon said, "Sox fans gotta stick together."

"Yankees suck," the guy said.

Brandon lifted his glass and sipped. Betts had moved to third on a grounder to the right side. A guy two stools to the left leaned closer and started talking baseball, too. The two of them chatted and then the tire guy ordered beers for all three of them. Glasses came up again. "Go Sox."

The tire guy said, "New around here?"

"No, just doing some work for a couple of days."

"A lot of new people these days. Apartments in the mill."

"Oh, yeah," Brandon said. "Get me a latte."

"Right. Kid came in here with this girl. He's got on these little tight pants, looked like he was wearing her clothes. Wanted some kind of fancy ale or whatnot. Gina goes, 'We got PBR, Bud, and Bud Lite.' They walked out."

"Good riddance."

"Got that right."

The third guy's beer came. He was older, handlebar moustache with gray in it. He drank, wiped foam off his moustache with the back of his hand and hunched over the beer. Mookie scored on a squeeze bunt. Red Sox 3-Tampa 2. The tire guy said, "That's the way you do it."

They watched the rest of the fifth, the moustached guy suddenly draining his glass, saying, "Gotta go to work." He slid off his stool and headed for the door. The tire guy said, "Works security. Guards this factory that closed last year. Made chains you use in the woods. Gets paid to guard nothing from nobody."

"Huh," Brandon said.

During the commercial, the guy asked Brandon, "So what do you do for work?"

Brandon took a long drink, wiped his mouth, too, the beer on his stubble.

"Gonna sound weird," he said. "But mostly I find stuff out. For insurance companies, lawyers. They don't want to leave their cushy offices."

"Huh," the guy said back.

"Was working construction, got hurt, while I was out on comp my girlfriend's father—she's not my girlfriend any more—he says, 'Why don't you try this? Better than sitting around killing your liver.'"

"Where you from?"

"Mass. Haverhill."

"Oh, yeah. So what are you asking about in Woodford?"

"Oh, no big deal. Just this lady, she's suing an insurance company, been battling over paying out life insurance for some biker guy got killed up here a few years back. They're saying they don't have to pay because he was killed committing a felony crime. She says there's no proof of that."

The guy watched the start of the sixth, the first batter for Tampa out on a called strike. The guy said, "So who hired you?"

"The lady. She's no dope, either, and her husband wasn't. People think bikers are these animals but this guy had an auto body business, nice truck, condo in Florida. She's smart, too. Got this big insurance outfit working their asses off."

"What does she want you to find out?"

"Whether there was a crime involved. I mean, everybody says it was drugs but the guys are dead and there was no drugs there, so who's to say?"

The bartender was back with another round, said "on the house." Brandon and his friend smiled and held up their glasses. A couple came in and the bartender turned and said, "Hey," and they stood by him and talked.

"So what do you do?" Brandon asked the tire-changer guy.

"Work in a garage. It's a chain, you know? Tires, brakes, exhaust. In and out. Pretty good money, no heavy lifting. Did the transmission, motor-rebuild thing. Work your ass off, people bitch about the bill. I mean, what do they make in a week?"

"Right," Brandon said. He drank. The next Tampa batter grounded to second.

"I'm Chris," Brandon said.

"Kenny," the guy said.

They bumped fists.

"What did the cops say?" Kenny said.

"About the biker? They don't care. More or less said they're glad the scumbag's dead."

"Goddamn cops."

"Yeah."

The Rays went down one, two, three. Brandon said, "Maybe you knew this guy. Damian Sash?"

"Sash? Sure. Went to school with some Sashes."

"Make 'em out to be like some kinda Colombian cartel," Brandon said.

"Just a buncha gearheads, really. Mighta sold dope. I don't know. I'm a beer guy."

"Yeah, that's what I pictured. Guys who liked trucks and bikes. This guy named Clutch, he was his buddy."

"Oh, yeah, there was a regular crew. This guy Smoker, they called him that 'cause he drove this big diesel Dodge pickup, belched out this cloud of black smoke. He's in jail now, like his fourth DWI. Dude's got an alcohol problem. Wolf Man, he's in Florida. Went down there for work, driving long haul. This guy Clutch, he's around. He's selling cars, got a wrecker. Him and his old lady run this little used-car lot."

"Mom and pop thing?"

"Oh, yeah," Kenny said. "Settled right down like old folks."

Brandon smiled. They looked at game, Sox up in the sixth. Sandy Leon teed off on a fastball, deep home run to center. Another fist bump. The bartender, who had been washing glasses, turned to them and said, "You all set?"

They nodded and she went out back.

"So must have been a big deal, those three guys getting killed here," Brandon said.

"Oh, yeah. I mean, we got your regular murders but usually one at a time, some asshole shoots his wife after she serves divorce papers. Three people get whacked, that'll get your attention."

"People talk about what happened?"

"Mostly that the Sash kid, talk was he was selling drugs, owed them some money. But come on. I mean, how friggin' stupid can you be, go up against those guys alone? I mean, hide the fuck out, you know? Or if you are gonna meet up, bring a crew."

"Yeah, seems like he must have been outmatched."

"Two on one. Ain't like the movies, you know? The bad guys, they're shooting all over the place, can't hit the side of a house. Good guys taking everybody out like they got lasers."

On the TV, Pedroia doubled. Tampa was going to the bullpen.

"I mean, any of those guys," Kenny said. "They ain't like trained killers but still, could've evened things up a little, you know? So those bikers—no offense to your lady there—three or four on two of them, they ain't just walking away."

"Which nobody did anyway," Brandon said.

"I guess to hell."

"Newspaper said they weren't killed outright. Sounded like everybody bled out."

"Wouldn't that suck, huh?" Kenny said. "Dying slow. I mean, shit for luck or what?"

Kenny said he had to get home, getting up early with his kid. With a last glance at the screen—Sox up two, batting in the eighth—he left. The bartender came over and asked Brandon if he was all set. Brandon nodded. He left a $20 bill on the bar and walked out.

The street was deserted and it was cold, the autumn night descending. Brandon felt the beers, was glad he hadn't driven in. He walked back to the main drag, lights showing in the side of the mill like portholes. There was a café open a half-block down so he walked that way, hoping to see a taxi. Cars passed and he wondered if Uber was in Woodford. He had his phone out, was searching for the app when a car horn honked. He looked up.

It was the white Focus, pulled up to the curb across the street. Danni was at the wheel. She waved like they were old friends.

Brandon crossed, and Danni buzzed the window down.

"Hey, I said, 'That looks like Brandon. What's he doing here?' You should've told me. I would have bought you that beer."

"Had to get out of Dodge," Brandon said. "Your town's growing on me."

"Good deal. It's got a bad rap, you know. I think of it as sort of this secret place."

He was standing in the street and a box truck slowed and passed.

"Hey, get in," Danni said. "You come down in the boat again? I'll give you a ride."

"No, I drove this time. Navigating at night isn't something you do if you can help it."

"Okay. Where you parked? I'll drop you."

"I got a ride," Brandon said.

"Then where you need to go?"

Brandon looked up the block, wavered.

"I'm staying on Route 1. Motel 5."

"Christ," Danni said. "Only time cops go there—"

"I know. To kick in doors."

NINETEEN

The car was small and he felt very close to Danni, more than on the boat at the Bowl or in his truck. She was chewing gum and it filled the car with the smell of mint. She pulled away and he heard bottles clink in the back seat. "Picked up some beers," she said. "Home alone. Clutch got a repo job in Mass. for the next coupla days. He does these three a.m. grabs down there. A little sketchy but wicked good money. New Range Rover this time. Some guy got up the downpayment, six months later, hasn't paid a cent."

"Cool," Brandon said.

Danni swung off Main Street, headed west to Route 1. Brandon waited for her to bring up the note, the diary, but she talked about the business, how it was getting harder to find good buys at the car auctions since everything was online. And then it was how Clutch still drank Bud Lite, but he had to drink like twelve of them to get a buzz.

"I say, 'Why don't you buy real beer. Something you can taste. Have three or four of 'em. Won't be peeing all night long, either.'"

Brandon nodded, wondered if she'd forgotten the last time he'd seen her boyfriend Clutch had been on the pavement with his arm jammed up to his neck.

"So I get a good IPA for me. Even a double IPA. I like the hoppy stuff," Danni said.

She swung into the motel parking lot, scanned the lot for Brandon's truck. Spotting it, she drove to the end of the lot, pulled up to the building. She shut the motor off, lowered the window halfway, took the gum from her mouth and tossed it out. She turned back to him.

"So," Danni said.

"Thanks for the ride," Brandon said.

"How 'bout one of those beers now? I owe you big time, for everything you've done. The diary and all."

Brandon looked away. "I don't know. I already had a few."

"Oh, yeah. Where?"

"Twilight Lounge."

"Jesus, Brandon. Motel 5 and the Twilight? What would those cool people in Portland say?"

He smiled. She leaned toward him, then reached into the back seat and brought out two beers. IPAs. She handed him one and took an opener out of the ashtray, leaned over and opened his beer, then her own. The caps went into the ashtray with the opener. Danni held her bottle up and clinked his and said, "To the good guys."

Brandon smiled and drank. Danni did, too, and then turned in her seat to face him. He smelled some sort of perfume, mixed with the mint.

"Because that's what you are, Brandon. A good guy."

"Yeah, right."

"No, you are. I know what you're going through. It's some serious shit so you don't see this, I know. But you're a wicked good person."

"About ten thousand people would disagree with that."

"Well, they don't know you like I know you," Danni said. She looked at him, fixed him with a long gaze.

"I'll come right out and say it. I like talking to you," she said. "And I think you like talking to me."

"Sure," Brandon said.

"This is gonna sound weird, but I think you need somebody like me right now. Somebody real, you know? Somebody who isn't connected to the whole rest of your life."

Brandon took a drink.

"I'm like this escape thing, you know?" Danni said. "I'm not a cop. I'm not a cop-hater, either. I'm not, like, judging you."

"No," Brandon said. "You're not."

She lifted the bottle, drank down a third of it.

"It's like we have this weird little bubble, you know what I'm saying? You know me from the diary. I mean, nobody else in the whole world has read that stuff."

Brandon thought of Mia and her writers group. Danni smiled, moved closer.

"I mean, it's weird but in some ways you know me way better than Clutch does. I've only known you what, three days? And I feel like we really, I don't know, we just get each other."

Danni reached over and touched her fingers to the top of his left hand.

"How 'bout we go inside and finish these beers."

She leaned closer, cleavage exposed. There was the edge of a tattoo, blue and unrecognizable. A bird's wing? Her lips were glossed and her mouth was slightly open. "Maybe nothing will happen. Maybe something will."

"Wow, Danni. I'm flattered. Really. But I can't do that," Brandon said. "I'm with this woman, Mia."

"And I have Clutch. But they aren't in our bubble. This doesn't have anything to do with the rest of our lives. We can just do it this once. Kinda seal our own secret deal. Like the blood brothers thing, except not."

The evergreen scent was cloying and Danni was still leaning toward him. More of the tattoo was exposed but he tried not to look, fixed his gaze on the pine-tree-shaped air freshener hanging from the heat control on the dash. The beers at the Twilight were spinning around in his head as she moved closer. When he turned he could see pores, a speck of stray eye-liner on her cheek, tiny welts where she had plucked her eyebrows.

"Just kiss me and we'll get this party started," Danni said. "I'm telling you, Brandon, I want you bad."

Her mouth was open, lips coming closer.

"The paper," Brandon said.

"We can get to that after," she said.

"No. I mean, is that why you're doing this? So you can have that note?"

She pulled back. Her mouth snapped shut. The amorous haze fell away from her eyes.

"Screw you," Danni said.

"Sorry."

"You think that's all this is? You have something I want?"

"I think I have something you need," Brandon said.

She looked at him—not angry, not seductive, just real. "What makes you think I need just one thing?" Danni said.

"How many things do you need?"

She smiled, snorted. "Ha."

And then her expression changed. Brandon waited. She started to tear up.

"Hey, okay. You want to fucking know? Okay. I need a life. I need a guy really loves me, not one who walks around like he's the jail guard. Not one who only talks to me when he needs something. 'What's for supper? I gotta go to friggin' Brockton. Make me a sandwich. You wanna jump in the sack before I go?' Hey, he had a half-hour. Why not get laid for the road?"

"So why are you still with him?" Brandon said.

Danni looked out of the window, turned quickly back as a car pulled in.

"All I need, one of his garage buddies showing up here."

A pickup, a beater Ford Ranger, pulled up a couple of rooms down. A skinny gray-haired guy got out. He reached a Miami Dolphins duffel out of the truck, walked to the door and knocked. The door opened and he went in. Danni drank the next third of the beer.

"Habit," she said. "Clutch is a habit, you know? Like smoking."

"You do this a lot? Come on to guys?"

"Last time was four years ago. That guy didn't turn me down. What are you, gay?"

"Every four years?" Brandon said.

"Fuckin' A, Brandon Blake. Don't you get it? I'm so fucking lonely."

"Why? You know half the people in this town. Lived here your whole life, right?"

"But they don't know me," Danni said. "And I just felt like, I don't know, that you did. Or you could. You know why?"

"No."

"Because you're lonely, too. You have this girl—"

"Mia."

"Right," Danni said. "Some rich chick, probably. Probably really pretty. I'm picturing a hard little body. Probably jogs. What's she do for work?"

"She teaches kids to write. At USM."

"A teacher. I get it."

"But she thinks of herself mostly as a writer. She writes stories."

Danni looked at him quizzically.

"Like fiction. Novels except shorter."

"She get paid for that?"

"A little. Not a lot."

"So it's like her hobby," Danni said.

"Sort of, but maybe more than that. She doesn't do it for money. She does it because she likes it. And she's good at it."

Danni looked at him and then she smiled.

"Okay. So here's the real story. She doesn't really know you. I can tell 'cause I'm the same way. We're both inside our heads. I mean, we talk to people, Clutch and Mia, but underneath it we're alone. Stuff in there you never tell her. Things you keep all to yourself."

It stunned him, the truth of it. He looked away, saw another car pulling up beside the pickup. A Nissan two-door something-or-other, after-market wheels and buzzing exhaust. Two guys got out, when to the same door where the guy went with the Dolphins duffel. They knocked. Waited. The door opened and they went in, closed it behind them. A door that needed to be kicked in, an MDEA case waiting to happen.

"You're not denying it," Danni said.

He looked back.

"Denying what?"

"What I just said. That we're the same. You're not saying I'm wrong."

Brandon sipped his beer. Danni finished hers, turned and leaned over and fished two more bottles out of the back. The tattoo was a dragonfly. She opened his beer and hers, handed his over. Danni drank. Brandon held the two beers in front of him.

"You know what I think?" Danni said.

"No."

"I think little shit turns into big shit. Things you decide or don't decide. Things that just happen for no reason. Turn into things that end up being like the most important things in your life. You didn't know it when it was happening. You said to yourself, 'Oh, this is what happened today. Something else will happen tomorrow.' But what you don't get is that it doesn't matter what happens tomorrow because what happened today is just too fucking key, or whatever the word is."

"Pivotal," Brandon said. "But I hate that word."

"Yeah, right. But it's like it turned you in a whole new direction and you never saw it coming. And there's no going back."

"Like hooking up with Clutch?"

Danni smiled, the rejection from Brandon a half-beer ago. "Yeah, like hooking up with Clutch. I was a kid, you know what I'm saying? I liked him 'cause he had a big truck."

"And you stayed with him," Brandon said.

Another smile, then a long pull on the beer. She wiped her mouth with the back of her hand. "Yeah, I stayed with him."

"He didn't screw you over like the other guys? The ones in the diary?"

"Oh, them? They just wanted to get into my pants. I was too young and dumb to know the difference. Clutch wanted that too but at least he stuck around."

The two guys came out of the room. Baseball hats on backwards, built like they lifted. One glanced over at Danni and Brandon, then got in the car and looked over again. Danni lifted her beer and the guy looked away.

She drank, stuck the beer bottle between her legs. "No, he didn't screw me over. He just friggin' locked me away."

Brandon waited. Danni looked at him and said, "So what's your story, Brandon Blake? Other than shooting this kid. And the other guy, the one in the paper. In the hotel or whatever. This Mia, you save her life and now she won't go away? I mean, that would totally suck. Like if you weren't really into her and this thing happens with this kidnapping and you save her and now you're stuck. I saw a movie like that once. Guy saves this other guy's life and the other guy follows him around for like years, trying to save him back. Finally the first guy shoves the second guy, to try to get away from him, and the guy lands in the street and he gets run over by a truck. It was some weird movie like with Cary Grant."

"It's not like that," Brandon said.

"What is it like then? What is it about you that makes me feel like we just fucking get each other?"

Brandon finished the one beer, put the bottle on the floor of the car. It fell over and rolled under the seat. He took a drink from the second beer and rested it in his lap.

"Killing someone?" he said.

Danni looked at him, suddenly serious, not dreamy.

"What?"

"Only thing you really know about me. I shot and killed someone. Twice."

"But why would that—"

"So what happened on that day? July 21, 2007?" Brandon said.

Danni looked away, took a quick, nervous drink. She put the bottle back down and looked at him and said, "It's a long story."

Brandon waited but she ended it there. He pushed on: "I was curious. Like maybe there was a car accident or somebody died, like your mother or something. I read the paper from back then."

Danni turned to him. "You read some old newspapers?"

"Yeah. Big news was three guys killed in a gravel pit."

She blanched, then added a quick shrug. "Maybe. I don't remember."

"Bikers from Lawrence and a local guy named Damian Sash. Cops decided they got in some shootout over drugs and all bled out."

"Oh, yeah. I guess I remember something about that. But I was just out of high school, doing my own thing. Some motorcycle gang guys get killed, I mean, who cares?"

"Clutch must have known this Sash guy, right? Same age, both car mechanics. Woodford isn't that big a place."

"What? Where are you getting all this shit?"

"It's the biggest thing that happened in Woodford that day. By a longshot."

"What the fuck are you doing?" Danni said. "Investigating me?"

"It's what I do, Danni," Brandon said. "I'm a cop."

"But you're not supposed to be working. You're suspended or whatever."

"I had time."

"Jesus Christ," Danni said. "And you come up with this crazy shit. Bikers and some old murders from a long time ago. All because I put something down with that day on it? Maybe I screwed my best friend's boyfriend, you know? Maybe I stole from a restaurant. Maybe I hit somebody with my car and took off. Maybe I ran over a cat. Maybe I even picked some guy up outside the Twilight, went back to his motel 'cause I thought he was a nice guy, dumb shit that I am."

She reached for the key in the ignition, sputtered, "Fuckin' A, man. I thought we were gonna be friends. Maybe even more."

"You can talk to me," Brandon said.

"Fuck you," Danni said. "I mean, sure I can talk to you. I been talking for a fucking half hour."

"About that night, I mean."

Danni flipped her beer up, finished it in two swallows. She flung the bottle into the back seat and it bounced, clinked against the others. As she reached for the shifter Brandon said, "I still have that paper."

"Yeah, well that paper is nothin'. Just a girl with some problems."

She put the car into reverse and it lurched. She jammed on the brakes and it lurched again.

"I gotta go," Danni said.

"Okay," Brandon said. "But I think you need some help."

He opened the door and hoisted himself out.

"Maybe I do," Danni said. "Maybe I don't. I don't know what I need. I just know I gotta get the fuck out of here. You know what? Like I said in the diary, guys are assholes. You included."

Brandon closed the door. Danni backed up, slid to a stop, squealed the tires and sped out of the lot, turning south. Brandon watched as the taillights moved up the highway and disappeared into traffic. And then he went to the room door, opened the door with the metal key. He went inside, put the key on the bureau, picked up his backpack off the bed, stepped outside. He left the door ajar.

A half-mile up the road, he pulled into a MacDonald's lot and circled around. Backed into a space and killed the lights. And watched the road. Five minutes went by. Nobody showed. Not Clutch. Not

Danni. He leaned forward to touch the butt of his gun, under the seat. He called Davey, Woodford P.D., and said, "You got a minute?"

"I think you've mistaken me for an Uber," Davey said.

"No," Brandon said. "I'll come to you."

It was the darkened lot of a closed-up burger stand on Route 1, a cop meet-up spot, a place to watch for drunken tourists trying to make it back from Old Orchard Beach. Brandon and Davey parked side-by-side, driver's doors lined up, windows buzzed down.

"How was the Twilight?" Davey said.

"Good. I made some new friends."

"Be careful. You don't know where they've been."

"I met an old one. Danni spotted me coming out. Drove me back to the motel."

"Is this one of those too-much-information things?" Davey said.

"Nothing happened," Brandon said.

"Hey, it's your business."

"Except that I mentioned the murders. The bikers and this Sash kid."

"You mentioned it?"

"Yeah. She freaked."

Davey listened, waited.

"Said she thought I was her friend and here I was investigating her and Clutch."

"Don't know about the friend part but hard to argue with that last thing."

"I said I was a cop. It's what we do."

Davey looked toward the road, the headlights streaming past. His radio barked and he turned it down.

"Not my business, but isn't it what you're supposed to not be doing?"

Brandon looked away and when he turned back Davey was staring at him like he was waiting for an answer. It was Brandon who broke the gaze and looked out at traffic, two lanes moving slow. When he looked back, Davey still was waiting.

"I touched a nerve," Brandon said. "It was like I jabbed a knife right in."

"What? She and her boyfriend killed all three of them?"

He was quick.

"I don't know. I just know her face went white. Then she got all pissed off to cover it up."

"They had money after that," Davey said.

"Maybe they just picked over the proceeds. Maybe they saw Sash was dead, knew where cash was hidden. Or more drugs. Maybe they just capitalized on the situation. Like looters."

"Be a project and a half to prove that."

"I have time," Brandon said.

The look again.

"Do you?" Davey said.

The motors idled, white vapor wafting into the night air like dry ice at a heavy-metal show. Davey looked preoccupied, staring through the mist at the highway, a distant neon sign in the shape of an ice-cream cone. This stretch of road was a ghost town, the ruins of a playground from a distant past. Danni and Clutch were throwbacks, too, Brandon thought, people right out of the Thirties. Bonnie and Clyde.

"Where do you think she went?" Davey said.

"I don't know. Home? She said Clutch was down in Mass. doing repos."

"Or he was home. He sent her to see you. Said, 'Get this freakin' cop off our backs.' Instead she has to go back and report to him that you're not off their backs. You're on their backs now. If it's anything like you think, you're a huge problem."

Brandon didn't answer.

"You didn't have to tell them. Could have just told me. Maybe we could have worked it some more. I'll still ask around but now they know you know."

"I wanted to see her reaction."

Davey hesitated, then said, "I think you just wanted some action. Distract you from everything that's happened. Catch a bad guy, even up the score a little."

"It wouldn't be even," Brandon said.

"It won't be even if you get yourself killed," Davey said. "In case that's what you're thinking."

"I'm trying not to."

"Get killed?"

"Think," Brandon said.

They sat for a moment, then another. Headlights came up fast from the south, a loud jacked-up Dodge pickup passing them at way past 60. The driver saw the cruiser, eased off the gas, then hit it hard. Davey flicked on the blue strobes.

"Gotta work," he said. "You don't."

And then Davey hit the throttle and the cruiser shot out of the lot and hissed, taking off down the road like a jet. Brandon sat in the dark, watched the blue lights recede. "Sure, I do," he said. And then he pulled out of the lot—and turned south.

Clutch Auto was four miles down, take a left onto Western Highway, a mile up on the right. Brandon slowed 50 yards shy of the lot, killed the lights, and coasted into the lot of a boarded-up diner. He let the truck roll to a stop and shut off the motor. No brake lights.

But lights were on in the little house. He leaned over, opened the glove box, and took out a pair of binoculars. Rested his elbows on the steering wheel and focused on the lights. Two windows on the end of the house, lights on and shades down. He moved the binoculars to the right. Waited for his eyes to adjust to the darkness.

At first it was all blackness. And then a shape materialized slowly, like an apparition. A glint from glass. Windshield. A rectangular blotch, something protruding above it.

Brandon reached up, flipped the switch for the dome light. He opened the door and slid out, reached back for his Glock, slipping it out from under the seat. He tucked the gun into the back of his waistband, let the door fall back noiselessly. Then he walked slowly to the side of the diner, into the darkness. There was a stake fence at the back of the lot, the top covered with vines. He stayed close to the fence, in the shadows, and moved toward the little house.

Six steps. Stop. Raise the binoculars. Still too far. Six more steps.

Then six more. A dog started to bark in the house, a frantic yipping. Brand hurried the next six steps and then he knew. He walked six more steps to make sure. Raised the binoculars.

It was there, backed deep into a space between the house and the garage.

Clutch's wrecker.

Danni was wrong. They couldn't have been friends.

TWENTY

O r maybe Clutch was right. Danni liked to screw around, made up the story about the Range Rover in Brockton just so Brandon wouldn't worry about Clutch bursting in on them.

Brandon didn't think so.

He was on Route 1, headed from Scarborough into South Portland. Traffic was steady and he leaned deep into the seat, his arm up on the driver's side window. Hiding, in plain view. He was turning onto Broadway—sandwich shops, service stations, hair salons—when his phone buzzed. He picked it up, looked at the number.

"Hey," Brandon said.

"Hey, Blake," Kat said. "Where are you?"

He told her.

"Come over the bridge. Commercial. East side of Harbor Marine."

"Gimme ten," Brandon said.

Kat was in the cruiser with Park, backed into the blackness. Behind them shrink-wrapped boats loomed like giant white cocoons. Brandon pulled in, did the door-to-door thing again.

"How you doing?" Kat said.

"Fine," Brandon said.

"Keep hanging in there, Blakesy," Park said, leaning forward to see.

"No choice."

"Where you been?" Kat said.

"Here and there," Brandon said, wondering, even as he said it, why he could confide in a Woodford cop he hardly knew but couldn't do the same with his partner. "Any more on our sniper?"

She shook her head, looked to Park. They both got out, no lights showing inside the SUV. Kat walked past Brandon, nodded for him to follow, out of the range of the cruiser's voice recorder. They walked under the bridge, stood in the rubble: broken glass, soiled clothes, an upturned shopping cart. Park joined them as Kat said, "They'll get him. Detectives are rousting the usual haters."

"Rawlings, the dad, he's some sort of big-game hunter."

"Yeah, but I heard he always has an alibi. Home with the wife."

"Maybe it's not him. Feel bad saying it, kind of."

"Could be any number of these assholes, just waiting for an excuse." Park said.

"Stay safe out there," Brandon said.

"We keep moving," Kat said. "Don't give anybody time to set up."

"Any other news?"

"Carew is working it hard, trying to get them off your back," she said.

"Bad enough what's happening," Park said. "Don't need to fight your own department."

Brandon smiled, barely.

"And we walked the route this afternoon, from the bar to the alley. Thought maybe we'd see a memory card on the ground."

"Didn't CSI do that?" Brandon said.

"Sure, but another set of eyes."

"Two sets," Park said.

"And?"

Kat shook her head.

"Sorry," she said.

Brandon shook his head.

"With you, Blakesy," Park said. "Gotta keep the blue line like a fucking wall."

"Appreciate it," Brandon said.

"This too shall pass," Park said. "It'll blow itself out. These dipshits, they'll get bored, find some other freakin' thing to march about. You'll be back on, everything back to normal."

Like that could ever happen, Brandon thought. He nodded. Kat put her hand on his arm, led him away from the cars over toward the boats. It smelled like mud flats, rotting seaweed, gasoline. Kat reached over and took his hand, opened the palm. She dropped something in it. He looked down.

A phone, cheap and light. A burner.

"Keep it on," Kat said. And then she turned, walked back to the cruiser. Brandon followed, stood as she slid in, equipment rattling and creaking.

Park put the cruiser in gear as Kat said, "Take good care, partner." The cruiser pulled away, lights off until it hit the road. Brandon walked back to his truck, got in and buzzed the window closed. He laid the phone on the seat beside him. He pulled out, drove a hundred yards, then pulled off the road again. He was under the bridge, the concrete piers standing around him like redwoods. He shut off the motor and sat in the darkness, this place as good as any. He waited.

His eyes adjusted to the dark. Lights flickered from cars above him. Down the road sailboat masts were reflected in security lights. If he listened hard he could hear rigging jingling in the wind. He looked over at the phone, a black spot on the seat. And just then it glowed, pale green like a firefly. Brandon picked it up.

"Yeah."

"It's me. Maddie."

"Hey. How you doing?"

"Good. Sorry about the cloak and dagger, the phone thing. I don't think I should be seen with you. And you know how phone records are."

"First thing they subpoena," Brandon said.

"Anyway, I had a productive day."

"That right?"

Brandon waited.

"I went door to door. In Moresby. For Maine Equality. Tried to talk to people about gay rights."

"How'd that go?"

"Pretty well. I think some of the old folks were actually kind of excited to meet a real live lesbian," Maddie said.

"So now there's Ellen DeGeneres and you."

"Right. I expanded their horizons a hundred percent."

"Good math for an English professor," Brandon said.

He waited.

"And I got some interesting stuff."

"About—"

"The Rawlings family."

"How'd you bring that up?"

"Worked my way down the street toward their house," Maddie said. "Then I started asking people about the next place. You know. 'Who's across the street? Should I stop there?' Everybody loves giving the lowdown on their neighbors."

Brandon thought of the marina. Boat gossip.

"What'd they say?"

"The family is screwed up."

"No surprise."

"Dad is some sort of financial advisor in town, acts like he's Gordon Gekko. When he isn't Mr. Macho. Goes around the world shooting exotic animals and hanging their heads in his man cave."

"Huh," Brandon said.

"A couple of people said he was a real jerk. Looks down on them, always making references to how his mother was wealthy, like they wouldn't even get how wealthy she was. Tiff Rawlings is a social climber. From some hardscrabble family in northern Maine and isn't going back. Latches on to people, then drops them when she gets another rung up the ladder."

"Who told you that?"

"The last part? This woman who got dropped. One week it was all hugs and muffins and then it was like Tiff Rawlings didn't know she existed."

"Tiff. Short for—?"

"Tiffany. I Googled her. Used to be spelled T-I-F-F-A-N-E-E. She changed it to a Y."

"Went upscale."

"Right."

"What else?" Brandon said.

"Son is—I mean was. Sorry. He was kind of a geek. Picture

emerged is he didn't play sports. Had one really close guy friend, they were into computer games and stuff. And old movies."

"*Blade Runner.*"

"Right. Kinda quirky. But not going around acting suicidal," Maddie said.

"He was when I met him."

A car went by slow, hit the truck with high beams and kept going. Brandon waited as the dark fell over him.

"Here's the thing," Maddie said, her voice lowering "About a month ago—August 9, to be exact—the husband's mother comes to visit. From a nursing home. A place in Deering. Twin Oaks. They'd bring her over for a day once in a great while."

"Sounds normal."

"Until she OD'd. Tiff Rawlings told one of the neighbors she had some sort of dementia. Story is she went in the bathroom, took a bunch of pills."

"Aren't you supposed to lock that stuff away?" Brandon said.

"Maybe they did. Maybe they put it up high but she stood on a chair."

The cars rattled above him. A tractor trailer passed, headed for the container port. Something scuffled in the weeds.

"So she dies," Brandon said.

"Neighbor said they had an oxygen mask on her when they took her to the ambulance. So I guess she was alive that long."

"O.D., they might've gotten a heart beat," Brandon said.

"Right," Maddie said. "But here's the thing. Two people told me that's when the son—Thatcher—went off the rails. Scraped his mother's car with a knife or something. Broke one of the windows. Some fancy Mercedes. Neighbors heard the alarm go off."

"Huh."

"It goes on from there. First the car, then he lights a fire in their trash can, burns the siding off the back of the house. Paints the cat with spray paint. Rides his bike up and down the driveway throwing bottles up in the air. Started throwing them against his own house."

"Cops?" Brandon said.

"I think for the fire. Because the fire trucks came. With the bottles, somebody called the parents first. They came home, dragged him inside."

"And then he goes and does the fake robbery and gets himself shot," Brandon said.

"Very self-destructive," Maddie said. "Like he doesn't care about his life anymore."

"And some of it's directed at his parents."

They paused, Brandon in the dark, Maddie—

"Where are you?" he said.

"Dunkin' Donuts, Forest Ave. I figured I shouldn't be home. You know how they triangulate and can trace a cell phone location."

"I've seen it on TV," Brandon said.

Something swooped out from under the bridge. Bats. There was more scuffling in the weeds.

"And he told Amanda something," Brandon said. "What was bothering him. And your student there—"

"I don't know if they got into specifics. I think my guy just knew something was wrong," Maddie said.

"The grandmother, maybe he was really close to her. If the parents are useless, maybe she was his surrogate mom or something. Until she started to lose it."

"And she dies," Maddie said, "because the useless parents were careless about leaving medication around."

"Would you kill yourself for that?" Brandon said. "A sixteen-year-old boy?"

Maddie didn't answer. Brandon mulled it, too, and then they came to the same conclusion.

"I don't know. Adolescents don't always think straight," Maddie said. "But probably not."

"There was something more," Brandon said.

"Unless he was really nuts."

"Which nobody is saying he was."

"Until now," Maddie said.

Brandon sat in the darkness, the cars rattling overhead. The rustling had moved behind his truck. He had an uneasy feeling, waited for the reason to slowly emerge. It did: Loose lips.

"Maddie," he said. "These people who gave you all this dirt—don't you think they'll talk about you?"

"And say what?"

He heard car doors closing in the Dunkin' lot. A motor started. A horn beeped. There was a distant siren but he couldn't tell if it was nearby or over the phone.

"I don't know. I can hear it. 'This nice woman came to the door today. Some gay rights thing. We talked for a while. I told her all about everybody on the street. The Smiths. The Rawlingses. I told her about the boy, how he went crazy.'"

"You think that—"

"It'll get back to the Rawlingses."

"But they can't tie me to you. That's why we're doing it this way. The phones."

"Did you use your car?" Brandon asked.

"Yeah. Kat said I should rent one but that seemed a little over the top. I just parked at the end of the street."

A red Honda Civic, plate POETIC, as in license.

"Give them your name?"

"I just said I was Madeleine. I didn't want to lie."

Scruples. They come back to bite you, Brandon thought.

"How long were you out there?"

"A couple of hours."

"People coming and going on the street?"

"I suppose," Maddie said, the excitement draining from her voice.

Brandon pictured it. The first person calling a neighbor after Maddie had left. Telling the story. Word getting around the neighborhood, then getting back to Thatcher's parents, them hearing that their problems are being hung out there for some stranger. Driving down the road to see if they could get a look at this person. Driving to the end of the street and seeing Maddie's car. Getting her ID off the plate. A friend at DMV. A cop in another town....Saying, "Blake's partner. She's married to this lady. What the hell? What are the chances?"

Risky, Brandon thought. "Thanks for your help, Maddie," he said.

"You're not happy," Maddie said.

"No, I am. It's all good to know."

"I can go back tomorrow," she said. "There are a few houses I didn't hit."

"That's okay."

"I think the grandmother's dying that way sent him off the deep end."

"Grandparents die," Brandon said. "It happens."

His own grandmother, Nessa, dying of alcoholism, liver gone, kidney failure what finally took her. A messy combo. Deep down, Brandon was still grieving.

Maddie didn't answer for a moment, then said, "I hope this isn't a problem. Kat and I thought it was the best way to get a look at these folks."

"Did you go to their house?"

Maddie hesitated. "Yeah. I figured it would look odd if I skipped them. But nobody answered. If their cars were there, they were in the garage."

"See anything from the craziness?"

"Some broken glass in the driveway. Burnt stuff in a trash can."

"Huh. Listen, thanks for doing all of this."

"You can't just roll over for them, Brandon," Maddie said. "I mean, I know it's hard. Taking a life and all but..."

"Not so hard," Brandon said. "You just pull the trigger."

He rang off, put the burner phone down on the console. Opened the truck door, then reached over to get his phone from the passenger seat. He missed once, leaned in further.

A boom.

The windshield shattered.

TWENTY-ONE

Another shot, the windshield spidering, the back window above his head, glass falling on his neck and ear. Rifle shots, slugs that would go through the back of the cab like it was tin foil. He kicked the door open behind him, wriggled out and grabbed his Glock from under he seat on the way by. Scrambled to the front of the truck, crouched by the bumper.

His phone. Still in the truck. His radio on the seat.

He crouched, gun out. Waited. Too long a pause now. The shooter would be running, driving off, not risking a third. Or would he?

Brandon waited. Heard the jingling of the rigging. Cars still passing overhead. The rustling in the brush. He turned, gun leveled. Something moved. A rat, oblivious to the shots, not the target.

He turned back. Looked across the street and up, the steep embankment between Commercial and Brackett. Someone could have spotted the cruiser, circled around and taken the high ground. But they didn't shoot at the cruiser, at Kat and Park. They waited for a clean shot at the pickup. Took so long to set up that the cruiser was gone? Brandon didn't think so.

When he heard sirens, he darted around the truck, staying low. Stretched out on the floor of the truck, reached up for his phone or the radio. Felt the phone and pulled it down, slid back out. Crouched low

216

and made it to the front of the truck again. Called 911. More sirens as he waited.

"Portland Police Department. How can I—"

"Chooch. It's Brandon Blake. Commercial Street, shots fired."

"Yeah, we know. Units are—"

"Two shots through my truck. Under the bridge."

"You okay?"

"Fine."

"Where are you now?"

"Same place. Outside the truck. For cover."

"We're coming," Chooch said. "Stay on the line."

He pictured her keying the mic. "All units responding to West End. Target is under the bridge on Commercial. It's Blake. They missed. Active shooter."

Blue lights around his truck, passing on Commercial, spots and flashlights flickering through the yards on top of the hill. Kat and Park pulled in, saw for themselves that he was okay, drove away fast. Sergeant Perry set up a command post, his SUV. Detectives in unmarked cars, drug cops in pickups, cruisers blocking the road. Brandon at the center of it all, feeling waves of déjà vu. The night of the Rawlings shooting. Sitting in the back of the cruiser.

They were standing in the darkness, thirty feet from Brandon's truck. Looking up at the embankment. The shots had hit halfway up the back window, lower on the windshield. A downward trajectory, from top of the hill.

"You don't reach for your phone, you're gone," Perry said. "Dodged that fucking bullet."

"As they say," Brandon said.

Cops were canvassing the houses at the top of the hill. Brandon heard the call. Dever had a woman said she heard a noise in her side yard, then the shots. She went to call 911. Didn't see anyone.

O'Farrell arrived. The chief right behind him. O'Farrell gave Brandon a pat on the shoulder, said, "We'll get him." He coached youth hockey. Brandon felt like a goalie, just let one go through his legs.

The chief ignored Brandon and went to Perry. "Go," he said.

"Lady hears something in her yard, right up there."

Perry pointed to lights on a house at the top of the hill, to the left.

"Books it out of there with a long gun," Perry said. "Car running. Back into town or out onto the interstate. He had three, four minutes."

"Or he's still there," Garcia said. "Remember that Boston bomber asshole hiding in the boat. I want you to drive that neighborhood like you're driving deer."

Perry was back on the radio. Brandon could hear cops signing on: day shift, desk guys, old fat guys, everybody coming in. Garcia walked over to him, turned and looked up at the hill.

"You probably feel like a eunuch standing there, not being able to chase him."

Thanks, Brandon thought.

"Something like that," he said.

"Gotta get this motherfucker before he kills a cop," the chief said.

He said it like Brandon wasn't one. Brandon nodded.

"What were you doing down here, Blake?"

"Stopped and said hi to Kat and Park."

"Like, 'Hey, how you doing?'"

"Exactly. Hang in there and all that."

"How long were you here?"

"Five minutes. Maybe a little longer," Brandon said.

"Where were you coming from?"

"South Portland side," Brandon said.

"Could you have been followed?"

Brandon pictured the drive from Woodford, traffic heavy on Route 1.

"I suppose. I didn't notice anything but I wasn't trying to shake anybody, either."

Perry walked over and joined them. "Got 20 on Brackett," he said to the chief. The chief nodded without looking at him.

"Where were you coming from?" Garcia said to Brandon.

"The south."

The chief waited.

"Woodford," Brandon said.

"Family down there?"

"No."

"Where is your family?"

"I don't have any," Brandon said.

Garcia caught himself, like he vaguely remembered Brandon' story. Mother killed in some drug smuggling thing with a boat. Grew up with grandparents but they were dysfunctional. Smart kid but maybe not the best hire. Too much baggage. Thank O'Farrell for that.

"So who is in Woodford?" the chief said.

"Friends," Brandon lied.

"Then maybe you oughta stay there, Blake," Garcia said. "No offense, but around here, you're a fucking lightning rod."

Brandon didn't answer, fingered the burner phone in his pocket.

The pickup was hauled off on a ramp truck. Cops were still going door to door when Mia called.

"You okay?"

"Fine," Brandon said, then caught himself. The word she now hated. "I'm okay. But it's after 12:30. Shouldn't you be asleep."

"I can't sleep. And this is all over the news. People are calling. They got the texts."

"All's well that ends well."

"Where are you going to go?"

"I don't know. The boat, maybe."

"You could come—"

"No."

"You need a car, right?"

"I'll get a rental."

"You should keep swapping them," Mia said. "Like every day."

"Now you're thinking," Brandon said. "Make a cop out of you yet."

They paused, and then Mia said. "How much did they miss by?"

"A few inches."

"My god."

"An inch is as good as a mile."

"I think you should go far away," Mia said. "Like out of state. California or something."

"I can't leave. The shooting. They need me here."

"I need you alive."

"I know."

Another pause.

"What have you been doing?" Mia said.

Images of Danni swept in. Leaning close, her lips parted. *Just kiss me and we'll get this party started.*

"Not much. Trying to keep moving."

"Is Kat staying in touch?"

"Yeah. She's got my back."

"I do, too, you know," Mia said. "I'm with you. If you'll let me be."

"I know that. But you can't be, and that's hard."

"I barely sleep," she said. "I need to see you."

Another image of Danni. *We're in our own bubble.*

"Soon," Brandon said. "They'll catch this guy and things will start to get back to normal. Or at least closer."

"I hope so."

"I know so," Brandon said. "He can run, but he can't hide."

"What makes you so sure it's a he," Mia said.

Danni again.

"We need to talk," Brandon said. "I'll call in a while."

———

He got a ride to the airport from O'Farrell in his unmarked SUV. O'Farrell went inside the terminal and rented a dark gray Jetta from Enterprise, put it on his personal credit card. They drove over to the lot and Brandon followed O'Farrell, in the Jetta, out of the airport. In the parking lot of the Comfort Inn, they switched vehicles. O'Farrell got in the passenger seat of the VW as the SUV idled beside them.

"Don't crash it," he said. "I didn't get the insurance."

Brandon nodded and said, "Sorry about this shitstorm."

O'Farrell shrugged. "Not your fault, Blake. It's a domino effect. Kid does something stupid, gets himself shot. Community goes ballistic but that's a domino effect from all this other stuff around the country. Race gets entered into the equation but that's a domino effect from civil rights and everything else."

He put his hands on his knees, tried to stretch out his legs.

"We're just the tail on the dog here."

"I think Rawlings was committing suicide," Brandon said.

"Hard to know what was going on in the kid's head," O'Farrell said.

Hard, Brandon thought. But not impossible.

"Just keep your nose clean, Blake. Ride this out. Someday it'll be in the rearview mirror. You'll file it away. We all will."

Another image of Danni, desperate for the anniversary paper. File it away? Sometimes you can't.

O'Farrell gave him a pat on the shoulder, got out and slammed the door behind him. Brandon waited until the SUV swung around him, then counted to 30 and drove out of the airport exit road. At the first light, he eased deeper into the seat and pulled his hat down. Called Mia.

"Headed into town. Gonna leave the car in the garage at Monument Square. We can talk there."

Mia said, "Okay," and rang off. Brandon swung up onto 295, drove into the city. Low tide at the Fore River, a trough of water, a swirling pattern in the mud. He glanced over, then, when a pickup passed, looked straight ahead. The car was anonymous, invisible. He got off at Congress, drove up past the bus station, the hospital. Even trying not to look, he counted six guys with a history, at least two he knew had outstanding warrants. Brandon watched the road, drove the speed limit.

At the light at Longfellow Square, a panhandler moved down the line of cars with the sign that said, "HOMELESS VETERAN." Brandon looked more closely and knew him: a perv they'd busted for indecent exposure, never in the military for a minute. Sat in his car with his pants down across from an elementary school. Brandon put his hand over his face as the guy passed.

And then he was in the garage, drove up to the third floor and parked next to the exit. It was deserted and dark, the restaurant crowd already at their tables. Brandon called Mia, said, "Drive up to the fifth, then back down to the third. If it's clear, I'll step out."

He waited. In five minutes, Mia's Volvo SUV passed him, continued to the spiraling ramp and disappeared. Nothing passed. In five more minutes, she swung around the corner. Brandon stepped out from between the cars and Mia stopped. He got in and she started off. On the second floor, he pointed to an empty space and she pulled in.

"I think you should back in," he said, and Mia hesitated, then pulled back out and in again. They faced the traffic lane, the motor running.

Mia turned to him. Waited. He watched the mirrors, counted to ten, then turned and they embraced. Brandon could feel the Glock in his waistband.

"God, you look awful, Brandon," Mia said. "Have you been eating?"

"Sure," Brandon said, but couldn't remember his last real meal.

"You've got to take care of yourself. This is hard enough without—"

"It's okay. I'm—let's just not go there."

Mia cooled, just a degree or two.

"Okay," she said. "Where *do* you want to go?"

"Back in time. A week ago."

"If only," Mia said.

She fell back into the seat.

"Thanks for coming," Brandon said.

"Are they close to catching him?" she said.

"I don't know. You can't just go around the city shooting at cops and get away with it."

"But they are."

"Matter of time."

Mia looked at him, left him a chance to elaborate. He didn't. She said, "You're still shutting me out."

Brandon shrugged. "There's nothing to let you into. Nothing good."

She waited.

He looked straight ahead. A car swung around the corner and he squinted against the headlights. And then it was dark again and he took a deep breath, tried to muster a reply. "Maddie asked around. On the Rawlings' road. The guy's mother died, Thatcher's grandmother. OD'd in their house. Got into the medicine cabinet. They said she had dementia or something. The kid wigged out."

"Like how?

Brandon told her. The fire. The bottles. The scraped-up Mercedes.

"And then he got himself shot?" Mia said. "That's pretty serious grieving."

"Yeah."

"Maybe he was messed up already."

"But nobody's saying that."

"Nobody who?" Mia said.

"The neighbors Maddie talked to. His friend Amanda."

"What happens to Kat if it gets out her wife is asking questions about the family of a shooting victim?"

"He's not a victim," Brandon said. "He's a suspect who got shot. That's the line I'm supposed to follow."

"So what happens?"

"Nothing good."

"Did you tell her to stop?" Mia said.

"No," Brandon said.

"Aren't you afraid this will—"

"Drag Kat down with me? Yes."

Brandon was quiet. Mia looked away.

"Where have you been?"

"Around. Keeping moving."

"That's not an answer," she said.

"It's true."

"It's like saying you're fine."

Brandon looked down at the console of the car, fiddled with the shifter.

"What's in Woodford?" Mia said.

"What?"

"I know you were there. Your phone. You put Find My Phone on my laptop."

"So you've been tracking me?"

"I got worried."

"Still—"

"I have good reason," Mia said.

Brandon looked out of the window, didn't answer.

"So what's in Woodford?" Mia asked again.

"Danni," Brandon said. "But not her personally. I went to talk to a cop down there. There was a big murder on that date she wrote down. Two bikers got killed, a local guy with them. Shot in a gravel pit."

Mia watched him and waited.

"So what does that have to do with—"

"I don't know," Brandon said. "Maybe nothing. But this dead kid

Sash knew Clutch, her boyfriend. A guy in a bar told me that. And then I was walking down the street and Danni drives by."

"Ah," Mia said.

"Kind of a small town."

Mia looked out at the deserted garage, the concrete walls, a sign that said, "Compact cars only."

"Don't tell me. She hit on you this time."

A pause, Brandon trying to figure out how to answer.

"Yeah, and then when I turned her down she wigged out. She's desperate to get that paper."

"God, Brandon," Mia said. "Don't you have enough going on in your life?"

Brandon didn't answer and they sat in the darkness. A couple popped out of the door by the elevator, a man and woman their age. They were both weaving, holding each other up. They fell into a white Passat, the woman behind the wheel. She drove off without turning on her headlights. A good DWI stop.

"Maybe this was a bad idea," Brandon said.

He looked away, toward the railing of the garage. Thought of Amanda, over the railing and down. What did they call it? Collateral damage?

They sat in silence for another minute, squinted into the glare of a passing pickup, headlights aimed high. Brandon could hear her the raspy noise of Mia breathing through her nose.

"I'll go," Brandon said.

"To where?"

"The boat."

She looked at him.

"It's on a mooring," Brandon said. "It's like having a giant moat around you."

"I'll drive you."

He shook his head.

"I'll get an Uber."

Mia had her hands on the wheel, clenched tightly.

"I feel like when we say goodbye, I won't see you again," she said.

"I'll be fine," Brandon said, the words like a gate swinging shut.

She turned the key and started the motor, said, her voice stone cold, "I'll bring you to the street."

The Uber driver was at Monument Square in two minutes, pulling up in a white Corolla, a cheap lease. Brandon gave Mia's hand a squeeze. They didn't say goodbye.

The driver was a Somali guy. He was on the phone and didn't glance over when Brandon slid into the back seat behind him. The Uber destination was Sunset Grille, a waterfront restaurant up the road from the marina. The guy stared at the GPS, sped past the P.D, the backside. The lot was nearly empty, everybody out hunting the guy who'd taken the shot. Or not a guy at all.

Amanda Shakespeare's mom? Tiff Rawlings? Some unknown nutjob, drawn to the cause by the stories? *Rogue cop gets away with murder.* Like the commenters said, *Somebody should take him out.*

They were on the bridge. Brandon peered over the railing and out over the harbor. The marina lights were on, a string of solar on the float. The mooring field was dark except for dim cabin lights on the Rockaways' motorsailer, three moorings west of *Bay Witch*. Helene would sit in the salon and watch movies, DVDs from the public library. George would sit in the cockpit for hours and smoke his pipe, very nautical. People complained about the smell.

The driver dropped him in the restaurant parking lot, a couple of cars left, the late crew. Brandon walked toward the door until the Corolla was out of sight, then turned around and walked out of the lot and onto the street. The street was dark away from the restaurant sign. Brandon walked on the harbor side, in the shadows, close to a chain-link fence covered in vines. When he approached the marina gate, he stopped. The parking lot was beyond the gate, behind rusting metal boatsheds. A single bug-spattered street lamp illuminated the boatyard. The Coke machine glowed outside the office. The yard was still.

Brandon stepped into the vines and stopped and listened. He could hear crickets. Traffic on the bridge. A siren from across the harbor. The distant sound of a forklift working on the Portland side. And once he had filtered those sounds out, nothing. He counted to 30, then walked quickly to the gate, punched in the code, swung the gate open and closed. In a half crouch, he hurried across the yard and down the ramp to the float.

The tide was out and the ramp was steep. He grabbed the rail, then swung down and untied into his dinghy. Slipping the oars into the oarlocks, he feathered the boat backward, then swung hard and started to pull. He rowed steadily but under control, keeping the oars from rattling the oarlocks. The boat skimmed away from the floats and into the darkness. Brandon stayed wide of the other moorings, close by the stumps of a rotting pier. He smelled George Rockaway's pipe, heard him cough and clear his throat. And then *Bay Witch* was coming up and Brandon gave a last pull and coasted up to the starboard side. He circled the boat silently, stopped to sit and listen.

He heard barely audible slaps, the ripples from the oars flicking the wooden hull. The bilge pump kicked on and water ran, trickling into the bay. He eased up to the stern, grabbed the transom and the painter and swung aboard. Listened again. Tied the dinghy on, moved across the stern deck to the cabin door.

He opened it, went inside, and closed it behind him. Stepped down to the galley and bent to take a Budweiser out of the fridge. Moved up to the helm and opened the chart book. Danni's note was there, tucked between Casco and Muscongus bays. He read it again. Went down to the stateroom, and through to the ladder leading up to the bow hatch. Tucking the bottle into his jeans, he climbed up, unhooked the hatch and pushed it open. Then he climbed out onto the foredeck, the bow pointed toward the Portland skyline, into the northwest wind.

Brandon sat on the deck, his back against the windscreen. He thought of medieval people cast out of city gates. Hence, the word. Outcast. Why did he think he and Danni had so much in common? Outsiders, even when they were with someone.

He shrugged off the thought, let the conversations with Mia replay. *You're wallowing...* Yeah, well, she hadn't killed two people. Two messed-up kids, probably needed counseling, instead they got—

He opened the beer, took a long drink, closing his eyes as he swallowed. When he opened them nothing had changed. The sign on top of the Time & Temp building across the harbor said 1:43, 56 degrees. There was a siren somewhere, but just one. Not the shooter.

Brandon drank again, swallowed and said aloud, "She's right."

He put the bottle down on the deck. Tapped his phone on, the screen lighting the darkness.

He searched for an obit for Rawlings, Portland, Maine. There were several, or there used to be. Men, women, old and not so old. All named Rawlings, all dead. One was named Alexandra. She was 89. She died unexpectedly.

Alexandra Rawlings was formerly of Bryn Mawr, Pennsylvania. Her husband, Thatcher T. Rawlings, died in 2001. She was survived by one son, Crawford Rawlings, and his wife, Tiffany, of Moresby, Maine, and a grandson, Thatcher D. Rawlings. Readers were asked to make a gift in her memory to the Woodford Bowl Historical Society, c/o of P. Ainsley Wethersfield...

"Huh," Brandon said. "Small world, these rich people."

He looked up the number of Twin Oaks Residential Care Center. Then he took out the burner phone and called.

TWENTY-TWO

A woman answered.
   "Twin Oaks."

Brandon could hear the faint sound of a television show in the background. Voices then laughter.

"Hi. This is Dave Joseph, I'm a reporter at the Review. Do you have a sec? I just have a question for you."

There were voices, somebody saying, "They need you in 309. He's out of bed again."

"Oh, Jesus," the woman said, then back to the phone, "Listen, I gotta go."

And she was gone.

Brandon waited, a 20-count. He called back.

"Twin Oaks. This is Tammy."

He introduced himself again.

"Boy, you guys work late. You really should call during the day. Talk to Mrs. Martine. She's the supervisor."

"Oh, I know. But I always figure the people who work nights know what's really going on. Not off in some office, pushing paper. Listen, Tammy, it's just a quick question."

Tammy hesitated. The TV sound was turned down, not off. Brandon pictured a movie on her phone.

"What'd you say your name is?"

He repeated it.

"So what's the question?" Tammy said.

She said it like she thought she might win something.

"So it's just that we do this thing in the paper where we talk about older folks, pick one out and write about them, the contribution they've made in their life, that sort of thing," Brandon said. "It's a feel-good piece. Somebody suggested Alexandra Rawlings."

"Mrs. R? You're about three weeks too late."

"Oh, no," Brandon said.

"She passed away."

"Sorry to hear that."

"Yeah, well..." Tammy said, like she wasn't. "Happens around here."

"I'm sure."

"So would she have been a good one for the story?" Brandon said.

No reply. The boat rocked softly. Brandon tightened his grip on his beer.

"Just curious. You wonder when people call in."

Still nothing, and then Tammy said, "This off the page or whatever they call it?"

"Off the record? Sure. I mean, she's gone. Not like there's anything to write."

"Then I can tell you. Mrs. R, she was a tough one. Walk in there, get ready to get your head taken off."

"No kidding."

"Yeah, I don't know what you would've wrote. I was scared of her. Everybody was. We called her 'the queen.'"

"Huh."

"Yeah. She lived on VIP, that's what we call the wing for the old folks with money. Two-room suites, big flat screens. Nice view of the woods and the shrubbery. They even get their own bird feeder."

"Sounds expensive."

"They got cash. Mrs. R., they said she had like millions," Tammy said.

"So Mrs. Rawlings was rich?"

"You have to be for VIP."

"Her family come to visit?"

"The son and his wife. Sometimes their kid. He was in high school."

"That's nice," Brandon said.

"Not really. You read about the kid got shot by the cop? Had a BB gun or something? That was this kid. Cops blew him away."

"Whoa."

"I know, right."

Brandon swallowed, said, "At least she didn't live to see that."

"Mrs. R, yeah, she would've freaked. She liked the grandson. They'd chat, the parents would be trying to leave, grabbing the kid by the arm. She didn't like the parents. Can't say I blamed her."

"That right?" Brandon said.

"Oh, yeah. It happens more than you think. People come in to visit their so-called loved one. Once a month. Stay for five minutes. You can tell they can't wait to get the heck out."

"The Rawlings folks were like that?"

"Oh yeah. When they were here, the dad and Mrs. R—they argued like you wouldn't believe."

"Really. About what?"

"Money, what else? This place is like a money hole."

"And that's money that isn't going to be in the inheritance," Brandon said.

"You said it, I didn't. You know nobody's even picked up her clothes and stuff? I'll email the guy again tonight. You know, if you don't want it, we give it away."

The TV show got slightly louder. Even buzzed, Tammy was losing interest.

"Anyway," she said. "This is my last night. I'm going to Pleasant View. Got a day job, seven to four. Two of the girls here, we went out for a goodbye margarita."

The chattiness.

"Six a.m., I'm out the door."

"Good for you," Brandon said.

"Nights do a number on your body. Plus, I'm on match.com. You tell a guy you work nights, end of conversation."

"I'm sure. Hey, listen, so how was Mrs. R before she passed. Pretty out of it?"

"Mrs. R? You kidding? That lady was sharp. Five minutes late with her tea, you'd catch hell. She called me 'Girl,' like I didn't have a name. 'Girl, I pay good money for service here. I could have you fired.'"

"So not just vegging out?"

"Heck no. Smart as hell. Read like a book a day. But wicked mean."

"How'd she die?"

The TV show got still louder.

"Went to visit her son. OD'd is what I heard. They said she took something out of the medicine cabinet or something. I'm like, 'Mrs. R? You sure?' She watched her pills like a hawk. Counted 'em a couple of times a day. She thought we were gonna steal her meds, sell 'em on the street."

There were voices in the background, the first woman who'd answered the phone. The TV sound cut off.

"Hey, I gotta run," Tammy said.

"So you don't think that she would—"

But Tammy was gone.

―――――――

Brandon sat on the deck, took a drink. The Time & Temp sign said 1:42 a.m., 53 degrees. He looked at the phone, tapped out a text. Put the phone down and waited. It rang.

"Yes," Maddie said, like it was the red phone at the White House.

"Did I wake you?"

"No. Breaking Bad, Season Six. We're bingeing."

"Kat doesn't get enough of that at work?"

"She's indulging the English professor."

"She right there?"

"In the other room," Maddie said. "Plausible deniability and all that."

"Right. Listen, I just wanted to let you know. I called the nursing home. The one where Mrs. Rawlings was."

A gull passed over in the darkness. Brandon had a flicker of a thought, that it was the Mrs. R's soul, on its way to wherever. Maddie didn't reply so Brandon kept going. Recounted the conversation with Tammy.

"She was chatty," Maddie said.

"A little drunk. And her last night," Brandon said.

"So let's just say the son was seeing his inheritance slip away."

Maddie, true detective.

"At twenty K a month."

"Would you kill your own mother for a million dollars?" Maddie said.

"If you hated her to begin with? Why not?"

Silence, Maddie thinking.

"If he's a narcissist," she said, "a personality disorder, he could rationalize it. Hey, she had a long life. Just laying around in bed, money wasted on years of a vegetative state."

"Except she was sharp, the woman said."

"He could rationalize that, too. Narcissists shape the world around them to fit their needs."

"Mom, time for your medicine," Brandon said.

"A couple of Oxycodones in the Manhattan. A couple more as she's starting to wobble."

"Then stir up some opiate paste, wash it down with water."

"And she's gone," Maddie said.

"Problem solved," Brandon said.

"Assuming he was the beneficiary."

"He was her only survivor, according to the obituary."

"Could have left it to the local food pantry or the animal shelter. Except—"

"Except what?" Brandon said.

"Except, maybe I forgot to tell you this. One of the neighbors said he seemed all cheerful after she was gone. She stops the car, he's getting the paper out of the box at the curb. She gives her condolences, he just smiles, says, 'It was time.'"

Brandon looked out at the skyline, felt the boat rocking from something unseen. A wake? A wave? The ghost of Mrs. R? Thatcher Rawlings? Amanda Shakespeare?

"And then Thatcher goes and gets himself killed," he said. "And spoils the party."

"Wills are public once they're filed in probate court," Maddie said. "I could..."

"You could," Brandon said.

"But you don't know that."

"No."

"We'll talk soon," Maddie said.

"Be discreet," Brandon said. "Like, go in and ask for five or six. Say you're from a law firm."

"I got it. Obfuscation. Like in Graham Greene. *The American.*"

"Because this is a pretty dangerous thing here, for Kat especially. I don't want to take her down with me."

"Nobody's going down," Maddie said. "It's all good."

But it wasn't. That much Brandon absolutely knew.

He sat and drank the beer, the boat swaying, a salty night-dew coming off the water. The wind shifted and *Bay Witch* swung and pointed at the bridge, its lights veiled by the almost imperceptible mist. An occasional car crossed, headlights fading to taillights, then darkness. The boat was making a gentle arc, with each swing turning a few degrees farther south. As Brandon sipped the beer, the moored boats came into view, then the end of the floats, boats tucked in their slips.

He was thinking about Maddie, the scandal that would erupt if she were found out. A court clerk who'd been in one of her classes. A former student in Probate to register an adoption. It was a gantlet Maddie was running, three careers on the line. Estusa would go crazy, more evidence of a giant police conspiracy, all of them trying to pin the blame on the victim. Brandon would be—

Someone moved on the float. A dark figure near his empty slip.

It disappeared behind the hulls, then showed again. The person was moving, stopping, moving again. Not walking to a boat.

Brandon leaned forward, turning as *Bay Witch* swung toward the bridge, then back. The person had reached the top of the T of floats, was moving right, closer. Brandon saw legs in the dim dock lights, then the figure at the end of the float. It stopped.

Arms came up.

A spotlight blazed.

Brandon dove to the deck.

A slug hummed close by his head. A rifle boomed.

He rolled, almost went overboard, one leg dangling. The light was out and he could hear footsteps, running on the float. The shot had come from the bridge side. He moved along the starboard side of the cabin in a crouch, flung himself onto the stern deck.

Another shot, a smack against the port hull. Then another. Brandon crawled to the hatch, down into the salon. He rolled to the far side, away from the shooter, protected by the thin plywood hull.

He thought of getting the hatch up, hiding in the bilge behind the engine.

But the next shot didn't come. Lying on his back, he dug his phone out. Tapped 911. The calm voice of the dispatcher, a woman, not Chooch.

"This is Brandon Blake. Somebody just took three shots at my boat." A millisecond to process. Who he was. Why someone would want to shoot him.

"Are you hit?"

"No."

"Are you on the boat?"

"Yes."

"Could you tell the direction of fire?"

"A rifle. I think toward the bridge. South Portland side. It was two people. Someone lit me up with a spotlight for the shooter. The spot was on the float at the marina. It's just up from the—"

"I know where you are," the dispatcher said.

Cops were on the float. Cruisers were on and under the bridge. The South Portland P.D. launch was drawn up alongside *Bay Witch*, strobes flashing, spotlights trained on the stern deck. An inflatable launch from the Coast Guard station was standing by fifty yards out.

There were two bullet holes in the plywood above the deck on the starboard side. Exit holes to port, slightly lower. The slugs had passed over Brandon as he crawled.

An evidence tech named Whalen was measuring the distance from the holes to the stern deck.

"Was the boat rocking?" she said.

"No," Brandon said.

"A couple of centimeters lower on the exit side."

"So he was shooting down," a SoPo detective said. His name was Rothstein. Like the rest of the cops, he was wearing a life jacket.

Everyone looked toward the bridge, the buttresses and supports. There were cruisers there, blue lights flashing. Another night, another set of cops.

"Climbed up?" Brandon said.

"Ballistics will be able to get some idea," Whalen said. "Ten feet? Fifteen?"

"In position when the light went on."

"And you just saw somebody in black?" Rothstein said. "Big? Small? Woman? Man?"

Brandon shrugged. "It was dark. They were behind the boats most of the time."

"Who knew your boat was on the buoy? Not on the dock, I mean."

"Anyone who knew where my slip was would know the boat was gone. You'd have to know the boat to spot it out here."

"Who knows your boat?" Rothstein said.

Brandon thought of Estusa's reporting, the photos, video.

"Anyone with a pulse," he said.

"Did you sail it in?"

"I came by Uber. Walked over from the restaurant. Rowed out."

He nodded toward the lights.

"What time?"

"One-thirty. Around then."

"So anybody who saw you walk in, get in the rowboat, they'd know which boat."

"Yes."

"Why didn't they shoot at you on land then?"

"I don't know," Brandon said.

"Seems like it would have been a lot easier. The spotlight and all that."

"It's been a sniper set up. Not somebody walking up and shooting point-blank."

"Easier getaway for a sniper," Rothstein said.

"Evidently," Brandon said.

TWENTY-THREE

The Portland police stood on the float until the South Portland launch came over and ferried them out. Bay Witch was low in the water, from the weight of cops. Kat and O'Farrell stood in the stern and eyed the bullet holes.

"This thing isn't gonna sink or anything, is it?" Kat said.

"No," Brandon said. "Way above the waterline. I'll fill them with silicone putty."

"How close was the first shot?" O'Farrell said.

"I don't know," Brandon said. "I could feel it first. Then I heard it. Hard for me to tell how close. I've never been in combat or anything."

"This is combat," O'Farrell said. "If you could feel it, I'd say within a foot of your head."

"The spotlight. That changes things," Rothstein said.

Nods all around.

"Not just one loner nut job," Kat said. "Coordinated and planned."

"Like an insurgency," O"Farrell said.

Kat turned to Rothstein, said, "He was in Iraq."

"Terrorists," Rothstein said.

They turned and looked toward the bridge, lights strung across the harbor. Envisioned the shot coming out of the darkness. Their eyes moved to the blackness of the shoreline. Nobody said anything but they knew. It wasn't a question of whether the shooter would try again. It was when.

O'Farrell looked at Brandon and said, "Theories, Blake?"

"You kill somebody's kid, the rules change," Brandon said.

"You shoot at cops, that changes the rules, too," O'Farrell said.

Kat said he couldn't stay there, not on the boat, not that night. It was an order, not a suggestion, and Brandon said, "I can go to a hotel."

"Negatory," Kat said. "Maddie's on her way."

She was, waiting at the marina gate when Kat and Brandon came off *Bay Witch* in the dinghy, tied it off in the slip, and made their way up the float. The yard was dark, the few operating lights dim and feeble. Maddie was in black, jeans and a fleece that, when Brandon opened the gate, he could see had USM on the chest. She reached for his shoulder like Kat was handing him off, then turned and pointed to the left, where her car was parked.

"Get some sleep," Kat said, and went right, toward her cruiser, parked next to the S.P. cars, O'Farrell's unmarked SUV. Maddie said, "Let's go," and they walked along the vine-covered fence.

And something moved to their left.

Brandon spun, crouched, pulled his gun from his waistband. A white light came on and a voice said, "Jesus, Blake. Is that always your first reaction?"

"Show yourself," Brandon said, and the light moved left, Estusa stepping from the shadows, his phone in his outstretched hand.

"Still carrying a gun, Officer Blake," he said. "Some cops would swear never to hold a gun again, after killing an unarmed teenager."

Maddie grabbed Brandon by the upper arm, his left, not his gun hand. She said, "Let's go, Brandon."

Estusa was moving closer, the camera panning from Brandon to Maddie. Estusa said, "Hello, Professor. Good of you to get up in the middle of the night to help out your friend."

He swung the phone back to Brandon.

"What happened out there, Officer Blake? Someone take a shot at you? What's it feel like to have some incoming? I imagine it's different from looking down the barrel. Have you ever been shot at before? I know you've had many physical altercations as a police officer. And the Rawlings fatal shooting, the fatal shooting of Joel Fuller, just missing Ms. Erickson. But how does it feel to be—"

Estusa broke off as Brandon set himself to swing at him, take Estusa's head right off his shoulders, break teeth, face, bones. But Maddie yanked him backwards, staggered, righted herself and grabbed his shoulder again, saying, "He's not worth it, Brandon."

She was pulling him away, Estusa following with the camera still rolling, saying, "When is it worth it to take a life, Officer Blake? How do you make that decision to pull the trigger? Why was Thatcher Rawlings worth shooting but I'm not? Have you learned something from this experience? If you could do it again..."

They were at the car, the red Honda. Estusa was still shooting video, the laser-white light glowing like an alien eye. Maddie slammed the car in gear and lurched past him, Estusa leaning down to get video of Brandon in the passenger seat.

Maddie snaked her way through the neighborhood of dark houses, a few lights showing. They were on Broadway when Maddie said, "What a vile creature."

Brandon didn't comment.

"I mean, to goad you like that. What would his editor say? Oh, I suppose he's his own editor. That's the problem. No checks. Somebody like that needs a grown-up reining him in. What sort of journalist is that?"

"He knew who you were," Brandon said.

Maddie drove through the lights, headed for the bridge.

"He called me—"

"Professor."

"So he must know I teach there. But do you think he knows?"

"Why else would we be together?" Brandon said.

"You can't hide everything," Maddie said.

"He saw the car, the license plate."

They were up on the bridge, both looking right out at the harbor. The police launch was still by *Bay Witch*, lighting the boat for the crime-scene crew. Brandon figured they'd be winding down. Maybe they'd tow the boat, could park it with his truck.

He turned away from the water, looked straight ahead.

"I'd jump up on the interstate," he said. "I'll watch behind us."

Maddie got on the highway at Forest Avenue, drove north to Falmouth, then backtracked through Deering. Nobody followed, and it was almost 4 a.m. when they pulled into the driveway of the house on William Street.

"What shift is Kat working?" Brandon said.

"All of them, I think," Maddie said. "I barely see her."

Brandon reached up and turned off the dome light. He got out and walked up the driveway along the house and into the backyard. There was a carriage house at the head of the driveway, a picket fence around the backyard. Brandon stood at the gate and listened and looked, gun at his side, finger on the trigger. The yard was quiet behind the chirping of crickets. And then rustling in the leaves in the garden.

He swung around, raised the gun. The rustling continued. Mice. Maybe voles.

Brandon walked to the back door, tried it. It was locked. He walked back down the driveway, past Maddie, wide-eyed in the car. He crossed the front lawn slowly, peering into the shrubs. Nothing, no one showed. He walked up the front steps and tried that door, too. It was locked.

He stepped back down, started to circle the house. There was a nightlight on in a room in the house next door. A bathroom. He walked to the rear of the house, found nothing. Retraced his steps to the car and said to Maddie, "All clear."

She got out, the lights still off. Brandon followed and she unlocked the back door and let them in. Turned on a small lamp on the kitchen counter and said, "You must be exhausted."

"I'm fine," Brandon said. "How 'bout you?"

"I'm good. There's a comforter on the end of the couch in the guest room."

"Thanks. I'll leave the door open."

"We should sleep," Maddie said.

"Yes."

"You know what Hemingway said. 'I love sleep. My life has—'"

She stopped herself.

"Has what?" Brandon said.

"Oh, nothing."

"It had to be something."

"Well, he said, 'I love sleep. My life has the tendency to fall apart when I'm awake.'"

Brandon smiled. "I know the feeling," he said.

Maddie gave him a pat on the shoulder, and then walked down the hall and up the stairs. Brandon opened the cupboard and got a glass and filled it with water at the sink. There was a photo on the counter, Maddie and Kat on the coast, arm in arm with the ocean sparkling behind them. They were smiling. Thoroughly happy. It seemed like it was from a different time, like nothing he'd seen lately. Not he and Mia, Brandon keeping her at arm's length. Not Danni and Clutch, holding each other in some weird captivity. Not the Rawlingses, calculating even in their loss.

They were the same, somehow. Kept together, it seemed, more by collusion than affection.

Brandon walked to the guest room, left the door open and the room dark. He sat down on the couch and put his gun on the cushion beside him. He took off his trainers and arranged them neatly. Leaned back and reached the comforter down and shook it loose. Still sitting, he pulled the comforter over him. Reached over and felt the gun.

He stared into the shadows, listened to the ticks and creaks of the house. What was it Estusa had said? Some people would never pick up a gun again? As if he had that luxury. He kept his hand on the butt as he stared into the shadows of the house. Live by the gun, die by the gun, he thought. Sometimes he thought he'd died by the gun already. As he drifted off to sleep, the Glock slid down the cushion and lodged against his thigh.

A hand on his shoulder. Brandon felt for the gun, heard a voice saying, "Easy. Easy, Blake. It's me."

Kat was bent over him, still in her uniform. His fingers found the Glock. Kat reached down and pushed it aside.

"I'm one of the good guys," she said.

"You catch 'em?"

"No. Everybody's pushing it but nothing. Figure they're local. Take a snap shot, slip back into the woodwork."

"With a thirty-ought," Brandon said.

"And a scope. And a handheld floodlight."

"I had an idea," Kat said, sitting down on the side of the couch. Brandon had a glimmer of déjà vu, his grandmother sitting down on the edge of his bed to say good night. She always reeked of alcohol.

"What if they didn't shoot from land? What if they shot from a boat?"

"There were no boats moving."

"What if it wasn't moving. What if it was anchored there."

"Moored," Brandon said. "Nobody was anchored."

"Alright. Whatever you call it. But the boat was stopped. They take a couple of shots, go down the hatch or whatever. We go beating the bushes while they're sitting in the bilge."

"Nobody at the marina would do that."

"How many of those boats are unoccupied at night?" Kat said.

"Almost all."

"Row up or whatever. Sit there and wait for Brandon Blake to get back to his cabin cruiser. He sits out on the deck. A nice target."

Brandon considered it.

"He'd have to be higher than your boat," Kat said.

"That narrows it down. Did you tell Perry?"

"I just thought of it as I was pulling into the driveway."

"They'd be gone by now," Brandon said. "Wait until everybody had left, slip away the way they arrived."

"Might leave some residue."

"Only two boats in that direction with higher vantage points. *Coyote*, she's a Parker with a tuna tower. And *Magellan*, that's a Silverton with a sedan bridge."

"Who owns them?"

"Rich people," Brandon said. "They generally like cops."

"They likely to be aboard last night?"

"No. Haven't seen them in weeks."

Brandon pulled himself up and they sat side by side. Brandon tucked the barrel of the Glock into the crack between the cushions. His stocking feet were next to Kat's black tactical boots. It seemed fitting—Kat still on the street, Brandon on the shelf.

"Maddie," he said. "That was a gamble."

"I thought it was just an idea," Kat said. "Then she comes home and says she's already been out there."

"Jesus."

"She wanted to help you."

"Yeah, well. Estusa saw her tonight. He knows who she is."

"Does he know we're married?" Kat said.

"I don't know. If he doesn't now, he will very soon."

Brandon reached for his running shoes.

"Where you going?"

"Out of here. I'm dragging us all down."

"'Us all.' You got that part right," Kat said. "We're in this together."

"I don't think so."

He laced the second shoe and stood, reached for his phone, his gun.

"Stay here. Hunker down. I've got lots of history books. Drink coffee and ride this goddamn thing out."

"I can do that by myself," Brandon said.

He took his flannel shirt from the end of the couch, put it and started buttoning it.

"So where are you going?"

"Doesn't matter."

"Who's this woman in Woodford?"

Brandon turned to her.

"Who told you about her?"

"Mia," Kat said. "She's afraid you're leaving her for some barfly, all part of flushing your life down the toilet."

"She's got that all wrong. I'm not leaving her."

"You're leaving all of us, Blake."

"Chief said it. I'm a lightning rod. Stand near me, you could get hurt."

"Stay."

"I need to move my boat. Next thing somebody will torch it."

"Only if you're on it, for god's sake," Kat said.

"I'll be a moving target," Brandon said. "And I'll look at those boats while I'm there."

"I don't like this."

"Yeah, well, nobody does."

She shook her head, then said, "The Rawlingses are having a press conference today. Monument Square."

"About what?"

"I don't know. Lawyer's been tweeting it, says it will be a major revelation in the case."

"Huh."

"It's going to be livestreamed on Facebook."

"What time?"

"Nine. We're supposed to stay in the background."

"Big crowd expected?"

"Social media and all that. The thing's taking off."

"Estusa must be coaching them," Brandon said.

"Team asshole," Kat said.

Brandon stood up.

"I still think you should stay, partner."

Brandon smiled, leaned down and gave her shoulder a squeeze. With his other hand he slipped the Glock out of the cushions, put it in the waistband of his jeans, at the back, slightly to the right.

"Stay safe," Kat said.

"Keep Maddie home," he said, and he was out the door, down the driveway.

TWENTY-FOUR

It was half-dark, shadows emerging from the gloom. He walked up the street, hit the Uber app. Only one driver close, but he was on Forest. Two minutes.

Brandon crossed the street to get out of the wash of a streetlight. He stood, stamped his feet, rubbed his unbrushed teeth with his tongue. The street was deserted, then it wasn't. A guy walking on the opposite side, a block down. Hoodie, hands in his pockets. He crossed, continued toward Brandon, hands still in his pockets.

Fifty feet away, he looked up, glanced at Brandon, held his gaze. The guy was white, in his 20s, tall and thin, a goatee. Timberlands and jeans and the black sweatshirt. His hands were moving in his pockets now, then he slipped his right hand out and reached behind him. Brandon did the same, slipping his right hand up under his shirt, gripping the Glock in his waistband.

Thirty feet, the guy's hand still behind him.

Twenty feet, the guy fiddling with something.

Fifteen feet, the guy's eyes locked onto Brandon's. His arm started to lift, the elbow coming up. Brandon turned, drew his gun, leveled it in two hands.

"Police," he said. "Turn around and show me your hands."

The guy was frozen, eyes fixed on the barrel of Brandon's gun. A

244

light went on, second floor of a house across the street. The guy still hadn't moved. Brandon trotted toward him, gun still leveled. When the guy started to bring his right arm out, Brandon lunged, locked the guy's arm up, spun him around.

There was something black in his right hand.

A phone.

"Jesus Christ," Brandon said. "Didn't you hear me?"

He patted the guy down, shoved him away. The guy stumbled, righted himself and turned back. The phone was up. He held it in two hands, shooting video.

"Random meeting with the famous Brandon Blake, Portland, Maine," he said. "In this case, Officer Blake did not pull the trigger. Thanks, Officer Blake. This is Trad Jones, for realportland.com"

Brandon turned his face away, stepped into the street as a car approached and slowed. A Prius. It stopped, the bearded Uber driver fiddling with his phone. Brandon got in, said, "Parking garage, Monument." The realportland guy was standing alongside, still shooting video.

That one would go viral, him with his gun drawn. He was being crucified in the court of social media, a gun-pulling nut-job cop. Never mind that somebody had taken shots at him twice in a period of hours. The mayor, the chief—they'd have to throw him to the crowd, give them at least that bone. Even if the shooting was justified, they'd fire him for the body cam, then let the civil stuff run its course.

"Shit," Brandon said. "Shit, shit, shit."

The garage was deserted, the VW where he'd left it. Brandon got in, put his gun on the passenger seat, then spiraled down and out onto Congress. A couple of people were picking through trash cans, a woman jogging before work, her headlamp bobbing. He went left, passed an oncoming cruiser but turned his head and didn't see the cops. He drove out to the bridge, looked out on the lights of the harbor. Would Estusa have someone posted there, too? That son of a bitch.

Brandon thought of the marina shooter, the trajectory. Tuna tower? Too high. The bridge of the Silverton? Maybe. He was at Mill Creek

Park, four people on road bikes, strobe lights blipping, a woman walking a big white dog and a small dark one. Life going on as usual. Surreal.

Brandon passed the park, the church, took a left and drove down to the water. The Coast Guard Station was lit up, lights on in the kitchens of the houses. But the marina was dark, the light over the yard sputtering. He slowed as he approached, looked left into the parking lot.

Three cars and two pickups. Nobody showing. He turned around at the restaurant and drove back, pulled into the lot and made a slow loop. He recognized four of the vehicles as belonging to boat owners; the fifth, a new Nissan with New York plates, looked like a rental. Brandon backed into the far corner of the lot, facing out. He shut the car off and sat in the gloom and watched. Waited. A truck passed on the street, headed into town. Then a car, and another, people going to work.

He watched the marina yard, but nothing moved. After 10 minutes the sky to the east was turning a pale gray and he made sure the dome light was switched off, then got out. He paused and scanned the lot. Walked five steps then sprinted for the gate, punched in the code and slipped through.

As he crossed the yard he heard a young woman's voice behind him: "Hey, Brandon. Brandon, it's me, Cindy."

He didn't know a Cindy. He did know that he'd just slipped past one of Estusa's cell phone sentries. "Fuck off," he mouthed.

And then he was trotting down the ramp, onto the float. At his slip, he untied the dinghy, stepped in, and dropped the oars into place. He turned the boat toward the harbor, his back to the woman with the phone, and started rowing. He could hear her talking, reporting in, presumably. He was past the floats, slipping silently through the moored boats.

He veered to port, wound past a couple of sailboats, approached the Parker. Drifting toward it, he looked at the tuna tower, then back at *Bay Witch*. If the shooter had been on the tower, he would have been too high. The bridge? Maybe.

Beyond the Parker was the Silverton with the sedan bridge. A big superstructure, plenty of cover. Brandon looked back, thought the trajectory would have been about right if the shooter had been prone on the foredeck. He spun the dinghy around and started rowing for his boat.

Bay Witch looked undisturbed, except for the wad of yellow crime-scene tape on the transom. Brandon slipped alongside, tied the dinghy off and stepped aboard. He hurried below, took the key from its place at the top of the map cabinet. Moved quickly up to the helm and hit the blower. Looked back at the marina once, and saw nothing moving, Cindy gone after missing her chance for viral stardom. He started the motor and it coughed and sputtered, then settled into an easy gurgling rumble.

Brandon slipped down and onto the sidedeck on the harbor side, moved forward and uncleated the mooring line and tossed it over. He hurried back to the helm, slipped the boat into gear and swung out, bow toward the gray of the harbor opening. He wanted to be out of sight of the marina as fast as possible, and he slipped along the South Portland shoreline, running lights still off.

He passed the Sunset Grille, the Saltwater marina alongside it, a lighter barge on the pier at the oil tanks. Then, still running without lights, he swung out and started across the harbor. As he approached the channel, he hit the lights and the bow was illuminated in red and green. It was a straight shot across to Custom House Wharf and the doctor's empty berth. He motored slowly, six knots, an outgoing island ferry passing to starboard. When he slipped between the wharves, the bait shack was lit up, a lobster boat idling as the crew loaded barrels aboard. No one paid him any mind as he eased the cruiser in, jumped onto the float and tied the boat off, stern first, then the bow. There was a big sail-boat, *Castaway*, from Marblehead, on the harbor side of *Bay Witch*, a Grady White cuddy cabin tucked just ahead. He glanced up at the condos above him, saw a guy on the third floor leaning on the rail of his veranda and smoking.

From above, the name *Bay Witch* wasn't visible. From above, Brandon was just another guy on a boat.

He jumped back aboard and went below, sat at the table with his phone. He flicked through his Twitter feed until he hit Estusa's morning news: the press conference.

big news in the #brandonblakeshooting case. Livestream 9am. Conspiracy to obstruct justice? #kidslivesmatter #justicenow

Stay tuned. Parents of executed teen thatcher rawlings speak out...

And then a new tweet:

Crazed cop pulls gun on reporter. Assault charges filed against brandonblake, will cops act? #brandonblakeshooting, video @ more realportland.com

"Reporter?" Brandon said. "It was a set up. The son of a bitch was bait, for god's sake."

He went to Estusa's website, saw the giant photo on the home page. He had his gun at his side, was caught in mid-snarl, the beard making him look like somebody who'd just been flushed from a cave. He clicked on the arrow, heard that asshole's voice. "Random meeting with the famous Brandon Blake, Portland, Maine, In this case, Officer Blake did not pull the trigger. Thanks, Officer Blake. This is Trad Jones, for real-portland.com

Brandon saw himself sliding the gun into his jeans, getting into the car, the car pulling away. The video ended. Under the window was text:

Renegade Portland cop Brandon Blake was loose on the streets early Sunday morning, pulling a gun on realportland.com reporter Trad Jones as Jones approached him on a residential street near the USM campus. Blake pointed the gun at Jones as he reached for his ID and his phone.

"Somebody took a shot at me, for god's sake," Brandon said. "Twice."

The Portland cop, under investigation in the shooting death of 16-year-old Thatcher Rawlings, grabbed Jones and bent his arm back, injuring the reporter. He then shoved Jones, causing him to twist his knee and ankle. A complaint has been filed with Portland PD.

All of this begs the question: Blake is on administrative leave for the duration of the Rawlings fatality probe. Why is this out-of-control and heavily armed rogue cop still roaming Portland's streets? A spokesperson for the police department declined comment. More to come as this story unfolds.

In six minutes, the story had been shared 49 times. Make that 51. There already were 43 comments. Brandon clicked and started to read, got as far as, *The Bible says eye for an eye and tooth for a tooth. Then why is killer cop Blake alive and well, while Thatcher Rawlings is dead? Blake should be—*

Brandon clicked the screen off. "You're being used," he said. "You're click bait."

It was time to bite back.

He got up from the table, walked to the stern and looked out. Traffic was moving on Commercial Street. The lobster boat put out from the bait-shack wharf and idled out toward the harbor. The sternman, a young guy with shorn hair and a beard, looked back at Brandon and stared. The video? Brandon went back inside, went forward and peeled off his clothes. He went to the head and brushed his teeth. Took the electric shaver off the shelf and started on the beard. He was half done when the shaver ran out of juice so he finished with a razor and cold water. Wiping his face, he went to the bureau under the berth, pulled out a gray plaid flannel shirt and jeans. He put them on, then hiking boots and a black hat that said Yanmar Diesels. Back down to the salon, he got sunglasses out of the writing desk, Oakley wraparounds. And his gun.

Brandon zigzagged his way through the Old Port. The streets were quiet, the restaurants closed, trucks unloading in the alleys. On the sidewalks people were hurrying to work, heads down, worrying about being late. Brandon kept his head down, too, the hat pulled low.

On Free Street, he went into the parking garage, crossed to the stairs, and started up. A young woman—pumps, suit, blonde—was coming down and she looked away, not because he was Brandon Blake, but because he was a guy. He was alone when he pushed through the door to the third floor, walked a few cars up, moved to the railing and looked out.

The crowd was gathering, maybe a hundred people standing in clumps, most of them clutching coffee cups. There were uniform cops across the street by the library, presumably plainclothes well to the rear of the crowd. TV crews were standing by tripods, the cameras aimed at a clutch of people huddled by a concrete bench. Brandon slipped the binoculars out and peered down. Tiff and Crawford Rawlings were standing with Kelly, his white mane of hair showing. Estusa was with them, too, the four of them talking intently. Going over the action plan. Standing in a semi-circle around them where five teen-age guys in jeans, black T-shirts with Rawlings' image on the front, and black armbands.

The Rawlingses were dressed in black, too—jacket and Thatcher T-shirt for him, jacket and Thatcher T-shirt for her, Thatcher's face peeking out. When the conversation paused they both looked at their phones. Checking the Facebook numbers? Retweets? Reading texts of support?

There was a small PA system: a box speaker and a handheld microphone. Trad Jones, now on crutches, was fiddling with the knobs on the speaker. He said, "Test, one, two." The crowd moved closer.

And Brandon's phone buzzed.

A call, not a text. He fished the phone out, didn't recognize the number. It went to voice mail. Brandon put the phone back in his pocket, looked out at the rally. The phone rang again. He scowled, took it out. Hesitated and tapped. Said, "Yeah?"

"Is this Brandon Blake? Brandon Blake the police officer?"

A guy's voice. Young.

"What?" Brandon said.

"Hey, Brandon. Listen, dude. We need to talk."

"Who's this?"

"Just somebody. Somebody who's got something you need."

"What's that?"

"It's a thirty-two gig memory card. Last will and testament, man. The kid you shot."

TWENTY-FIVE

Brandon stepped back from the rail, pressed the phone to his ear.
"The GoPro?" he said.

"You got it. The dude, Rawlings. Living color. Well, he was then."

"The robbery?"

"Yeah, but the real juicy shit is before that."

"Like what?" Brandon said, tense, trying to sound calm.

"Like some pretty weird shit," the guy said. "This dude's parents were messed up. Kid needed a freakin' shrink."

Brandon swallowed.

"How can I see this?" he said.

There was rattling in the background, the distant beeping of a truck backing up.

"Well, here's the thing, Brandon," the guy said. "I, like, try to do the right thing in my life, you know? Be chill, not screw people over."

He paused, like he expected a reply.

"Right," Brandon said.

"So that's why I'm not on the phone to those people and their lawyer. I mean, they would pay serious dinero for this thing. I'm like, call the cop. Don't get greedy."

"Okay."

"So this is mega, just so you know."

"Where did you get it?" Brandon said.

"Let's just say it fell in my lap. I mean, not literally in my lap. Just landed in my life."

"I see."

"Really, it landed in the back of my truck. There it is. I'm like, what's this shit? Stick it in the laptop, thinking it's somebody's porn video or something. Instead, it's the kid, spilling his guts."

"Really."

"Oh, yeah. Turns the camera on and starts talking. Really messed-up. I mean, the situation. Not the kid as much."

"Right."

"So," the guy said. "I been watching this thing of yours a little bit. Seen the shit on YouTube. They got you by the short hairs or what, dude?"

Brandon didn't answer.

"I'm telling you, you gotta see this. You are gonna freak."

"I'm sure," Brandon said.

More rattling. The truck beeping again.

"Like I said, I'm not out to screw anybody over."

"Right."

"And I could sell this to the parents, their lawyer. I could freakin' retire."

"Uh-huh."

"But I want to do the right thing."

"How much?" Brandon said.

"Five grand. That's like dirt cheap. Just something for my trouble."

"I see."

"You got that kinda cash, Brandon?"

"Not carrying it around," Brandon said.

"But can you get it? Go to the bank? Borrow it from somebody?"

"Yeah."

"Sweet," the guy said. "Then we have a deal?"

"Sure. When and where?" Brandon said.

"Text me when you got the money. We'll go from there."

The beeping stopped. There was a hiss, air brakes on a truck. The guy said, away from the phone, "Jesus, dude. Why don't you get a little closer."

A door clicked closed and then it was quieter, faint voices in the background.

"So how long?" the guy said. "Just so I know."

"I don't know. A half hour," Brandon said. "Maybe less."

"Perfect. Pleasure doing business, Officer Blake."

And then there was the sound of a door slamming shut.

A clank.

Three digital notes.

A whooshing sound.

For an instant, Brandon was back in the alley, Rawlings somewhere in the dark. It was the same sound. The dishwasher starting in the bar. The sports bar. Strike Two.

Brandon trotted to the stairwell, slammed the door open and started down, two stairs at a time. On the ground floor, he made for the Spring Street side, passed two women carrying signs that said, "Say NO To Violence."

On the street, he went west, walking fast. He thought of calling Kat for back-up, shrugged it off. He cut through a parking lot, hurried down Cross Street. Slowed as he approached the bar, Strike Two. Stayed on the far side of the street, head down. Cut over and down a driveway, through the lot of an electrical supply place, and doubled back.

The same alley, the night rushing back. Rawlings coming out of the darkness. Them talking. Brandon shooting. Rawlings blood. Rawlings dead.

Brandon swallowed hard, forced the images back down like bile. He was behind the bar, saw two cars parked. A box truck with a cartoon fish on the side. And a pickup.

It was an old Nissan, black with a white driver's door, tailgate rusted. He watched the restaurant door, slipped to the front of the box truck. Leaned against the cab and took out his phone. Texted:

`got the money.`

Waited.

`that was f'in fast.`

`i was downtown. banks across the street. savings acct now empty.`

Brandon peered at the phone. Didn't want to spook him but didn't want to lose him, either.

good deal for u.

right. where can we meet?

the oaks in 20. by the basketball court. what you driving?

chevy pickup. blue.

i'll find u.

Brandon moved to the Nissan, tried the passenger door. It was unlocked, the inside of the cab strewn with food wrappers, Red Bull cans. He moved back and leaned against the box truck and waited.

For four minutes. And then the back door of the bar rattled open, a guy came striding out. He was tall, lanky, a wispy beard and a blue bandanna, worn pirate style. He was whistling as he came around the end of the truck and got in. He reached to the console and rummaged and was lighting a joint when Brandon moved to the passenger door, yanked it open and got in, wrappers crunching underneath him.

The butt of his gun showed at the top of his jeans.

The guy looked over at him, said, "You don't have the money, do you?"

Brandon shook his head.

"You want to go get it?" the guy said.

Brandon shook his head again.

"Drive," he said.

———

"Fuckin' A, man. I thought you were one of the good guys."

The guy pulled out of the alley, drove up the hill, a left on Congress. He had the driver's window open, was blowing the marijuana smoke out.

"You don't mind, do you?" he said, nodding toward the joint.

Brandon shook his head.

"I don't have the card," the guy said. "I left it with a friend. For safe-keeping."

Holding his breath, he held the joint out to Brandon.

"No thanks," Brandon said.

The guy exhaled.

"Figured you ain't working. So what are you gonna do? Search me?"

"Not necessary," Brandon said. "You're gonna give it to me."

"Dude, we had a deal. A man's word, you know?"

"Attempted extortion," Brandon said. "First offense, you might get a year, the rest suspended. But then you get out, every job you apply for. Ever been convicted of a felony? You'll be washing dishes the rest of your life."

The guy turned. Indignant.

"I was trying to help you out, man. I didn't have to do any of this."

A pause.

"Besides, it's your word against mine."

"I recorded your call," Brandon said. "I record everything these days."

"Dude," the guy said. "That is low."

They were sitting at the light at Longfellow Square. The guy drew on the joint, turned toward the window. Lunged toward the door, yanked it open.

Brandon got him by the neck, a forearm lock, pulled him back in. The truck started to roll as the light turned green. A horn honked somewhere behind them. The guy flopped back into the seat and put the truck in gear, the joint smoldering on the floor at this feet. He glanced into the rearview as he pulled through the intersection, leaned down and fished the joint up, put it in his mouth and toked. The horn honked again.

"Chill, back there," the guy said, exhaling. "Everybody in this town is in such a freakin' hurry."

"You're out of your league," Brandon said.

"No shit."

"Drive to the P.D.," Brandon said.

"Oh, come on, Blake. Don't be such a hardass."

He turned right, headed down the hill through Bayside, headed for the Oaks. The original plan, Brandon thought. A set-up?

"Pull over," he said.

"Shit, dude. No need to get all macho."

He pulled to the curb, stopped in front of a hydrant.

"Your ID."

"No way."

"I have to know who I'm dealing with," Brandon said. "Let me see your license."

"What?"

"I'm a cop, remember?"

"Listen, Blake. How 'bout I just give you the fucking thing, we pretend like we never met."

"I'm not gonna touch the card," Brandon said. "You're gonna hand it over and you're gonna tell them the whole story."

"The money, you mean? I was just seeing what was out there, man. I got friends, they're going to Tahoe for the winter. Just needed a little cash, carry me for a few months, you know?"

"Not the money part. Just how you found it."

"You can tell them."

"Chain of evidence," Brandon said. "They could say I altered it or something."

"Can't really alter it. Well, I guess you could. But then you'd have to put the file back on the card and the dates would be——"

"Drive."

The guy put the truck in gear, pulled out into traffic. "Dude, this was not how it was supposed to go down at all."

"You could be a hero," Brandon said. "The guy who found the card, cleared up the mystery of Thatcher Rawlings."

The guy frowned, took a deep breath.

"I got warrants," he said. "Failure to appear out of Mass. Nothing big. Disorderly. Criminal mischief except it wasn't me for that. Total bullshit."

"I'll tell them you helped. Good intentions. Get those filed."

The guy was thinking. When they stopped at intersections, Brandon turned, ready for the guy to try to bail again.

They were past Market, approaching Pearl. The guy took another deep breath, squirmed in his seat.

"Don't you have *any* money?" he said.

Brandon hesitated, like someone mulling a panhandler. He reached into his pocket, took out his wallet. Fished out all the bills. He handed them over.

"How much is this?"

"A hundred-fifty. Maybe a little more."

"Ain't going cross country on that."

He folded the bills and stuffed them in his jeans. When he took his hand out, he was holding a memory card. The label was smudged and the card was dirty. It said 32 gigabytes.

"This is it, Blake," the guy said. "Just take it, dude."

"Right on Pearl."

"But I don't want to be a hero," he said. "Not my style. I'm like wicked self-effacing."

"Too late," Brandon said.

They were a couple of blocks away from the P.D., the intersection at Congress, waiting for traffic. Brandon could sense the guy tensing, one last chance to run. Brandon reached out and opened the glove box, pulled out an envelope. He took out the registration. The guy's name was Elery Slamm. He was 27. He lived on Sherman Street, right around the corner. Brandon knew the building. It was a dump. Brandon put the registration in his pocket.

"Hey," Elery said. "I might need that."

"The P.D., Elery," Brandon said.

He looked over at Elery and held his gaze.

"And if this isn't the real card, if this was some kind of set up, I'll hunt you down myself."

TWENTY-SIX

They drove in silence, passed people walking toward Congress Street, headed east. Their signs *Kids Lives Matter....Portland PD=Gestapo*. One said *Thatcher Rawlings Did Not Die in Vain*. The rally was a half-hour off, at Monument Square.

Brandon told Elery to drive up to the Middle Street entrance. He did and Brandon reached over and shut off the motor and yanked the keys out.

"You sit there," he said. "I'll come around."

He got out, circled the truck and opened the driver's door, like the guy was in custody. He almost put a hand on Elery's head, keep him from banging it. But he did walk close to him, one hand on his arm, all the way up the steps.

"Don't worry, Elery," Brandon said, smiling. "You're doing the right thing."

Sherri at the window buzzed them in, nodded to Brandon as they as he passed. Brandon kept Elery in front of him as they went down the corridor and up the stairs, two at a time. They went through the door, headed for the chief's office. As they approached, the chief's admin looked up from her computer, said, "He's not in there. He had a meeting."

Brandon kept going, down the corridor. He stopped at Lieutenant

Searles office, heard voices behind the door. He knocked once, opened the door and nodded to Elery. He stepped in, Brandon behind him. Searles was talking to O'Farrell and Chief Garcia and Sergeant Perry.

They turned in unison.

"Blake," O'Farrell said.

"This is Elery Slamm," Brandon said. "He has the card."

They looked at Elery. He hesitated, then smiled and said, "Hey there, officers. How's your day going?"

"From the GoPro," Brandon said. "Elery works at Strike Two, the bar where the shooting happened, out back. He found this card in the back of his pickup."

Elery fished in his pocket, took out the card, held it out.

"I thought it was, like, my civic duty and everything to make sure this wasn't lost or whatever. So I called Officer Blake here and reported it."

Perry took two steps and took the card. "Did you look at it?"

"Yessir," Elery said, opting to go military in the presence of so many uniforms. "Some messed up shit, sir."

O'Farrell took the card from Perry and handed it to Searles, who fumbled as he tried to slide it into the side of his laptop.

"Have you seen it?" Garcia asked Brandon.

Brandon shook his head.

"Never touched it," he said. "We came directly here."

Garcia said, "Record this, in case it blows up or something." Searles took a small tripod out of this desk drawer, set it up, and plugged his phone onto it. He fiddled and then leaned forward and hit play.

They crowded around the back of the desk, the cops in front, Brandon and Elery at the back.

"Jesus," Perry said. "There he is."

Thatcher Rawlings was in the middle of the screen, the GoPro on his head. He was filming himself in a mirror, sitting on a bed. He moved and the springs squeaked.

"I'm Thatcher Rawlings," he began. "I live in Moresby, Maine. I'm sixteen years old. This is like my last testament. By the time you see this, I'll be gone. Unless I chicken out. But I don't think so."

He looked away, licked his lips, then looked back.

"It's like this. My parents, they don't like me. I mean, I don't like them much, either, but they started it. It's not like they hate me or anything but they just would rather I wasn't around. It's like animals, you know? Failure to bond. They just think I'm a pain in the ass. My mother was really pissed when my dad blew like almost all their money with some stupid investment thing—he's like this really lousy stockbroker—and they could only afford to send me to like one semester of boarding school."

Thatcher smiled. "He's back!"

"Anyway, this isn't funny. I don't mean the part about me. I mean the rest of it. There's only three of us. I don't think they meant to have me and then they were stuck. But it's four if you count my grandmother. She's this wicked cool old lady, my father's mother. How she had him, I don't know. Her husband must've been a real dickhead and it all rubbed off on my dad."

"You know how kids play catch with their dads? I remember the one time my dad played catch with me. Somebody must've told him it was one of those things dads and their sons have to do. So we get out there and I suck at it and I'm missing the ball and throwing it over his head and he says, 'Wow. You are really bad.' And he walks away. Leaves me out there in the yard with the stupid glove on my hand. I thought he was coming back and he didn't. I waited a long time and then I went in and cried. I know it's a small thing but I never forgot it."

He licked his lips then pursed them, like he was gearing up.

"But enough about me, right? The real story is that me and my parents, we have separate lives. I have my friends, they have the rich people they suck up to. It's pathetic. Anyway, they've been arguing for like months. Okay, so my grandmother is really rich. But she hangs on to her money, bails out my parents once in a while, but not the whole wad, not 'til she's gone. She says my dad is such a fuck-up that she doesn't want to enable him. But then like two years ago, she goes into this assisted living place. It's like forty-thousand a month, with all these fancy meals and a whirlpool bath and a massage person and this lady playing classical music on the piano in the community room.

"So my parents, they're pissed because the money is like going steadily down the drain. And then my grandmother, she falls and breaks her hip and that's even more money and my parents, they can see her chewing through the whole thing and she dies and they get nothing. My mother, she always hated my grandmother, thought she was a total snob. Which she was. She used to call my mom trailer trash. Not to her face, but that's beside the fact."

Thatcher took a deep breath, reached up and adjusted the camera on the band around his head. The picture shook like there was an earthquake. The cops in the room stared intently, Elery, too.

"Here's the deal."

A swallow and a breath, inhale slowly, exhale slowly.

"My parents are real assholes. I mean, they are just evil. Totally into themselves, think the world owes them everything, you know? Like the fact that they're losers is somebody else's fault. Everything is somebody else's fault. In psychology in school, they were talking about these disorders and they came to narcissists and I'm like, 'Hey, that's my 'rents.' Except they're like narcissistic together. Which is exponentially more bad."

Thatcher looked away. O'Farrell said, "Come on, kid. Don't quit now."

"So listen now. Right now 'cause I'm laying it out. My parents killed my grandmother. They brought her home like it was this nice thing to do. Give her a change of scenery, is what they told the assisted-living place. And then they made her a Manhattan—that's what she's always drank—and they made it like really strong, and then they told her she had to take her meds. And they gave her like all this shit, Oxycodone and codeine and all this stuff, and she passes out and chokes on her own vomit. This nice lady, she pukes to death. I mean, what is more evil than that?"

Thatcher started to tear up, pulled himself together.

"So I'm ratting them out, you know? That's what I'm doing. I heard them talking about it a few days after, the night after the funeral. I was on the roof outside my bedroom window, I go out there to look at the stars and think and get away from them, and I hear them on the patio and they're telling each other how it was for the best. Mostly my mom talking because my dad, he was feeling kind of guilty. Killing his own mother and all. She says shit like like, 'What kind of life was it anyway? It was time for her to go. It's the quality of life.' And how the place and the doctors were gonna bleed her dry and what a waste that was. And how in some cultures, old people just go off in the woods and croak, it's just America that hooks you up to machines and keeps you going until you're just a beating heart hooked up to this decrepit body. I heard my mom say, 'We had to do it, baby. It was the merciful thing to do.' I heard that. This is my sworn testimony."

"Jesus," Garcia said.

"So I'm gonna go now. I mean, really go. I had this idea for a video. It's based on surveillance camera footage. You know how they always show robbers and they're at the bank counter or whatever, and the camera is looking down at them and it's all fisheye and distorted? Well, I thought, what if the camera was from the robber's POV? Wouldn't that be totally cool?"

He jiggled up and down excitedly.

"So I'm gonna do that before I die. And if it all works out and I don't wuss out, my parents will see their son in this cool video, I mean, it would go totally viral. I searched and searched and I never found anything like this."

A grin.

"And then they'll see their son die. The muzzle flash. The thud as I hit the ground."

A wider grin. "Thanks, Mom. Thanks, Dad. It's been real. You made me what I am today."

He laughed. "It's like *Blade Runner*, you know. I'm a replicant gone off the rails. Somebody's gotta take me out."

And then he was serious, leaning to the mirror.

"One thing before I peace out. Apologies to whatever cop has to do the deed. Not your fault. So sorry. For everything. And oh, yeah, bye Amanda. You've been totally cool. I wish I could've been a better boyfriend."

The screen went black. The room was silent. Searles shifted in his chair and it creaked. Finally O'Farrell said, "Jesus, Mary and Joseph."

And then the screen brightened to gray, the audio crackled. Running shoes flashed in and out of view, and then a door swung open. Music was playing. The Pogues, Brandon thought. The Irish pub. Two women were washing table tops. A guy was sweeping the floor. They looked up. Thatcher said, "Hands where I can see 'em. You're being robbed."

One of the woman said, "You're shitting me."

It was four minutes long. Thatcher gathering everyone up in front of the bar. Five of them. They stood with their hands up and Thatcher walked up and down the line and said, "This is what a robbery looks like, POV." In the last minute, Thatcher ran behind the bar and found the bartender, a woman with big horn-rimmed glasses, and herded her out with the others. The bartender said, "You'd better get out of there. Cops are coming for you, you little prick."

Thatcher said, "Great." And then he was quiet, told the group to stop moving. And then the camera pivoted and the door came into view, then it was banging open and he was running, the images swinging wildly, streetlights flashing. A siren sounded and then went off. "That's us," Brandon said.

More movement, the sound of shoes slapping on the street. And then Thatcher slowed and heaved himself up. There was a shot of lights and then a truck cab, the back window. "He's jumped into the bed of a truck," Perry said.

And then there was more dizzy swinging and Thatcher, breathing hard said, "Holy shit. What if they shoot the GoPro?" There was a clatter and the screen went black.

"He took the card out and tossed it," Brandon said. "And kept running."

"And you came up behind him."

"I guess he wanted to make sure the thing about the parents was on the video more than he wanted to record his own death," O'Farrell said.

There was a long pause, the room gone quiet.

"I think you're off the hook, Blake," Garcia said.

"If only," Brandon said.

TWENTY-SEVEN

The news spread fast. Before Brandon left the building a meeting was called with Charlie Carew for the union and Esli Hernandez for the city. Another meeting was scheduled for the next morning with Jim Beam from the AG's office. Searles and O'Farrell went directly to the DA's office with the memory card. Sergeant Perry took Elery into an interview room to take his statement. "You did the right thing, son," Perry said, and he patted Elery on the back.

"This," Searles said to Brandon as they left the room, "changes everything."

In the conference room, it was Carew and Hernandez and Brandon. Carew said it was too bad the shooting itself wasn't recorded but the intent to commit suicide by cop was pretty clear. "It was a good shoot all along," he said, "but this is icing on the cake."

"We go from defense to offense," Hernandez said. "If they're convicted of killing the old lady, you can sue them civilly for damages. Emotional, psychological, damage to your reputation."

"How do you fix that?" Brandon said.

And then they broke off, the plan for coming days set in motion. At some point, Kelly would be informed of the new evidence against his clients. The rallies would likely die a natural death. Brandon would be called to testify as to Thatcher's demeanor in the confrontation that led to the shooting. A judge would rule on the admissibility of Thatcher's allegations, given that he couldn't be in court to be questioned by the defense.

"All good, Brandon," Carew said, reaching across the conference table to shake Brandon's hand. Hernandez smiled. Brandon thanked them for their help. They said they'd be talking.

"No doubt," Brandon said.

Brandon went out the way he came, the woman at the front desk giving him a thumbs up. The word was spreading.

His phone was buzzing as he crossed Middle Street, headed for the waterfront and his boat. Kat, a text: "CALL ME TONIGHT!" Mia, a voice mail: "Kat called me looking for you. She said you had good news?"

And then an actual call. Danni. He hesitated. Answered it.

"Brandon, this is Danni. Hey, we were just looking at this Facebook page, the cop-haters. Fucking-A, dude, what a shitshow. Are these people out of control or what?"

"They don't know the whole story."

"Well, that still sucks, the things they're saying about you I almost commenting, sticking up for you."

"Thanks, almost," Brandon said.

A pause. In the background he could hear traffic noise. He waited.

"Listen, that's not the only reason I'm calling. I was thinking about what you said. About that day. I think we need to talk."

"OK."

"Because I can't just carry this shit around anymore. It's like this giant thing on my back. It's freakin' crushing me."

"I understand," Brandon said.

"So listen, where are you?"

"I'm in Portland. Downtown."

"Can you just walk around? I mean, with everything going on?"

"Sort of. I'm careful."

"You oughta take that boat back down here," Danni said.

"It's ready and waiting."

"Yeah, take old *Bay Watch* and—"

"*Bay Witch*," Brandon said.

"Right. Sorry. But listen, can I meet you?"

Brandon considered it.

"I need more info," he said. "What are you carrying around?"

"Jeez, Brand. I'd rather tell you in person."

"Was I right about that day? The bikers?"

He waited. Heard traffic noise, and then Danni said, "You weren't totally wrong."

So they had been involved. Three people dead. Hard to can a cop who just solved three murders.

"Were you there when it went down?"

"Listen, Brandon. It's complicated. I'd rather do this face to face. I mean, this is a big deal to me. I mean, I been holding this inside for a long time."

"I'm sure."

"You going back across the harbor there? Back to the boat?"

"No, it's here."

"Want to meet there?"

The safest place, Brandon thought. Not like they could go for coffee.

"Custom House Wharf. All the way to the end. There's a bunch of trucks parked out there."

He heard her start off, shifting through the gears. "Okay. How long?"

"Twenty minutes," Brandon said. "I gotta get a coffee."

Danni said. "I won't hold you up, if you want to get the hell out of Dodge."

"We'll talk. I'll head out from there," Brandon said.

"I appreciate this," Danni said. "It's like I'm gonna get to live again, after being, like, the walking fucking dead."

They rang off. Brandon looked at his phone. Eighty-two percent. Enough juice to record what Danni had to say. Life turning on what was recorded and what wasn't. He pocketed the phone, felt for the Glock at the back of his waist.

Making his way to Commercial Street, he went left, headed for Arabica for coffee. Pulled his hat down low. The shop was crowded, people hunched over laptops, engrossed in conversation. The baristas were busy, the woman behind the counter barely looking up. Brandon ordered an Americano, turned away and waited. When the coffee came, he reached for his wallet, remembered he'd given his cash to the guy with the video.

He turned and walked out.

Walking back down Commercial Street, he felt lighter, weirdly liberated. One of these days the news would come out. He could picture the headline: "Portland Police Shooting Victim Wanted to Commit Suicide by Cop, Investigators say."

How would Estusa twist it? How would he keep Brandon in his sights?

Still, Brandon felt like the truth would come out. He could take whatever came his way in the meantime. Ride it out and emerge almost intact, or closer to it. He took out his phone, called Mia, got voicemail. "Hey. Some pretty good news, sort of. Call me."

He didn't want to miss Danni, didn't want to give her time to get cold feet, her secret locked away again. Nobody noticed him as he walked in the shade of the storefronts, crossing the street, walked a block up to Custom House Wharf.

He was starting down the wharf when his phone buzzed. The call had gone to voice mail: Mia. He decided to call her back, after Danni. Maybe even more news to report.

He kept walking, looking for Danni's car, Danni herself. He went to the end of the wharf. Nothing. He turned back, walked more slowly. At the corner of a warehouse he paused. Still no Danni. No white Focus.

"Damn it," he said.

He stood and watched for her coming down the wharf. Walked across the wharf to the water's edge, and looked up and down the walkway over the boats. He walked back and down the wharf, stopped outside Harbor Fish. People were coming and going, but no Danni. He took his phone out and called her. It went to voicemail. He said, "I'm here. Where are you? Call me back."

He walked back up the wharf. There was a wooden gate with a sign that said, *Private Dock*, and he reached over and unsnapped the latch, pushed through, and walked down the ramp. He saw that the big sailboat from Marblehead had left, the Grady White, too. *Bay Witch* looked conspicuously alone on the stretch of float and Brandon decided to leave, maybe find a mooring, maybe anchor again off Cushing Island. He'd call Mia, hunker down. If he had to, he'd meet Danni at Woodford Bowl again.

He stepped aboard, thinking he'd need fuel if he were going outside the harbor. He could cut across and gas up at the marina and, if he were lucky, not have to talk to anyone there.

Opening the cabin door, he crossed the salon, stepped down into the cabin. Saw someone sitting on the starboard berth.

Danni. Her left eye was purple and yellow, her mouth cut and swollen.

"What are you—"

A gun pressed against his head from behind.

"I'm really sorry," Danni said.

TWENTY-EIGHT

Clutch kept the gun hard against Brandon's neck.

"Don't shoot. It's not worth it," Brandon said.

"You should know," Clutch said. Danni came off the berth, a strip of duct tape hanging.

"Put out your hands, Brandon," she said. "Please."

The gun pressed harder. Brandon held his hands out and Danni wrapped the tape around his wrists, concentrating like she was wrapping a package.

"Search him," Clutch said.

"He's not working. He's not gonna be carrying."

"Search him."

Danni leaned close, patted Brandon down. Last time she'd tried to kiss him. She patted his waist, front and back, pulled the Glock out with two fingers, holding it by the butt.

"What'd I tell you," Clutch said. "Son of a bitch ain't walking around unarmed. People hate his guts. Put it over there, on the couch."

Danni laid the gun on the port berth. She turned to Brandon and smiled, like things would be okay now.

"So what is it I can do for you guys?" Brandon said.

"The paper, Brandon," Danni said. "Just give us the paper and we'll go."

"That all?" Brandon said. "You could have asked. No need for all this. I would have—"

"Shut the fuck up," Clutch said and he whipped the barrel across Brandon's forehead. "That's for the parking lot, asshole."

A long barrel. Revolver, Brandon thought. Blood was running through Brandon's eyebrows, into his left eye. He blinked it away but it kept coming.

"The paper," Danni said.

Brandon smiled.

"So I give it to you, you take the tape off, your boyfriend puts the gun away and we shake hands. No hard feelings."

"Right," Danni said.

"Right," Brandon said.

"Just tell her where it is," Clutch said. "Or I start shooting. Your knees first."

"You'll put a big hole in the bottom of the boat. That'll really start the clock ticking."

"I'm counting to ten," Clutch said.

"Please, Brandon," Danni said. "He'll hurt you."

Clutch spun Brandon around, shoved him down on the edge of the berth. Brandon's head hit the bulkhead, and bounced back.

"Jesus," Danni said. "Go easy."

"Shut up," Clutch said, and to Brandon, "Last chance, dipshit. Where is it?"

"Gone," Brandon said. "I decided you guys are nothing but trouble. I tossed it."

The barrel again, the right side this time. Brandon blinked blood away.

"No bullshit," Clutch said.

"Please, Brandon, please."

"Don't want to see your boyfriend chopped up?" Clutch said, and Brandon saw the sadist side. Just a glimpse.

"Can't produce what I don't have," Brandon said.

"Jesus," Clutch said, pressed the barrel of the gun against Brandon's chin. A .357, Brandon thought. Used to be a bad-ass gun, Dirty Harry days.

"I'll do it," Clutch said.

"Half the Old Port will hear that shot," Brandon said. "Shouldn't've brought that bazooka."

Clutch hesitated, looked out of the cabin door toward the salon. "Then we'll go out where we can have some quiet," he said. He motioned to Danni with the gun. "His ankles. And his mouth."

"Please, Brandon. Just tell him. Just tell him and we can go."

"Okay," Brandon said. "It's in a purple trash bag, last seen being heaved into the dumpster outside the marina in South Portland."

Another slash with the gun barrel, blood running down Brandon's temples, dripping off his chin.

"Oh, god," Danni said, but she was tearing strips off the roll of tape. She moved close and pressed the strip against Brandon's mouth, said, "It won't stick."

She was crouched in front of him, the tape stretched in front of her. Clutch reached for a T-shirt from the shelf, stepped in and swiped Brandon's face, like a rough dad with a messy kid. Danni tried again and the tape stuck. Brandon took a long breath through his nose, watched as Clutch—jeans, workboots, camo hoodie—stuffed the gun in his waistband, stepped out into the salon. Brandon heard thumping, lockers opening and closing and then Clutch was back, a toolbox in front of him, *Bay Witch* written in marker across the lid.

"Ankles, too," he said, and Danni knelt in front of Brandon, started peeling tape off the roll. She looped it around his ankles, pulled it tight and strapped it down. "Some people just ain't got the sense to leave shit alone," Clutch said, unsnapping the lid, digging through the tools. "Everything was great. For years. And this son of a bitch cop has to stick his nose in. You have to write shit down in some fucking book."

He took out a pair of vice-grips, needle-nosed.

"Oh, Clutch, don't," Danni said. "Let me talk to him."

"Too late for talk, babe."

"No. Brandon, just tell him where it is. We'll get out of here. Don't you have enough crap to deal with? I mean, you don't need this."

Understatement, Brandon thought. He breathed slowly, in and out. A diesel rumbled outside, moving on the water. Maybe nobody would hear a shot.

Clutch snapped the pliers shut, said, "Last chance. You want to talk, just nod your head."

Brandon stared at him.

"Your choice. After this we get out the saw, start cutting off fingers."

"No," Danni said. "He'll tell us, won't you, Brandon."

Clutch stepped closer as the boat rocked. He reached out and steadied himself on the bulkhead and Brandon kicked out straight and hard, both legs, aimed for the groin but hit the knee. Clutch shouted, punched Brandon in the head, knocking him sideways. Pain shot from his ear, radiating inside his head. Clutch hit him again, same place, kicked him in the shin.

"Wanna play rough, freakin' cop? We can play rough."

He yanked Brandon's hands up, pulled his left index finger out and clamped the pliers on. Brandon screamed into the tape while Danni said, "Oh, my god, stop."

The pliers were still on, the pain burning, shooting up Brandon's arm.

"Like that?" Clutch said, taking the gun out, pressing the barrel to Brandon's forehead. "Want me to put you out of your misery? Cause I'll do it, I swear. Just like I did with those biker assholes. Put them down like dogs, but they was half dead already. No loss, those pieces of shit. They were murderers, for Christ's sake. Sash, too. They worth getting jammed up like this for? A couple of biker murderers, Blake? Is it? Is it?"

Brandon shook his head, his teeth clenched under the tape.

"There you go," Danni said. "You can stop now. He'll tell us."

Clutch still had the gun on Brandon's head, and he didn't answer. Brandon looked at her and their eyes met. She wasn't getting it, that the paper was only half the problem, and the other half wasn't going away by letting Brandon go. He gasped through his nose, mucus spurting. Danni wiped it for him, said to Clutch, "Please. Stop it."

He did, unclasping the pliers. Brandon's finger was crushed, throbbing, turning black-red.

"Ready to talk?" Clutch said.

"Sure he is," Danni said, and slipped a finger under one end of the tape and pulled. Brandon gasped again, panted for air. His finger was paralyzed, the pain spreading to his whole hand.

"Where is it, Blake?" Clutch said, the gun pointed at Brandon's forehead.

"It's gone," Brandon said. "I'm telling you, I threw it away. Mia, my girlfriend, she was pissed because I found Danni. It was nothing but trouble."

The gun, lashing across his mouth, his lip splitting, blood spurting.

"Oh, god," Danni said. "Don't. Please don't."

"You're next, bitch," Clutch said, "he don't start talking."

The blood was dripping off of Brandon's chin onto his lap, his wrists, beading on the tape.

"It's true," Brandon said, blood spittle spraying. "You think some stupid bikers from years ago are worth this? What do I care about them, or you, or any of it. I don't. If I had it, I'd give it to you in a second. It's not my problem."

"Is now," Clutch said, and he slapped Brandon, a left-handed back-hand. Brandon's head rocked back, and Clutch clamped the pliers again, the middle finger. Brandon grimaced and Clutch said, "The tape, you idiot."

Danni tried to put the old piece back on but it wouldn't stick, folded on itself. "Get a new piece for fuck's sake," Clutch said, and she did, tearing it off, wiping Brandon's bloody mouth, pressing the tape on. It stuck, one end trailing off.

"Somebody's gonna hear," Clutch said.

"He doesn't have it," Danni said.

"You don't know that," Clutch said.

"I do, too. I know him."

"I'll bet you do, you slut. We gotta get outta here."

Were they leaving? Brandon grimaced, a glimmer of hope.

"I'll get this tub started," Clutch said.

"You don't know how to drive a boat," Danni said.

"I can drive anything," Clutch said. "Tape him down."

"What?"

"Around his neck and around that wood thing."

It was the shelf above the berth, a handhold cut out for hoisting yourself out. Danni said, "Oh, Jesus," but she started to unwind the tape. She wrapped it around Brandon's neck, one loop.

"Again," Clutch said. "Then through the hole."

She did it, feeding the tape through three times before yanking it back to Brandon's neck and making a final wrap. He was short-leashed like a dog.

"I'm really sorry about this, Brandon," Danni said.

"You'll be wicked sorry, I oughta give you what you deserve, starting all this," Clutch said.

She recoiled as he feinted a swing of the gun.

"Way I take care of you, I don't know why I do it. Lying bitch."

He took two steps back. The pliers were still clamped, the pain turning to numbness. Danni said, "Can't you take those off now?"

"Shut up," Clutch said. "You watch him. He moves an inch, you're both dead."

He turned and crouched as he moved through the door and into the salon. Brandon heard him stepping up to the helm, then metallic creaks and thunks as he moved the controls. The starter cranked and stopped. Cranked again. Brandon wondered if Clutch could figure out the choke, the throttle setting. Another crank. Nothing. Then another, and the big Chevy coughed and stalled. Coughed again and roared to life.

It idled while Clutch bounded down the steps and out to the stern. The boat rocked slightly as he stepped off, untying the docklines, then rocked again as he jumped back on, trotted back to the helm.

The motor throttled back, then stalled. Brandon thought, please flood it. Out in the bay, he'd be alone. He'd be done.

The motor started again, and this time didn't stall as Clutch put the boat in gear. It surged forward, ground the fenders into the float. "Shit," Clutch shouted. He reversed and there was more grinding but the stern was moving away from the float. The boat was going sideways in the passage between the wharves, and Clutch shifted, and the boat surged forward again. The bow hit the float and the boat shuddered, and the motor rumbled as Clutch reversed. He jockeyed back and forth twice, and then *Bay Witch* swung around and started out into the harbor.

Brandon looked at Danni, held out his hand, the plier hanging from his finger.

"I can't, Brandon," she said. "He'll kill me. He really will."

The motor surged, Clutch shoving the throttle forward. The boat lifted and through the crack in the cabin curtains Brandon could see the wharf and then open water. Clutch turned east, headed out of the harbor. He pushed it faster and they passed the ferry terminal, passed outside of the mooring field. Brandon looked at Danni and implored her again, grunting through the tape.

"I'm sorry," she said, and sat still on the berth, the roll of tape on her lap.

And the motor stopped. The boat settled. Clutch cranked the starter. Nothing.

The tank, Brandon thought. It's drained and he doesn't know how to switch over.

They were drifting at the edge of the channel, the outgoing tide swinging the bow to the east. Clutch was clicking switches, hammering at the controls. "Goddamn it," he bellowed.

He came down the steps, into the cabin.

"Goddamn piece of crap is out of gas, Blake," Clutch said. "You stupid shit."

He cuffed Brandon on the side of the head, said, "Is there a gas tank on here?"

Brandon shook his head. A disabled boat drifting into the channel. Someone would notice. Someone would check. Call the Coast Guard.

Clutch hit him again, said to Danni, "Watch him." He moved out of the cabin, out to the stern deck. The boat was drifting but moving closer to the moorings. Danni looked out between the curtains, saw the top of a sailboat mast.

Brandon couldn't feel his finger, some nerve thing that relieved him of the pain. Clutch was still flicking switches, trying the starter. The switch to the tanks was amid all the others, the markings long worn off. Brandon held his hands out to Danni, and she looked away.

They heard the motor rumble to life. Clutch thrust the boat into gear and they motored for 20 seconds, then slowed. The motor cut out and they saw Clutch moving onto the deck, his legs passing the window. He was scrambling forward, boat hook in hand. They heard him on the bow deck, grunting and saying, "Goddamn thing." And then they felt the boat swing, the stern coming around. Clutch had hooked something. Brandon glanced out. They were at the outer edge of the mooring field of the Portland Yacht Basin, tied up to an empty mooring.

Clutch came by the window again, carrying the boat hook. And then he clumped down onto the stern deck, threw the hook aside and stepped back up to the helm. They heard the VHF radio blare, channel

16, the hailing emergency channel. Static, scratchy voices. A tanker hailing a pilot boat, a lobsterman telling *Miss Betsy* to go to channel 9. Brandon listened with a sinking feeling. The radio was cover for any sound he might make.

Clutch was back, bending and bumping his head on the bulkhead as he entered the cabin. "Goddamn piece of junk," he said. "But we're good now. Nobody gonna hear you out here, Blake. Nobody out here but the seagulls, peck your goddamn eyes out. Maybe that's what I should do. Scrape your nosy eyes out with a friggin' spoon, feed 'em to the fish."

He pulled the gun out again, jammed it against Brandon's throat.

"Gonna ask again. Still being a nice guy."

Brandon looked at him, blinked against the coagulating blood.

"Where is it?"

Brandon shook his head slowly.

"Okay," Clutch said. "Let's see what other toys you got on this tub."

He tucked the gun in his jeans, moved to the galley, started opening cupboards. Brandon heard the drawer slide open, the utensils and knives. "Here we go," he said. "Slice and dice time."

"Clutch, what if he's telling the truth?" Danni said. "What if he threw the stupid thing away? He can't snap his fingers and make it just appear."

Brandon felt the pliers on his finger, his hand numb. He wasn't snapping anything.

"Then it sucks to be him," Clutch said, coming back into the cabin.

He had a fileting knife, a butcher knife, a propane torch. He held the torch up.

"I figure we're out here, might as well do some grilling," he said.

"No," Danni said.

"Shut up," Clutch said. "Trouble you started, just shut your mouth."

She did. Clutch turned the valve on the torch and the gas hissed. He fished in his pocket for a lighter. Snapped the flame on and the torch lit, the flame a blue-white point.

Brandon heard the radio crackle, the pilot and tanker talking. A sailboat looking for U.S. Customs. A woman's voice say, "Motor vessel *Bay Witch*, motor vessel *Bay Witch*. This is Munjoy dinghy. Go to channel 9."

Mia.

Clutch was adjusting the flame. Danni said, "Please, Brandon. Just tell him. Let's end this right here."

It would be the end of him, Brandon knew. Nothing to sell, he was dead. And once they had it, he was dead anyway.

"Motor vessel *Bay Witch*, motor vessel *Bay Witch*. This is Munjoy dinghy. Go to channel 9, captain."

Danni said, "Isn't that the name of this boat? Who's that?"

She looked to Clutch. He nodded and she ripped the tape from Brandon's mouth. He grimaced and Danni said, "Sorry." Brandon flexed his jaw, said, "Melissa. She and her husband Lowell have a boat at the marina," Brandon said. "I have the keys to the fuel dock."

"They can call you way over here?" Danni said.

"Three or four miles, depending on the height of the antenna."

"Motor vessel *Bay Witch*, motor vessel *Bay Witch*. This is Munjoy dinghy. Go to channel 9, please." Mia's voice was more clear. She was getting closer.

"They can call all day," Clutch said. "You're all tied up."

The torch sputtered out. He tried to relight it but the gas canister was empty.

"Christ," Clutch said, throwing it aside, clanging off the hull. "Does anything work on this piece of junk?"

He took the filet knife off of the berth, the blade long and thin and razor sharp. He reached out and drew it hard across Brandon's knuckles, the left hand. Brandon gasped as the flesh parted to the bone and blood began to seep.

"Whoa, that's sharp. We can cut your balls off, one slice."

"Please, no," Danni said. "Just stop."

"Motor vessel *Bay Witch*, motor vessel *Bay Witch*. This is Munjoy dinghy. Go to channel 9." Mia, the signal strong now. She was close. Brandon had to warn her. He had to get them topsides where they could be seen.

"Bitch won't take no for answer," Clutch said.

Brandon looked at Danni and nodded.

"What?" she said. "Are we done?"

He nodded again.

"Oh, thank god," Danni said. "Let's get the goddam paper and get out of here."

. . .

"Spill it before I cut your tongue out," Clutch said. He pressed the point of the knife into the flesh under Brandon's chin. Brandon felt the warmth of blood running. He took a deep breath through his mouth, his nose clogged with more blood, now drying. The boat rocked, almost imperceptibly.

"The helm," he said.

"Where's that?" Clutch said. "Speak goddamn English."

"Where the wheel is. Where you were driving."

"Okay."

"There's a chart book in the cupboard to the left of the wheel. It's tucked in there. The chart for Muscongus Bay. It's about halfway in."

"Get it," Clutch said to Danni, and she slipped behind him and out of the cabin. They heard her footsteps as she started up the ladder. And then there were other footsteps. And then none at all.

Danni came back into the cabin, walking backwards slowly, her hands up.

"What the—"Clutch said.

He reached for the revolver. Brandon lunged at him, swung his arms, the pliers yanking on his finger. The tape on his neck jerked him back and Clutch shoved him off and he fell back onto the berth. Tried again, the tape snapping his head backwards.

And then Mia was in the doorway. She was holding the Glock, Brandon's Glock from the closet, in front of her with both hands. Clutch reached for the handle of the revolver and she screamed, "Don't."

Danni backed past him, said, "It wasn't me. It was him. He did it."

Mia glanced at Brandon, his bloody head and face and hands. Clutch smiled at her, kept his hand on the butt of his gun. "No harm done," he said. "Just a little dickering. Your boyfriend here delivered his end of the deal, so now we can just move along."

"Put your hands up," Mia said. "Or I'll kill you."

Clutch grinned, kept his hand on the gun. "Jesus, must run in the family, shooting people. Ever fired that thing, honey? Got the safety off? Don't want to—"

His arm tensed and he started to jerk the gun out but it caught on the denim. He looked down, shook it loose, had it halfway out when Mia fired.

One, two, three, four shots.

Danni screamed, kept screaming. Clutch staggered backwards, looked up at Mia, his mouth agape. Back down at the holes in his shirt. Brandon saw Thatcher Rawlings and Joel Fuller. Clutch dropped to his knees, wobbled, and then pitched forward, flat on his face, blood running from underneath him like the boat had sprung a terrible leak.

Mia trained the gun on Danni. She stopped screaming, put her hands back up.

"Take that thing off him," Mia said, "or I swear to god I'll kill you, too."

TWENTY-NINE

It was the phone-finder app on Brandon's old laptop, Mia told O'Farrell and the CID detectives. The GPS showed his phone out in the harbor. She took the handheld radio and gun from the apartment, drove down the hill to the docks. When Brandon didn't answer her first call, she called 911, then took a dinghy and motored out to Bay Witch. Fifty yards off, she switched to oars. She knew something was wrong because Brandon would never leave the boat's fenders hanging.

"What was Mr. Tedeschi doing when you shot him?" O'Farrell said.

"He was trying to pull that big gun out of his pants," Mia said. "It got stuck."

"So that gave you time?"

"I would have shot him first anyway," she said.

The cops looked at her.

"I know this is hard," a CID detective named Liegner said.

"No, it isn't," Mia said, her voice cold as steel. "I'm a writer. It's what we call a happy ending."

The interviews lasted hours. They first talked to Brandon outside the

ER at Maine Med, where they used metal clamps to close the cut on his knuckles and splinted his broken fingers. Later he'd need surgery.

Brandon told the whole story, from reading the diary to the dead bikers, and Clutch's friend. He'd later find that Danni had filled in the gaps, saying all three guys were wounded, but Clutch, who had run when the shooting started, went back and finished them off. He took the money and Danni, who'd been waiting in the truck, helped him count it. Clutch told her she was a murderer, too, that this was their secret. She'd kept it, except for the time she wrote that stuff down. Brandon said Danni had been forced to help with his abduction and torture. As near as he could tell.

Mia's parents called from Alexandria, said they were coming that night. Mia told them to wait, she needed time. She was with Brandon. She'd call.

A day passed, then another. Brandon and Mia holed up in her apartment, friends bringing meals like someone had died. Which was true.

No one stayed to visit, just dropped casserole dishes covered with foil, takeout from food trucks, bottles of wine. They flashed sad, awkward smiles, said to call if there was anything they could do. A couple of the old cops, day-shift guys consigned to the airport and the mall, brought whiskey, nodded and left. Brandon lined up the unopened bottles on the counter beside the laptops, which were unopened, too.

Brandon and Mia slept like it was the only possible escape. They sat on the couch, Brandon's bandaged hand on his lap, and looked out at the harbor like it was infinitely interesting. They took naps. Mia very occasionally cried silently but mostly just stared. Brandon took her hand and said, "I know."

On the morning of the third day, O'Farrell called and said he was coming over. He came with Kat. They sat in chairs in front of the couch. They looked like they had bad news.

"It's gonna take some time, sorry to say," O'Farrell said. "D.A. says Kelly will fight tooth and nail to keep that video away from a jury. You have a right to confront your accuser, and all that."

"What if you caused his death, too?" Brandon said.

"Oh, we'll fight like hell, too. But she wants to have some stuff to back it up. They're redoing the toxicology. Interviewing the nursing home people about her state of mind. And her physical abilities. It may be that she not only wasn't demented, but she wasn't strong enough to get that medicine cabinet open. Heard they had to dress her because she couldn't do buttons or zippers."

"Or child-proof pill bottles," Mia said.

O'Farrell smiled.

"They're building a case," Kat said. "First you line up the zippers and bottles. Then you introduce the video because it has relevance."

"How much time?" Brandon said.

"Weeks. A couple of months," O'Farrell said.

"And what about the protests and all that?" Brandon said. "They just go on, them strutting around like they're the victims."

"They got word to Kelly and the Rawlingses, back channel. That there may be new evidence in the old lady's death," Kat said.

"How'd they do that?"

"Estusa," Kat said. "The turd ran right over to tell them. Hasn't been a peep about a protest since. Or a story."

"And Tedeschi?" Mia said.

"Self-defense," O'Farrell said. "Slam dunk."

He looked at Mia. She had her tough face back on as she said, "Yeah, it was."

The cops took a up a collection that netted $3,800. Brandon and Mia left town. First stop was a cabin they found online. It was near the New Hampshire border, at the edge of the White Mountains. It had a view of Mt. Washington, which was already snow-capped, and a big field-stone fireplace. They hiked during the day and Brandon built fires at night. They sat side by side on a different couch and read books set in another century and watched the flames. For the first couple of days they said almost nothing.

And then on the third day, it was raining. They stayed in bed and held hands and listened to the patter on the roof. Finally, Brandon said, "Are we okay?"

"No," Mia said. "But we're not okay together."

"Some couples share a hobby. Like bowling or riding a Harley."

"Motorcycles scare me."

"I don't think much scares you."

"Yeah, one thing really does," Mia said. "The idea of losing you scares the heck out of me."

Brandon thought for a moment.

"We have to make the best of what we've got. Time, I mean."

"Yeah."

They lay there, and Mia said, "Why is life such a big mess sometimes?"

"The nature of it," Brandon said. "Always has been. I was just reading about the battle of Argonne Forest in World War I. More than fifty thousand people killed. Most people today have never heard of it."

Mia considered that and said, "It's this big random spinning thing—the world I mean. We try to make sense of it but there really isn't any. And some people don't make it."

"Amanda Shakespeare."

"You don't think she killed herself."

"I don't know. But if she did, if they take the Rawlingses down, for her mother that's some kind of justice."

"Some," Mia said. "Not much."

"And they go to prison. With their secrets. Until one of them cracks."

"And writes something down," Mia said.

"In a diary or something," Brandon said.

"Yes," she said, squeezing his hand. "What goes around, comes around."

"Sometimes," Brandon said. "Sometimes."

EPILOGUE

One year later:

There were no more sniper attacks on Portland police. The task force remained in place but, with no new leads, there wasn't much to be done. The slugs from Brandon's truck were in evidence bags. The ballistics were compared any time a 30.06 rifle was seized in connection with a crime.

The AG's office investigated Crawford and Tiffanee Rawlings in the death of Alexandra Rawlings. They denied any role, said their son was distraught after his grandmother's death, and was given to flights of imagination. Investigators concluded the evidence—the video—wasn't enough to move the case forward.

The threatened civil suit against Brandon Blake, the Portland Police Department, and the City of Portland never happened. The house in Moresby was sold. Tiff and Crawford Rawlings were said to have moved to Charleston, South Carolina. Brandon returned to duty, still working the night shift with his partner, Kat . Park was reassigned.

And then, a break.

Tiff Rawlings called Chief Garcia. She said she and her husband had split up. He had found someone else, a waitress in the U.S. on a work visa. Her name was Alina. She was twenty-eight, from Moldova, strikingly pretty. She quit her job at Tequila Sunrise, and they left the country. Tiff Rawlings hired a P.I. who tracked them to Tiraspol, in the wine country of Moldova. Crawford Rawlings had emptied all of their accounts, sold his Jeep for cash, and had taken all of the money with him.

He didn't take his Remington Model 783 rifle, one of his favorite firearms. He kept it in a storage unit in Charleston but it was gone when he went to retrieve it. Tiff Rawlings had beaten him to it.

This was the rifle Crawford Rawlings had used to shoot at the cops, Tiff said. She'd provided him with an alibi on those nights, but she knew where he was, what he was doing. Hitting the cop hadn't been the plan. The whole idea had been to create havoc, she said.

"What about Blake, in his truck?" she was asked.

"Him? Crawford just missed," she said.

Detectives flew to Charleston, took custody of the Remington, and interviewed Tiff Rawlings. She said Crawford killed his mother with the overdose, threatened that she'd be next if she said anything. He made her put the light on Blake's boat. She was glad he missed, not because she cared if Blake lived, but because she figured killing Blake would be like poking the bear one too many times. Which, it turned out, it almost was.

Tiff Rawlings came back to Portland with the detectives, was put up in Eastland Hotel. The Remington was a match. She told the story of the shootings over and over. Asked about Amanda Shakespeare, she said she didn't know anything about her death. If that had been her husband, he'd kept it to himself.

Based on her story, Crawford Rawlings was charged with murder, attempted murder, reckless conduct with a firearm. The indictment was secret but Interpol was notified on the chance that one day, he'd leave Moldova.

Brandon Blake, among others, would be waiting.

PORT CITY RAT TRAP

A BRANDON BLAKE MYSTERY, BOOK 2

Almost seven on Sunday morning, January 4. A long night, the latest robbery in a long string called in at 3:45.

The Pop-In store on outer Congress Street. Same description, tall thin man with a calm, almost soothing voice. Same silver gun. Brandon on scene at 4:01, the second unit. Circle the block, see no one. Check parked cars, all cold as ice. Units converge so fast that the area has to be choked off.

Nobody and nothing moving. The patrol sergeant pissed off, everyone frustrated. K-9 on track around the corner and down the side street, losing the guy in the middle of the snow-covered sidewalk. Detectives to follow up with security camera footage, which always made it look like the photos were taken from Mars, not from six feet over the perp's head.

It was dark, cold, the sun just a pale gray glow to the east, as Brandon made his way down the icy float, the water black, the plastic-shrouded boats still. He climbed aboard *Bay Witch*, ice crackling against the hull. Opened the door in the plastic canopy and slipped inside his icy cocoon, then into the cabin and down.

His gun went into the starboard cupboard. His radio went on the table by his berth. He sat and took off his boots, hung his uniform trousers and shirt in the tiny closet. Put on jeans and was buttoning his flannel shirt—when he heard a woman scream.

He tugged on a pair of running shoes, heard her again, this time the scream turning into a shout, the woman saying, "Oh, my god. Oh, my god."

It was on the float, only two other live-aboards this winter. Evie from Canada, her partner overboard? Then Sadie, the partner shouting, too, saying, "No, don't lean over. Wait. They're coming."

Brandon grabbed his gun and radio, leaned back for a flashlight. He plunged through the plastic door, stumbled and turned, then scrambled toward the floating T. At the intersection of the floating dock, he went left. Saw the two women on the float near the bow of their sailboat, both peering into the water.

He slowed to a trot on the ice and snow, said, "Guys, what's the matter?"

They didn't turn to him, just stared down at the water, Evie leaning on the dock line. Sadie standing with her hands on her knees.

Brandon moved close, said, "Back away."

They did, eyes still transfixed. Brandon moved between them and the edge of the dock and flicked the light on, played the beam on the oil-black water. At first he saw nothing. And then the pale gray shape came into focus.

A woman, head down, her parka buoyed above her, her hair floating on the surface.

He put the radio to his mouth, reported a subject in the water, So-Po Marina. Not moving.

"Boat hook," he said, and Sadie ran to get one off the boat.

"Did you hear someone go in?" he said.

Evie shook her head.

"No. I just got up and was checking the lines."

Sadie was back with the pole and Brandon hooked it onto the back of the woman's parka and eased her closer to the edge of the dock. He leaned down and grabbed the neck of the jacket, then the woman's wrist. It was cold and slippery, like thawing chicken.

He lifted and the woman raised from the water, the smell of fish and salt and diesel wafting from her. He dragged her onto the float and she lay there, face down, water streaming from her jacket, her jeans, her high-heeled shoes. He turned her over and she stared up at him, eyes wide open like she was about to speak. Sea water was running from her open mouth. Her hair was dark and stuck to her forehead. Her face was oval shaped, her nose bobbed in a way that made her look surprised.

He started pumping her chest, counting to ten. Then another set. Then he took a deep breath and leaned down, sealed her mouth and blew. Nothing.

He blew again. Nothing. Told himself he'd do ten of those, too.

He was on eight when he heard an approaching siren, leaned back and started CPR again. The South Portland cruiser was skidding into the marina lot when he fell back.

Looked at her, frozen in time, staring like she'd died in middle of a thought. And then he noticed something entangled in her hair. It was gold, a wire headband. He pulled her hair aside and stared.

Sadie said, "Oh, no." Evie said, "Oh, good lord."

The headband was a sort of tiara. In twisted cursive, the wire said, "Bride."

Available in Paperback and eBook From Your Favorite Online Retailer or Bookstore

ALSO BY GERRY BOYLE

ABOUT THE AUTHOR

Gerry Boyle is the author of more than a dozen acclaimed crime novels. His work, including the Jack McMorrow mystery series, has been translated into six languages.

A former newspaper reporter and columnist, Boyle lives in a small town in Maine. He is at work on the next Brandon Blake novel. Many of his novels are inspired by his own crime reporting.

gerryboyle.com

facebook.com/gerry.boyle2

instagram.com/mcmorrowsmaine

Made in the USA
Las Vegas, NV
11 July 2021